IRON COFFIN

JOHN MANNOCK

A SIGNET BOOK

SIGNET
Published by New American Library, a division of
Penguin Group (USA) Inc., 375 Hudson Street,
New York, New York 10014, U.S.A.
Penguin Books Ltd, 80 Strand,
London WC2R 0RL, England
Penguin Books Australia Ltd, 250 Camberwell Road,
Camberwell, Victoria 3124, Australia
Penguin Books Canada Ltd, 10 Alcorn Avenue,
Toronto, Ontario, Canada M4V 3B2
Penguin Books (N.Z.) Ltd, Cnr Rosedale and Airborne Roads,
Albany, Auckland 1310, New Zealand

Penguin Books Ltd, Registered Offices:
80 Strand, London WC2R 0RL, England

First published by Signet, an imprint of New American Library,
a division of Penguin Group (USA) Inc.

First Printing, January 2004
10 9 8 7 6 5 4 3 2 1

PUBLISHER'S NOTE
This is a work of fiction. Names, characters, places, and incidents either are the product of the author's imagination or are used fictitiously, and any resemblance to actual persons, living or dead, business establishments, events, or locales is entirely coincidental.

BOOKS ARE AVAILABLE AT QUANTITY DISCOUNTS WHEN USED TO PROMOTE PRODUCTS OR SERVICES. FOR INFORMATION PLEASE WRITE TO PREMIUM MARKETING DIVISION, PENGUIN GROUP (USA) INC., 375 HUDSON STREET, NEW YORK, NEW YORK 10014.

Acknowledgments

Many Thanks to my Literary Agent and Friend, Jimmy Vines.
And
Additional Thanks to my Editor at NAL, Doug Grad.
And also
Special Thanks to my Father-in-Law,
Master Sergeant Richard E. Durrance, USMC (ret.),
For Editorial Advice on Military Content.
And of course
All my Love and Gratitude to my wife, Teresa,
For whom all my books are written.

Author's Note

This book is a work of fiction set against the backdrop of World War Two. To provide the necessary realism, occasional references are made to historical events and, in particular, to the military technology of the time. It is quite possible that a significant number of men (and women) who knew these vessels, airplanes, and weapons first-hand may discover this novel. For any and all inaccuracies in the relating of these technical details, whether engineered intentionally by me for the purpose of smoothing out the narrative, or perpetrated unintentionally as a result of my own ignorance, I claim Sanctuary in the Cathedral of Fiction.

Prologue

I spent nearly ten years as a commercial diver in the oil fields of the Gulf of Mexico. Ten years of offshore deepwater diving will give you a lifetime's worth of stories to tell, and most of the time you only have to embellish the truth a *little* bit to make them worth hearing. Walk into any bar or roadhouse from Corpus Christi to Pensacola—as long as it isn't in the better part of town—and chances are you'll find some ex–oil field diver holding court over in the far corner near the busted jukebox, telling sea stories for free drinks. Me, I put mine down on paper. It pays better.

What's that old saying? *Truth is stranger than fiction.* Absolutely.

It was the late summer of 1991, the year before Hurricane Andrew roared across the southern tip of Florida, swept through the Gulf oil fields, and smashed into the quiet bayous and coastal shallows of Louisiana's Atchafalaya River delta. I was employed at that time by one of the large offshore-diving contractors based in Morgan City, an oil industry and shrimping town southwest of New Orleans.

My small crew of divers and I had just completed a nineteen-day pipeline-jetting job in seventy feet of water off the Chandeleur Islands. Too shallow for any decent depth pay, but the work had been steady and the weather fair, and nobody had gotten hurt. Good enough, I thought, looking down at the corroded steel bow of the oil field workboat as it butted through the murky, green brown coastal water toward home. No harm, no foul. Though land wasn't visible yet, I could smell it on the light wind.

"Hey, John!" I turned and looked up at the wheel-house. The Cajun captain was leaning out the starboard door, waving the hand mike of the VHF radio at me. "Call for you, *mon ami*."

"Thanks, Cap." I squeezed past the anchor winch, walked down the port rail, and·climbed the steel-grating steps up to the bridge. The workboat bucked gently as she crossed the wake of one of the faraway freighters heading up the Mississippi to New Orleans. I leaned against the door briefly until she settled down again, then picked the hand mike off its clip and thumbed the talk button.

"Mannock."

"John? Cal Walker at the office in Morgan City." The dive company operations manager.

"How you doing, Cal? What's up? Social call?"

The operations manager chuckled. "You wish." A burst of static interrupted the transmission as a flash of pink heat lightning illuminated the afternoon thunder-heads to the north. "Got something else for you to do on your way in. A *little* something."

I sighed. We'd just pulled nineteen days of exhausting, tedious work in black water, carving pipeline trenches in the gumbo-mud bottom of the Gulf with handheld water-jet nozzles. To a man, we were ready to hit the beach and have a beer or three.

"What's that, Cal? Wheel job?" I had visions of spending the rest of the day and most of the night rafted up beside some stinking oil field tugboat, hacking away with knives and saws at a never-ending ball of rope or cable she'd gotten tangled in her screws.

The pink heat lightning flickered in the far-off clouds again, causing a fresh burst of radio static. "Nope, no wheel job," Cal said. "Coast Guard wants us to check out a sighting of an oil slick reported by one of its coastal-patrol planes this morning. Something's causing a small but consistent sheen on the water out off the entrance to the Atchafalaya. It's right on your way in. I've got the position where the slick's originating right here."

"No pipelines in the area?" I asked.

"Nope. No lines within eight miles. No wrecks on the chart, either. They don't know what it is."

"Probably a fifty-five-gallon drum of oil that fell off one of these scows out here," I groused. It had happened before. Even a small container of oil could sit on the bottom for months, rust through eventually, and begin to leak its contents. A slow but continuous bleed could produce a surface slick that was miles long, particularly in calm weather, giving Coast Guard air patrols the impression that the *Exxon Valdez* herself was lying beneath the surface, spilling her guts.

I sighed again, pulling my job notebook from the hip pocket of my jeans. "Okay, Cal. So the Guard wants us to drop down on the source of the slick and see what it is, right? The usual. When I find that it's a half-empty fuel can some shrimper's tossed overboard, who do you want me to inform? Report in triplicate to the Coast Guard office in Morgan City, or just call it in to you and let you handle the paper?"

Cal chuckled evilly. "Not me, bro. I'm taking the wife and kids down I-10 to Disney World at four this afternoon. By the time y'all are done grubbing around in the mud out there, I'll be trying to peek up Minnie Mouse's dress in Or-lan-*DO!* Don't try to call me, 'cause I won't be here."

"You bastard," I said.

"Now, now," Cal laughed. "Let's try to keep the profanity off the public maritime channels. It ain't professional, you know."

"You bastard," I repeated.

He snickered, then cleared his throat. "Okay. Got a pen?"

"Yeah."

"Here's the position." He rattled off a latitude and longitude, which I jotted down.

"All right, got it," I said. "Anything else, O great operations manager?"

"Nope, that's about it. Just let the Coast Guard know what you found first thing in the morning by radio—the CO of the Morgan City office should be in by eight, I think—and then file the paperwork with them by Monday or Tuesday, after the weekend. Okay?"

"Okay, Cal. Will do."

"Oh, and one other thing . . ."

"Uh-huh?"

"Make sure you tell all the guys that while I'm walking around the Epcot center getting pie-eyed on fuzzy-peach margaritas, I'll be thinking of y'all and the fine job you're doing."

"You're a funny man, Cal. I'm leaving now."

He was laughing so hard he could barely get the words out. "Roger that, John. Over and out."

"Out," I chuckled, and hung the mike back on its clip.

Down below in the cramped crew's quarters, my loyal friends and coworkers didn't take the news of an unexpected delay in reaching shore well at all.

"You're fuckin' kiddin' me," Gaston Messier grumbled, squinting as the smoke from his Camel trickled up around his eyes. He threw the handful of cards down on top of the game of solitaire he'd been playing and pushed his chair back from the gimballed galley table. "Dis is Friday night, cuz. I ain't had a drink in over two weeks, and now I'm gonna miss de wet T-shirt finals at Titty City Grille." The grizzled old veteran diver went into a sulk. "Dem was some nice titties I seen on dem ol' gals at de end of last month."

"You're breaking my heart, Gaston," I said. "Look, it's only going to take one dive to see what's leaking the oil. Then we drag up the hook and continue on into Dulac. You left your pickup in the oil dock parking lot. You'll probably be back in Morgan City for last call, if you don't drink too many six-packs on the way home."

"Aaarrgh," Gaston commented. He folded his arms and glowered at the opposite bulkhead.

"Who's gonna do the dive, John?" Perry Flagg was

lying in his bunk, peering at me over the top edge of an outdated *Newsweek*. He smiled. Whoever had to get wet, it wasn't going to be him. The pecking order of seniority took over whenever the need to do a shallow, low-paying dive arose, and Perry had more years in the company than anyone except Gaston.

I fished a Camel out of Gaston's crumpled pack without asking him and tipped back my chair. Gaston tossed me his Zippo. I lit the smoke and let my eyes travel slowly over to the far bunk on the port side, where Dave Bledsoe was trying to make himself small behind his pillow. Dave had only recently broken out as a diver, and as such was low man on the totem pole.

He'd also been the last diver to pull a shift on the jetting assignment we'd just completed, and had done one hell of a job finishing up for us. He'd already spent nearly six hours in the water earlier in the day. I thought about it for a moment.

"Dave," I said.

He gave a long, piteous sigh and propped himself up on one elbow. "Yeah?" he murmured, resigned to his fate.

"I'm doing the dive myself," I said. "You mind helping me hook the compressors back up? Won't take long with two of us."

He swung his legs out of his bunk, looking like a man who'd just been reprieved from the electric chair. "Sure, no problem."

"Whoa!" Perry chortled from behind his *Newsweek*. "Designated job supervisor's gonna do a shit-ass mud dive? You buckin' for sainthood, Mannock?"

"That's right, Pericles," I shot back as Dave and I picked our way over gear bags toward the companionway ladder. Perry was touchy about his unusual first name. "And when Saint Peter gives me the fast pass-through at the pearly gates, I'll be sure to tell him just how quick you were to move your fat butt out of your rack to help out a tired junior diver."

"Dat don't worry him none," Gaston growled, throwing a dirty sock at Perry. "He ain't even gonna be dere, cuz. He's goin' where I'm goin'. Straight to hell."

"Yeah, and me and the devil will be takin' turns with your sister while you kiss my ass, Gaston. . . ."

I stepped out onto the back deck behind Dave, leaving behind the raucous, good-natured ribbing, and dogged shut the hatch. On the northern horizon, the heat lightning flickered like a distant warning signal in the towering thunderheads.

An hour later the workboat was anchored directly on the position Cal had given me, with bubbles of oil rising slowly to the surface and blooming into iridescent circles behind the open stern. The slick wandered off down current toward the setting sun, creating a smooth, glassy path through the rills and wavelets of the darkening sea. We'd been lucky to find it when we did; another thirty minutes and the slick would have been invisible until morning.

I locked down the neck cam of my heavy fiberglass dive hat, adjusted the free-flow valve, and checked that the umbilical hose containing my air line, pneumofathometer line, and communications cable was shackled securely to my dive harness. Putting a hand on Dave's shoulder to steady myself, I moved to the edge of the stern.

"You hear me okay, Gaston?" I said into the oral/nasal mike. The Cajun was in the dive shack with Perry, running the radio and the air manifold for my dive.

"Roger dat, cuz." Gaston's gravelly voice crackled in the ear speakers. "Good comms in dat hat."

"Just replaced the speaker," I replied. "Okay. I'm going in."

We'd dropped a weight, line, and small Styrofoam buoy on the oil blooms when we'd first arrived. I reached up, snapped on the underwater flashlight clamped to the top of my hat, and jumped toward the bobbing marker.

As the familiar explosion of silvery bubbles and sudden cold enveloped me, I hooked the thin Manila line below the buoy with one elbow. The water was dark green and shadowy, heading for dead black as the ambient light decreased with the setting of the sun. There was surprisingly little suspended sediment up near the surface. It would be different closer to the bottom, some fifty feet below. I inverted myself and began to pull my way down the line, my umbilical hose trailing after me.

Twenty seconds later my leading hand sank into the dense, cold mud of the seafloor, and a cloud of brown sediment boiled up against my faceplate. I set a glove on top of the small buoy weight, righted myself, and glanced around quickly, the glare of my hat light probing the darkness. Visibility was about eight feet.

"On bottom," I said.

"On bottom," Gaston repeated, following the rote procedure.

"Well, I don't see anything right here," I told him. "Guess I'll have to sweep."

"Sho'," Gaston grumbled. "It couldn't be dat easy, cuz. We wanna get out of here as quick as we can, so naturally you ain't gonna drop right down on top of whatever's leaking de fuckin' oil."

"Of course." I laughed, pulling the duct tape off the small coil of search line we'd secured to the buoy weight. I backed away, letting the line slip through my fingers until I felt the knot marking the first ten-foot section, my booted feet skidding on the slippery mud. "If you *didn't* want to be on the beach as soon as possible, Gaston, I'd have landed right on it. Law of the sea, right, *mon ami?*"

"Story of my effin' life," the veteran diver bitched on.

"I'm sweeping," I said. "Ten-foot radius, counterclockwise." Keeping the line taut, I churned along the bottom, digging in with my feet and free hand, looking right and left with my hat light as I went. Half a minute and 360 degrees later, I'd found nothing. A beer can and one highly indignant mud crab.

"Backing out to a twenty-foot radius, Gaston," I said, letting the search line slip through my hand again. "Sweeping clockwise this time." Alternating the direction of my sweeps would help to keep my hose from twisting and wrapping in the buoy line.

"Roger, roger, whatever," Gaston muttered. I heard the metallic click of his Zippo as he lit a Camel.

"You're not bored up there, are you?" I panted as I toiled along in a billow of mud. "You—"

I stopped abruptly just before I ran headfirst into a huge, curving wall of barnacle-encrusted steel.

"What the hell . . . ," I muttered, putting a gloved hand against it. I tipped my hat back, looking up. The wall, or hull, curved up into the darkness like the side of some huge cylindrical tank, half buried in the bottom.

"Got something here," I said. "A vessel or container of some kind. Big."

"Oh, yeah?"

"Uh-huh. Hang on, I'm going to try to get on top of it."

The barnacles and other marine growth provided just enough purchase for me to scramble upward until I reached a point where the curving steel became horizontal. I looked one way, then the other. In either direction, the hull extended off into the darkness. Long and slender. Like an immense torpedo.

"Strange-looking thing," I said, moving along the steel plate. "Slack the diver." The strain at the shackle of my dive harness disappeared as Dave fed more umbilical hose into the water topside. "It's not a sunken barge or wrecked shrimp boat, nothing like that."

"See any oil leakin' out of it?"

"Not yet."

A small stingray flapped out of the darkness and through the pool of light in front of me, kicking up a little swirl of sediment from the encrusted steel plate. As I continued along, I noticed a secondary bulge running down the long axis of the hull, just below me and to my left.

And then, on the surface of that secondary bulge, my light caught a long, snaky thread of black oil rising from a foot-long fracture in the steel. It popped free of the jagged tear and coalesced into three large, undulating globules, which then rose unhurriedly toward the surface. I moved in for a closer look and probed the crack with a gloved finger, dislodging several more bubbles that floated upward, trailing sticky threads.

"Found the leak," I said, "and judging from the little bit of oil we saw on the surface, this is probably the only one."

"Fan-fuckin'-tastic!" Gaston enthused. "Plug it up and let's get de hell out of here."

I reached into the mesh bag hanging from my weight belt and extracted a small hammer, a cold chisel, and a handful of lead wool—soft lead that had been shredded into something resembling very dense metallic oakum or caulking cotton.

"I can't figure out what this thing is," I said as I kneaded a long piece of lead wool down into the crack. "It doesn't look like any oil field boat or barge I've ever seen out here." I pushed more lead wool into the fracture and began to tap it down with the cold chisel and the hammer. "We're going to have to set a more permanent buoy on it. Whatever it is, it's big enough to hold a serious amount of oil. Actually"—I cupped a hand over another rising globule, caught it, and watched the glistening threads of oil snake upward between my fingers as it disintegrated—"this stuff sort of looks like thick diesel fuel."

"That's what I thought." Perry's voice broke in. "The wind switched around a little bit as the sun went down. Smelled like diesel to me."

"You guys got a large flag buoy rigged?" I asked, pushing the rest of the filler lead into place. I tapped it out smooth and flush over the length of the crack with the hammer.

"Yeah, and by de way, you're still no-de," Gaston said. "You won't need to decompress on the way back up if you only stay down another five minutes."

"Okay," I replied, bagging the tools and the remaining lead wool. "Leak's plugged. I'm going to head along the hull and find a place to secure the flag buoy, then get off bottom."

"Roger dat, cuz."

Leaving the crack location behind, I headed off into the gloom again, following the hull. After a minute or so of scrambling along in silence, I paused to pull more umbilical-hose slack to me and cinch up my weight belt. Standing alone in the nocturnal ocean on top of the unknown vessel, I was seized by a sudden chill. Odd, I thought. The water wasn't particularly cold.

Then I looked down and to my right and saw the unmistakable outline of a conning tower lying on its side in the mud bottom. I blinked. It had been split open vertically from top to bottom. On the twisted remains of its railed bridge were two large, twin-barreled antiaircraft guns. Four muzzles pointed off into the black water at random angles. From the top of the conning tower, a broken periscope extended out like a lance.

I was standing on the deeply canted hull of a sunken submarine.

"You got two minutes to get off bottom, John, or you're doin' decompression time." Gaston's rough voice jarred my ears. "You want de buoy?"

"Yeah, yeah," I replied, turning and pulling the slack out of my hose, "send it on down."

The heavy shackle with the buoy line attached came slipping and bumping down the umbilical a minute later. Hurriedly, I gripped the line and slashed it free with my dive knife. Then I lunged outward and soared down in a controlled fall toward the conning tower.

Landing on the bridge railing, I wrapped the buoy line around one of the growth-encrusted barrels of the nearest antiaircraft gun and secured it with four quick half hitches. Then I gathered the slack in my umbilical and leaned clear of the rusty metal.

"Pick up the diver," I instructed. Instantly, my hose began to move upward. A few seconds later it tightened at the shackle on my dive harness and plucked me off the corroded railing.

"Leaving bottom," I informed Gaston.

As I ascended, I watched the ghostly outline of the conning tower recede into the cold darkness. And then the nighttime sea closed in, and it was gone.

The workboat reached the dock in Dulac at 2100 hours. Gaston, Perry, and Dave made a beeline for their vehicles and wasted little time in getting up the road toward Morgan City's Friday night bar scene. I stayed behind to oversee the off-loading of our dive equipment from the boat to the dock. By the time the

crane operator completed the final lift, it was nearly
eleven p.m.

The operator killed the crane's big diesel and jumped
down from the cab. Nodding to me, he shuffled off toward
the parking lot. A profound silence settled over the oil
dock compound, broken only by the croaking of bull-
frogs, the lapping of bayou water against wooden pilings,
and the humming of the insects that swarmed in clouds
around the few security lights.

I was tired, too tired to consider lugging my gear off
the docked workboat, loading it into the company truck,
and driving all the way up to Morgan City. Just outside
the compound's chain-link fence, built on wobbly pilings
right over the bayou, was the dilapidated wooden structure known as Oswald's Beer, Bait, and Gas. The *s* in
Gas was painted backward, like a rounded *z*.

I'd been in the place a thousand times. A thousand
and one wouldn't hurt. I decided to have a couple of
beers, maybe a plate of deep-fried shrimp or catfish, and
sleep one more night on the boat. Tucking my clipboard
under my arm, I zipped up my work jacket and set off
across the compound toward the gates, my steel-toed
boots scuffing on the hard dirt.

The crooked wooden catwalk creaked under me as I
walked around the outside of the shack and onto the
galvanized-roofed back deck. A single long bar of sun-
bleached cypress planks ran across the rear of the ancient structure, a half-dozen battered stools in front of
it. Several upended cable spools that served as tables
were set next to the wooden railing overlooking the
water, surrounded by cheap plastic chairs. The deck and
the bar were dimly illuminated by two yellow ship's lanterns and a crookedly hung string of blue, green, and
red Christmas lights.

The woman sitting behind the bar looked up from her
National Enquirer and acknowledged me with a tip of
her peroxide-blond head. Somewhere between forty and
two hundred years of age, she was a prime example of
that hard-faced, flinty-eyed, impossibly lean species of
Southerner one finds in every oil town, trailer park, and

roadhouse below the Mason-Dixon line. The multitude of wrinkles around her thin lips deepened as she drew on her cigarette and looked me up and down, as if daring me to disturb her with a drink request.

I gazed at her for a moment, then settled back on a stool and tossed my clipboard onto the bar. "So Maggie, you gonna pull me down a draft or let me die of thirst?"

Her seamed face split into a black-toothed grin and she plucked the cigarette from her mouth between two scarlet-painted talons, erupting into a rattling, emphysematous guffaw that lasted half a minute and made the overhead Christmas lights tremble.

"Have another cigarette, Mag," I suggested.

She hoisted herself off her stool, still hacking, and stuck the smoke in the corner of her mouth before shoving a draft glass under the beer tap and pulling the carved wooden lever. "I'm quittin' as soon as I finish this pack, John," she wheezed in her East Texas accent. "I think my habit might be affectin' my looks some." She patted her perm-fried hair and cackled, showing her black teeth again.

"Nah, you're a doll, Mag." I grinned at her. "Run me a tab, will you? I think I'll have two or three."

"Sho' thing, hon." She glanced past my shoulder. "Hi, Al."

I turned to see a gray-haired man wearing steel-rimmed glasses and a khaki hunting jacket moving silently past me. "Evenin', Maggie," he said. He took a seat at one of the cable spools at the far end of the little deck.

Maggie butted her cigarette and leaned over toward me. "Boss man," she whispered conspiratorially. "He owns this place, along with six shrimp boats and that fish-packing warehouse down the bayou toward the state road." She reached under the bar and came up with a bottle of very expensive scotch and a glass. "The last Friday of every month, he comes in late, sits there by hisself, and has a few drinks. Never talks to nobody. If I didn't know him pretty good, I'd say he was a mite touched in the head."

She carried the bottle and the glass over to the gray-haired man and set them down in front of him. He thanked her with a smile, then turned to gaze out across the bayou again. Past the mangroves and the cypress trees on the far side, the moonlight glittered on the velvety surface of the Gulf of Mexico.

Nice night, I thought, turning back to the bar. I'd taken a sip of my beer and was beginning to peruse the job log attached to my clipboard when I felt a hand on my shoulder.

"Mr. Mannock?" The old man was standing behind me again. "Pardon me if I'm interruptin' you." The Cajun accent was strong, but more refined than Gaston's.

I shifted to face him. "You're not interrupting me, sir. Can I do something for you?"

He smiled pleasantly, almost shyly. "Well, I was wonderin' if you'd care to join me for a drink." He nodded toward his table, then extended a hand. "Al. Al Mandy."

I shook with him. He had to be well over seventy, but age hadn't diminished his grip. It was like iron. "John," I said. "You already know my last name, apparently."

"Only as of this evenin'," he laughed. "I asked the workboat captain, whom I happen to have known since he was a little boy. He was born here in Dulac."

He reached over the bar and picked up another whisky glass, and we walked over to the spool-table and sat down. Al Mandy poured himself a generous shot from the scotch bottle, then tipped it toward me inquiringly.

"Not just yet, thanks," I said, holding up my beer. "I'll finish this first."

"Of course." He set the bottle down and picked up his glass. *"Salut."*

"Cheers." We drank. Then I rested the draft on my leg and waited expectantly for him to begin, looking him over. Mid-seventies at the very least, but well preserved. A full head of thick gray hair topping a lean, intelligent face that had weathered many days outdoors. Dark brows and eyes that were almost fierce in their intensity. The sun-and-wind-whipped eyes of a man who had looked long and hard into far, bright distances.

He shifted his chair so that his right side was toward

me. "I'm a little deaf in my left ear," he explained, tapping it. Then he smiled and looked down at his feet, as if deciding whether or not he really wanted to pursue the conversation.

The beer was cold and it was a nice night. I settled back in my chair and waited.

"John," he said finally, "I know you found something out on the bottom of the Gulf today. Something . . . unusual."

I gazed at him. "Well, we located an oil leak. Nothing unusual about that in an oil field."

"Of course not, of course not." He paused. "May I ask what the source of the leak was? A pipeline?"

"Since you've been chatting with the workboat captain," I said, "I imagine you know that it was a sunken vessel of some kind, half buried in the mud."

Al Mandy leaned back and picked up his scotch glass. "I know that's what you told the other divers and the boat crew." He looked sharply at me. "That's *all* you told them?"

"What more is there to tell?" I took a sip of beer. "There's an old hull out there with a crack in it, leaking oil. I put a temporary plug in it and buoyed it off. End of story."

The old man leaned closer again. "Shall I tell you what you found out there, my friend?"

"If you like."

"A submarine."

I held his gaze over the rim of my glass as I took a long drink. He waited for me. "Might have been," I said, my guard up in response to being questioned so directly.

"And you didn't tell the others that it was a submarine, did you? Why not?"

I was still trying to figure that out myself. For some reason, I hadn't wanted to. But Al Mandy was different. "I don't know," I said quietly.

He smiled and settled back in his chair. A night-flying heron whiffed out of the darkness and landed on the far end of the deck railing with a prehistoric croak. It stared at us for a moment, then took off again, sailing down and across the bayou's black surface on silent wings.

"More'n forty-five year I been runnin' shrimpers in and out of this bayou," Mandy mused. "Started with nearly nothin'." He seemed lost in thought for a few seconds, then smiled at me. "That's not just a submarine on the bottom out there," he said softly.

"No?" I replied. "What is it, then?"

"A U-boat."

I raised an eyebrow. This was interesting. "A Nazi submarine?"

He nodded slowly. "German. World War Two. The Nazis were in charge of Germany at the time, so you're right—a Nazi submarine."

Al Mandy sipped his scotch and was silent for a long time. He kept looking me over, as if trying to make up his mind about something. I let him look.

Finally, his expression relaxed. "Do you have to get out of here anytime soon?" he asked. "I have a story I'd like to tell you, if you wouldn't mind listenin'."

"I've got all night, Al," I replied.

Al Mandy talked long into the night and on into the early hours of the morning, with only occasional interruptions from me. The scotch bottle emptied, along with most of another, and when dawn began to break in the eastern sky, he was still talking and I was still listening.

The story he told me that night was at times rambling, at other times—when memory served him better—incredibly detailed and coherent. I promise you one thing—nothing short of a hurricane could have moved me from that chair until he was finished.

In the following pages, I've tried to present Al Mandy's story in a way that I think does it justice. Some additional historical research and several private interviews with a few of Al's close friends helped to flesh out the details here and there. But the story is his.

Imagine how it must have been . . .

Chapter One

Kapitänleutnant Kurt Stuermer rubbed the grit and fatigue from his eyes, reversed the weather-beaten captain's cap on his head, and quickly squinted into the attack periscope again. The lone freighter between the bearing crosshairs was silhouetted perfectly against the silvery dawn sky, brazenly churning her way across the wartime Atlantic as if out for a Sunday sail.

"She's fat," Stuermer said, his voice controlled, quietly commanding. "At least six thousand tons. Panamanian flagged. We're—what? One hundred and fifty miles east of the South Carolina coast? She probably left the naval yard in Jacksonville last night." He scratched his five-week growth of beard and shook his head slightly. "Even now, at this late date, the Americans still occasionally try to send out individual ships, unescorted and out of convoy. Suicide."

"Personally, Captain, I don't mind a bit," growled Otto Dekker, the U-boat's chief engineer. "You recall that last little affair south of Iceland six months ago, when we attacked that huge convoy out of Halifax? Those bloody Canadians and their corvettes. I never thought we'd get out of that alive. Depth charges, sonar, deck guns. Those bastards know their business."

"Let's hope it takes the Americans a while longer to catch on," Stuermer said.

"I wouldn't count on it," the chief muttered gloomily.

"Frankly, neither would I," the captain replied. "They're improving all the time." Stuermer focused the periscope's optics slightly. "Exec! Anything on the sky 'scope?"

"No, Captain," *Oberleutnant zur See* Erich Bock called down from the conning tower compartment above the control room. "Not a plane in sight so far."

"Very well, Erich," Stuermer continued. "Hold the boat at this depth, Chief. Helmsman, come around to zero-eight-five degrees and maintain. We'll take her at one thousand meters with a single torpedo, then surface and finish her off with the deck gun if she doesn't want to sink."

"Aye."

The U-113 heeled slightly as the helmsman brought her around onto the new bearing. Bock slid down the ladder from the upper compartment and maneuvered his slim six-foot frame across the cramped control room to a position at the firing panel. Leaning over to an intercom, he began to speak rapidly: "Forward torpedo room, load tubes one and two." He glanced over at Stuermer quickly. "One backup in case of a dud, Captain, since we're not firing the usual spread."

"Good idea, Erich," the *Kapitänleutnant* replied, intent on his target. "Hold her steady, helm. Range now fourteen hundred meters."

"Aye, sir."

"Tubes one and two loaded, Captain," Bock said.

"Flood tubes. Open outer doors," came Stuermer's order.

"Aye." Bock repeated the command into the intercom.

A slight heaving motion began to develop as U-113 surged along silently at periscope depth on her battery-driven electric motors. Stuermer swore under his breath and began to manipulate the periscope up and down in order to keep the freighter in the crosshairs.

"*Verdammt!* Steady on zero-eight-five, helm. Chief,

can't you hold the boat at consistent depth? There isn't even a six-foot sea running!"

"Trim has been disturbed, Captain," Dekker answered. "It's this damned Gulf Stream—we've encountered a seawater density change. Probably another water temperature fluctuation." He cursed fluently, manipulating the myriad bronze flywheels and levers that controlled the U-boat's overall balance. "Worse here than the North Sea ever was. . . ."

"Keep her calmed down until after the eel is away," Stuermer said, the tension in his voice growing as the attack progressed. "Stand by to launch from tube one."

The dank control room was silent but for the hum of the electric motors and the occasional creak of flexing steel as the U-113 stalked her prey through the final seconds of the attack. Stuermer watched with icy concentration as the doomed freighter's gray bulk filled the periscope's viewing field. Nine hundred meters. At this range, they could not miss.

"Los," he ordered quietly.

"Los!" Bock repeated, jerking back the firing lever to launch the torpedo.

The U-boat shook slightly and a sudden change in air pressure popped the ears of all fifty-two men aboard as a blast of compressed air ejected the torpedo from its tube. A bundle of moldy bratwurst fell from where it had been hanging on an overhead valve and bounced onto the chief's boot. He kicked the reeking sausages from underfoot, continuing to adjust the trim controls.

"Reduce throttle to one-quarter speed," Stuermer barked. His jaw was set. "Now we'll see. . . ."

Bock was holding a stopwatch. "Twenty seconds to impact, Captain."

"Let's hope it's not another dud," piped up the teen-age helmsman from his seat at the main wheel.

"Quiet in the control room!" Chief Dekker shouted. "You haven't been out here long enough to talk during an attack, boy!"

At the periscope, in spite of the tension, Stuermer smiled. A boat chief like Otto Dekker always made a captain's job easier. And the young executive officer, Erich Bock, was a great asset as well: cool and efficient. He'd have a command of his own soon enough, at the rate U-boat captains and crews were dying in the North Sea.

"Ten seconds to impact," Bock intoned.

"No change in her course or speed," Stuermer muttered, his gray green eyes glued to the periscope's viewfinder. "They haven't seen it."

"Or us," added Dekker.

"Five . . . four . . . three . . . two . . . one," Bock recited. *"Impact."*

As Stuermer watched, a sudden explosion of white water and flame erupted up the side of the freighter, staggering her. A second later, the hull of U-113 resonated with a distant *boom*, confirming the hit for the rest of the crew. The torpedo had struck dead amidships, a lethal blow.

The freighter's forward progress halted almost immediately and she began to list to starboard, billowing clouds of white steam and black smoke. Tongues of fire flickered along her rails, and on her sloping decks men began to appear like ants from a stirred-up nest, scrambling and tumbling over each other in their haste to abandon ship.

Stuermer leaned back and slapped the hinged handgrips of the periscope up against the side of the housing. "Down 'scope," he ordered, reversing his battered white captain's cap so that the brim faced forward again. "Blow tanks, Chief. Take her up and let's have a look." He turned to Bock with a weary smile on his lean face. "I want a gun crew on the eighty-eight, in case she needs the coup de grâce, and Lothar Wolfe on one of the bridge machine guns, in case of planes."

Bock nodded. "At once, Captain." He stepped through the forward control room hatch and began barking orders.

The U-113 corkscrewed slightly as she broke through the surface and steadied herself on an even keel. "She's up, Captain," the chief announced, spinning two bronze flywheels on the trim panel.

"Good, Otto." Stuermer slipped on a salt-stained great-coat made of heavy gray leather and turned up the collar. "Make ready to crash-dive in case we spot any planes. All set, Erich?"

"I'm here, Captain," the exec said, stepping back through the forward hatch. He was buttoning up a great-coat similar to Stuermer's, but made of khaki-colored oilcloth. Behind him appeared a bald-headed, bull-necked torpedoman clad in greasy coveralls, wiping his hands on a dirty rag.

"Ah, there you are, Lothar," Stuermer said. "All right, gentlemen, follow me."

He began climbing up the steel ladder that led to the conning tower compartment and the bridge hatch above, his seaboots clumping on the rungs, greatcoat dangling. Bock and Wolfe followed, shouldering their way past the net hammock of mildewed black bread that partially blocked the overhead hatchway.

Locking a leg around the ladder, Stuermer reached up and undogged the bridge hatch. Seawater cascaded down onto his shoulders as he pushed it open, and the cold, pale light of dawn flooded into the dark tower compartment. The sharp tang of fresh salt air cut through the dank, fetid atmosphere within the U-boat like the breath of life.

Filling his lungs gratefully with the clean air, Stuermer climbed out of the hatch and stepped to one side of the bridge, making room for his exec and gunner. Wolfe squeezed his wide shoulders through the small hatch with a grunt, got to his feet, and took up station behind one of the double-barreled antiaircraft machine guns.

Stuermer lifted to his eyes the finely crafted Zeiss binoculars that hung around his neck. Less than a quarter of a mile off the U-113's port bow, the stricken freighter was settling rapidly on an even keel, listing nearly thirty degrees to starboard and burning. A plume of black, oily smoke rose like a signal marker into the clear morning sky.

"She's not down by her bow or stern," the *Kapitänleutnant* mused, adjusting the binoculars. "They must not have had all the internal bulkhead hatches closed. Either that or the bulkheads gave way when the eel exploded. She's flooding evenly." He dropped the binoculars to his chest. "Come around to two-seven-five degrees. Ahead one-quarter speed."

Bock flipped up the watertight cap on one of the bridge speaking tubes and repeated the order. As the U-113's sharklike black bow swung slowly toward the dying vessel and nosed ahead through the light swell, her foredeck hatch popped open and a half-dozen crewmen scrambled into the sunlight to man the eighty-eight-millimeter deck cannon mounted in front of the conning tower. Even as they worked to prepare the gun for action, their relief at having been freed—however temporarily—from the stinking, claustrophobia-inducing interior of the U-boat was apparent on their pale faces.

Stuermer ran his eyes over his men with concern. He bent to the speaking tube. "Ventilators all operating, Chief?"

"Yes, Captain," came the muffled reply. "Ventilating interior, under diesel power, recharging batteries."

"Very well." Stuermer turned to Bock, who was shaking a black-paper Turkish cigarette from a damp pack. He offered it to his commander. "Thank you, Erich," the U-boat captain said, taking it. Bock lit a match for him, cupping the flame against the gentle breeze. Stuermer drew heavily on it, luxuriating momentarily in the rare opportunity to smoke, then brought the binoculars up to his eyes again.

"Three lifeboats away," he said. "At least twenty men in the water, along with a lot of oil. We've cracked her fuel tanks."

"Lucky for them they weren't carrying aviation fuel," Bock muttered, looking through his own binoculars. "Unlike that Dutch tanker out of Aruba we torpedoed last month. *Mein Gott*, what an inferno."

Stuermer nodded. "I doubt if any of the crew survived the initial explosion. That high-octane aviation gasoline is so volatile. Like sailing along on a bomb."

On the machine gun, Lothar Wolfe grunted: "That was one shipload of fuel the Yanks and Tommies won't be able to use in their bombers."

"I wonder what was on this freighter," Bock said. "Not munitions. She'd have blown up on torpedo impact."

"We'll ask," Stuermer replied. "If we get a chance." He glanced over at his exec. "Planes?"

"Nothing yet, sir. Sky is clear."

"Radar?"

Bock shook his head, tapping a finger on the small wire-strung wooden cross that he'd brought up through the hatch and hurriedly mounted on the bridge. "No radar impulses detected on Metox, either," he said, referring to the German radar-detection device. Its antenna wires were supported by a crude wooden cross that had to be taken down and passed through the conning tower hatch before every dive, then reinstalled upon surfacing.

"Come around to three-five-zero degrees and idle engines in neutral," Stuermer ordered. He rested the binoculars against his chest and set his elbows on the bridge rail, smoking and watching the officers and the crew of the burning freighter flounder in the oily water. The U-113's slender black hull drifted nearer, prompting a number of the life jacketed men to thrash and kick in the opposite direction. The three lifeboats that had been successfully deployed were dangerously overcrowded, near capsizing, in spite of the fact that many of the crewmen, some badly burned, were still in the water. The fourth lifeboat hung by one cable from a damaged davit beside the ship's stern superstructure.

A sudden explosion rocked the air. A ball of black-and-orange fire erupted from the deck of the dying freighter, accompanied by shards of wood and steel. Instinctively, Stuermer, Bock, and Wolfe ducked low behind the armored rail of the bridge, then cautiously rose again. The freighter had begun to sag in the middle as well as list, black smoke billowing ever more furiously from her cargo hatches.

"Her back's broken," Bock observed. "She'll go down quickly now."

The merchant-marine captain of the torpedoed freighter knelt in the bow of one of the wallowing lifeboats, looking at his worst nightmare. A German submarine, black and deadly in appearance, had surfaced at her leisure after mortally wounding his ship and was now idling right up on him and his struggling crew. The screams of the burned, broken, and drowning echoed in his ears. And there was *nothing* he could do: no help to be had, no way to fight back. Nothing to do but wait.

As he watched, the faces of his enemies came into view. Standing on the bridge of the conning tower was the captain, identifiable by the white peaked cap that only U-boat commanders wore. He could not have been more than thirty, with a lean, scraggly-bearded face and broad shoulders under his dark gray overcoat. His expression aged him far beyond his years: his visage composed of hard horizontal lines—brows, mouth, eyes—all permanently set by strain and resolve. In appearance, he was the very embodiment of the icy, northern sea raider.

Beside him stood another officer in a tan overcoat, slightly taller and more slender, his dark hair and beard partly disguising his youth. He was a younger version of the commander, with the same weary, hard expression dominating his face. A bald-headed crewman, a powerful man with huge arms and shoulders, stood behind a heavy double-barreled antiaircraft gun, flexing his hands on its grips.

At a massive deck gun mounted below the conning tower, six more Germans clad in greasy coveralls and engine-room leathers stared in his direction, their pale faces devoid of expression.

As the captain watched, swallowing hard, the big gunner on the conning tower swung his twin-barreled weapon around and lowered it to the horizontal.

"All right, Erich," Stuermer said quietly, "that looks like the captain in the bow of that lifeboat. Ask him."

Bock brought a hand up beside his mouth and shouted, in perfect American-accented English, "Is the captain present? I want to speak to the captain."

The merchant-marine captain hesitated, then raised his hand. "I am the captain of the vessel you just torpe-

doed," he shouted angrily, his own English heavily
Dutch-accented. "What do you want?"

"We know what you were carrying aboard your ship,"
Bock called. "We wish you to confirm it for us. We
know it was not fuel or munitions."

The merchant-marine captain didn't answer. Stuermer
could see him thinking as he steadied himself in the bow
of the rocking lifeboat.

"Do you think the explosion scrambled his brains
enough to fall for that?" Wolfe growled from behind
his gun.

Stuermer watched his beaten counterpart silently,
studying his face. Another Dutch career mariner, as
tough a breed as any. The man was nobody's fool, and
probably no coward, either. "He isn't going to tell us
anything," he said.

He received confirmation of his assessment a second
later. "You can go straight to hell!" the freighter's captain shouted.

They floated opposite each other in silence for a moment, in a sea littered with groaning, injured men, scattered debris, and oil. Nearby, the dying ship began to
emit a loud hissing sound as hot steel began to touch
cold water, accompanied by clouds of steam and the
shriek of rending metal. Stuermer's gray green eyes
flickered over the teetering lifeboats, the vainly struggling men in the water, and the burning hulk behind.

He turned to Wolfe at the machine gun. "Lothar," he
said, pointing outward toward the helpless men. "Not
difficult shooting, eh?" He grinned.

The big torpedoman/gunner returned the grin. "Child's
play, Captain," he replied in his coarse baritone. He
trained the twin barrels down at a low angle and
squinted through the weapon's ring sight, his shoulders
firmly against the recoil pads. Bock covered his ears,
smiling.

A look of horrified realization came over the freighter
captain's face as he saw the machine gun swing down. He
had no time even to bellow a protest before the heavy
weapon opened up with an ear-shattering burst of gunfire.

The lifeboats rocked precariously as men dove for cover on top of each other. Those in the water tried in vain to thrash their way beneath the surface. Cries of alarm rose in a ragged chorus.

The deadly hail of heavy-caliber bullets passed ten feet above the survivors' heads and hammered into the damaged davit that held the fourth lifeboat to the sinking freighter. Amid a cloud of sparks and metal fragments, the davit cable parted and the lifeboat plummeted into the water stern first. It bobbed to the surface immediately, self-righting, and drifted toward a small knot of crewmen floating together around a charred wooden hatch. Immediately, they began to flounder toward it.

"Not bad, Lothar," Stuermer said, "not bad."

"Personally, I think he could have used a little less ammunition, Captain," Bock commented with a smile. He glanced over at the big torpedoman. "You may be slipping, Lothar."

"Too much time locked up in this stinking tub without shore leave, sir," Wolfe growled, leaning casually on his weapon. "My skills are deteriorating due to overwork." He grinned, showing strong white teeth.

"You and all the rest of us, Lothar," Stuermer pointed out. "Good shooting, Torpedoman."

"Thank you, sir."

The merchant-marine captain was just getting to his feet in the bow of his boat. He looked slowly over at the last of his men climbing into the safety of the fourth lifeboat, then gazed back up at Stuermer.

Stuermer cleared his throat, flipped his cigarette butt over the rail, and cupped his hands around his mouth. His English, unlike Bock's, was guttural and more typically German-accented: "We must be leaving shortly, Captain. How much food and water do you have aboard your lifeboats? And do you have a compass with you?"

The merchant-marine captain responded after an incredulous pause: "We are short of both water and food. And we lack sufficient medical supplies to tend to all the injuries. I have a man lying in the stern with his lower leg off at the knee. Also, there are many burns."

"Have you oars?"

"Yes."

"Come alongside," Stuermer called, "but I request that you control your men. Do not attempt to board my vessel. Agreed?"

The merchant-marine captain nodded. "Agreed."

Steurmer waved him in. "Erich," he said, "have twenty cans of lard and ten cans of bully beef passed up through the forward hatch, along with forty gallons of fresh water. Water's the main thing. Being a little hungry until they're picked up won't kill them." He looked back at the bobbing lifeboat as its oars were clumsily deployed, the men rearranging themselves to pull toward the U-113. "And give them a box of bandages and burn salve, six bottles of blood plasma with an intravenous needle, and a dozen ampules of morphine. That's all we can spare."

"Right away, Captain." Bock stepped onto the conning tower's outer ladder and slid down fifteen feet to the U-boat's slatted foredeck. He trotted past the deck gun crew, knelt at the open forward hatch, and began to shout orders.

The lifeboat bumped alongside the U-113. "Keep a close watch on them, Lothar," Steurmer cautioned. "The captain knows what's good for him, but some of his crewmen look a little wild-eyed."

There was a whirring of ball bearings as Wolfe swung the heavy weapon around, and a loud clack-*clack* as he checked the breech. "Anyone who tries to rush our foredeck will find his bad morning suddenly getting even worse, Captain," he rumbled, lining up the lifeboat in the machine gun's ring sight.

"I doubt that it will be necessary," the *Kapitänleutnant* replied. "And keep an eye on the sky. All that smoke will bring someone eventually." He bent to the speaking tube. "Still nothing registering on Metox? Radar?"

"Nothing so far, Captain," came the muffled answer.

"Hmmm." Stuermer scanned the skies. "It can't last. We're not staying here much longer, hanging about on the surface like a sitting duck."

Down on the foredeck, Bock was passing a small wooden crate of medical supplies to the soaking, oil-covered crewmen in the lifeboat. In the stern of the low-riding craft, a young man barely more than twenty was stretched out under the thwarts, the bleeding stump of his leg tourniqueted and wadded with wet shirts. He had screamed himself faint, and was now simply moaning into the forearm of the older crewman who cradled his head in his hands. The older man locked eyes momentarily with Bock in silent accusation, but the hard-faced young exec steeled himself, turned away, and began to pass over five-gallon jerricans of freshwater.

When the supplies had all been transferred, Bock stepped back and called up to the bridge: "Boat is provisioned, Captain."

"Very well, Exec." Stuermer leaned over the rail. "Stand clear of my vessel, Captain," he shouted, again in English. "We are leaving." He paused. "I must ask you if you managed to radio a distress signal before abandoning ship, sir."

The merchant-marine captain looked up at him as the lifeboat bobbed away from the U-boat's side, his bearded face solemn. "I regret that I cannot give you that information, Captain."

"It is for your own good, sir," Stuermer replied. "If I knew that you did not, I could broadcast a standard SOS signal on the six-hundred-meter international wavelength, insuring that you and your men would be picked up quickly."

The other captain gazed at him with penetrating dark eyes. "And you would also know whether or not submarine-hunting planes and vessels are likely to be heading to this position as we speak." He smiled thinly. "We are at war, Captain. I repeat: I regret that I cannot give you that information."

"Very well," Stuermer said. "Then I must leave now. I am sorry for your misfortune this morning, Captain. I wish you and your men all luck in making the U.S. coast or—better yet—being rescued without delay." He brought a hand sharply to the brim of his cap in a standard military salute.

The merchant-marine captain hesitated, then returned

the salute. "I thank you for your chivalry, Captain, but I cannot wish you well."

"Understood. Good luck." Stuermer shifted his attention to the U-113's foredeck. "Secure deck gun! Prepare to dive!" As the six-man gun crew plugged and locked down the eighty-eight, he leaned over to the speaking tube. "Ahead half speed. Helm, come around to course zero-six-five and maintain. Prepare to dive." He looked up as Bock mounted the last few rungs of the bridge ladder and stepped inboard. "All secure, Erich?"

"Yes, sir," the exec replied. "Gun secure, closing forward hatch." Ahead of the conning tower, the last member of the gun crew dropped through the foredeck hatch, pulling it shut after him. The U-boat gathered speed as she settled onto her new heading, her sharp hull foaming through the light Gulf Stream swells. Bock lifted the wooden-cross antennae of the Metox out of its bracket and turned to Wolfe, who had just finished locking down his antiaircraft gun. "I'll pass this damn thing down to you, Lothar."

"Mmpf," grunted the big torpedoman. He squeezed himself through the tight hatchway of the tower compartment and disappeared below. Bock lowered the antennae down to him a moment later, then stepped over beside Stuermer.

The two officers stood in the salty wind, savoring their last few seconds of clean air and light before descending into the stifling, dim world of the U-boat's interior.

"That Dutch captain was a tough nut to crack," Stuermer said, looking astern at the shrinking spectacle of the still-burning freighter and the wallowing lifeboats. The decks of the stricken vessel were awash; she'd be gone in minutes.

Bock laughed. "Did you see the look on his face when Lothar opened up with the bridge gun? He thought we were going to murder them all in the water."

Stuermer shook his head. "Disturbing, isn't it, that he would assume that? War puts strange fears into men's heads. We're sailors and soldiers, not assassins. This far offshore, with relatively little danger to my boat and crew, I can afford to be magnanimous. What sailor would leave another marooned and helpless on the open sea when he was able to render assistance, much less attempt to murder him?" He scowled. "We'll leave the wholesale slaughter of innocent people to the experts in the *Gestapo* and the *Waffen SS*. We sank the freighter, and our duty ends there."

Bock didn't even wince. Two years earlier, such talk would have been unthinkable. But two years was an eternity when you lived each day and night locked in an iron coffin floating through a wartime sea. And everyone knew, even now, that the tide of war was turning against Germany.

"All right, Erich," Stuermer said, sighing deeply, "let's get below. We'll go deep, to two hundred and twenty meters, and alter course underwater away from the heading the freighter survivors will report seeing us take on the surface."

"Yes, Captain," the exec replied, lowering himself through the tiny hatchway.

"And one other thing," the *Kapitänleutnant* continued. "Have the radioman broadcast a standard SOS on six-hundred-meter international wavelength with the position of those survivors. Fifteen minutes only. We're not making a target out of ourselves with a radio signal the Americans can home in on."

The steel hatch banged shut on top of Stuermer, and the long black hull of the U-113 began to slide beneath the waves as she went bow down in a shallow, unhurried dive.

Chapter
Two

One week later, the U-113 was idling in calm, sapphire blue water some two hundred miles east of the Windward Passage, the fabled northern route into the Caribbean Sea between Cuba and Haiti. Cargo netting had been deployed along the starboard bow so that it hung into the water, and the U-boat's foredeck was packed with naked, soap-covered sailors, laughing and jostling as they took turns leaping into the ocean. A few thrashing strokes and they would scramble up the netting, accompanied by the hoots and cheers of their comrades.

"*Ach*, Horst! You still smell like the south end of a northbound pig! Try again!"

"Still have both your feet, Max?"

"There, Lothar, *there!* There's another one, see him?"

"Get him, Lothar! *Gott in Himmel*, this mob needs to wash their asses some more!"

The big torpedoman, standing at the starboard rail and clad only in a pair of khaki shorts, brought a beautifully crafted German hunting rifle to his shoulder and squeezed off a quick shot. Fifty feet away, the round smacked into the shiny brown dorsal fin of one of the large pelagic sharks that were circling the U-113, attracted by the sounds and the vibrations of the bathing sailors. A sudden thrash, and the fin was gone.

"Bravo, Lothar!"

"Three cheers for the Black Forest huntsman!"

"Forget the cheers, Paul. Finish soaping down and get your rank ass in the water!"

Up on the conning tower bridge, Erich Bock turned to his captain. "They're enjoying themselves, sir. A bath—even a saltwater bath—and a half hour to horse around in the sun will do wonders for morale. I'm glad you decided to chance it."

Stuermer lowered the Zeiss binoculars from his eyes. "Well, it was time. They were starting to look like human moles, and smell much worse." There was a sharp *crack* as Lothar Wolfe snapped off another shot at a shark. "Keep your eyes peeled, though. The Americans are improving their coastal defense systems all the time. The air patrols are getting too well organized and frequent."

"Still," Bock mused, "it's not very likely they'd be out this far. Grid number DN-47 puts us well east and south of the Bahamas."

"Yes, but you and I can't afford to be lax, can we, Erich?" Stuermer flashed a wry smile at the younger man, the crow's-feet at the corners of his eyes crinkling. "All we need is some wandering PBY to happen upon us while the entire crew is cavorting like children on the bow. Not a pretty picture." The PBY-5 "Catalina" flying boat was one of the most effective antisub aircraft. He glanced at his watch. "Another ten minutes, that's all."

"Yes, sir," Bock grinned. "Chief!" Down on the foredeck, Otto Dekker looked up at the conning tower. "Ten minutes more," the exec called, tapping his watch. Dekker nodded, toweling his wet, thinning hair, and stalked off into the crowd of sailors like a patrolling bear.

The thin blond hair and bony shoulders of Jonas Winkler appeared in the bridge hatchway. He blinked up from behind his thick, round glasses, wincing in the bright sun. The radio/hydrophone operator had a distinctly indoor, academic appearance, with a frail build, stooped posture, and skin the color of parchment. A former flutist with the Berlin Philharmonic Orchestra, he had been the ears of U-113 since her first patrol in the early days of the war. Musicians like Winkler were much sought after as sonar and hydrophone operators. Their trained ears gave them an advantage in using technology in which one "saw" the enemy by interpreting sounds.

"Radio communication from U-395, Captain," Winkler said, holding up a piece of paper.

"Good, good," Stuermer replied, taking the paper. "Kessler's made the rendezvous in one piece, at least." He stepped back from the hatch. "Come up out of that hole, Jonas, for God's sake. Even you need a little sun once in a while."

"Thank you, sir," Winkler said. The rake-thin man clambered awkwardly up onto the bridge deck and stood there, blinking rapidly. "It *is* bright out here, isn't it?"

Stuermer smiled. "Don't worry, Jonas. We'll all be locked up in our tin drum again, soon enough." He ran his eyes over the piece of paper. "Kessler says he's dangerously low on fuel, and has spent all his torpedoes." The *Kapitänleutnant* gave a snort of laughter. "Only twelve days out of Lorient and already he's fired off all his eels? Either it's like shooting rabbits up near Long Island where he's been operating, or our old friend Hans is starting to miss what he's aiming at."

"Knowing Captain Kessler, sir, I doubt that very much." Bock smiled.

Down on the foredeck, Chief Dekker began to herd the crewmen toward the open hatch, barking admonitions at the few stragglers. Four sailors hauled on the cargo netting, recovering it to the deck and rolling it up.

"Any communication from the *Milchkuh* yet?" Stuermer inquired. The large, noncombatant U-boats were designed as refueling and reprovisioning vessels. *Milchkuh,* literally "milk cow," submarines enabled the smaller attack boats to operate far from their European bases for extended periods of time.

"Not yet, sir," Winkler answered. Bock shook a Turkish cigarette out of his pack and offered it to him, but the radio/hydrophone man politely declined. "No, thank you, Lieutenant. I've given it up. It makes me cough."

Bock shrugged and stuck the cigarette between his own lips. "Probably better for you, anyway," he said.

"Captain!" Chief Dekker hailed from the foredeck. "All below, sir. I'm going down myself."

"Very good, Chief," Stuermer called back. "Let's have the men back on station, but you can leave the hatch open and rotate them up on deck to smoke, four at a time. We're going to stay on the surface and look for the *Milchkuh*."

"Aye, sir." The chief engineer snapped off a quick salute and walked toward the forward hatch.

"Well, let's have a look around for Kessler," Stuermer said. "Ahead one-quarter speed, come around to course heading two-four-five." He brought the powerful Zeiss binoculars to his eyes again and began searching the horizon.

Bock repeated the order into the speaking tube and began to look in the opposite direction with his own binoculars. There was a muted metallic *thung* as the shafts were engaged, and the U-113 began to make way under diesel power, her black bow cleaving the sparkling blue water into twin trails of foam. As the U-boat gained speed, a gentle breeze wafted over the conning tower, dissipating some of the eighty-degree heat.

Winkler shivered, folding his bony, blue-veined arms to his stomach. "Brr," he said, "I'm cold. Permission to leave the bridge, Captain?"

Stuermer smiled at Bock. "Of course, Jonas. Go below before you get frostbite."

Winkler grinned, accustomed to jokes about his preference for indoor life. "Thank you, sir." He twisted through the hatch to the tower compartment. "Standing by on radio for contact with the *Milchkuh*."

"Very good, Jonas." Stuermer resumed scanning the horizon with his binoculars. "We'll proceed to the western edge of the grid square," he said to Bock, "then backtrack to the southeast. Sooner or later we're going to encounter Kessler's boat, and maybe the *Milchkuh* as well."

"Aye, sir."

The U-113 cruised on a westward heading for nearly two hours before Stuermer ordered her into a wide turn that put her on a southeasterly course. He, Bock, and two additional lookouts had seen no indication of other U-boats in the area. After another hour and a half, with the U-113 entering the center of the map grid square, the *Kapitänleutnant* called Jonas Winkler back to the bridge.

"You wanted to see me, sir?" the slender radioman inquired, the breeze tossing his limp blond hair.

"Yes, Jonas," Stuermer said. "Look, are you sure we have the right grid square? That broken rotor on the *Schlüssel* machine isn't causing us to get our messages scrambled?"

"Absolutely not, sir," Winkler replied, shaking his head vehemently. "I checked the rotor's function after I made the repair. It's as good as new. And we have the correct rotor and plug settings for this date. Messages are being received and decoded correctly. We are supposed to rendezvous with the *Milchkuh* today, at this map location."

Stuermer sighed. "All right, Jonas. Thank you."

A sudden shout came from the hatchway beneath their feet. "Mr. Winkler! Mr. Winkler! Hydrophone contact! Diesels right on top of us!" The young radioman second-class who served as Winkler's backup was nearly incoherent with fright.

Everyone on the bridge started in alarm and began searching the surrounding ocean frantically in an effort to locate the source of the sound, minds suddenly sharp with the memory of being hunted by relentless Canadian corvettes. Just as quickly, their panic faded as it became obvious that all the way to the horizon, 360 degrees around, there was nothing but empty sea.

"What the hell is that young fool screaming about, Jonas?" Bock growled, unable to conceal his annoyance. "There's nothing out here but flying fish. How can he have diesel sounds right on top of us, unless he's listening to our own engines?"

"Check on it, Jonas," Stuermer directed, but the radioman was already disappearing through the hatchway.

A moment later, his head reappeared. "Diesel sounds confirmed, Captain. I can't explain it, but the hydrophone is vibrating with the sound of another diesel-powered vessel close behind our starboard stern quarter."

Four heads swiveled in unison as everyone on the bridge examined the ocean to the left of the U-113's wake.

Bock squinted, then brought his binoculars up to his eyes. "What the hell is that?" he exclaimed, pointing astern.

Expecting to see a large surface vessel upon hearing the report of diesel sounds, the men hadn't noticed the small white V of a secondary wake cutting along unobtrusively in the U-113's wide foamy trail. At its apex was the upper end of a periscope, and beside that another length of larger-diameter tubing that supported an unusual float-valve assembly.

Stuermer grinned. "Well, I suppose if that were an American submarine, we'd all be swimming for our lives right now." He glanced over at Bock. "I think Captain Kessler is playing a little cat and mouse with us."

As if on cue, the periscope and the float tube began to rise out of the water, until finally the conning tower of another Type VII U-boat broke the surface in a froth of white foam. It continued to rise until the entire hull of the second boat was exposed, pacing the U-113 at a distance of less than one hundred feet. Like the U-113, the U-395 carried no identifying numbers, only a faded *Kriegsmarine/Ubootwaffe* crest painted in red and black on the armored plating of her bridge.

"Kessler will have something to say about this, no doubt," Stuermer mused, smiling.

A tall, red-bearded man wearing a black leather jacket and the distinctive white cap of a U-boat commander appeared on the bridge. Bock could see his teeth flash in a wide grin as he leaned forward, hands on the rail, his body posture aggressive and confident.

"Aaaaah, Kurt!" he roared. "You're dead, you bastard! I sneaked up and killed you!"

Stuermer laughed and waved back. "You have an unfair advantage, Hans! We were expecting you to rendezvous on the surface, not stalk us like a schoolboy hunting rabbits!" He pointed at the long, tubular mast that supported the odd-looking float-valve assembly. "When did that old tub of yours get outfitted with the new *Schnorkel?*"

Kessler reached over and with gusto slapped the vertical tube that allowed his sub to run at periscope depth using its diesel engines. "Two weeks ago, when we were refitting in Lorient. The Lion is going to see to it that every U-boat gets one as soon as possible. That damned Allied radar can't see us when we're submerged, Kurt—its wavelength is too long to pick up something as small as the *Schnorkel* float on the surface." He laughed like a drunken Viking. "When we left, we went straight through the Bay of Biscay, up the English Channel, and around the tips of Scotland and Ireland, close enough to spit on British soil! We must have bypassed a hundred corvettes and destroyers as we ran the blockade, and not a single one of those bastards saw us! Oh, they were pinging away like mad with ASDIC, but they weren't actually *sure* we were there, so they were never able to pinpoint us. We alternated between diesel and silent running and left them far behind, chasing echoes and jockeying around like so many bumper cars at the carnival! Hilarious!"

"That's good news," Bock remarked quietly to his captain.

"Hans has a selective memory," Stuermer replied, smiling across the water gap at the red-bearded commander on the opposite tower. "If two or three corvettes triangulate you with confirmed ASDIC reflections, the *Schnorkel* isn't going to do you much good. They'll run accurate depth charge patterns until you're blown to bits. All the *Schnorkel* does is prevent you from being located visually on the surface."

"Well, that's something," Bock went on. "At least they can't see you motoring along topside like a clay pigeon."

"Oh, by all means." Stuermer nodded. "I'm not saying it won't be nice to have one, just that it isn't the magic cloak Hans is making it out to be. It has some technical problems, too. Last year, I went out on a trial cruise on a *Schnorkel*-equipped boat. It works fine when the weather is good, but when the sea gets rough and waves start to pass over the top of the tube—or worse, the chief engineer lets the boat get too deep—the float valve closes automatically and cuts off the air. The diesels keep sucking air out of the boat's interior, so you suddenly find yourself gasping for breath, your ears rupturing, and your eyes about to pop out of your head. Less than enjoyable, to say the least." He raised a hand to his mouth and shouted, "Where the hell is the *Milchkuh?* I'm not going to float around out here forever waiting for it!"

"What choice do you have?" yelled Kessler. "Neither you nor I have enough fuel left to make it to the Azores, much less Lorient! If it doesn't show up, we'll have to transfer all remaining fuel to one boat and leave the other floating with a skeleton crew until we can find another *Milchkuh*, or even an attack boat we can pinch fuel from! Bloody hell, that'd make *three* boats having to share fuel and shorten patrols in order to get home!"

"Do you know whose boat we're supposed to meet out here? The message we got didn't specify."

"Bauer, on U-496." Kessler cast his gaze around impatiently. "God knows where that bastard's got to."

"I hope it's not another unreported sinking," Bock muttered. "One direct depth charge hit and you're dead too soon to let anyone know about it on the radio."

"I don't think so," Stuermer said. "Bauer was operating his floating grocery store in the mid-Atlantic, well south of the convoy routes. He shouldn't have encountered any escorts or patrols that far away from the action." He looked at the sun. "I wish he'd show up, though. We're going to lose the light in another couple of hours."

. "Kurt!" Kessler's bellow came echoing across the water. "I have something to discuss with you. Can you transfer over here for a few minutes after we rendezvous with Bauer? It's important."

"Of course," Stuermer shouted back. "Let's give him another hour to put in an appearance. What do you say to continuing along together at this speed to the far side of the grid square?"

Kessler raised a hand in agreement, nodding his head, and turned to speak to his exec.

"And Hans," Stuermer added. The tall captain looked back. "Good to see you alive."

"You, too, you bastard," came the gruff reply.

The twin U-boats cruised along side by side for another forty minutes, black metal sharks patrolling a calm azure sea, before one of the lookouts on Kessler's bridge shouted that a third boat was surfacing approximately a quarter mile to the south. All eyes were quickly directed to that area.

"That's the *Milchkuh*, sir," Bock said, focusing his binoculars.

"About time," Stuermer replied. "Helm, full right rudder. Come around to heading one-eight-zero."

"One-eight-zero degrees, aye," came the muffled confirmation through the speaking tube.

The two attack boats turned together like a pair of predatory fish homing in on a blood trail and headed for the new arrival. Sailors began to emerge from the forward hatches and muster on the decks fore and aft of the conning towers, in preparation for the upcoming transfer of fuel hoses, torpedoes, and provisions. The large bow and stern torpedo-loading hatches were swung open, ready to receive the new cargo.

Kessler let his boat drop behind Stuermer's, waving him on as they approached the *Milchkuh*. "Go ahead, Kurt! If Bauer can handle two of us at once I'll come in on his opposite side!"

Stuermer nodded, and issuing a few succinct commands to helm and engine room, brought the U-113 neatly alongside the supply sub. Up close, the difference between the two designs was apparent: while the Type VII attack boat and the Type XIV tanker were roughly the same length overall, the U-496 lacked the U-113's slender, knifelike hull shape. Rather, she was thick and fat, her integral hull tanks oversized in order to carry the additional 635 tons of diesel fuel that could resupply up to a dozen attack boats. At 1,690 tons, she had nearly two and a half times the bulk of either the U-113 or the U-395.

Though she carried numerous torpedoes, she had no firing tubes of her own. Bridge-mounted antiaircraft guns were her only armament. Comparatively slow and unmaneuverable, her role was one of support and supply, her only real defense, stealth.

As the U-113 settled beside the bulkier U-496, a steady stream of sailors began to pour from the *Milchkuh*'s bridge hatches, most of them quite young and clad in shorts and undershirts, arraying themselves along the bridge railings like schoolboys out on a field trip. On deck, the duty crews in their greasy coveralls began to lay out the heavy fuel hoses for transfer, as well as open cargo bays that would disgorge new torpedoes and provisions.

"*Gott*, Martin!" Kessler's hoarse bellow resounded over the water as the U-395 came sliding up on the U-496's opposite side. The black-jacketed *Kapitänleutnant* grinned in mock horror from his conning tower bridge. "Are you running a kindergarten aboard that ark of yours? Who are all these hairless children?"

"Ah, Hans," came Martin Bauer's laconic reply, "I could tell it was you without even looking." It was difficult to pick Bauer out among his crew; he was not wearing his white U-boat commander's cap. "And good day to you, Kurt. And you too, Exec Bock."

Stuermer and Bock finally singled out the short, stocky captain with the blond crew cut and waved to him. "Glad you could make it, Martin," Stuermer called. "And don't mind Hans. He's shot off all his eels and is feeling a little hot-blooded today."

"Yes, but did he hit anything?" Bauer returned. "That is the question."

"Fourteen eels expended and nine ships sunk!" Kessler shouted from the opposite side of U-496. "Nearly forty thousand tons in four days, you pair of condescending bastards! I expect to overtake Kretschmer in another week or two, so be damned to you both!" *Kapitänleutnant* Otto Kretschmer was Germany's leading U-boat ace of World War Two, sinking 266, 629 tons of Allied shipping before being captured in the North Atlantic on March 16, 1941.

A ripple of laughter ran through the men who were

crowding the bridges and decks of the three U-boats. In addition to being a top commander, Hans Kessler was regarded fondly throughout the fleet as something of a character—a role he relished and played to the hilt.

"If you're done making jokes, Captain," Bauer laughed, "perhaps you'd like to receive a refueling line?" He gestured to the crewmen who were handling a secondary diesel hose on the afterdeck, having already transferred the first one to the bow of Stuermer's boat.

"Pass it over, my friend, pass it over!" Kessler leaned toward the U-395's bow and glared down at his foredeck crew. "Look sharp, now, boys!"

As his men hurried to retrieve the hose and connect it to the fuel tank fill-valve, Bock turned to Stuermer and said, "I wonder what it would be like to have to serve a whole tour of duty with Captain Kessler."

Stuermer shrugged. "His men love him," he said simply. "His exec once told me that they'd follow him across the devil's doorstep if that was where he led them."

He clapped a hand on Bock's shoulder. "Supervise the fueling and provisioning for me, Erich. I'm going to transfer over to U-395 for a few minutes. Kessler wants to talk to me."

Kessler pulled the mildewed curtain across the entrance to the U-395's tiny captain's nook and leaned back against its small metal sink, folding his arms. Stuermer brushed by him in the closetlike space and sat on the green leather mattress of the single bunk. From the deck overhead, there came a constant thumping and banging as the crew worked to onload the torpedoes and foodstuffs.

Stuermer peered up at his fellow captain. "All of a sudden you don't look happy, Hans," he said.

Kessler frowned, unsure of how to begin. "Well, I'm not," he growled. He shook his head. Stuermer waited patiently, studying him.

"Look, here's the thing," Kessler said at last. "When I was in Lorient, I came by some information that disturbs me greatly. And damned if I don't have mixed feelings about passing it on to you."

"What, Hans?" Stuermer said, with a matter-of-fact expiration of breath. "Are you going to tell me that we aren't going to get the new wonder boats we've been promised? That the führer in his infinite wisdom would rather build tanks to get stuck in the mud on the Russian front than follow Dönitz's sane advice to cut the Atlantic supply lines from North America to the British Isles and Murmansk? That the Allies' U-boat detection technology is improving so quickly that we'll all be lucky to live through the New Year? That Goebbels, Himmler, and that fat degenerate Göring may, in spite of our best efforts, lose the war for us by whispering the wrong advice into Hitler's ear? We already know all that, Hans, even if we don't want to admit it to ourselves."

"No, no!" Kessler whispered angrily. "And keep your voice down when you talk like that. I was assigned a couple of new junior officers in Lorient whose sole function on my boat, it seems, is to dispense Nazi Party propaganda to my crew. The other side of that coin, Kurt, is that they're likely to report any political sarcasm they overhear back to their Party supervisors. You want the *Gestapo* coming to visit you some night when you're on shore leave?"

Stuermer's eyes flashed. "The *Gestapo* can go hang!" he snarled, then abruptly lowered his voice and regained his usual calm. "I apologize, Hans; this is your boat. I just don't equate myself, you, or most of the men in the *Ubootwaffe* with that gang of uniformed political buffoons in Berlin. I know you feel the same way."

"*Ach,* Kurt, we conduct ourselves like honorable navy men and serve Germany as best we can," Kessler rasped, shifting against the sink. "But look, you've gotten me off track. What I wanted to tell you has nothing to do with problems of military strategy and equipment. It's something more immediate, more personal."

Stuermer spread his hands. "So?"

"Your exec, Bock . . . how's he doing?"

"Erich Bock?" Stuermer shrugged. "Lieutenant Bock has in the past and continues at present to perform his duties admirably. It's like having a second captain aboard U-113. Exactly like it, as a matter of fact: he's long overdue for a boat of his own. Intelligent, observant, cool and brave under fire—a first-class officer."

"Aaaargh," Kessler groaned, rubbing his eyes. "You like him."

"Yes, and so do you. What the hell is this all about, Hans?"

Kessler sighed and looked directly at his comrade.

"About Bock . . ." he began.

The sun was a flame-colored ball hanging just above the purple water of the western horizon when the U-113 completed her refueling and provisioning and locked down her loading hatches once more. From bow to stern, the U-boat's interior was packed with foodstuffs. Sausages, hams, bundles of vegetables, and hammocks stuffed with bread loaves hung from overhead valves and conduits. Crates of eggs and potatoes were jammed among the newly racked torpedoes, and jugs of wine and juice were wrapped in blankets and lashed into the narrow bunks shared by the crew. Because the weight of supplies had to be distributed evenly throughout the vessel in order to maintain its trim and there was little storage space, U-boat men worked and slept with their rations.

Bock, on the bridge, looked toward the stern just in time to see Stuermer jump from the slightly higher deck of the *Milchkuh* to the top of his own boat's starboard saddle tank. The captain looked decidedly unhappy as he strode toward the conning tower, habitually casting a critical eye over the condition of his vessel's hatches and access ports.

"All secure, Erich?" he asked briskly as he reached the top of the bridge ladder, consciously lightening his grave expression.

"All secure, sir," Bock reported. He gave his commander a second look. "Everything all right, Captain?"

Stuermer hesitated, his hard gray green eyes softening a little as he met his exec's inquiring gaze. It seemed to Bock as if he wanted to say something, but couldn't find the right words.

And then it didn't matter.

"Captain!" came a frantic shout from the control room below. "Six radar contacts bearing north-northwest, coming in fast! *Aircraft!"*

Chapter Three

U.S. Navy Chief Aviation Machinist's Mate Eugene Moffitt, piloting the lead PBY-5 Catalina bomber in the six-plane formation, pressed the throat mike to his larynx with a leather-gloved hand. "Damn, y'all. Intelligence was bang on; they really can decode all that U-boat gibberish comin' out of Europe. There's three of them sumbitches lyin' side by side dead ahead." He began to dive his aircraft toward the water. "Follow my lead, flight. Take it right down on the deck, full throttle. Everyone drop a stick of six surface bombs right across their asses, then bank around, three right and three left, and hose 'em down with your nose and blister guns."

"Roger that, Chief," the response crackled in Moffitt's headphones.

"Roger, Mr. Moffitt."

"Yee-haw, Chief."

"Save your depth charges for when they dive," Moffitt shouted, barely able to hear himself over the high-pitched roar of his own engines.

"They ain't gonna get a chance to dive, Chief, once we get done with 'em!" came the breathless, excited voice of one of the younger pilots.

"Shut up, Yablonski! Keep the radio clear and concentrate on what you're doin'!"

*   *   *

"Verdammt!" Stuermer swore as he saw the black silhouettes of the six approaching Catalinas spread across the fiery disk of the setting sun. "Full ahead! Bow planes down!" he shouted into the open hatchway at his feet. "All crew forward! Dive, Chief! *Dive!*" Bock started for one of the bridge antiaircraft guns, but Stuermer grabbed him by the shoulder. "No, Erich! Too little, too late! Get below—we're going to run!"

"Aye, sir." The lithe exec slipped down through the hatchway and disappeared as the U-113 slid away from the U-496, her screws churning the water into white foam.

Stuermer waved wildly at Bauer and Kessler, who were both on the conning towers of their boats. "Split up in three different directions!" he yelled. "I'm going west! Make them divide their formation!" His heart sank as he saw that the *Milchkuh* and the U-395 were still yoked together by mooring lines and fuel hoses.

"Get out of here, Kurt!" Kessler bellowed, taking up position behind one of the three double-barreled antiaircraft guns mounted on the U-395's bridge. On both linked U-boats, sailors scrambled to man all available guns while their comrades on the decks below worked frantically to turn the two vessels loose from each other.

The staccato blast of heavy-caliber gunfire shattered the stillness of the gathering dusk as the U-boat gunners opened up, pouring streams of tracer shells into the sky. The line of bomb-heavy Catalinas closed with frightening speed, barely fifty feet off the water.

The U-113 tilted down under Stuermer's feet as she gained enough speed to power into her crash dive, dark water surging over her bow and up the foredeck. Stuermer yelled again at the two other commanders: "Go *deep* when you dive! This is Caribbean water! *Don't run from planes near the surface, especially at night! Don't Schnorkel, Hans!*"

His words were lost as the Catalina on the extreme left of the formation simply exploded in a huge ball of flame. The other planes never wavered, flying on relentlessly into the hail of tracers like great black bats. Kessler's U-395 had just separated from Bauer's lumbering

U-496 when Moffitt's lead bomber overflew them, nose and blister guns blazing. A series of rapid splashes erupted on the water behind the plane, some fifty feet apart, as the Catalina dropped its surface bombs. Stuermer ducked low behind the armor plate of the bridge, one hand on the hatch and a foot on the top rung of the compartment ladder, watching the attack progress in slow, unreal time.

Crump crump crump crump crump crump! Six towering geysers of white water bracketed the U-496, some closer than others. Both the *Milchkuh* and the nearby U-395 rocked violently, their conning towers swaying. Kessler's boat pulled away rapidly with guns hammering as the second Catalina roared overhead, dropping her stick of bombs, but the U-496 was not moving. Stuermer thought he could see Martin Bauer reel across his bridge in a sparking cloud of bullet strikes as the aircraft's machine guns raked the conning tower, but he wasn't sure. And then the second stick of bombs detonated.

Crump crump crump . . .

BANG!

With a thunderous, air-heaving concussion the U-496 blew up, disintegrating instantly on the surface as her huge fuel tanks and ammunition stores exploded. Stuermer felt the blast flatten the skin of his face against his skull and drive the breath from his lungs. Behind the giant column of boiling fire, he could see the conning tower of the U-395 knocked nearly horizontal by the shock wave, the keel of Kessler's boat rolling up into the air.

And then dark, foaming seawater began to swirl into the bridge as his own U-boat arced down into the depths. The *Kapitänleutnant* ducked through the opening to the tower compartment and slammed the hatch cover shut behind him as the huge black shape of a third bomber roared overhead, machine guns chattering.

The rain of slugs impacted on the bridge and the hull plates of the U-113 with a sound like that of a thousand ball bearings flung from a pail, hurting Stuermer's already traumatized ears. He slid down the ladder to the control room, nearly falling as he landed on the tilting deck. "Hang on!" he shouted. "A Catalina just went right overhead! She dropped a stick of—"

WHAM WHAM WHAM WHAM WHAM WHAM!

Six shattering explosions kicked the U-113 like a tin can, blowing her stern up toward the surface and sending Stuermer, Bock, Dekker, the hydroplane operator, and the teenage helmsman—the only five men of the fifty-two aboard who weren't packed into the forward torpedo room as human ballast—sprawling across the cramped control room. As the battle lanterns flickered wildly, the helmsman went headfirst into a ballast control flywheel, his neck wrenching at an unnatural angle, and lay still. The other four were bowled into the forward bulkhead, crashing on top of each other in a jumble of arms, legs, loose equipment, and foodstuffs as the U-boat went nearly vertical in the water.

The U-113 plummeted toward the bottom nearly four miles below at an angle of more than eighty degrees. Already ballasted bow down for a crash dive by flooded forward tanks, steeply angled bow planes, and the weight of her crew, the sudden lifting of her stern by the explosions had turned her into a huge iron javelin hurtling into the depths, completely out of control.

"Catch the boat, Chief!" Stuermer roared, clawing his way up the slanting deck plates. "Catch her or we'll pass crush depth before we know it!" Dekker fought his way up to the ballast control panel, pulling himself up the deck literally by his fingernails. Behind him, Bock shoved on his feet, giving him something to push against. There was a blast of compressed air as the chief threw the valves to the forward tanks.

"Erich! Bow planes up, *verdammt!*" Stuermer gestured wildly at the hydroplane station next to Bock. The exec released his grip on the foot of the tower compartment ladder and flung himself across the deck toward the controls. Seizing the base of the tiny hydroplane operator's stool, he reached up and yanked on the bow plane manipulator with all his might. It wouldn't budge.

"Too much water pressure on the planing surfaces, Captain!" he gasped. "She's falling too hard!"

Stuermer kicked away from his purchase at the base

of the attack periscope and sprawled next to Bock, heaving on the manipulator with all his strength. The combined weight of the two men slowly moved the planes into an upward orientation. Still the boat fell, accompanied by a growing cacophony of metallic creaks, groans, and squeals as the increasing external pressure of the sea stressed the hull to its limit.

"Otto . . . ," Stuermer said loudly, his voice rising with alarm.

"I'm trying, Captain!" the chief panted, spinning flywheels madly. "Boat's extreme position is overcoming her own buoyancy! Too much momentum!"

Stuermer turned toward the forward hatch, hanging on with one elbow hooked through the hydroplane controls. "All crew astern!" he bellowed at the top of his voice. "Get to the aft torpedo room, boys! Hurry, *verdammt*, hurry!"

A hull rivet gave way with a report like a gunshot, followed quickly by two others. The U-113 moaned in her iron and steel bones as she began to contort under the incredible pressure exerted on her outer shell. Bock's eyes jerked over to the depth gauge mounted on the buoyancy control panel. The indicator needle was just passing 275 meters. Official crush depth for the Type VII hull was 250 meters.

"Twenty-five meters past design crush depth, Captain," Bock reported, his voice shaking only slightly.

"Aye," Stuermer growled. The first crewman from the forward torpedo room appeared in the control room hatch. It was Lothar Wolfe, battling his way up the slippery deck plates, followed closely by the rest of the ship's company. "Go, Lothar, go!" urged the *Kapitänleutnant*. "All the way back, or we'll never catch her!"

The big torpedoman clawed his way up the control room and through the aft hatch, a line of sweating, gasping, battered, and bleeding men following him, their faces drawn and pale with fear. At the ballast panel, Dekker juggled the controls like a man possessed, sweat pouring down his craggy face. "Flooding aft tanks," he rasped. "Come on, you bitch. . . . Level off . . ."

Almost imperceptibly, the extreme slope of the deck

began to lessen. As more men scrambled aft and the
stern tanks filled with seawater, the U-113 began to de-
crease her downward angle. Still, she was dropping into
the abyss at a fatal speed, heading for a sudden and
violent end when her hull finally ruptured.

Bock stared at the depth gauge. "Three hundred and
ten meters, Captain, and still falling."

Stuermer got to his feet as the deck leveled to the
point where he could just barely stand, his arms locked
around the periscope housing. "Faster, Chief," he urged.

"She's coming back, Captain," Dekker gritted. "Come
on, you sweet bitch. . . ."

Pow! Another rivet blew. Shrieks of straining metal
echoed throughout the boat.

"Three hundred and twenty-five meters, Captain,"
Bock whispered, "and still falling."

"Water rising in the aft compartment, Captain!" came
a yell from astern. "Batteries in danger of being
flooded!" Flooding of a submarine's batteries was feared
by all sailors. Seawater coming into contact with battery
acid produced deadly poisonous chlorine gas.

"Distribute Dräger gear to all crewmen!" Stuermer
shouted. The underwater escape gear consisting of a
hose and mouthpiece, nose clip, oxygen cylinder, and
inflatale life jacket was quickly broken out. "Do not turn
on oxygen bottles unless someone smells toxic gas!"

"Three thirty-five," Bock said hollowly. "Still falling."

"If there is water rising in the aft bilges, Captain,"
Dekker muttered, "there may be leaks in the forward
compartment as well, weighing our bow down."

"And if there aren't," Stuermer responded, wiping a
trickle of sweat from his temple, "the extra weight in
the stern should help us recover from this dive." He
managed a quick grin. "Think in positive terms, Otto."

The U-boat was still sliding downward at an angle of
twenty degrees. Bock bit his lip. "Three hundred and
forty meters. The naval architects claim our crush depth
is two fifty. You wouldn't happen to know what it *really*
is, would you, Captain?"

"No, I wouldn't, Lieutenant," Stuermer replied, his
eyes glued to the down-angle gauge on the bulkhead.

"When I was an exec like you in thirty-nine, my captain, August Heydemann, took the U-116 down to three hundred meters to escape a depth charge attack by a British destroyer. The boat screamed bloody murder, just like now"—his terse monologue was punctuated by the sharp report of another bursting rivet—"but the hull held." He looked over at Bock. "The only men who really know the crush depth of these boats are the ones who never made it back to the surface."

The interior of the U-113 continued to echo with the grinding moans of stressed metal as she finally came level. "Got her," Dekker said hoarsely. He threw more valves and spun flywheels. "Balancing her out, Captain." The boat shuddered as compressed air blasted into her aft tanks.

"All crew to resume battle stations!" Stuermer shouted through the aft hatch. He gestured toward the hydroplane station. "Level out those bow planes, Erich."

"Aye, sir."

An unhealthy-sounding *thumpthumpthumpthump* accompanied by a troublesome vibration became apparent. Stuermer caught Dekker's eye. "Shaft damage," he muttered, turning to an intercom mounted on the periscope housing. "Engine room, disengage electric motors. Report status."

"Three hundred and fifty-seven meters," Bock said softly. He licked his lips. "Nearly one thousand two hundred feet deep." He was interrupted by a long, drawnout screech as the U-113's iron bones complained once more.

Stuermer nodded at Dekker. "Let's not punish her anymore, Chief. Bring her up to two thirty. Easy."

Dekker puffed his cheeks and blew out a long breath. "Aye."

One of the senior engineers, stripped to the waist with blood dripping from a cut on his temple, stepped into the aft hatchway. More men filed past him, hurrying forward to their battle stations, Dräger gear dangling. "Damage report, Captain," the engineer said. "Stuffing boxes, glands, and seals have been ruptured around both shafts. Port shaft will not turn at all; it's jammed from the outside. Starboard shaft turns, but has external damage as well. It's probably bent, and I'm certain the propeller is damaged, too. That was the thumping sound we were hearing. The bent shaft was making its stuffing box leak worse with every revolution."

"The leaks?"

"Under control, Captain."

"Batteries?"

"Batteries are intact. No cracks in the housings. Seawater has not flooded them, and we're pumping out the bilges now." The engineer wiped his forehead with the back of a grimy hand. "No chlorine gas formed, Captain. It was close, but we were lucky." He stared at the dead body of the teenage helmsman, sprawled on the deck with his head stuck through the spokes of the flywheel, his neck clearly broken.

"All right, Richter. See what you can do about getting me some propulsion, if any."

"Aye, sir." The engineer disappeared back through the hatchway.

"Twelve hundred feet, with bomb damage, and still holding together," Bock said. He patted the ballast control panel. "I love this old boat, rust stains and all."

"She held," Stuermer concurred. He looked upward, as though he could see through the hull, through the dark water, and up into the nighttime skies. "But let's hope those planes don't get any more help once they exhaust their supply of depth charges."

"They must still be after us," Bock said, "unless they think they killed us on the first run. Or that we got away clean."

"Planes don't have ASDIC or sonar," Stuermer muttered. "They can't hunt us underwater like corvettes. They have to make their kill on the first rush, on the surface, or they miss their chance. Once we go deep, they have no way of locating us. The most they can do is salt the area at random with depth charges set to go off at different depths, and they can't carry an endless supply of those."

Bock nodded. At that moment, a series of distant concussions reverberated through the hull plates of the U-

113. The control room was silent until the last echo died away.

"Those are depth charges," Stuermer said, "not surface bombs."

"They're a long way from us," Bock remarked. "Maybe they're just dropping them at random, like you said, Captain."

"Maybe," Stuermer replied. He looked up at the control room ceiling again. "Or, more likely, they're after Kessler."

Moffitt banked wide after overflying the submerging U-boat, in time to see the bombs from the third Catalina in the flight blow her nearly vertical, lifting her stern and rotating screws clear of the water. In an instant, she was gone, plummeting straight down into the depths as white water thrown into the sky by the explosions rained back down onto the sea's churning surface. Already jubilant after seeing Yablonski's stick destroy the fat U-tanker, he turned his attention to the third boat, wallowing back upright after being knocked over by the tremendous explosion.

"I think that makes two of these sumbitches sunk!" he radioed. "Flight, concentrate on that Kraut that's still on the surface! I want a hat trick tonight, y'all!"

"Yee-haw!" Yablonski's high-pitched voice chattered through everyone's earphones. "Y'all see that fat tub get blowed up? She done blowed up real good!"

"Shut up, Yablonski!" Moffitt shouted. "Carter! Bodean! Wheel to the south! The rest of you follow me around to the north! Make them gunners divide their fire! Approach from opposite directions! I'm goin' high! Carter, Bodean, you two come in low! Nail that sumbitch and don't let's fuckin' fly into each other, got it?"

"Roger that, Mr. Moffitt, sir!"

"Aye, aye, Mr. Moffitt!"

"All right." Moffitt brought the Catalina out of its steep bank and lined it up on the remaining U-boat, which was now moving forward in an apparent attempt to dive. Yablonski and O'Meara brought their planes around tight on his flanks, while off in the distance, on the far side of the enemy vessel, Carter and Bodean were wheeling into position in tandem, their black aircraft hard to pick out in the gathering dusk. Perelli was gone; the junior lieutenant from Yonkers and his Catalina blown to ash by the German antiaircraft guns. From the bridge of the U-boat, red-and-orange tracers streamed into the evening sky, tracking the planes like ribbons of fire.

Kessler grabbed the young ensign manning the antiaircraft gun opposite him by the back of his shirt and jerked him back toward the tower compartment hatch. "Get below, Paulsen!" he roared. "Get the men forward for the crash dive!"

He swung the heavy-caliber machine gun to the south as he saw two of the Catalinas approaching low, no more than fifty feet off the water. Lining them up through the weapon's ring sight, he depressed the trigger. The gun chugged, spitting out long, graceful lines of tracer bullets that curved up toward their targets with illusory slowness. With steely concentration, Kessler walked the deadly spray of fire across the sky and into the leading plane.

The aircraft jinked as the shells hit it, and its port engine burst into flames. A second later the port wing broke off and the doomed Catalina fell out of the air, hitting the water and cartwheeling across the surface in a whirl of fire.

"*Haaaa!*" Kessler yelled, delighted. He shook his fist at the remaining bomber before jerking the gun back up and hurriedly targeting it. The deck angled sharply under his feet and dark water began to boil up the sides of the conning tower as the U-395 powered into her crash dive.

The Catalina roared overhead before Kessler could get a good lead on it, but by incredible luck released its depth charges too late. The explosive canisters—four of them—tumbled through the air over the U-boat and hit the water more than two hundred feet from their intended target. The big *Kapitänleutnant* ducked through the conning tower hatch, cackling with glee, and slammed the lid shut. Seconds later, black water gurgled over the hatch, and the U-395 slipped beneath the waves, well ahead of the other flight of attacking planes, as the wasted charges detonated harmlessly off to her starboard side.

"Goddammit!" Moffitt cursed, as he saw Bodean's plane shed a wing and come apart on the water in a fiery explosion. "Get that sumbitch, Carter!"

He swore again, more eloquently, as he watched Carter's spread of depth charges miss the disappearing U-boat completely. In helpless rage, he pounded his glove on the already fully depressed throttle levers. The German was going to escape; they were too far away. Once submerged, the U-boat would go deep and there was no way in hell they were going to locate it in the nighttime sea.

"Spread out to my starboard flank and drop your cans along the Kraut's estimated course line!" Moffitt ordered as he watched the enemy vessel dive out of sight. "Maybe we'll nail him before he gets too deep!"

Kessler hugged the periscope housing as the U-395 angled steeply downward, snapping off orders to the control room personnel: "Bow planes down full! Full port rudder! Full speed ahead!" He gave his chief engineer a tense grin. "Corkscrew her off to the left as she goes down, Chief. As hard as you can." Locking his hands around the periscope, he shouted over his shoulder, "All hands prepare to receive depth charges!"

The U-boat spiraled off to port as she fell through the lightless water, diverging farther from her original course line with each passing second. No one spoke. The interior of the U-395 was silent but for the creak of flexing metal and the light thrum of the electric motors.

Whan wham wham wham wham wham wham . . .

The multiple depth charge detonations hammered the U-boat and her crew mercilessly, rattling teeth, blurring vision, and shattering eardrums. And they went on and on and on and on. . . .

And then they stopped.

Kessler and his men stood motionless, hardly daring

to breathe, their eyes flickering over one another. The U-395 moaned eerily as she continued her steep dive, taking her human cargo farther and farther into the depths, away from the surface and the planes above that swarmed like angry hornets, frustrated.

Kessler relaxed his grip on the periscope and nodded to his chief engineer. "All right, Chief. Level her out." He glanced at the depth gauge. "One hundred and seventy-five meters. Hold her at this depth. Helm, zig once to the southeast for two minutes, then zag to the southwest and maintain."

He clapped the sweating chief—a swarthy Rhinelander named Goethe—on the shoulder. "Battery power?"

"Low, sir," Goethe answered. He pursed his lips. "We were servicing the linkages from the generators the whole time we were on the surface today. I'm surprised we've got enough juice stored to light a lantern bulb."

"Christ." The *Kapitänleutnant* gazed at Paulsen, the young ensign. "Well, we could kill all power and just hover at depth for a few hours. Those planes don't have enough fuel to buzz us forever. Of course, we'd still be hanging about near our last known position."

"And those planes have almost certainly called for reinforcements," Paulsen added pointedly. "Maybe even destroyers with sonar." He shrugged and lifted an eyebrow. "Much tougher to shake, Captain."

"Aye." Kessler thought a moment. "Our best option, it seems, is to *Schnorkel* away under diesel power. We'll put distance between ourselves and this hot location, and recharge our batteries at the same time. Planes can't spot a *Schnorkel* float and its small wake at night, no matter how calm the sea is. Funny, though . . ." He paused, scratching his red beard.

"Sir?" Paulsen prompted.

"Mmm? Nothing, Ensign. It's just that when Captain Stuermer was pulling away at the beginning of the attack, I thought he yelled something about not running shallow—especially from planes—at night. That this was Caribbean water."

"What possible difference could that make?" the chief

said over his shoulder. "Water's water. If you've got enough to hide your boat without hitting bottom, you've got everything you need." He spun a ballast control flywheel. "Perhaps you misheard, Captain."

"I suppose, Chief," Kessler mused. "All right. Bring her up to *Schnorkeling* depth. Prepare to switch to diesel power. I want those batteries charged up as soon as possible."

Eugene Moffitt was not a happy man. Two planes of the six he'd led out of the new airstrip on the southeastern tip of Cuba—Perelli's and Bodean's—had been destroyed. Carter's and Yablonski's had been shot up pretty badly, and his own controls were mushy, as though his ailerons had been sieved by the withering ack-ack fire sent up by the U-boats. Only O'Meara's plane had gotten through unscathed. Moffitt spat onto the floor between his legs. Fuckin' mick had a charmed life.

"Not good, you guys!" he fumed into the throat mike. "Two buddies and their crews blown to hell, along with two planes, and only one sure kill. We had the jump on them sumbitches! What the hell happened? Carter, you forget how to aim a stick of cans, or what?"

"No, Mr. Moffitt. Just had trouble maintainin' altitude is all. Caught a burst of ack-ack in the starboard wing just before that bastard got Bodean. Threw off our depth charge run some."

"Fuck!" Moffitt shouted to no one in particular, pounding his glove on his plane's instrument panel. "Fuck, fuck, *fuck!*"

The battered flight of Catalinas rumbled on through the night sky, maintaining a loose formation in case someone lost control of a damaged plane and veered into a wingman. Moffitt was rehearsing what he was going to say during the upcoming debriefing, visualizing his CO asking him to justify his battle tactics and account for his flight's heavy losses, when Yablonski's adenoidal yelp came over the airwaves: "Holy shit, y'all! Ten o'clock low! What the hell's that down there?"

*   *   *

The warm waters of the Gulf of Mexico, Caribbean, and southern Atlantic are rich with life, from the great whales to the tiny plankton on which they feed. At frequent intervals, for no known reason, these minute planktonic organisms suddenly begin to reproduce at an astonishing rate, blooming into living tides that extend for miles throughout the surface water of the open sea. Of the many fascinating characteristics exhibited by plankton, one of the most unusual is its capacity to bioluminesce.

Particularly when disturbed.

As the U-395 *Schnorkel*ed along under diesel power at a depth of forty feet, her forward progress through the water disturbed millions upon millions of tiny, transparent zooplankton, causing each one to emit a miniscule flash of greenish white light. In untold numbers, each flash combined with others to produce a swirling cloak of living light that sheathed the hull of the U-boat as it moved forward just under the ocean's black surface.

From an altitude of 700 hundred feet, it looked to Moffitt and his pilots as if a brightly glowing 130-foot cigar was cruising along beneath them, leaving a shimmering trail of liquid light in its wake. The shape was unmistakable.

"Approach from dead astern," Moffitt radioed, trying to control his elation. "Let go all your remaining cans. This sumbitch is ours, boys."

Aboard the U-113, Stuermer and Bock glanced up at each other sharply as the telltale rumble of faraway depth charge explosions reverberated faintly through the hull. The barrage lasted nearly ten seconds, then faded away.

The *Kapitänleutnant* felt the eyes of everyone in the control room upon him, but made no comment. His gaze moved over to the depth gauge, then to Chief Dekker, sitting on the metal stool in front of the buoyancy control panel.

"Maintain our depth at two hundred meters until further notice, Otto. Stay deep."

*   *   *

The shattered hull of the U-395 spun downward, torn into three barely connected sections by the sudden onslaught of airborne depth charges. Some of the bodies whirled out of the fractured U-boat, to drift aimlessly through the black void of the sea, perhaps to rise to the surface eventually and give grim testimony to the fate of their vessel and comrades—if any human eyes happened by to discover them.

But *Kapitänleutnant* Hans Kessler and most of his crew remained trapped inside their iron coffin, taking one final ride into the abyss, down to the devil's doorstep.

The ocean into which the U-395 sank was over four miles deep. It took nearly an hour for the mangled wreckage to hit the bottom.

Chapter
Four

The U-113 had been limping northward at a depth of two hundred meters for more than four hours, her single functioning shaft, damaged as it was, setting up an alarming vibration that thumped ceaselessly throughout the hull's interior. Stuermer, poring over a chart in his tiny quarters, paused to rub his eyes and tell himself yet again that the air inside the U-boat wasn't nearly as unbreathable as it tasted. There was a soft knock on the bulkhead outside, and the curtain to his sleeping nook was pulled back.

"A word with you, Captain," Chief Dekker said, his face and burly forearms streaked with diesel fuel and grease. Behind him, Bock, Winkler, and Wolfe crowded in close. Stuermer made room, and Dekker and Bock squeezed into the closetlike space. Winkler and Wolfe stayed at the entrance, leaning against the jambs. All four crewmen looked close to exhaustion.

"What's the situation, Otto?" Stuermer asked, trying to keep the weariness out of his voice. "Overall status."

Dekker puffed his grimy cheeks and blew out a long breath. "We've got problems, Captain. As you know, only one propeller shaft would still turn freely after the attack. We made it more or less operable by dropping it from its coupling to the main drive, sliding it back through the stuffing box and gland until the bent section was well clear of the hull, and then reconnecting it to the drive with a meter-long extension piece.

"The trouble is, the vibration caused by the bend is going to wear the seals out eventually, and we won't be able to support the shaft. The leakage is already a bloody nightmare." The chief mopped his dripping forehead with a dirty rag, breathing with effort in the thick, rancid air. "We won't make it one-quarter of the way back across the Atlantic with that shaft, Captain.

"Problem number two: we have no fuel in the starboard saddle tank, and less than half in the port saddle tank."

"What?" Stuermer's face registered surprise. "We'd completed refueling from Bauer's *Milchkuh* just before the Catalinas attacked."

"That's true, sir, but we must have sustained damage to the tanks. They've either been cracked or holed, or both. We were so busy trying to deal with the shaft repair and leaks that we didn't notice we were losing fuel. Torpedoman Wolfe just discovered it a few minutes ago, when he sounded the tanks."

"Lots of seawater, Captain," Wolfe muttered wryly, "but very little diesel."

"Did you transfer the remainder?" Stuermer asked Dekker.

"Yes, sir. When we determined that fuel was leaking steadily out of the saddle tanks, I checked the integrity of the keel ballast tanks and then pumped all remaining diesel into them." He wiped his brow again. "It wasn't much, I'm sorry to report."

"How much have we got?"

"About one-fifth of our capacity, sir. Maybe a little less."

"*Verdammt.*" Stuermer rubbed his eyes again.

There was a moment of respectful silence. From overhead, condensation that had formed on the inside of the hull dripped with a steady *plink . . . plink . . . plink* onto the deck plates, nearly keeping time with the thumping of the damaged propeller shaft. The yellowish light from

the battle lanterns flickered for a few seconds, and then
Stuermer looked up at Winkler.

"Jonas. Please tell me that you were able to repair
the radio and the *Schlüssel* machine."

The thin ex-musician shook his head forlornly. "I'm
sorry, Captain. I'm still trying, but the concussion from
the surface bombs jarred both pieces of equipment off
their mounts and threw them across the sound room.
The radio is completely smashed. The *Schlüssel* I might
be able to repair, but without the radio it's useless." He
raised a hand helplessly into the air. "It's nothing but a
tangle of shattered tubes and wire."

Stuermer leaned back against the edge of his bunk,
his pale face expressionless but for something that might
have been a hint of black amusement. He locked his
hands behind his head and gazed up at his executive
officer.

"All right. Why don't you summarize for me, Erich?
Then we'll discuss our options." He permitted himself a
thin smile.

Bock cleared his throat. "Well, Captain, it looks like
this: we have one jury-rigged propeller shaft that won't
get us even partway across the Atlantic, and less than a
week's worth of diesel fuel running at half speed on one
engine. The batteries are undamaged, but they're only
useful as long as we have fuel to run the engines and
keep them charged up. In addition, the added load on
the shaft will drain them more quickly than usual, restricting our range even further.

"We have an unknown amount of damage to the external hull and tanks, which may affect our ability to
maneuver, submerge, and resurface. The time will come
when we have no more diesel fuel, and must proceed
solely on battery power. When the batteries run down
that one final time, we're going to have to surface and
remain dead in the water—a sitting duck. We won't even
be able to handle the boat in bad weather."

"You make it sound cheery, Lieutenant," grumbled
Wolfe. He spat into the small trash can beside Stuermer's chart table.

"The worst thing, it seems to me," Bock went on, "is

the loss of the radio. Without it, we can't contact either *Ubootwaffe* Command or any other U-boats at sea to arrange a rendezvous. We have no way of letting anyone know where we are or that we need assistance."

"And it's highly unlikely," Stuermer added, "that we'll run into another U-boat in this area. As you know, Dönitz is keeping the bulk of the attack fleet into the North Atlantic, targeting the convoys from Halifax. Ours is one of the last boats still operating this far south."

"More likely we'll find another American air patrol than one of our own vessels," Dekker grunted.

"Exactly," Stuermer concurred. "Anything else?"

"Yes, Captain," Bock said. "Machinist Feldstein is dead. The internal injuries he sustained when the torpedo fell on him during the crash dive were too severe. Hartmann just informed me that he died in his sleep a few minutes ago." Hartmann was the U-113's cook/barber/field surgeon. "Including Helmsman Preiss, that brings our casualty total from the air attack to two."

"Plus Seaman Roth's broken leg," Wolfe mentioned.

"Right, Lothar. That, too." Bock thought for a moment. "That's everything I can think of, Captain."

Stuermer nodded silently, scratching his unshaved neck. From down the passageway came the sound of coughing. The atmosphere within the U-boat was becoming intolerable: humid, heavy with carbon dioxide, and reeking of engine-room fumes.

"All right, gentlemen," Stuermer said, rising to his feet, "let's see about getting this boat on the surface so we can ventilate the interior before we all choke to death, and can charge batteries and check for external damage. We'll go to periscope depth first, Chief." He glanced at his watch. "Just after midnight. Stop engines. No forward momentum, no propeller rotation. We're not going to risk kicking up any phosphorescence, at least not until we have a good look around with the sky periscope. I'm not lighting this boat up like a Roman candle in the middle of the night." Stuermer put a hand on Dekker's shoulder. "Blow the tanks easily, Otto. I want to float straight up to the surface with a minimum of water disturbance."

"Aye, Captain." The chief stepped out of the sleeping quarters and headed down the passageway to the control room, followed by Winkler. Wolfe went aft toward the engine room. As Stuermer moved into the passageway, Bock touched his elbow.

"Sir, about the phosphorescence . . . you think Captain Kessler was aware of it? How it can illuminate a shallow-running U-boat?"

Stuermer hesitated for a moment. "I don't know, Erich. Hans never operated this far south. We only found out ourselves by accident, remember? That night in the Straits of Florida when we were running on the surface and the water glowed like liquid fire? Phosphorescent plankton occurs in the North Atlantic, but not as frequently and not with this kind of intensity." He shook his head. "I don't think Hans knew. If he was running from the planes at *Schnorkel* depth, they may have killed him." A sad smile crossed his face. "But maybe they didn't."

"I hope not, sir."

Bock started toward the control room, but this time it was Stuermer who paused.

"By the way, Erich, your father—he's a fisherman, isn't he?"

"Yes, sir," the exec replied. "He owns three small herring boats that fish the Baltic out of Kiel. He runs one himself; his two brothers—my uncles—run the others. But it's my father's business."

Stuermer's hard eyes softened imperceptibly. "A hard-working fisherman. And his son a top graduate of the Naval Academy at Flensburg. That must have been a proud day for him."

Bock nodded, slightly puzzled. "Yes, sir. It was. For my mother, as well."

For the second time that day, the young exec got the impression that Stuermer was searching for words that eluded him. And then, abruptly, the *Kapitänleutnant* grinned and clapped Bock on the upper arm.

"There, you see, Erich? No wonder you have such an aptitude for the seafaring life. It's in your blood." He turned away and headed for the control room.

"Yes, sir. Thank you, Captain," Bock replied, pleased but slightly taken aback by the unexpected compliment. He stepped out of the captain's quarters and followed Stuermer forward, moving quickly and carefully along the dank passageway.

The U-113 hung motionless just below the surface of the dead calm midnight sea with only the bulky head of her sky periscope exposed, a huge black predator lurking hidden, testing its surroundings with a single slender antenna. For a full ten minutes the periscope rotated slowly, scanning from horizon to zenith, but no airborne hunters wheeled overhead across the glittering carpet of stars.

Clouds of air bubbles began to froth the surface, setting off flickers of phosphorescence, and in the midst of the roiling water the conning tower of the U-113 appeared, rising straight up into the air. The U-boat heaved gently as her decks came clear; then she stabilized with a slight list to port. Around her waterline, the gleam of bioluminescing plankton gradually subsided into the occasional pinpoint flash as gentle ripples lapped the hull.

The bridge hatch undogged with a clank and swung open. Bock emerged first, followed by Stuermer, Winkler, Wolfe, and Dekker, all five men breathing in the sweet night air like the elixir it was. Moments later the forward hatch cracked and crewmen began to clamber wearily out onto the foredeck, lighting cigarettes and stretching their cramped bodies.

"Beautiful night," Winkler said, gazing up at the sky through his wire-framed glasses.

"Yes, and it looks as though we have it all to ourselves," Stuermer replied. He turned to Wolfe. "Lothar. Mount the Biscay Cross anyway. We don't want any surprises."

"Aye, Captain." The big torpedoman bent down over the bridge hatchway and called for the wooden Metox radar-detection antennae to be passed up.

Dekker and Bock moved to the conning tower's external ladder, preparing to descend to the deck for a walk-around inspection of the upper hull. Stuermer touched Winkler's elbow before following. "A special assignment for you, I think, Jonas. We'll be lying on the surface for an hour or so while we assess the damage. On such a fine night, perhaps a little solo recital might be in order. Uplifting to the spirit, eh?"

Winkler smiled broadly. "I'll see to it right away, Captain," he said, stepping toward the open hatch.

Stuermer smiled back and moved to the top of the external ladder. Hooking the insteps of his seaboots around its vertical supports, he slid quickly down to the deck with practiced ease. Dekker and Bock were already walking forward along opposite sides of the boat, checking every inch of the hull for damage.

The *Kapitänleutnant* moved slowly up the deck among his men, pausing here and there to offer an encouraging word. He stopped at the forward hatch as the canvas-wrapped bodies of the two dead seamen, Preiss and Feldstein, were passed up through the arms of their crewmates from the compartment below.

"Put them there, together," he said. "After we complete our inspection of the hull, we'll give them a proper sailor's burial. I'll read a few words."

The men nodded silently, trying not to look at the two six-foot bundles of cloth lying side by side on the deck slats. Stuermer continued on up toward the bow of his boat, his eyes roving left and right. At the bow, Dekker and Bock waited for him, leaning on the heavy rigging cable that ran from the prow chain plate to the upper edge of the conning tower.

"Well, we know where the fuel went," Stuermer commented. He gestured at the three-quarter-inch holes that riddled the tops of the two saddle tanks. "I counted seventeen in the port tank and forty-one in the starboard. And that's just the forward half of the boat." He knelt and stuck a finger in a single random hole at his feet. "This was no light machine gun. Those Catalinas were carrying at least one heavier-caliber automatic weapon. Armor-piercing shells, too."

Dekker squatted beside him. "Twenty-millimeter cannon?"

"Possibly."

"Did you notice the crumpled section of the starboard tank, Captain?" Bock inquired. "There's a three-foot-long split in the middle of it, right at the waterline."

"How wide?"

"I'd say not more than one inch, sir."

"Good. That and the bullet holes we can patch without too much difficulty. If we have to, we'll ballast the boat over into a more pronounced port list in order to expose the split and make it easier to repair." He looked at Bock and then Dekker. "Anything else forward of the conning tower?"

"Not above the waterline, Captain," Bock answered. Dekker shook his head.

"All right. Chief, the saddle tanks are flooded with seawater right now?"

"Yes, sir. All fuel transferred to keel tanks. Water only."

"Good," Stuermer said. "No ignitable fumes. Put one two-man crew to work welding up those holes, Otto, and get a second crew to rig a working platform around the split. Come astern when you get the men organized, and join Erich and me to complete the damage inspection."

"Aye, sir," Dekker grunted. He strode off toward the foredeck hatch, calling out orders.

"Let's have a look at the stern, Erich," Stuermer said. "We'll probably find something even more interesting back there."

At that moment, a series of pure, silvery notes began to float through the midnight air. The entire crew turned their heads toward the bridge, where Jonas Winkler sat playing his flute. The starlight glinted off the polished keys of the instrument as his skilled fingers moved across them. It was an old tune, very recognizable, and several of the men began to whistle along, smiling and nodding their heads. But as Stuermer and Bock walked aft, one of the crewmen standing near the canvas-wrapped bodies scowled and shook his head.

"I don't mean to complain, Captain," he said under his breath, "but does Mr. Winkler have to play that particular piece just now?"

The *Kapitänleutnant* looked puzzled for a moment. Then realization dawned and he nodded in agreement, a faint smile on his lips.

"Jonas!" he called. "A lovely melody, to be sure, but would you mind playing something other than Mozart's *Requiem*?"

Winkler stopped abruptly. "Sorry, Captain," he said. "I wasn't thinking." He raised the flute again and began to play the haunting melody to "Lili Marlene."

Stuermer and Bock made their way aft along opposing gunwales, visually checking every inch of steel above the waterline. There were more bullet holes and another split in the starboard saddle tank—this one only a foot long—where the shock wave from a bomb had buckled the steel plate. But the most extreme damage was at the stern, where the torn bronze of the port propeller was imbedded in a tangle of crushed steel. The force of the explosion had ripped the propeller blades away from their hub like petals from a flower, hopelessly binding up the port shaft.

"I can't believe the hull held at nearly three hundred and sixty meters after sustaining this kind of damage," Bock said. "Incredible."

"Not only that," Stuermer replied, "but the rudder seems to be completely intact. I'd have thought it would have been more fragile than the screw." He shook his head. "There's no telling with near-miss explosions. Sometimes they kill you; sometimes they don't even wrinkle your shirt."

Stuermer straightened up, stretching his back. "We need to take a good look at those screws and shafts, underwater. At dawn, when there's a little light, you, the chief, and I will all go for a short swim in Dräger masks to inspect the damage. Then we'll discuss what we can do about it, if anything." He looked toward the bow. "In the meantime, tell Otto to have the crew stop working for a few minutes and muster on the foredeck. We have two men to bury."

The sun was still obscured by low-lying clouds on the eastern horizon when Bock, clad in black athletic shorts, a heavy fabric belt, and canvas deck shoes, pushed the rubber skirt of the Dräger mask up against his face, wiggling it to ensure a good seal. Behind him, a crewman secured the buckles of the leather straps that held it in place. Another shackled the single air hose into a bronze D ring on the belt, some four feet back from where it entered the mask. Air began to free-flow across Bock's face behind the triangular plate of glass, making his eyes water slightly.

Cutting the flow down by twisting the small valve on the air supply fitting, he put a hand on one crewman's shoulder and stepped to the starboard stern rail. As he was looking down at the dark water lapping along the U-boat's side, a finger tapped the thick glass of the faceplate. He turned and saw Stuermer, whose hair was wet and matted from his own dive, standing beside him.

"Have a look at the propeller and shaft damage," the *Kapitänleutnant* said, "and then swim up the port underside of the hull to the bow and back again. Otto and I have covered the starboard half. See if we've missed anything."

"Aye, sir," Bock said, his voice muffled behind the full-face mask. He gathered a loop of air hose at his side, looked down, and stepped off the rail of the U-boat.

Keeping the mask pressed tightly to his face with one hand, he plunged through the surface in a sheath of whirling bubbles. When his downward momentum ceased, he found himself even with the U-113's keel, surrounded by a dim gray blue void that flickered with faint shafts of sunlight. Below his pale legs and feet yawned the shadowy abyss of the open sea.

Suddenly feeling very small and vulnerable, Bock breaststroked rapidly toward the propellers, focusing his attention on the underside of the hull. Damage aside, it was badly in need of a dry-docking to remove the buildup of barnacles below the waterline; such accumulations could reduce a boat's hull speed by as much as a third.

Of more immediate concern, however, was the bomb damage to the stern. Bock swam to the rudder, grabbed it, and rested momentarily, looking over the shafts and propellers.

If it had appeared bad from the surface, underwater it was far worse. The port screw was little more than a smear of torn bronze imbedded in the crumpled steel of the stern plates, its shaft irreparably twisted and jammed. The starboard propeller was missing one of its three blades, as well as half of another. Though it hung clear of the hull, its shaft exhibited an obvious warp. That it provided any propulsion at all, Bock thought, was something of a miracle.

He moved in and ran his hands around the shaft where it penetrated the hull. There was definite metal-on-metal wear. It would be only a matter of time before the shaft's rotation wallowed out the stuffing box and allowed the sea to rush in, particularly at depth, under pressure.

He shivered, suddenly conscious of the water's chill, and began to swim along the port side of the hull, checking for additional damage. With the exception of a few older indentations caused by groundings, it looked fine below the waterline; even the barnacles were undisturbed. Reaching the bow, he turned around and paused to look down before heading back.

Less than a fathom below him, the gray black shape of a fourteen-foot oceanic whitetip shark soared lazily through the watery void, a cloud of striped pilot fish enveloping its head. Bock froze, holding on to the edge of the starboard torpedo tube door, staring down in fear and fascination. The great animal gave an unhurried flick of its tail and curved off into the shadows, the broad, white-tipped pectoral fins that were the inspiration for its name spread out like the wings of a Heinkel bomber. Bock watched it until it disappeared at the edge of visibility.

His trip back to the U-113's stern was accomplished rather more briskly than his initial swim forward. Locating the short boarding ladder that had been secured over the side, he wasted little time in getting his body and legs clear of the water. The sun was warm on his arms and chest as he reached the deck and pulled the Dräger mask off his head.

"All clear on the port underside of the hull, Captain,"

he reported, spitting salt water. "A few dents here and there from groundings, that's all. No bomb damage." Dekker stepped in and handed him a towel. "Thank you, Chief."

"You took a good look at the damage to the shafts and screws?" Stuermer asked. Bock nodded. "Good. Quite a mess, don't you think?"

"Captain, it amazes me that the starboard shaft and propeller give us any propulsion at all. And most definitely, they won't last under constant use."

Stuermer glanced at Dekker. "Exactly what the chief and I thought." He drew a deep breath. "Finish drying off and come to the captain's nook. Hartmann's concocting some kind of soup to warm us up. We'll put our heads together and try to come up with a plan of action."

He started up the deck toward the conning tower. "I want two lookouts on the bridge and both antiaircraft guns manned, plus constant radar and Metox surveillance. Secure the boat for rapid submergence. It's daylight now, and we're too close to the United States for comfort."

With the batteries now fully charged, Stuermer ordered the diesels shut down in order to conserve fuel. He, Bock, and Dekker sat together in his cramped quarters, wearing fresh clothing, luxuriating in the fresh air that was wafting through the U-113 from the ventilators.

"We could simply head north," Bock ventured, "and trust that we'll encounter another U-boat. I know there's at least an equal chance that we'll run into Allied ships or planes, but what choice have we got? Trying to head for South America—say Argentina—is just as bad. It's a long way, beyond the range of this damaged boat, and there's no guarantee of security in Buenos Aires. The British have destroyers all through that area. We'd probably end up cornered like the *Graf Spee* was at the start of the war."

"Too far, that's the main point," Stuermer said. "We don't have the range to reach any known *Kriegsmarine* support facility, on either side of the Atlantic."

"The radio," Dekker fumed quietly, bouncing his fist on his knee. "We need the damned radio."

"I spoke to Jonas about it again when we came below," Stuermer said. "It's broken beyond repair. And incidentally, so is the *Schlüssel.* We can't encode or decode, even if we manage to pirate a radio from some passing ship." He raised an eyebrow and smiled at Dekker. "I read your mind, didn't I, Otto?"

The burly chief engineer snorted with laughter. "Well, I was thinking we might be able to sneak up on some small coastal tub, surface right beside her, and bluff her into surrendering by waving our deck gun. A boarding party would be able to send an encoded message requesting a rendezvous at sea, since the *Schlüssel* is portable, and we might even be able to pull her radio and reinstall it on this boat."

"And if we don't locate a cooperative ship?" Stuermer countered. "We'll burn up precious fuel chasing a vessel that's either running or fighting—probably screaming for help over the airwaves at the same time, bringing the air patrols down on us—and if she doesn't stop, or we sink her, we still don't get a radio for all our trouble."

Dekker looked somewhat deflated. "Just a thought."

"Maybe we could pull into one of these uninhabited islands in the Bahamas or Caribbean," Bock said. "Beach the boat, camouflage her, and take our time with a more involved repair. If we just had one reliable shaft and screw, plus a full load of diesel fuel, we'd be able to make our way back across the Atlantic to Lorient. Maybe we could hijack a fishing boat from a nearby port and siphon its fuel." The young exec shrugged helplessly. He was grasping at straws and he knew it.

"No," Stuermer replied, shaking his head. "Too great a chance of being spotted. The Bahamas are overflown daily by American planes. And if we do pull up on an isolated island, what do we do then? We still can't effect repairs. This U-boat is a ship of war, the property of the Reich; we have been entrusted with it and charged with the task of waging war against the fatherland's enemies. Germany is under attack. We do not have the option of arbitrarily removing ourselves from the conflict when our families and countrymen so desperately need us to do our duty.

"It's not sufficient for us to simply ensure our own survival. We need to choose a course of action that will result in the U-113's continued existence as a German military asset."

"Then we need to repair the boat," Dekker said simply. "How?"

"And get fuel," Bock added. "Without getting caught."

Stuermer shifted to one side as the curtain parted and Hartmann, the cook, appeared carrying a large pot of thick stew. Setting it down on the edge of the chart table, he reached inside his apron and withdrew three bowls and spoons. "Here you are, gentlemen," he said, steam from the pot curling up around his red face. "Something to warm you up from the inside out."

Dekker sniffed the pungent aroma as he took his bowl and spoon. "Ah, those odd ingredients again," he said. "I thought we'd eaten them all, Hartmann. We haven't operated in the Gulf of Mexico for over a year now."

"Not since U-166 was sunk near the mouth of the Mississippi in September of 'forty-two," Bock interjected. He inhaled deeply. "I'd almost forgotten that smell. What's in this again, Hartmann?"

"I had one small crate of the dry supplies left," the cook said, looking pleased. "It was underneath a sack of potatoes. I just scraped a little green mold off the sausages, and the rest was fine. The dehydrated vegetable—the slimy one—is called okra. The sausage is called boudin, and the hot spice that's tickling your nose is cayenne pepper."

"And what's it called? That funny name . . ."

"Jambalaya."

"Yes." Bock smiled as the cook ladled some of the stew into his bowl. "That's it. Jambalaya."

Stuermer gazed at the bulkhead as the cook finished serving and departed. Pungent steam filled the tiny cabin, temporarily overpowering the ubiquitous reek of diesel fumes and sweat. Bock and Dekker began to eat, savoring the unusual meal.

The *Kapitänleutnant* turned the spoon in his stew, thinking. Slowly, a smile began to dawn on his lean face.

"I do believe Hartmann's just given us the solution to our problem," he said suddenly. Bock and Dekker looked up from their bowls.

"Eh?" Dekker grunted. "How's that, Captain?"

Stuermer's smile split into a broad grin.

"Papa Luc," he said.

Chapter
Five

September 1943

The lone figure in the pirogue leaned hard on the long wooden pole, propelling the narrow, canoelike boat diagonally into the scurrying whitecaps that dotted the muddy water of the coastal flats. An afternoon sea breeze had come up unexpectedly, ruffling the mangrove foliage and roiling the shallows all across the vast expanse of the Atchafalaya River delta. The fresh wind whipped the gray cotton shirt and baggy brown trousers against lean arms and legs as the poler turned chin into shoulder so that a battered fedora, brim fluttering, would not be carried away.

The pirogue made laborious progress across the open flat until it reached the wind shadow of one of the delta's innumerable small mangrove-covered headlands. Once in calmer water it began to glide more easily, the lone figure in the stern standing erect and poling with far less effort. A flock of snowy egrets stopped wading through the shallows near the dangling mangrove roots and took off in a coordinated chaos of white wings, spooked by the pirogue's approach.

The slender craft rounded a small hook of land and slid into the entrance of a tiny semicircular inlet. Across the inlet bobbed a line of tan-colored cork floats, spaced about eight feet apart, with a large, green-glass jug en-

cased in a sleeve of woven rope marking one end. As
the pirogue glided up to the jug, the occupant shipped
the long pole and walked nimbly forward along the cen-
terline of the tipsy craft, maintaining balance with practiced ease.

Stooping down, the figure in the baggy clothes and the
weather-beaten fedora hauled the glass jug inboard and
recovered the short rope and the stone weight that
served to anchor it in place. Then, shifting to a sitting
position at the center of the pirogue, the occupant began
to haul on the float line hand over hand, pulling in the
thin mesh net that hung beneath it. It was hard work:
the net didn't come across the bottom into the boat so
much as the boat was dragged under the net, across the
little inlet, as it was retrieved.

The catch was good. Several dozen spotted sea trout
came into the pirogue, dangling from the net by their
gills like silver icicles, along with seven fat redfish, their
bronze sides' with the characteristic black tail ocellus
gleaming in the afternoon sun. The fisherman rose to
one knee as a stingray appeared near the end of the net,
very much alive, thrashing its whiplike tail and flapping
its pectoral fins. After a cautious disentanglement of the
thin mesh, it was set free.

The fisherman brought in the last few feet of mesh,
hauled up the small grappling hook that anchored the
far end of the net, and stepped over the still-wriggling
catch to the stern of the boat. With a shove of the long
pole, the pirogue moved off inland, following the contour of the mangrove-choked headland. Overhead, a few
yellow white clouds scudded across the warm blue sky,
riding the fast breeze.

A mullet leaped clear of the water just ahead of the
pirogue, then—typically—leaped twice more. Without
warning, an osprey shot into view like a small brown
thunderbolt, spreading its raptor's wings and air-braking
as its talons smacked down on the rippling water that
marked the mullet's last location. Nothing. With powerful flaps it rose into the air again, venting its frustration
with a high-pitched, keening cry. The poler paused to

watch it soar away on the gusting wind, looking upward with a hand holding the old fedora in place.

The osprey sailed off across the shallow bay and the pirogue continued its slow, gliding progress along the irregular shore of the headland, keeping to the shelter of the wind shadow. The tide was going out, and even with most of the wind blocked by the mangroves it took forty-five minutes for the lone occupant to pole the boat all the way to the top of the bay.

Up here the water was less salty, diluted as it was by the outflow of fresh water from the great Louisiana swamps formed by the deltas of the Mississippi and Atchafalaya Rivers and their countless associated bayous. The foliage was different, too—more dense, taller, with numerous moss-draped cypress trees guarding the edge of the swamp like gray-clad sentinels. The brackish water was a transition zone, where the ocean gave way to the land and a different variety of plants and animals flourished.

Though not as salt tolerant as their relatives the crocodiles, alligators lived on the edge of the seawater penetration zone, the big males asserting their territoriality and claiming small stretches of bayou as their own. The pirogue turned up one of these narrow, deep channels, saw grass waving in the breeze on one bank, dense undergrowth interspersed with cypress trees choking the other. The poler searched the banks carefully as the boat slid along the ten-foot-wide pathway of dark water.

There was a gator here, one particular gator with a gleaming brown black hide and a fat, succulent tail, clever enough to have survived long enough to have grown a full fourteen feet in length . . . but not as clever as a human. The poler chuckled in anticipation. The hook snare was just around the next bend. There would be gator tail stewed with onions, tomatoes, and small hot peppers for several weeks, and a huge, nearly flawless hide to sell to the city men for cash money.

The pirogue ghosted around the bend, leaving barely a ripple on the black water. Then the poler's shoulders sagged. Just ahead, dangling a foot above the water from the branch of a deadfall tree, was a short length of line

ending in a large black iron treble hook. A small shred
of bloody nutria hide about the size of a man's palm
hung from one barb. No gator.

The poler sighed, grabbing the branches of the deadfall as the pirogue slid up beside the stripped hook.
Smart old gator. Stuck his big head out of the water and
yanked the bait nutria right off the barbs without sticking himself. Not one in a hundred could do that with a
properly set hook snare.

Where you at? the poler wondered, looking around.
*Down the bayou a ways? Up on land, thirty feet back in
the bush, bein' lazy in a patch of sunlight, your belly full
of free nutria? Layin' on bottom five feet below this pirogue, keepin' real still, waitin' for me to move along?*

Where you at, old Mr. Gator?

Another sigh. *Nothin' to do but try again. Ain't no
gator really smarter than no human. Leastways, a person
has to believe that.*

Lean brown hands checked the snare line back from
the eye of the treble hook. No nicks or gashes, chafing
or wear. Good as new. A thumb touched the tines of
the three barbs. Sharper than porcupine quills. All that
was needed was fresh bait.

The skinned carcass of a nutria was lying under the
center thwart of the pirogue, wrapped in dampened
Spanish moss to slow the ripening process. The poler
extracted the bloody bait, set it on top of the thwart,
and whacked it in half with one swift blow of a rusty
machete. Then the two gory pieces were threaded carefully over the three barbs of the treble hook, the sharp
tines unobtrusively exposed.

Proper baiting was only half the battle. The real trick
to hook-snaring a gator was positioning the hook just
so. It had to be inaccessible enough from shore that
patrolling raccoons wouldn't steal the easy meat. The
hook and the bait had to be placed above the water so
that catfish and turtles wouldn't gnaw the slaughtered
nutria away to nothing in the first half hour, but not so
high that a gator couldn't find and seize it. For a really
big gator like this one, the hook should be set even a
little higher than usual, so that when he bit down and

hung himself he'd be held well up out of the water, his own weight keeping him stuck on the barbs. Eventually, after thrashing for hours with his great tail, he'd just give up and hang from the black iron, waiting.

With the baited hook dangling in just the right place, the poler shoved the pirogue gently away from the deadfall and assumed a standing position in the stern once again. A couple of hard thrusts and the narrow craft moved off down the bayou, back toward the open bay. The high saw grass along the southern bank surged back and forth in the hard breeze, a rustling green sea of leaves and stalks, as the boat slid past.

It was the golden hour of the afternoon, when the sun hangs the thickness of two fingers above the horizon and drapes the earth in warm gilt light and long, friendly shadows. The whitecaps crisscrossing the open flats were smaller now, and the tide's outward rush had slackened. The pirogue made good time in the wind shadow of the taller foliage, heading for the barely discernible mouth of a larger bayou that drained into the very top of the bay.

As the little craft reached the entrance of the second bayou, the lone figure in the stern abruptly stopped thrusting with the push pole and stood up straight, staring at the shore. On the nearer of the small points of land formed by the intersection of bayou and bay stood a huge, ancient cypress tree, its flaring base and roots nearly seven feet in diameter. On a spike driven into its smooth gray trunk, at about the height of a tall man's eyes, hung a black nylon stocking, fluttering in the breeze.

"Les Allemands!" the poler whispered. *"Les Allemands . . ."*

A couple of quick thrusts with the pole and the pirogue was beside the cypress tree. Stepping out onto the spongy ground, the poler unknotted the stocking from around the spike, examined it, and then gazed out across the bay toward the open Gulf of Mexico. From the brown shallows of the inshore flats all the way to the far horizon, there was nothing on the water but the familiar drifting pattern of small whitecaps.

Hurriedly, the lone figure stepped back into the pirogue, jamming the stocking into a pants pocket, and kicked away from the bank. Though there was little wind or tide to overcome this far up in the headwaters of the bay, the pole flexed and dark water gurgled under the stern of the narrow boat as it was propelled up the quiet bayou as fast as the poler's muscles could drive it.

The interior of the U-113 was almost completely silent; only the occasional echoing creak of metal expanding or contracting in response to mild changes in temperature disturbed the quiet. In the captain's nook, Kurt Stuermer put down the copy of Thomas Mann's *Buddenbrooks* he had been reading and looked at his watch. He sighed deeply, rubbing his tired eyes, and was about to get out of his bunk when Erich Bock appeared at the entrance to his tiny quarters.

"It's time, Captain," the young exec said. His eyes roamed down to the book that lay inverted on the gray military blanket covering the bunk. "Forgive me for saying so, sir"—he smiled, keeping his voice low—"but it seems as though every book you read is on the banned list." Frank literary discussions that transcended rank were one of the bonds shared by the *Kapitänleutnant* and his young *Oberleutnant zur See.*

A look of cynical amusement spread across Stuermer's lean face. "I like a good read," he said, "by an author who actually has something to say, and says it well. It relaxes me, which in turn helps me perform my duties more efficiently." He waved his hand dismissively. "You can only read so much Nietzsche and listen to so much Wagner. They both become quite frighteningly ponderous after a while. And the minor writers sanctioned by the Nazi Party—unreadable. To a man, they've got their heads so far up their own asses they can hardly breathe." He ran his fingers over the cover of *Buddenbrooks.* "Nobel Prize in Literature, 1929." A faraway look came into his eyes and he fell silent.

"A lot of Thomas Mann fed the bonfires when the party faithful burned the books back in the thirties," Bock commented gloomily.

Stuermer batted the book cover with his fingertips. "But not this one," he said, brightening. "You can have it when I'm finished. Next for me, *The Sun Also Rises*. A fairly good German translation, I was told when I picked it up."

"Hemingway?"

"Hemingway." Stuermer grinned. "A dissolute fellow, with a typically American inability to control his drinking, but an interesting writer all the same."

"Where were you able to come by a German translation of Hemingway these days?" Bock inquired. "That's quite a find, Captain."

"Spain," Stuermer replied. "Last year, when we put into Vigo Bay to do the clandestine refueling from that, quote, *interned*, unquote, German tanker. I found a bookseller the night I went ashore, just two streets up from the city wharf."

"Sometimes I wonder just exactly how much trouble we'd be in if any meddlers from the party found out that we had authors like Mann and Hemingway in our possession." Bock frowned. "I mean, what would they really do, Captain? Take seasoned U-boat officers out of action just for reading a few banned novels?"

"I hardly think so," Stuermer said, swinging his legs down to the deck plates, "but we won't tell them anyway." He glanced at his watch again. "Back to work, Lieutenant. We'll continue this chat at a later date." He got to his feet. "Let's extend the *Spargel* and have a look around."

"Aye, Captain." With a grin Bock stepped back into the passageway.

They made their way forward, stepping over the splayed legs of a sleeping crewman, wrapped in a blanket, who had made a niche for himself against the aft bulkhead of the control room, his head resting on a sack of dried lentils. Chief Dekker was at the ballast control panel, tightening the seal of a valve with a small wrench.

"All well, Otto?" Stuermer inquired.

"Aye, sir," Dekker replied. "Routine maintenance."

The *Kapitänleutnant* reached over and tapped the main depth gauge. The indicator needle quivered, but did not move off the seven-meter mark. "No shifting, apparently."

"No, sir," Dekker confirmed. "She's sitting in the mud right where you parked her." He grinned, the creases deepening in his broad, seamed face.

"Good," Bock said. "I was wondering if the tide would move her. It was flowing pretty fast when we set her down. You could hear it gurgling outside the hull."

"So was I," Stuermer said, reversing the white cap on his head and snapping down the periscope's handgrips. He smiled as he squinted into the eyepieces. "On the other hand, maybe we're stuck in the mud now."

"I wouldn't be surprised," Dekker grumbled, removing the wrench from the valve. "The amount of silt that's suspended in this water is incredible. It's completely ruined our trim, Captain. You're going to have to let me rebalance the boat before we perform any fancy diving maneuvers."

"Noted, Chief," Stuermer said, adjusting the periscope's eyepieces. "Noted."

The U-113 was sitting firmly on a mudbank at the mouth of a wide, shallow bay, barely enough water over her conning tower to cover her two periscopes when retracted. In clear water, her position would have been obvious to any patrolling planes; in the muddy water of coastal Louisiana, she was invisible. Both the attack periscope and the sky periscope were extended, protruding through the light chop on the surface like wayward marker pilings.

Stuermer took his time at the *Spargel*—literally "asparagus"—walking first the sky 'scope, then the attack 'scope around through a 360-degree inspection of the U-boat's surroundings. Finally, he slapped the handgrips up against the shaft of the attack periscope and spun his cap so that the brim faced forward again. "Retract both," he said, stepping away as the shaft descended into its bilge housing.

"All right, gentlemen," he said. "Let's have the crew on station. Prepare the dinghy for launch. Switch to red. Chief—bring her to the surface." He turned to Bock.

"Erich, do you think you can find the entrance to that bayou at the top of the bay once more and then make it back again, mostly in the dark?"

The young exec nodded. "Yes, Captain. I refreshed my memory when I hung the stocking early this morning. It's been nearly a year, but it all came back to me. I can move around the bay without getting lost."

"Good. Take your side arm and Lothar with his rifle again, plus one other crewman—mmmm—that young Hofstetter this time. He looks like he needs some fresh air. Issue him a *Schmeisser* and a couple of clips of ammunition, just to bolster his confidence. But for God's sake don't let him shoot at anything."

"Aye, sir."

"It's just after sunset now. The same procedure as this morning: we'll surface under cover of darkness, launch the dinghy with you and your shore party, then submerge immediately and sit back down on this mudbank with the periscope extended. I'll have a constant watch run on it, looking up the bay for you. This time, because you'll be coming back at night, I want you to take a portable signaling lamp and double-flash to seaward every ten seconds as you approach the mouth of the bay. We'll see you and give you a return double flash using the signaling lamp in the head of the periscope. That will guide you right to us, and when you're close enough, give a series of multiple flashes and stand off. We'll surface and pick you up."

"Aye, Captain."

"Any comments? Suggestions?"

"No, sir. A good plan."

"All right, Erich." Stuermer clapped a hand on his exec's shoulder. "Carry on."

As Bock turned and began to issue orders to several crewmen standing near the forward passageway hatch, Dekker cleared his gravelly throat. "Boat is breaking bottom suction, Captain. Rising to the surface now."

"Very well, Chief."

The U-113 listed slightly to port, creaking in her metal bones as she broke free of the bottom, then steadied on an even keel as she floated up a scant four meters. There was a familiar rushing sound as water streamed off the hull.

"Boat is on the surface, Captain," Dekker intoned, manipulating ballast control valves.

"Very well," Stuermer said. "Keep idling starboard electric motor; prepare to engage starboard shaft in case the tidal current starts to move us off our present position." He put a foot up on the rung of the control room ladder. "I'm going to the bridge."

Stuermer climbed through the conning tower compartment to the bridge hatch, spun the dog, and broke the watertight seal. Only a small amount of water trickled down onto his shoulders; in calm weather, without boarding seas, the bridge drained almost immediately through its scuppers. He pushed back the lid and hoisted himself through into the night air.

The sky to the west was still lit with the smoldering violet remnants of the sunset, and the dying wind was ripe with the scent of land. Overhead, the first stars were twinkling against the blue-black sky, and to the east a slender crescent moon gleamed like an illuminated fingernail clipping. Perfect, Stuermer thought. Just enough moonlight on the water to let Bock find his way around. Not so much that the U-113 would be highly silhouetted and in danger of being spotted by patrolling planes.

But he wouldn't remain on the surface, even at night, any longer than necessary. Not here. Water this shallow was a death trap for any U-boat targeted by an enemy. With barely enough depth to cover the conning tower when resting on bottom, there was nowhere to hide, no room to maneuver, no way to escape.

He watched as the forward cargo hatch was cracked open and swung back, disgorging several seamen who muscled a small collapsible dinghy—made of wooden frames and a rubberized canvas skin—out onto the foredeck. A few practiced tugs accompanied by a few muttered profanities, and the little craft was assembled. Finally, a small outboard motor was passed up through the hatch and clamped to the dinghy's transom.

Bock climbed out onto the foredeck, dressed in a

short black leather jacket and dark officer's cap, a Walther pistol holstered on one hip and his Zeiss binoculars dangling from a strap around his neck. In his left hand he carried a battery-powered signaling lamp equipped with a shuttering mechanism that enabled the user to transmit information in visual Morse code.

Behind him came Lothar Wolfe, huge and hulking in black engine-room coveralls, carrying his prized hunting rifle. Straddling the hatch, he reached down with one hand and virtually plucked a third man out of the boat by his collar. It was the newest and youngest member of the crew, the oiler's assistant named Hofstetter. Wolfe set the boy on his feet on the deck plates, steadying him, a look of long-suffering patience on his face. The flustered Hofstetter nodded his thanks, floundered for balance as the U-boat rocked gently on the light chop, and dropped several ammunition clips for the *Schmeisser* that hung awkwardly around his neck, all but strangling him.

Bock looked up wordlessly at Stuermer on the bridge, who smiled, and bent to pick up the dropped magazines. Stuffing them into Hofstetter's coat pockets, he conferred briefly with Wolfe and then ordered the dinghy lowered away. The knot of seamen eased the canvas craft over the side and into the dark water, holding it by its short painter.

"All right, Erich, Lothar; let's see if Papa Luc knows we're here yet." Stuermer waved. "Good luck."

Both Bock and Wolfe touched their temples briefly in quick military salutes and climbed down into the dinghy, followed by Hofstetter, who just barely managed not to fall in. Wolfe yanked once on the starter cord, and the motor sputtered into life.

And then the dinghy was away, nosing off into the darkness ahead of the U-113's bow. Stuermer watched until the little craft faded to a small black blot on the windswept bay, then stepped back to the bridge hatchway. Leaning over, his lean face bathed in the red glow of the tower compartment's night-vision lights, he called down to the control room: "Secure all hatches. Stand by to submerge the boat, Chief. Put her back on the bottom."

Chapter
Six

The pirogue ghosted along swiftly near the left bank of the thirty-foot-wide bayou; the middle was far too deep for poling. The water was utterly still, an oily black mirror snaking deep into the swamp beneath a canopy of immense, moss-hung cypress trees. The crescent moon and the stars offered scant light, but the poler was navigating more by feel than by sight. A water moccasin wriggled out ahead of the pirogue, making for the far bank, scribing a continuous sequence of S-shaped ripples on the dark, glassy surface.

The bayou led into a large grove of ancient cypress trees, then abruptly widened into a sizable pond. Clustered together around its banks were numerous shacks and shanties, many of them built out over the black water on stilts. Pirogues and flatboats were tied off everywhere, and here and there the flickering lights of candles and kerosene lanterns glowed from hut windows. Nets and strings of cork floats were draped over lines and tree branches outside most of the shanties, and on a small islet at the far end of the pond four large alligator hides were stretched out on vertical frames. Similar smaller frames held dozens of nutria hides, most with the fur still attached, some scraped clean and gleaming palely in the faint moonlight.

From farther up the pond, where the bayou narrowed once again, away from the main cluster of shanties, came the sound of singing. Not so much true singing as a cracked, lilting chant with no discernible words, delivered in a high, quavering voice, it echoed over the black water and through the sentinel cypress trees like a wisp of audible mist.

The pirogue slid past the larger concentration of stilt shacks and headed straight for the source of the curious vocalizing.

At the far end of the pond, where the bayou narrowed into little more than a ten-foot-wide creek, a dilapidated one-room shack stood on four-foot-high cypress stilts. Like most of the other shanties, it had a roof of rusty corrugated metal extending out over a wide porch that doubled as a dock. The pirogue slipped up beside the porch and bumped gently into the weathered wood.

The poler leaped nimbly out of the little boat, wrapped its painter around a wooden cleat, and hurried up to the door of the shack. The glimmer of candlelight was emanating from the single open window that faced the porch, along with the quavering of the strange, singsong chant.

The lean figure in the baggy clothes and fedora opened the door partway and leaned inside. "Estelle?"

The keening chant continued, accompanied by a rhythmic creaking sound.

"Estelle." Louder this time.

The singsong chant halted; the rhythmic creaking went on. "That you, child?" a hoarse female voice inquired.

"Yes, ma'am. It's me." The door opened wide and the slender figure in the baggy clothes stepped forward. The broad-brimmed fedora came off. "It's Jolene."

"Come closer, into the light, child. My old eyes can't see you way over there."

The girl moved across the coarse wooden floor of the shack, nearer the lone candle that burned on top of an upended wood-slat crab trap. She was not more than seventeen, the oversized male clothing completely concealing the curves of her slim frame. Her forearms and hands were slender but strong, and her neck above the threadbare collar of the gray shirt was long and elegant. Her face revealed the mixed heritage not uncommon among people who live in the bayou country of Louisiana: a blend of Spanish, French, Choctaw, and African blood. Creole. By far the strongest influence was the African, as revealed by her almond-shaped brown eyes, high cheekbones, full lips, and smooth, mahogany-colored skin. Her hair, jet-black and straight, was more typically Native American, and her nose was thin and narrow after the European design. She lowered herself to one knee and smiled, showing a generous mouthful of even white teeth.

"Something's happened, Estelle," she said softly, barely able to contain herself.

A withered claw of a hand reached out to her, a ragged shawl dangling, and there was a long creak as a wooden rocking chair tipped forward. A raspy chuckle, not unkindly, filled the interior of the little shanty.

"Oh, I know, child. I know."

The speaker was an old woman, so incredibly wrinkled that even her approximate age was indeterminate. Time had transformed her face, crosshatching it with seams and creases, padding its already broad features, until she resembled nothing so much as a large, benevolent toad. Small eyes glittered like black garnets behind squinting lids, missing nothing. A shapeless robe of black-and-red-patterned calico covered her from jowl to floor; a hooked shawl of beige wool was draped over her shoulders.

From the shawl hung the tiny skulls, bones, and sundry body parts of small animals—mammalian, reptilian, avian, and insectile. When the old woman moved, the dangling bones made a light clattering sound. On her head was a battered fedora identical to the one worn by the girl—with the exception of a small desiccated water moccasin sewn around it in place of a hatband, the shrunken head facing forward and bent up into a striking position, mouth wide open, needlelike fangs intact.

Jolene reached out and took the old woman's hand in both of hers. "You know what I seen, Estelle? How you know?"

Estelle shifted in her rocking chair and let out a short cackle. "Brother cottonmouth and sister wildcat done told me. *C'est vrai*. It's true."

Jolene doubted it, but long experience had taught her never to challenge Estelle's assertions. The old woman could lead you in circles, answering a question with a question, until your head spun.

The girl sat back on her haunches and smiled quizzically. "Estelle, you really a witch?"

"So they say. People's gonna believe what pleases 'em anyway, child, so I just let 'em talk." She leaned forward conspiratorially. "I'm too old too be anything but what I am, now, and what I am ain't got no name, *ma chérie*. But when I was young and beautiful like you, like I done told you, I was a voodoo priestess. *C'est vrai.*"

Jolene pursed her lips, half doubting, half afraid not to believe. An impish grin passed over her face, and she put a hand into the pocket of her baggy trousers. "You know things, don't you, Estelle? Sometimes before they happen?"

The old woman nodded. "I got the gift, child. Got it from my mother, and her mother before her. I always been able to look into the future."

"Then tell me what I'm gonna take out of my pocket." Jolene couldn't believe her own words; she'd never had the nerve to test Estelle before. Maybe the old witch would fly into a rage. . . .

Estelle laughed, a wheezing cackle that came from deep in her throat. She stared down at the girl kneeling before her, her small black eyes glittering. The maze of wrinkles on her face rearranged itself into a patient smile, and she leaned slowly forward.

"A stockin'," she said, her tone precise. "A stockin' for the leg of a city gal."

Jolene drew out the ball of dark nylon, held it up, and let it unroll. "You knew," she said. "How'd you know, Estelle?"

"I done told you," the old woman replied. "Brother cottonmouth and sister wildcat . . ."

Jolene sighed and crumpled the stocking into a ball in her lap. She was not going to set out in pursuit of an answer she would never get.

"*Les Allemands,*" Estelle said. "They've come back."

Jolene nodded, leaning forward, her eyes wide with

excitement. "That's right, Estelle. I was out in the bay, tendin' the traps and jug lines, and didn't see nothin'. But when I passed by the granddaddy cypress at the mouth of the bayou, I done seen the stockin', just like last year, flappin' in the wind." She peered hopefully at the old woman. "We gonna get to do some more tradin', ain't we, Estelle? Like last time? Get money for new nets and lines, and maybe some new traps and rifles for some of the men? And maybe even some pretty cloth for some of the women to . . ." Her voice trailed off suddenly and she looked at the floor.

The old woman waited a moment, then leaned forward and put a crooked finger under Jolene's pointed chin, lifting her face up. "To make pretty dresses?" she asked softly. "To make themselves feel pretty, too?"

Jolene nodded, her eyes bright, and turned her head away. There was a snuffling sound as she wiped her forearm angrily across her nose. The old woman sat back, appraising her.

"You didn't tell Luc yet, did you, *chérie*? He don't even know you're back."

Jolene rose to her feet, rubbing a knuckle at the corner of her eye. "No, Estelle. Papa Luc never saw me come in, I'm pretty sure." She looked at the stocking, then shoved it back into her pocket. "I gotta go tell him. He's gonna miss me, it gets much later. He'll get angry."

The old woman's eyes narrowed. "He get angry often these days, child?"

Jolene kicked at the floor with the toe of her homemade leather shoe. "Not much, I guess."

"You been livin' with him ever since he took you in after your mama and papa died of the consumption nine years back. You been a good child. He ain't got no cause to get angry with you."

Jolene glanced up and then down again. "I don't guess."

Estelle peered at her in the dim candlelight, her eyes flickering over the young curves that swelled beneath the rough clothes. "He ever done anything 'sides get angry?"

Jolene looked confused. "No, ma'am," she said, uncertain of the old woman's meaning. She frowned. "He ain't never beat me or nothin' like that."

There was a silence. Then Estelle nodded slowly. "All right, child. All right."

"I gotta go now, Estelle."

"I know, child."

"I gotta tell Papa Luc what I done found."

"Yes, child."

"But I'll come visit you again real soon, Estelle."

"I'll look for you, *ma chérie.*"

Jolene smiled at her from the doorway, raised a hand, and stepped out into the night. There was a wooden clumping sound as she got into the pirogue, and then a little swish of water as the boat was poled away from the dock.

Estelle gazed out into the darkness through the open door, and began to rock gently again. The rails of the chair creaked rhythmically on the rough wooden floor.

"Ainsi soit-il," she whispered, and began to sing.

"Verdammt!" Erich Bock swore as he batted at the insects whirling in a cloud around his head, attracted instantly by the probing beam of the signaling lamp. They were everywhere—on his face, in his eyes, ears, and nose, in his mouth when he tried to talk, in his windpipe when he tried to breathe. He'd forgotten about the bugs in the Louisiana delta country. Absolutely beyond belief.

"Perhaps if you turned off the lamp, sir," Hofstetter squeaked helpfully, his collar tugged up around his ears.

"Thank you for that insight, crewman," Bock commented, puffing and squinting at the dark vegetation along the shoreline. "Perhaps you'd care to tell me how we're going to pick out the correct cypress tree in pitch darkness without a light."

Hofstetter winced as Wolfe batted him lightly on the back of the head. "Don't be so helpful, junior," the big torpedoman growled, shifting his rifle between his knees and throttling up the little outboard motor slightly. "The lieutenant knows what he's doing."

Bock sneezed a couple of mosquitoes out of his nose

and aimed the lamp farther ahead off the dinghy's port
bow. "Try to bring us in a little closer to shore, Lothar,"
he said. "It's blacker than the bottom of the Skagerrak
over there."

Frowning over the side at the dark water, Wolfe let
the bow of the boat swing to port as it motored forward.
There was a sudden smack as he crushed a mosquito
against the top of his bald head. "Can't see a thing
through this water," he muttered. "No telling how shallow it is."

As if in response, the motor began to grind and vibrate, then kicked up on its tilt mechanism. Mud and
shells boiled up behind the dinghy's stern. *"Aghh,"*
Wolfe grunted, and yanked the shaft clear of the water
so that the small propeller wouldn't beat itself to pieces
on the invisible oyster bed just beneath them. "Not even
two feet deep here, Lieutenant."

Bock nodded, aiming the lamp dead ahead. "Can you
work us back out again? Or do we need to get out
and push?"

"No, sir. I'll get us clear."

White foam churned behind the boat as Wolfe lowered the propeller just past the surface and revved the
engine. The dinghy inched away from the shore into
slightly deeper water, where the shaft could be lowered
back down into a vertical position.

They continued along, straining their eyes to pinpoint
the one large cypress tree they wanted among the hundreds—thousands—lining the shore. Bock chewed his
lip, frustrated. Out in the middle of the bay, with open
water all around and a little moonlight illuminating the
surface, it was possible to move around by general feel—
north, south, east, west; closer to or farther from one
shore or the other. But picking out detail in the dark
masses of swamp foliage was something else again. He'd
been to the damned tree once already, just after dawn,
but it appeared as though it would be sheer luck if they
found it again in the dark.

Hofstetter slapped at his face, leaving little streaks of
blood on his cheeks where he'd crushed several ravenous
mosquitoes, and pulled his collar up around his ears.

Looking much like a turtle with its head half-retracted, he clambered around on his seat on the center thwart, the machine pistol banging on his knees, and faced Wolfe in the stern.

"I'm getting eaten alive, Lothar," he said, not exactly whining, but his voice loaded with that adolescent pleading quality common to young people who are in the process of discovering, to their dismay, that some circumstances in adult life simply have to be endured.

The big man nodded, searching the dark shoreline. "Mm."

"I *mean* it," Hofstetter mourned under his breath. "I don't think I can take much more of this."

"Yes, you can," Wolfe said flatly.

"I swear if these things don't stop biting me I'm going to jump into the water!"

"No, you won't," Wolfe replied. He checked a fuel fitting on the outboard, impassively swatted a mosquito attempting to feed from his jugular vein, and peered out into the night again.

Hofstetter blew out a pitiful sigh. His eyes fell on the beautifully carved stock of the hunting rifle resting between Wolfe's knees. "Why do you take such good care of that rifle, Lothar?" he asked.

Wolfe's prizefighter's face softened slightly. "My father made it for me," he said. "He's dead, so this is what I have left of him."

"Oh." Hofstetter looked lost, unsure of how to follow up.

Wolfe let him off the hook. "He was a gunsmith, one of the best, and the head gamekeeper for the Baron von Clausen at his Black Forest estates. Our family has been gamekeeping for the Clausens for nine generations. My father served in the baron's own regiment during the Great War, fought side by side with him."

" 'The War to End All Wars,' " Bock said from the bow. He chuckled grimly. "And here we are fighting the war after that. . . ."

"Huh!" Wolfe snorted. "I can imagine what kind of pointy-headed intellectual dreamed *that* nonsense up. Wars will never end—I can tell you that from watching wild animals all my life. They fight to eat, fight to mate, fight to live. And what are men but another kind of animal? War and fighting are part of human nature."

Bock turned and looked aft. "My God, Lothar," he said with a smile, "that's the longest speech I've ever heard you give. You may be in danger of turning into a philosopher on us."

Wolfe scowled. "Christ, anything but that, Lieutenant," he grunted. "Shoot me if that happens."

Bock turned forward again, aiming the lamp and brushing away insects. Hofstetter sat silently for a moment, then pointed at the rifle. "Is it really as accurate as everyone says?" he inquired timidly.

Wolfe fixed him with an even gaze. "With this," he said, patting the stock, "I could clip every hair off your head, one at a time, from four hundred meters. As long as the ammunition didn't run out, and"—he grinned, showing his teeth—"you didn't move."

Hofstetter swallowed, thoroughly impressed. He was trying to think of something else to say when Bock spoke abruptly from the bow: "There it is. See it, Lothar? I'll keep the light on it while you head inshore."

The dinghy puttered toward the great pillar of gray wood that was centered in the lamp's beam. As they approached, something large slipped off the low bank and hit the water with a loud splash. Hofstetter gripped the gunwales nervously, his eyes darting around. A few seconds later the bow of the dinghy eased into a tangle of half-sunken brambles with a wet crackling sound.

Bock steadied the light on the cypress trunk, illuminating the metal spike. The stocking he'd knotted around it earlier in the day was gone. He lowered the light and scanned the ground, just to be sure that it hadn't simply fallen off. It hadn't. He'd made sure it was secure. One of Papa Luc's people had taken it off.

He turned around and sat down in the bow, tipping the light toward his feet so as not to blind Wolfe and Hofstetter. "All right," he said, shrugging. "That's it. They must know we're here. Let's go tell the captain."

There was another violent splash a mere ten feet from the boat, back in the tangle of fallen branches and driftwood. A deep baritone rumbling began, and rose quickly to a roar. Concentric ripples began to brim across the water toward the dinghy.

Hofstetter looked ready to faint. "Wha—what's *that?*" he stammered, his eyes as wide as saucers.

Bock flicked the light over toward the sunken brush. "Alligator, most likely."

"What?" Hofstetter grappled for the handgrip of the machine pistol hanging from his neck, rocking the little boat with his contortions.

"Stop kicking around, you idiot," Wolfe muttered, scowling. "Or I'll feed you to the damn thing. And don't fool with that Schmeisser, either—you'll do yourself an injury."

Bock lowered his face to hide the grin. "Get us back out into the center of the bay, Lothar," he said. "And crewman Hofstetter, relax. The alligator isn't armed."

The little outboard revved up as Wolfe backed the dinghy away from shore, leaving behind a small cloud of exhaust fumes. There were no more roars or splashes. Rotating the boat onto a southward heading, he began to pilot it out into open water.

Chapter
Seven

Jolene poled the pirogue back across the pond toward the main cluster of stilt shanties, humming the odd melody to Estelle's chant under her breath. A pair of night-hunting owls somewhere back in the cypress set up a chorus of hooting, the queer sounds echoing through the trees and over the glassy surface of the ink black water. She ducked under a sheaf of low-hanging Spanish moss as the pirogue glided up to the dock of the largest shanty on the pond, and she shipped the pole.

After tying the boat off, she stood up straight, squared her shoulders, and drew a deep breath. In her right pocket she squeezed the balled-up stocking in one hand. The inside of the sprawling shanty was completely dark, even though it was too early for Papa Luc to retire. She pursed her lips and let out the lungful of air in a long, controlled stream.

The place had been home to her since she'd been a child of eight, but lately—maybe for the past year and a half—something hadn't felt right about it. The atmosphere had changed. It was Papa Luc. He kept looking at her funny, with eyes that were almost angry. Accusing. These days, constantly, she carried around the feeling that she'd done something wrong, although she had no idea what. It was very confusing.

No one wanted to upset Papa Luc, ever. He was their leader—their father, like his nickname said. He alone dealt with the city men, trading nutria pelts and alligator hides for cash money that could buy some of the tools and the utensils they couldn't make for themselves. He kept the outsiders, with their rules and laws and taxes and govern-*mint* that threatened to destroy their way of life, at bay. He headed up the thrice-weekly Bible meetings that everyone in the tiny community had to attend, quoting liberally from the Scriptures as he reassured them that they need not concern themselves with anything but their own day-to-day existence. That he was proud to be their protector and intermediary with the outside world. And everyone would sit agog as Papa Luc worked himself up into a righteous fury, thundering like the gray storm clouds that rolled in off the Gulf in the heat of the late afternoon.

Jolene bit her lip as she stood on the dock. It was that primal thunder she was afraid of. These days it was almost as if every time he looked at her, he was on the verge of releasing it—in her direction.

A nearby owl let go its wailing night cry, startling her. She *tsked* into the darkness at it and walked over to the front door of the shanty. Opening it as quietly as she could, she slipped inside.

The interior was pitch-black. She knew her way around, though, and decided to go to her tiny bedroom at the rear of the shanty and wash her face. Making no sound, she padded across the main room, stepped around the huge leather chair that she couldn't see but knew was there, and pushed open the door to her bedroom. With a sigh, she felt on top of the rough table beside her narrow cot for matches to light the bedside candle. As she found them, she pulled at the neck of her threadbare shirt, opening it down to her navel. Outside, the wind had died to almost nothing; it was becoming humid and sticky.

She nearly jumped out of her skin as a match flared into life at the foot of her bed with a harsh, scratching sound. She started back against the table, clutching her shirt across her breasts, as Papa Luc set the match to the bowl of his pipe, his severe, aquiline features highlighted by the sputtering orange glow.

He took his time, getting the tobacco going nicely before settling back in his chair at the end of her cot. She
struck a match and lit the bedside candle and, as the
little flame cast a warm light around the room, turned
to face him. He sucked several times on the pipe, making
a wet sound, before withdrawing it from his lips and
pointing the stem at her.

"Where you been, girl?" he demanded, his deep voice
filling her ears. With his arching black brows, piercing
blue eyes, and flowing gray white hair and beard, he
looked like the painting of Jehovah on the center page
of the huge leather-bound Bible that was a permanent
fixture on the preacher's pulpit in the main meeting hall,
Jolene thought. A few tendrils of dense pipe smoke hung
in the air between them, the acrid smell tickling her
nostrils.

"Mindin' the nets and jug lines," she answered. She
didn't mention the rebaiting of the alligator hook. Though
it wasn't expressly forbidden, it was pretty much accepted that only the men trapped, hunted, and killed the
big reptiles. But Jolene had never felt much affinity for
the drudging life of domestic chores and childbearing led
by nearly all of the women in the community. She much
preferred the solitude and the freedom of the deep
swamp and the coastal flats.

"You know I don't like you bein' gone so long after
sundown," Papa Luc rumbled. "A girl child could get
lost real easy out in the swamp so late. You understand
me? *Perdue totalement!*"

Jolene looked down as she rebuttoned her shirt. All
the way to the neck. "I ain't no girl, nor no child neither,
Papa Luc. Not no more." She glanced up at him, smiling
a little as if to defuse the directness of her response.
" 'Sides, I found somethin' I need to give to you." She
pulled the stocking from her pocket. "Look."

Papa Luc's stern, Old Testament visage registered
genuine surprise. He leaned forward and grabbed the
stocking from her hand. His face reddened in the dim
light, and he glanced up at her sharply. "Garment of a
temptress," he intoned. His hand shot out and grabbed
her forearm, yanking her close. In spite of his age, he

was very strong, his grip as unyielding as the jaws of a sprung trap. "Where you get this? I let you wander free—you pick up the habits of a Jezebel?" He yanked her arm again. "You been travelin' farther than you tell? Out to the roads and such, consortin' with men of low character?" *Yank.* "Well, girl?"

Jolene grimaced and tried to pull free. "No, no, Papa Luc! I ain't done nothin' like that! And you're hurtin' me!" She stamped a foot and ripped her arm out of his grasp. Rubbing it, she backed up against the night table. "You didn't let me say: I done found the stockin' at the granddaddy cypress tree, out on the point! It was hangin' on the nail, like last year!"

Papa Luc stared at her for moment, then sat back in his chair. Smoke billowed around his head as he drew heavily on his pipe, his brows knitting together. "You tell anyone else about this, girl?"

"Just Estelle."

"You told that old witch?" Papa Luc scowled around the stem of his pipe. "You stay away from her, girl. She's dangerous. *Folle.*"

Jolene didn't know where her newfound wellspring of nerve was coming from. The words were out before she could bite them off: "You afraid of Estelle, Papa Luc?"

The old man rose to his full height, like a huge, wrinkled black scarecrow. "Don't vex me, girl," he rumbled, his eyes flashing. "Don't you vex me."

He stalked to the door of the little room. "You sleep, girl, but before you do, you think on your loose words and ingratitude to the one who's protected and provided for you all these years." He reached out and grazed a finger along her cheek, and a haunted look came into his eyes. "You're in my debt. You must respect that, girl."

Jolene nodded silently, looking at the floor, her arms folded across her chest. Papa Luc stepped out into the main room. "Rest. Tomorrow, we go to find *les Allemands.*"

It wasn't until she heard the door to his room open and close on the other side of the dwelling that she let herself sag down to a sitting position on the bed, her heart fluttering in her throat.

* * *

It was well past one a.m. when the young seaman assigned to sit in the control room and take an hour's turn watching for Bock's signal lamp through the extended periscope blinked, straightened up, and moved the steel housing slightly.

"A double flash at three-five-seven degrees, Chief," he reported. Dekker, who never seemed to sleep, looked up from the electrical circuitry he'd disassembled at one of the damaged breaker panels.

"All right, Hansen," he said, getting to his feet, "go wake up Captain Stuermer." He took the seaman's place at the periscope, resting his forearms on the handgrips and squinting into the eyepieces. He spotted the repeating double flash immediately and responded by twice clicking the button, on the left handgrip, that activated the periscope's own signaling light. When the pinpoint of light flashed again in the darkness, it was somewhat brighter, closer. Dekker repeated his own double flash, guiding them in.

Stuermer stepped through the aft hatch into the control room, adjusting his white captain's cap. "Do you have them, Otto?"

"Aye, sir," Dekker replied, moving the 'scope slightly. He straightened and stepped aside. "Dead center, coming this way. Intermittent double-flash signal, as arranged. I've already responded twice."

"Good, good." Stuermer peered through the eyepieces, then double-clicked the signaling-light button. "They see us. Bring the boat to the surface. Nice and easy."

"Yes, Captain." There was a gentle hiss as the chief cranked open the compressed-air valves and began to displace the seawater that filled the U-boat's ballast tanks. Resting men began to stir as the familiar sounds of motion—the rushing gurgle of water, the creak of metal under stress—echoed through the hull. The deck tilted slightly, and then the U-113 was free of the bottom.

"Rising, Captain," Dekker said, watching the depth gauge. He began to close the valves, cutting off the flow of compressed air to the tanks and limiting the boat's buoyancy. "Five meters, three meters . . . on surface."

"Start electric motors," Stuermer ordered. "Stand by to engage starboard shaft and put some way on if necessary."

"Aye, sir." Dekker repeated the order into the engine-room intercom. Then he turned to Stuermer, who was adjusting the periscope height so as to keep Bock's lamp in view. "Before you go to the bridge, Captain, I have a new problem to report."

"What now, Otto?" Stuermer sighed, gazing into the eyepieces.

"The electrician and I have determined that even though the housings of the main batteries were not cracked during the attack last week, the extreme maneuvering we did must have caused them to suffer some internal damage." Stuermer looked at him, one eyebrow raised. "The reason I say this, Captain, is that we are having ongoing voltage problems. The batteries should still be fully charged after our long surface run up the Gulf from the Straits of Florida to Louisiana. Apparently, however, they take a charge but do not hold it. Port battery is down to thirty-nine percent, starboard battery is worse: only twenty-three percent. Probable cause: internal shifting of the batteries' zinc plates."

Stuermer's jaw muscles worked. "Impossible to repair," he said quietly.

Dekker nodded. "Impossible to repair."

Stuermer glanced back into the periscope and quickly double-clicked the light button. "How much time will we have to maneuver underwater if we have to dive and evade?"

"Even with one shaft functioning, not more than forty-five minutes."

There was a moment of silence. Both men knew only too well that it wasn't nearly long enough to shake off a pursuing destroyer, should one detect them on the passage back across the Atlantic to Lorient, or even an attacking plane. They couldn't even hang dead in the water at a safe depth, the electric motors shut down, without battery power—not for long. The scrubbers that removed excess carbon dioxide from the air during long submergences were powered by the main batteries.

"Well, then," Stuermer remarked offhandedly, "we'll just have to repair what we can and sail for home on the surface under diesel power—and hope we can avoid being spotted by any unfriendly eyes. Or dive just long enough to let them pass us by."

Dekker looked skeptical. "The whole way?"

Stuermer slapped the handgrips up against the periscope housing and retracted it. "The whole way, Chief," he said grimly. He picked up a handheld signaling lamp. "Join me on the bridge?"

They mounted the internal ladder that rose up through the conning tower, and paused at the top as Stuermer cracked the bridge hatch. Water dripping down on their heads and shoulders, they climbed out into the night air, still and humid now, and scanned the darkness ahead of the boat. In a few seconds Dekker pointed. "There."

Forty degrees off the port bow a double flash pierced the night, and then the silhouette of the dinghy bobbed into view, outlined against the reflection of moonlight on the water.

Stuermer flipped up the cover of the bridge speaking tube. "Open forward hatch," he said. "Three men on deck to help recover the dinghy."

The hatch in the foredeck popped almost immediately and three seamen hoisted themselves through it. The dinghy puttered up along the port side, Bock standing in the bow. He stepped out onto the top of the saddle tank, holding the short painter. Wolfe, in the stern, killed the motor and began to unclamp it from the transom. The young oiler's assistant, Hofstetter, tried to rise, then fell backward over the center thwart on the seat of his pants. A ripple of laughter rose from the three seamen who'd emerged from the forward hatch.

"*Gott in Himmel,*" Dekker muttered, shaking his head. He drew a battered tin cigarette case from his breast pocket and, opening it, offered it to Stuermer. "This is a good crew, Captain, the old hands. But the half-dozen or so replacements we received after the last war patrol—absolutely bone-chilling. They literally can't get out of their own way. Look at that poor schoolboy we lost on the helm the other day. Broke his neck going headfirst into a flywheel; I mean, how clumsy can you get? And now this baggage . . ." He waved his free hand at Hofstetter, who was clawing his way up the saddle tank, machine pistol clunking on the steel plates.

The *Kapitänleutnant* accepted the light Dekker held out, then blew a long stream of smoke into the night air. "A bit harsh, Otto. The boy lost his balance as the boat was diving out of control. As for Hofstetter and the remaining junior hands, we need to remind ourselves that they've been more hurriedly trained than we were before the war. Too young and green to be stuck out here, really. And it's only going to get worse before it gets better, so we might as well get used to it. Help them along as best we can."

"Well, we've got forty-six aboard who know the ropes," Dekker growled. "Maybe with the devil's luck that will be enough to get us home one more time."

They stepped aside as Bock reached the top of the external ladder and touched the brim of his cap in a salute that was more reflex than necessity. His jawline was streaked with blood from numerous mosquito bites. "They've found it, Captain," he said. "The stocking we hung this morning is gone."

Stuermer drew on his cigarette and exhaled. "Fine. Well, I think we have to assume that Papa Luc knows we're here. Maybe he'll be as receptive to a little illegal wartime commerce now as he was last year."

"Five times last year," Dekker commented wryly.

"Yes, I remember," Bock said. "His sense of patriotism conveniently evaporates when you're willing to buy supplies from him at premium prices, paid for in German gold." He looked at Stuermer. "This may be more expensive than a few links of sausage or a couple of sacks of rice, Captain. Pardon me for asking, but do we carry enough gold to make him happy and cooperative?"

The *Kapitänleutnant* smiled. "Twenty-five thousand dollars in U.S. currency, a tiny fraction of the millions in assets frozen by the Reichsbank at the outbreak of hostilities in 'forty-one, and nineteen kilos of high-carat gold bullion, cast into five-hundred-gram ingots." He arched an eyebrow. "The thing to remember about Papa Luc is that he is, by nature, acquisitive."

"Greedy," Bock interjected.

Stuermer nodded. "Exactly. Once he sees *some* of the currency and gold, he'll want more . . . and more, and then more. Our big advantage is that he doesn't know how much we have. Nor can he find out." He paused to draw on his cigarette. "As long as the money and gold keep coming in a thin stream, he'll keep us his little secret."

Dekker shook his head. "These people are strange," he said. "What is it they call themselves? *Les* something . . ."

"Les Isolates," Stuermer replied, rolling the word off his tongue in a continentally perfect Gallic accent. "It's not quite proper French, but in their odd dialect it means 'the Isolated,' or 'the Separated.' " He looked at Bock. "I'm not too worried about their patriotic instincts," he said. "Based on our past dealings with them, I'm not sure they even consider themselves to be Americans. More like a remnant of the French colonials from seventeenth-century Canada. Many of them don't even speak English."

"That's right," Bock added. "They don't even recognize the U.S. government or its political crises. Remember what Papa Luc said the last time we went in for supplies? He keeps his people separate so that the men can't be drafted into the military and killed in someone else's war. If we wanted to buy meat and fish and rice from him, and pay well for it, he had no quarrel with that; *he* wasn't at war with us."

Dekker nodded. "I remember. But the way they live, stuck out in the middle of nowhere in that swamp, trapping and hunting like some tribe of wild Indians . . . bizarre."

"But good for us," Stuermer concluded. "And now, maybe our salvation." He watched as the men on the foredeck finished disassembling the collapsible dinghy and passed it through the hatch into the forward torpedo room. Done, they looked up at him expectantly.

"Go below!" he called. "Seal forward hatch!" As they began to descend into the boat one at a time, he gazed out past the U-113's sharp bow, tapping his fingers on the rail. "Chief, we need to run the diesels more regularly than usual in order to keep the batteries at some kind of functional capacity, however limited that may be, correct?"

"That's right, Captain," Dekker said.

"If we let them discharge by sitting on the bottom, we'll lose the ability to cruise submerged . . . which in this shallow, muddy water would be our only means of escape should we be discovered by an air patrol."

"Correct."

"What we need to do," Stuermer mused, "since we don't have a *Schnorkel*, is conceal the boat so that we can get air to the diesels through the conning tower hatch, but not have the bulk of the hull exposed." He turned to Bock. "We need to find a way inshore to an inlet or a creek mouth that gives us just enough water to rest the boat on bottom and leave only the bridge above the surface. We camouflage it with mangrove branches and there we have it: the hull submerged, hidden, but with air to the diesels to keep the boat ventilated and the batteries charged in case we have to make a run for it." He looked from Bock to Dekker and back again. "Comments, gentlemen?"

Dekker shrugged. "It sounds like a good idea, Captain. Soft mud bottom here—there should be no chance of damaging the hull. At worst, we might get stuck until I could rock us clear by blowing and flooding the ballast tanks. But in the meantime, we'd be hidden."

"I agree, Captain," Bock said. He turned and looked up the moonlit bay. "And I believe I know just the place."

Chapter Eight

It was still dark, more than an hour before dawn, when Papa Luc stepped into the pirogue carrying a spindle-backed wooden chair that just barely fit between the boat's gunwales, and settled into it in the bow. Jolene, wearing her familiar baggy clothes and floppy fedora, got into the stern, pushed away from the dock with one foot, and picked up the pole. A few skillful thrusts rotated the narrow craft and sent it skimming across the pond toward the shanties on the far bank.

Jolene switched to a short, broad-bladed paddle to traverse the middle of the pond; like the bayou out to the bay, it was too deep for poling more than a few feet from shore. A gauzy mist steamed off the dark water in the cool predawn air, coiling around the pirogue, and somewhere nearby a mullet jumped, fell back, and hit the surface with a muted smack.

Papa Luc extended a long black-clad arm and pointed at a small shanty with a sagging roofline and a dozen fresh nutria skins, still bloody, hanging from the railing of its front porch. "Pull up there, girl," he commanded. "Right in front of Claude's place. *Rapidement.*"

Jolene bit off the retort that rose to her lips. This was a big part of it, the change in him that she couldn't stand or understand; he was always issuing orders, telling her how to do the obvious. And berating her whenever she went ahead and made her own choices.

And why Papa Luc needed Claude to come along she couldn't comprehend. She could move and maneuver the pirogue as well as any man—she practically lived in it. Besides, she didn't like Claude. Few people did.

"Claude!" Papa Luc shouted as the boat slid up to the small porch-front dock. "*Leve-toi!* I'm waiting!"

The front door of the shanty was kicked open and a man whose physique resembled that of an upright bear waddled out. Of middle height, his chest, trunk, and arms appeared to comprise ninety percent of his body weight. His huge torso was supported by incredibly short, bandy legs, which were encased in pants and moccasins of sewn hide. A bullet-shaped head, the dark hair thin and straggly, sat on his immense shoulders with no apparent neck in between. His features were simian, with heavy, bony brows, a massive jaw, and small, close-set eyes. Black hair curled up out of the neck of his plaid shirt, poked from his ears and nose, and covered his thick forearms.

He carried a battered, heavy-caliber hunting rifle in one hand. Waddling down the few steps to the little dock, he paused before stepping into the pirogue and grinned toward the stern. "*Bonjour,* Mademoiselle Jolene," he said, his tone dripping with sarcasm. The boat rocked as he boarded it and propped the rifle up on the center thwart.

Jolene rolled her eyes. She'd already had a couple of run-ins with Claude, during which he'd made it plain that he was interested in her and she'd made it equally plain that she was *anything* but interested in him—or any man, for that matter. She couldn't understand what was wrong with most of them, why they got so agitated around her these days. Of course, she hadn't told Papa Luc about the incidents, or anyone else. Only Estelle.

The broad, squat trapper moved toward her and extended a hand. "*Donnez-moi,*" he grunted, his eyes traveling over her rapidly. Like his father and mother before him, and like many others in the community who had lived their whole lives in the deep swamp, Claude spoke mostly French, with only a smattering of English. He grinned at the brief contact between them as Jolene

handed him the pole and slipped past to the center
thwart. Seating herself, she stared forward at Papa Luc's
back, feeling Claude's eyes on her. It was a comfort to
remind herself that Claude's loutish brain made him
somewhat monosyllabic; he rarely did more than mutter
short phrases in French and grunt unintelligibly. She'd
be able to pretend he wasn't there for a while.

"*Et maintenant, allons-y,* Claude," Papa Luc ordered,
pointing down the bayou in the direction of the bay.
"Jolene, keep your pretty eyes *en garde pour les Allemands, comprends-tu?* You mind, now, girl, you hear
me?" Depending upon to whom he was speaking and his
mood at the time, it wasn't uncommon for the leader of *les
Isolates* to employ two languages in the same sentence.

Jolene huddled on the center thwart and buried her
chin in the collar of her baggy shirt. "Yes, Papa Luc,"
she said. "*J'entends.*"

"I'm impressed that you were able to get us in here
without running the boat aground on a mudbank, Exec,"
Stuermer commented, leaning over the rail of the bridge
and eyeing the muddy water that lapped around the conning tower barely eighteen inches below the scupper
drains. "Particularly in the dark."

Bock ducked as a crewman—perched precariously in
a thick black mangrove tree just above them—tossed
down another leaf-laden branch that he'd chopped free
with a ship's ax. Stuermer picked it up and, with Bock's
help, stuffed the cut end under the lines that had been
run tightly around the conning tower just below the
bridge. It joined several dozen other branches that were
fast turning the exposed top third of the U-113's tower
into just another tangled mass of mangrove foliage along
the small inlet's overgrown shoreline.

Bock grinned at the *Kapitänleutnant*'s good-natured
use of his rank title. Privately, he wondered himself how
he'd navigated into the bay at night. Somehow, he'd read
the water accurately during his two trips inland to the
cypress tree, and luck had been with him. This little
inlet, about halfway up the bay on the western shore,

had been perfect: a sufficiently deep channel leading up to it, and just enough water to set the hull on the bottom with only the very top of the conning tower exposed.

"I'm amazed that I spotted this inlet in the first place, sir," he said, "and I have to admit that the gods were smiling on us when we didn't ground ourselves coming in." He smiled ruefully. "Very little to do with me, I'm afraid."

Stuermer gave a short laugh. "It takes an exceptional man to admit that his success was due to luck when all those around him are patting him on the back and crediting his skill." Reaching out, he clapped Bock briefly on the shoulder. "I'd say it was a little of both, Erich."

The crewman's feet came kicking down out of the overhanging foliage, along with a shower of thick, succulent black mangrove leaves. The two officers grabbed his legs and steadied him as he dropped out of the tree with a muffled curse, panting. Yellow pollen and light scratches covered his head and bare arms.

"The tree is winning, I take it, Mohler?" Stuermer inquired.

The seaman turned and spat pollen over the side. "Your pardon, Captain. No, sir, I just think I need to transfer to another tree. If I cut any more from this one I'll expose the inshore side of the bridge."

Bock nodded, scanning the overhead branches. "You're right, Mohler. We need to move to this tree back here, by the AA guns. Have you got a few more cuts in you?"

"Yes, Lieutenant. I think so."

"Good man."

Stuermer and Bock locked fingers, bending down, and Mohler set a foot on the step formed by their hands. On the count of three they hoisted him up into the foliage, ax and all, and waited until he'd braced his feet securely. A moment later, the tree began to shake as the seaman resumed his chopping.

Bock lit one of his black-paper Turkish cigarettes and extended the pack toward Stuermer, who shook his head. Both men took a moment to gaze eastward at the rising sun as its first rays beamed out from the horizon. It was going to be a perfect day, with a cloudless sky and little wind. Perfect for flying.

The *Kapitänleutnant* moved across the bridge, grasped the edge of the light camouflage netting that had been draped over the attack periscope and drawn down like a shroud to the rails, and pulled it around the after section of the conning tower. Small branches and clusters of foliage had been stuck through the loose mesh. Bock stooped down and gathered a few of the loose sticks that had fallen to the bridge deck, and he and Stuermer proceeded to thread them into the netting as well. Experienced wartime submariners accustomed to the hunt, hit, and hide tactics of the open sea, both men felt distinctly uncomfortable at being boxed into so restricted a space. Neither would be able to relax until the boat was completely and thoroughly camouflaged.

"It's looking good," Stuermer remarked, securing the overhead netting to the rail by one of its ties. "At least it gives us some relative security while we see what we can do about fuel and repairs."

"Captain!" Jonas Winkler's reedy voice echoed up from the conning tower hatch. "Radar contact on aerial target bearing two-seven-zero degrees! Distance two kilometers and closing fast!"

The radioman's last few words were nearly obscured by the rising drone of an aircraft engine. Stuermer and Bock ducked automatically, their eyes searching the sky to the west through the netting, the dense mangroves restricting their view.

The tree above shook violently as Mohler noticed the approaching plane. "Single bomber approaching, Captain!" he called softly, as if he might be heard by the enemy pilot and crew. The tree shook again, sending leaves tumbling onto and through the netting.

"Keep still, Mohler!" Bock hissed, frozen in place. "Stay up there and don't move the tree!"

The drone rose quickly to a roar, and then the pale underbelly and broad wings of a single-engine, two-seater seaplane abruptly shot into view over the tops of the mangroves. A curious-looking design with a single fat ski-like float built into the underside of its main fuse-lage, and a smaller float under each wingtip, it bore the U.S. Navy star-and-bar insignia clearly on its blue-painted side. Two racks of depth charges were clearly visible beneath its wings. It continued eastward, follow-ing the Gulf coastline, without giving any indication that it had spotted the U-113.

"Vought-Sikorsky OS2U-3 observation seaplane," Bock recited. "Converted to carry bombs or depth charges. Single four-hundred-fifty-horsepower Pratt and Whitney engine, crew of two. The Americans call it the King-fisher."

Stuermer nodded. "Right out of the aircraft silhouette identification handbook, Erich." He smiled thinly and let out a long breath, watching as the seaplane shrank into the distance. "Good memory."

"That's a hard one to forget, Captain. Very odd-looking. I recall seeing several of them during our war patrols in this area back in 'forty-two. Slow and clumsy, particularly when retrofitted with depth charge racks. An easy plane to shoot down, more so if you happen to have a Lothar Wolfe on one of the AA guns."

"True," Stuermer said, "but think of how much good it would do us to knock that or any other plane down if, before we did, they managed to radio in our position. Our goose would be well and truly cooked then."

"Lieutenant," Mohler ventured from the tree above, "can I come down now?"

"*Verdammt,* yes," Bock replied, remembering the sea-man. "We've got enough branches to finish the camou-flaging. Can you still see the plane?"

"Barely, sir. It's flying on straight as an arrow toward the horizon."

"Good. Climb down by the gun. It'll be easier."

Mohler clambered out of the tree without difficulty this time, carrying his ax, and stood at ease beside the tower hatch. "Shall I go below, sir?" he asked Stuermer.

"No, no, Mohler," the *Kapitänleutnant* said. "Have one of Lieutenant Bock's vile Turkish cigarettes and rest up here in the fresh air for a few minutes."

Bock smiled, dug out a cigarette, and lit it for the

seaman, who retired gratefully to the far side of the bridge. Stuermer glanced at his watch, then up at the rising sun.

"All right, Erich," he said. "If Papa Luc follows the rendezvous procedure we established last year, we should see twin fires at the top end of the bay at noon, then again at sunset. After the second signal, under cover of darkness, we'll head out in the tender to make contact. It will be myself, you, and Wolfe. Any more than three and that dinghy is liable to capsize. Chief Dekker, assisted by *Puster* Winkler, will take command of the boat—not that there'll be much they can do if it's discovered. Dark clothing and side arms, and of course Wolfe will have his rifle."

"Understood, sir," Bock acknowledged. He paused. "Captain, have you decided just exactly *how* we're going to effect repairs on the starboard shaft and screw, with no dry dock and no replacement parts? What are we going to do? Strand the boat intentionally on a mudbank at low tide, careen it, and risk being discovered while we try to straighten out the shaft and hammer the bent propeller back into shape?

"And what about fuel? We're down to one-tenth of our capacity. That's ninety percent empty, sir. We'll need full tanks to get back across the Atlantic to Lorient. Where are we going to find in excess of two hundred cubic meters of diesel fuel in this God-forsaken swamp? In the heart of an enemy nation, no less?" Bock drew on the stub of his cigarette and flicked it over the rail. "Pardon my directness, Captain, but now that we've made it here, just exactly *what* are we going to do?"

Stuermer gazed out across the inlet. "Well, you'll be relieved to know that I've been considering our options all the way up here, Lieutenant," he replied. "Our first priority is to repair the propulsion systems—the starboard shaft and screw, certainly, but also the port shaft, if possible. With a deep, quiet location in which to work, preferably concealed by overhanging trees from discovery by patrolling aircraft, we should be able—with the right kind of bottom under us—to perform a ballasting inversion and get the screws and shafts clear of the water. You recall the theory?"

Bock whistled. "Yes, sir, from textbooks. But I've never seen or even heard of it actually being done."

"Then we'll be the first," Stuermer averred. "At any rate, once we're inverted we can set the men to work effecting repairs on the entire exterior of the stern, and with a little ambitious rigging—again, hopefully, with the help of a few conveniently located trees—we should be able to pull out the damaged shafts and screws."

"Since I'm playing devil's advocate," Bock said, "may I point out that we have no *replacement* shafts or screws? Surely you're not suggesting that we should even bother trying to straighten out that starboard shaft. And the port shaft and propeller? Scrap metal, Captain."

Stuermer smiled, reached out, and extracted Bock's cigarettes from his breast pocket. The exec dug for his lighter as the *Kapitänleutnant* slipped one between his lips and returned the pack to Bock's shirt. "I've been thinking about that as well," he said, taking the proffered light, "and I believe I've come up with something. It's far-fetched, but it just may work. Besides—it's the only chance we've got to completely restore twin-screw propulsion to the boat."

Dekker's crewcut head emerged from the conning tower hatch. "Come up here, Chief," Stuermer told him, "you need to hear this, too." The burly chief engineer grunted and climbed out onto the deck to join them.

"I was going over the KTBs from last year's war patrol in the Gulf of Mexico, as well as my own personal diary, and was reminded of the night we picked up the final communication from Captain Rolf Schecter in U-115. Do either of you remember?"

Both Bock and Dekker nodded. "Of course, sir," Dekker replied. "He was on patrol off the Mississippi Delta and radioed that he was under heavy attack by aircraft. Not far from here. That was the last anyone ever heard from him."

Bock smiled grimly. "He got thirteen vessels out of Houston, New Orleans, and Gulfport for nearly sixty thousand tons before they got him," he said with satisfaction.

Stuermer drew on his cigarette. "The exact wording—

I wrote it in the KTB—was 'Attacked by aircraft, depth-charged, sinking.' Then he broadcast the exact latitude and longitude of his position." He paused. "And then he was gone. To the best of our knowledge, there were no survivors. All fifty-two men went down with the boat.

"Now, here's my point: the boat should still be there. The Americans hardly have time to go chasing after U-boats that may or may not have been sunk from the air, particularly if they're thought to be lying well offshore. They have only the pilot's recollection of his approximate location at the time of the attack. We have Schecter's coded transmission to *Ubootwaffe* headquarters of his exact plotted position immediately prior to the boat's sinking."

"Amazing that he got a message out, considering that he sank too fast for anyone to escape," Bock said. "There must have been a top *Puster* aboard U-115."

"Karl-Heinz Hufnagel," Stuermer said. "A friend of mine from the Naval Academy. He was very good, a first-class radio officer. But now he's dead, and there's nothing that can be done about it. So we put him, Rolf Schecter, and fifty other U-boatmen out of our minds and concentrate on keeping ourselves alive.

"I checked the last reported position of U-115 on the chart. It's twenty-six nautical miles from here, about fourteen offshore, in only twenty-two meters of water. That's within the working range of a salvage diver."

Bock and Dekker glanced at each other, but said nothing.

"The U-115 is a Type VII boat, just like this one. As a matter of fact, they came down the ways in the same Bremen shipyard within three days of each other. Their parts are virtually interchangeable—including, gentlemen, their shafts and screws.

"Assuming we can find Schecter's boat, we should be able to determine quite quickly whether or not her shafts and propellers are usable. If they are, we simply enter the aft portion of the hull and unbolt the shafts from their drives on the MAN engines. We recover them to the surface, bring them ashore, and install them on the U-113."

The *Kapitänleutnant* smiled and looked back and forth between his executive officer and chief engineer. With the exception of the faint, keening cry of a far-off osprey, there was complete silence on the bridge.

"I detect a lack of enthusiasm," Stuermer said at last. "Come on, gentlemen, I know you have concerns. Let's hear them."

It was Bock who spoke first: "I just have one, Captain. We are going to attempt to mount a surface-based salvage diving operation from a U-boat, in American coastal waters, barely a stone's throw from New Orleans? Without deepwater hardhat diving equipment?" His voice trailed off.

"Let me get even more to the point," Dekker said, his face pale, "and exercise—for once—my privileges of familiarity, since we've known each other for nearly ten years. Kurt, have you lost your mind?"

Stuermer drew on the cigarette. "Both fair questions. The answer to yours, Otto, is 'quite possibly.'" He smiled, exhaling smoke. "As for your concerns, Erich, I never said that we were going to run a salvage operation off the U-113. And you're right; heavy diving equipment is needed. We certainly wouldn't undertake such a task using only Dräger gear."

Bock shrugged helplessly. "Then I don't understand, Captain. How are we going to recover the U-115's shafts if we don't use our own boat?"

The *Kapitänleutnant*'s hard, resolute smile returned. "Well, Exec," he said, "I thought we'd contract some help."

Chapter Nine

The sun had just dropped below the horizon when the dinghy appeared around the point of the little inlet, hugging the mangroves, and motored toward the clump of foliage that was the top of the U-113's conning tower. Bock was sitting in the bow, with crewman Mohler handling the outboard. Dekker moved the camouflage netting aside as the little boat approached, and extended a hand to Bock. On the bridge behind the chief, Stuermer, Wolfe, and Winkler stepped back, making room for the two men to board.

The little tender bumped into the side of the conning tower. Bock climbed over the rail, holding the painter, and secured it to one of the rigging turnbuckles. A moment later Mohler followed.

"So?" Stuermer inquired, the expectant eyebrow raised once more.

"Two fires, Captain," Bock said, "just as before. Right at the top of the bay, like the fires at noon. The same signal we used all through the 'forty-two Gulf war patrol."

Stuermer smiled. "Then we have a social engagement with Papa Luc and *les Isolates*." He adjusted the belt and the holster of the Walther pistol on his hip, tugged down the waist of the short black leather jacket he wore, and turned to Wolfe. "Lothar, you have the sounding line?"

Wolfe, dressed again in his black coveralls, held up a

coil of thin cord with a small lead weight tied to one end. "Right here, Captain. And the tool case you prepared is ready to go, too." He touched a toe to the large, scarred metal chest at his feet.

"Good man." Stuermer put a hand on the rail. "All right. Chief, I leave the U-113 in your capable hands. Jonas, you're Chief Dekker's second. Rotate the men up to the bridge six at a time as long as it's dark, and let them smoke. Twenty minutes per group—that will give each member of the crew a turn up in the fresh air over three hours. We should be back by then, hopefully with a good idea of our next move."

"Understood, Captain," Dekker acknowledged. Beside him Winkler nodded, the fiery orange of the sunset glinting off his steel-rimmed glasses.

Wolfe climbed over the rail and down into the dinghy, his hunting rifle slung across his broad back. He moved immediately to the stern and pull-started the little motor. Bock boarded after him, followed by Stuermer, who received the heavy tool case handed over by the chief engineer and set it atop the forward thwart.

"Planes," the *Kapitänleutnant* said. "Watch for planes." Dekker nodded, raising a hand. Stuermer pushed the dinghy away from the conning tower and seated himself in the bow as Wolfe reversed the outboard. Spinning the boat on a dime, the big torpedoman throttled up and headed out toward the mouth of the inlet.

The burly chief engineer and the slender senior radioman watched until the dinghy disappeared around the point. Winkler reached down through the bridge hatch and retrieved his cloth-bagged flute from behind a couple of electrical conduits, one of many places he often wedged it for safekeeping. He blew a quick two-octave minor scale, up and down, then lowered the instrument and appraised Dekker for a moment.

"You look worried, Otto."

The chief scratched his beard. "I am, Jonas, old friend, I am. It's been nearly eighteen months since we were last here."

"Mmm." Winkler fiddled with a loose flute key. "You don't think they're going to have any trouble, do you?"

"I don't know what to think," Dekker answered. "I just hope that these weird Cajuns who live all alone out in the swamp haven't been infected with a sudden case of patriotism while we've been away. Maybe they've changed their minds about cooperating since we were here in 'forty-two. We're asking for a lot more than sausages and rice this time."

"I see your point." Winkler blew another silvery run of notes. "However, we have a few hours of waiting ahead of us, and there's nothing we can do about that. Any requests?"

Dekker tapped his fingers on the rail. "Yes. Nonmusical. That they come back healthy, with good news for us all." He paused. "If they don't, then this boat might as well be stranded on the dark side of the moon. That's about how far we are from home, Jonas."

Jolene sat on the log and frowned into the fire. Claude was really getting on her nerves. Here he came again: "A little bit o' gator tail, Jolene? Got him cut up an' roasted real good. *C'est bon.*"

Earlier, as they'd approached the big cypress tree on the point, they'd noticed three or four juvenile alligators, each about two feet long, basking in the first rays of the morning sun. Claude had amused himself for most of the day by gigging them out one by one with a sharpened wooden pole. Pieces of tail sizzled on sticks propped up beside the fire, and four small fresh hides were tacked out and drying on nearby trees.

"I said *no*, Claude!"

"But you like gator tail."

"Not from you, I don't! Now will you let me be?" Jolene got abruptly to her feet and strode around the fire toward the water.

Claude's dull face twisted. "You think you somethin' special? You oughta be nicer to me, girl! You don't wanna make me angry, no sir!"

Papa Luc, sitting in his chair and chewing slowly on a piece of charred tail, fixed the trapper with a black stare. "Let the girl alone, Claude," he rumbled. "She don't want no part of you, *tu comprends?* And keep the other fire burning as high as this one. *Les Allemands* need to find their way to us in the dark."

Claude muttered something sullenly and wandered off in the direction of the second fire. Papa Luc watched him for a moment from beneath his fierce brows, then went back to gnawing on his chunk of alligator tail.

Jolene stood on the bank, her hands jammed into her pockets, looking out over the dark water. It was as though she was trapped, like an animal in a cage, surrounded by invisible bars that were closing in on her more and more with each passing day. Papa Luc, Claude, other men of the community—the community itself . . . she wasn't sure exactly when it had started to feel like a prison instead of a home. Just that it did now.

She was so preoccupied with her own smoldering thoughts that she didn't notice the dinghy until it was barely fifty feet away, gliding out of the darkness toward the point with its small motor puttering faintly. A thrill seized her and she stared as the little craft approached. It was them. *Les Allemands.*

She hadn't actually seen them when they'd visited before; they'd never ventured up the bayou as far as the shanty settlement, and she hadn't been invited to any of the meetings on the shores of the bay, during which Papa Luc traded food supplies for money and gold. She'd only heard about the strange men from the war in the Old Country, who appeared on the sea out of nowhere and came ashore to buy all the food *les Isolates* could sell them, at any price.

The dinghy slowed as it neared the bank. Jolene had never seen men like these before. The one in the bow was slender, though broad in the shoulders, with a lean, lined face and a pointed beard. His eyes were hard and quick, and his mouth was grim, a horizontal seam above his chin. He was dressed in a black leather jacket, black pants, and boots. On his head was a weather-beaten white cap, and he wore a gun in a leather holster on his hip. An odd-looking ornament, like a thick, heavy X, dangled at his throat. She drew an involuntary breath.

It was difficult to even *imagine* trifling with such a man: an aura of authority, of lethal ability, emanated from him like heat from a glowing coal.

The man standing behind him, one knee on the center thwart, was dressed the same way, except that his peaked cap was dark. Though younger and taller, he had the same hard-eyed demeanor, the same grim set to his mouth. Jolene looked at him again. It was too bad he looked so serious. A smile would have made him almost . . . handsome.

The man in the stern reminded her of Claude because of the size of his chest and arms, but there the similarity ended. This man had long legs, a bald head, and a clean, angular jaw beneath his scraggly beard. And unlike Claude, there wasn't the least hint of dullness in his expression. He looked as keenly alert as a hunting hawk.

The hard-faced man with the white cap raised a black-gloved hand as the dinghy nudged the bank. "*Comment ça va*, Papa Luc?" he said in fluent French. "*Avez-vous quelque café sur le feu?*"

"*Malheureusement, non,*" Papa Luc replied. "*Mais j'ai un morceau de viande. Viande de gator.*" He casually waved the skewered piece of alligator tail in the air.

"*Gott in Himmel,*" Bock muttered under his breath in German. "These Cajuns will eat anything."

"I had some the last time we were here," Wolfe grunted. "Tastes like chicken. A little chewier."

Bock turned and looked at him in horror. "Remind me to put you on medical report when we get back to Lorient, Lothar." He tugged at the brim of his cap and eyed the three raggedly dressed people standing near the fire.

Stuermer smiled as he stepped out of the dinghy, spreading his hands. "*Chacun à son goût,* Papa Luc," he said. He switched to his guttural English: "It's not to my taste."

"A pity, my friend," Papa Luc declared, chewing. "You miss out."

Stuermer pulled the black glove off his right hand and extended it. "It's good to see you again. Perhaps we can transact a little more business." He shook Papa Luc's hand more firmly than necessary. "Assuming nothing about your situation has changed since the last time we were here."

The gray-bearded man turned and spat a piece of gristle into the fire. "Nothing ever change in the deep swamp, my friend. Outsiders come, outsiders get scared—or lost, or hurt—and outsiders go. Only we, *les Isolates,* live here. Nobody bother with us, not for long. Always been this way. Always will." His bushy brows narrowed and he grinned.

There was a sharp crackle of dead brush as Bock stepped ashore. He turned to steady the dinghy for Wolfe, who climbed forward over the thwarts and gained the bank. The two men moved up on either side of their commander and stood silently, the firelight flickering off creased black leather, verdigris-stained buckles, and the dark, heavy metal of weapons. Jolene thought she had never seen a trio of men look quite so formidable.

Stuermer reached inside his jacket, just beneath the Knight's Cross that dangled at his throat, and extracted a small cloth bag. He held it up in front of Papa Luc's eyes, suspending it from his black-gloved fingers by its drawstring. "Have a look at this, my friend," he said.

Papa Luc's bony fingers were trembling slightly as he took the bag and opened it. Two slender six-inch-long ingots of pure gold slid out into his open palm, their burnished surfaces glowing deep yellow in the light of the fire. Papa Luc's eyes widened at the sight as Stuermer's narrowed, watching.

The Cajun licked his lips. "A strange thing about gold, Captain. It's as lovely to touch as it is to look at, *n'est-ce pas?*" He hefted the small bars, savoring their weight. "Not unlike a good woman, eh?"

Stuermer smiled. "Not unlike."

Papa Luc gazed down for a long moment, then slid the bars back into their cloth bag. With some degree of difficulty, he returned them to the *Kapitänleutnant.* "Those will buy you a dozen sacks of rice, maybe a hundred pounds of dried venison, and all the salt fish you want. But if you want fresh fruits and vegetables, canned goods, well . . ." He gave a Gallic shrug and

peered sideways at Stuermer from beneath his brows.
"They tell us there's a war on. Many things are rationed—very difficult to come by. You . . . have more gold, maybe some money, Captain?"

Stuermer held up a hand. "We want to buy something more from you this time, my friend. Of course, we're quite willing to pay." He gestured over his shoulder with a finger. "*Oberleutnant.* The case."

Bock stepped back to the bow of the dinghy and with considerable effort lifted the battered engine-room tool case out with both hands. Stooping slightly under the weight, he walked it over and set it down on the ground in front of Stuermer, then looked up. The *Kapitänleutnant* nodded. Bock flicked open the catches and pulled up the lid.

The three-foot-long-by-one-foot-deep case was divided into thirds by vertical metal partitions. The two left-hand sections were piled to the top with neatly stacked gold bars identical to those Stuermer had just shown Papa Luc. The right-hand section was piled equally high with bundles of U.S. currency—fifties and hundreds.

Papa Luc stared down at the mother lode in silence. Jolene felt her breath catch in her throat. *So much gold and cash money.* A thousand times—maybe ten thousand times—more than she had ever seen before, all at once. A treasure chest.

Claude moved forward a few steps, drawn to the gleaming bars like a rodent hypnotized by a snake, his eyes glazing over. One hand clenched and unclenched at his side, and he glanced over at the rifle he'd left propped against a tree stump. Then he looked up and saw Lothar Wolfe regarding him with gimlet eyes, his own rifle slung loosely over one massive shoulder. Whatever ill-advised impulse was coagulating in Claude's dull mind vanished like a puff of smoke in a high wind under the big torpedoman's withering stare.

Stuermer tipped back the brim of his hat as he squatted on his haunches beside the tool case and watched Papa Luc coolly, giving him a few more seconds to absorb what he was seeing. Then he selected a gold bar from the loosely packed array and held it up. "More of the same, my friend," he said. He patted the bundles of currency. "And cash, too. You see, we can pay well for what we want."

The gray-haired Cajun took the gold bar. Standing to one side, Bock could practically hear the wheels spinning in his wily head. *Careful, Captain,* he thought.

"And what is it we can do for you," Papa Luc said, "that would be worth a good-sized share of . . . this?" He waved the bar at the tool case.

Stuermer stood up. "All of it," he remarked casually. "If you agree to give us what we want, all of it will be yours."

Papa Luc licked his lips. "And what is it you want?"

"Cooperation," the *Kapitänleutnant* said, "from *les Isolates.* And a safe spot on a deep waterway that has enough trees around it to make a large vessel difficult to spot from the air."

The Cajun leader thought a moment. "You want a place to hide your boat," he surmised. "Maybe to fix it, yeah?"

Stuermer nodded. "That's right."

"For how long?"

"As long as it takes."

Papa Luc grinned. "And you give us all that gold and cash money?" He laughed. "It sound too easy, my friend."

"That's all we want," Stuermer repeated, "and, as I said, some cooperation from your people to help us do what we need to do."

Papa Luc turned and gestured at the dark bayou. "We call this Bayou Profond. You understand?"

Stuermer nodded. "Deep Bayou."

The Cajun chuckled into his beard. "We call it that because it is."

"How deep?"

"Twenty foot in some places. Couple of holes with no bottom that we can find. If you stay in the middle, you always got at least fourteen foot. All the way to our houses up yonder in a big grove of cypress. And the pond there is much deeper."

Stuermer nodded slowly. "If we can get this far up the bay, it sounds perfect." He extended a hand. "Then we have a—what is it you Americans say?—a deal?"

Papa Luc's dark eyes glittered as he took the *Kapitänleutnant*'s hand. *"Mais oui, mon ami,"* he chuckled. "A deal." He glanced around at Jolene and Claude, then bent toward the tool case.

Stuermer's booted foot kicked shut the lid with a metallic bang. Papa Luc flinched and recoiled. "What the hell you do?" he exclaimed angrily.

Stuermer kept his boot on top of the lid. "I forgot to mention," he said evenly, "that you get all of this *after* we get the help we need. Not before."

Papa Luc straightened, regaining his composure. *"Non,* my friend. Suppose we help you fix your boat, and then you point your guns at us and leave without paying. Nothing to stop you from doing that."

"We've been here five times in the past," Stuermer said, "and we've never cheated you before."

Papa Luc shook his head. "That was straight-up barter and trade, goods for cash money and gold. This time, you want a *service.* You pay first, my friend."

Stuermer considered for a moment. "Fair enough. But if I give you all this, there is nothing to stop you from hiding it, then running to the U.S. Navy. After all, you would have the money, so why do the work?" He smiled thinly.

"We've never cheated you before," Papa Luc said pointedly.

The *Kapitänleutnant* laughed out loud for the first time. "Listen, Papa Luc, this is what we'll do: you keep that bar"—he indicated the single ingot the Cajun held in his right hand—"as a down payment. All of this"—he tapped the toe of his boot on the tool case lid—"will go with us. But there will be a payment plan. Once our boat is safely up the bayou, you get two more bars of gold. Each time you help us with another task, you get another two bars, and so on until we leave, when you get all the rest."

Papa Luc glanced down at the gold ingot. "Three bars each time," he said.

"No. Two."

The Cajun shook his head. "You must pay more."

Stuermer shrugged and folded his arms, his boot still on top of the tool case. "That is the best I can do. Take . . . umm . . . take . . ." He looked over his shoulder at Bock. "What is that American saying, *Oberleutnant?*"

" 'Take it or leave it,' " Bock recited in his unaccented English.

"Thank you," Stuermer said, turning back to Papa Luc. "As my officer said, *mon ami,* you can take it or leave it."

Papa Luc stared at him darkly for a long moment, his jaw working. The low-burning fires popped and crackled, the only sounds in the still night air. Finally, the Cajun spoke.

"I will take it, Captain," he growled. "On your word."

Stuermer extended his hand again, and they shook. "My word is good, Papa Luc," he said. "You can count on it, as I know I can count on yours."

"Mmm," the Cajun replied.

Stuermer bent over and lifted the heavy case with some effort. Bock stepped forward and took one end of it, and together they moved toward the dinghy. Wolfe backpedaled with them, eyeing Claude.

"You can expect us before dawn," Stuermer called. "We would appreciate someone meeting us at the mouth of this bayou to help guide us upstream. Our vessel is quite large."

Papa Luc nodded. "Someone will be here."

"Good," Stuermer replied, climbing into the bow after Wolfe and Bock and shoving the dinghy away from the bank with one foot. "I'd hate to have to withhold your very first installment." The little boat drifted out into the darkness. "*Jusqu'à demain,* Papa Luc," he called as the night closed in around him. "Until tomorrow."

Out in the middle of the midnight bay, there wasn't a breath of wind to stir even the smallest wave. The dinghy sat quietly on a flat, watery plane, reflections of stars dotting the black, oily-still surface here and there. Only the occasional movements of the men it carried caused the small boat to rock at all.

Bock knelt in the bow, swinging a lead weight on the end of its thin line. He heaved it forward some fifteen feet, letting the line uncoil from his other hand. It hit the water with a light splash. "Come ahead, Lothar," the exec said, retrieving the line carefully. "Easy, now."

The dinghy puttered forward until the line went vertical. Bock pinched it at the water's surface as Wolfe throttled down and took the motor out of gear. The exec glanced at the line and looked at Stuermer, sitting on the center thwart with a small notebook. "Four meters, Captain. Just barely."

Stuermer wrote it down. "Barely enough," he said. "But enough."

Bock re-coiled the line over his left hand and dangled the dripping weight from his right. "Again, sir?"

The *Kapitänleutnant* glanced around briefly. "No, Erich, that's good. By my reckoning we've sounded all the way from the mouth of the bayou to a point on the course you maintained for us when we first brought the boat inshore. There should be enough water for us to feel our way up the bay just before dawn. That'll be high tide."

He put the notebook into his jacket pocket and rubbed his eyes. "Take us home, Lothar."

"Aye, sir," the torpedoman replied, and throttled up the little engine.

As the dinghy puttered across the calm water, Stuermer unclasped the catches on the tool case at his feet and pulled open the lid. Bock dug into his jacket pockets and withdrew a couple of heavy cloth bags. Bending down, he began to scoop up the bundles of cash and deposit them into one of the bags. There were only five bundles. The rest of the money section of the tool case was filled with flat pieces of wood broken from vegetable crates.

Stuermer helped him transfer the slender gold bars into the other bag. As with the cash, there were far fewer bars in the case than there appeared to be at first glance—beneath the single upper layer of gold ingots were several large pig iron ballast weights.

"It fooled him, Captain," Bock said, "just as you said

it would. You made a few thousand dollars worth of gold bullion and cash look like a few million." He picked the last two bars off the ballast weights. "I guess you didn't need to use these damned heavy iron pigs, though."

"Well, I wasn't going to let him dig into the gold or money," Stuermer said, "but I wanted it to *feel* heavy enough in case he helped us lift it in or out of the boat. However, he didn't. Just as well."

"I don't think he does much lifting, Captain," Wolfe growled from the stern. "Just talking."

"I'd say you're right, Torpedoman," Stuermer agreed. He squinted into the night as the silhouette of the U-113's camouflaged conning tower came into view. "In any case, now he thinks we've got a boatload of gold and cash with us. That's what we want him to think. He'll keep cooperating with us until he decides he's got it all, or thinks he's figured out a way to take it from us."

"Huh," Wolfe snorted. "Let him try."

Stuermer smiled as the dinghy bumped gently into the conning tower. "I don't want any of us to underestimate Papa Luc, Lothar. We have to stay a couple of steps ahead of him, anticipate him." He rose to his feet. "Low cunning—after all—is still cunning."

Chapter
Ten

Dawn was less than a half hour away as the fully surfaced U-113, ballasted as high out of the water as
Dekker could float her, began a slow turn that would
line her up with the deep center of Bayou Profond. Two
Cajun guides, black-bearded and wary, sat in a pirogue
at midchannel to confirm the route, paddles resting
across their knees. Clearly in awe of the U-boat's lethal
appearance, they began stroking energetically up the
bayou as the war vessel nosed forward, her single damaged screw thrumming.

Stuermer, on the bridge, looked anxiously up at the
lightening sky. "I know he's already doing it, Erich," he
told Bock, "but remind Jonas to keep an extra-sharp eye
out for aircraft on radar and Metox. We're as exposed as
hell right now."

Bock nodded. "Right away, Captain." He glanced at
the encroaching banks as the U-113 slid completely into
the bayou. "Maybe these cypress trees will overhang
more as we go upstream."

"So Papa Luc said," Stuermer mused. "We'll see."

Bock knelt at the open conning tower hatchway and
called down to the control room. A muffled response
came back, and he looked at his captain. "*Puster* Winkler says all clear so far, sir. Chief Dekker reports that
the boat is stable and fully ballasted up to her minimum
draft of three and a half meters. Diesel number one is

running well. Shaft and screw are operating no worse than before . . . which is to say, poorly."

The *Kapitänleutnant* tipped his white cap back by the brim. "As expected. Very well, Exec, we continue. And hope that we have every bit of that fourteen feet of depth Papa Luc promised us."

"Fourteen feet," Bock repeated. "A little over four meters." He blew a sigh out between his teeth. "Maybe a half—three-quarters of a meter of bottom clearance."

"Correct." Stuermer bent to the bridge speaking tube. "Helm, one degree to port. Easy, now." He watched as the U-boat's sharklike bow moved imperceptibly to the left. "We'd better pray that we don't run hard aground before we move up under some tree cover. If we get caught here by an air patrol, we're as good as dead."

Bock put a hand on the conning tower's forward wind baffle, his eyes flickering over the channel of black water that meandered through the shadowy, moss-hung cypress trees ahead of them. The two Cajuns in the pirogue had slowed their paddling and were now pacing the U-113, keeping to the center of the waterway.

There was a gentle bump and the conning tower leaned slightly to the left. Stuermer and Bock shot each other quick glances. A sensation of gradual lifting came up through the soles of their seaboots, then ebbed back down as the U-boat slid over the high spot in the bayou's bottom. As the conning tower eased back into a vertical orientation, the two officers looked astern to see a cloud of mud, leaves, and detritus billow up in the boat's propeller turbulence.

Stuermer turned back toward the bow, his mouth set in its familiar grim line. "Wonderful," he muttered. "Just wonderful."

"They're comin', Estelle!" Jolene exclaimed, her eyes wide with excitement. Her fingers flexed on the sill of the shanty's open window as she looked quickly over her shoulder. "Don't you want to see them?"

The old woman smiled patiently and eased her rocking chair forward. With painful slowness she got to her feet, supporting her weight on an ornate cane carved from a twisted cypress root. The animal-bone charms dangling from her worn shawl clicked together softly as she shuffled forward, her back hunched with age. " 'Course I want to see them, child," she said. " 'Course I do."

She moved up beside the girl and peered out the window, squinting into the dawn light until her small black eyes nearly disappeared. At the far end of the mist-covered pond, sliding through the moss-draped cypress trees, was the huge black conning tower of the U-113. Just ahead of it was the pirogue containing the two men Papa Luc had chosen as guides. The U-boat rotated slowly as it navigated the final bend in the waterway, then straightened out as it emerged from the bayou, its long black hull fully visible.

People began to emerge from the other shanties, coming out onto the docks and porches to gape at the unfamiliar vessel invading their quiet pond. Estelle's sharp eyes ran over the U-boat, taking in the two sets of twin-barreled antiaircraft guns mounted on the conning tower and the big eighty-eight-millimeter cannon locked down securely on the foredeck.

"Arrrgghh," she growled deep in her throat, shaking her head.

Jolene could hardly contain herself. "You ever seen anything like it, Estelle? It's so . . . so . . . *big!"*

Estelle continued shaking her head, making noises of disapproval. "I don't got to have seen it before to know about it, child. I can *feel* it." She held up one clawlike hand, palm out. "Bad juju."

Jolene looked at her. "Bad juju? You feel that?"

The old woman nodded gravely, closing her eyes. "That thing there, that big black boat—it came from something evil. Maybe not the boat itself, maybe not the men on it, but the thing that caused it to be brought into bein'—evil. Stone-cold black evil."

Jolene's face paled slightly. "Can it hurt us, Estelle?"

Estelle swayed a little, letting her head rock back. "This kinda evil lives far away, across the sea, but it can reach out and strangle a person no matter where they're at. Strangle the whole world." She opened her eyes and stared at Jolene suddenly. "Can't you feel it, child?"

Jolene waited a few seconds to make sure. "No," she whispered timidly, "I don't feel nothin'. But I believe you, Estelle," she added.

The old woman seemed to come out of her curious half trance. "That's all right, *ma chérie*. Not everyone got the gift." She smiled at the girl. "Just you trust me, though."

"I do, Estelle."

On the bridge of the U-113, Stuermer raised a hand as the boat eased quietly out into the center of the pond formed by the widening of the bayou. "All stop. Engine neutral."

Bock, standing near the speaking tube, leaned down. "All stop. Idle in neutral."

"Reverse one-quarter speed."

Again, Bock repeated the order. The engine vibration under their feet changed as the screw went into reverse, throwing up a slurry of white water under the stern. The U-boat's forward drift gradually slowed to nothing.

"All stop," Stuermer said crisply. "Neutral." He scanned the shoreline, taking in the massive cypress trees, their tops grown together and hanging with curtains of Spanish moss, forming a virtual canopy over all but the very center of the pond. The corners of his mouth lifted slightly. "Good," he muttered. "Good cover near the bank."

Bock gazed around at the stilt shanties in amazement. The entire settlement looked like something out of a fairy tale by the Brothers Grimm. All it needed was the odd troll or gnome waddling around to complete the picture. Even nature, it seemed, had conspired to give the setting an aura of ethereality: layers of mist drifted off the black water and through the cathedral-spire cypress trees, dampening the reams of moss that hung from limb to limb like giant cobwebs. Here and there, a silver shaft of sunlight penetrated the deep shadows of the primordial swamp.

Dekker had come up from the control room. "Not exactly the Lorient U-boat pens," he observed dryly.

"No, Chief," Stuermer said, "but it has possibilities.

Look, over there." He pointed at an uninhabited section
of shoreline opposite Estelle's rickety shanty. "See? In
between those two giant cypress trees, that miniature
cove cut back into the bank. It's—what?—maybe thirty
meters long and eight wide? Tailor-made for the stern
half of the boat. If it has enough depth, we can use it
as our repair slip."

"Mmm," the chief mused, scratching his beard.
"Could work. If the pond's deep enough under the bow
after we back her in, we could perform the ballasting
inversion right there."

"Precisely," Stuermer confirmed.

"And we could rig cables and block and tackle off the
trees," Bock added. "Also stretch a camouflage net over
top of the whole operation, for extra concealment."

"Absolutely," Stuermer said, "although that canopy
of foliage gives us excellent cover anyway. But we'll take
all we can get." He wiped a trickle of sweat from his
temple with one finger. "But this is all moot if there
isn't enough water over there. Get me a sounding right
here, Erich."

Bock bent to the speaking tube. "Control room.
Sound bottom and report depth."

The reply came back almost immediately: "Depth beneath the keel twenty-one to thirty-three meters. Vari-
able. The readings are changing by the second, sir."

Bock looked over at Stuermer and Dekker in surprise.
"What could be causing that variation, I wonder?"

"Hmm," Stuermer replied. "We're reading a changing
bottom, eh? This is a swamp. I'd guess that the pond
bed isn't really hard, just a loosely packed mix of rotting
vegetation and muck. If there's a spring down there, or
some kind of underground river, it could be roiling the
bottom constantly. We're probably pinging off a cloud
of sediment and debris. That would explain the varying
depth."

"*Mein Gott,*" Dekker said slowly, looking around.
"Who'd have thought this reeking little puddle was so
deep? Most of the water around here is shallow enough
to wade through."

"If it's got similar depth in that little cut," the *Kapitänleutnant* said, "we're going to be in good shape." He glanced at Bock. "So let's find out. Wave that pirogue over here, Erich. Take a sounding line and check the depth in there."

"Yes, sir," Bock replied. He switched to his flawless American English: "Hey, you guys! Come over here!" He waved, beckoning to the paddlers.

They sat in the pirogue at a comfortable distance, looking up at him blankly, not moving. After a few seconds, Bock gave up and switched to French: *"Eh! Venez ici! J'ai besoin de votre bateau!"*

That got their attention. With tentative glances at one another, they dug in with their paddles and brought the narrow craft skimming over the mirrorlike surface of the pond to the side of the U-boat.

"How long have the Cajun people been living here, Captain?" Dekker inquired. "I know you've read the history."

Stuermer was kneeling at the open bridge hatchway. "Pass up a sounding lead!" He looked up at the chief. "Since the British kicked them out of eastern Canada in 1763," he said. "It's called the Expulsion of the Acadians. When the British took Canada from the French, they uprooted and deported thousands of French settlers who'd been living in Acadia for generations. A sort of ethnic cleansing, you might say."

"And they sent them here? To this swamp?"

Stuermer nodded. "Yes. At the time, Louisiana was still a French possession." He took the sounding lead from a crewman in the conning tower compartment. "Thank you."

"Not unlike what we're doing in the countries we've overrun," Bock commented. There was an acid tinge to his voice. "Slavs, gypsies . . ."

"Jews," continued Jonas Winkler, emerging from the bridge hatchway and blinking in the morning light. "Anyone who happens to be an inconvenience for the political powers that be, eh? Just make them disappear. Bloody Nazis." The treasonous words rang through the morning air, delivered with uncharacteristic vehemence by the mild-mannered radioman. Stuermer, Bock, and Dekker all looked at him.

No one said anything. It was true. It was frightening. It was something that decent Germans couldn't bear to admit about their country. It was distracting and troubling to warriors trying to fight and win a war. To a man, they shared the haunting, inescapable feeling that Germany was headed, deservedly, for the gutter of history. And there wasn't a damn thing any of them could do about it.

Dekker cleared his throat. "Well, let's not think about all that," he growled. "I just wanted to ask how it is that there are Americans who've been here for nearly two hundred years, but still can't understand English. I don't see how that's possible."

Stuermer handed Bock the sounding lead with its long coiled line. "I believe it's an anomaly, Chief. Most Cajuns live like typical U.S. citizens, but small pockets of them have remained in isolation out in the swamp for generations, hunting and fishing to survive. They've kept most of their old ways, including their original language. Strange but true."

"Why doesn't the government force them to become normal members of society?"

An ironic smile crossed the *Kapitänleutnant*'s face, and his gray green eyes were amused, almost sad. "This is America, Otto."

Bock descended the outer ladder of the conning tower and traversed the deck to where the two Cajuns were steadying the pirogue alongside the U-113's port saddle tank. Squatting down on his heels, he spoke rapidly in French to the paddler in the stern, then nodded and stepped into the center of the narrow boat. The bow man pushed off, and a few quick strokes sent the pirogue skimming across the pond toward the cut in the far bank.

Up on the bridge, an uncomfortable silence hung in the air. Winkler peered out through his thick eyeglasses at the U-boat's surreal surroundings, then turned to Stuermer. "I've got two men on radar and Metox, Captain," he said quietly, "but everything was clear just before I came up. No activity whatsoever in the sky. Metox senses no enemy radar impulses coming in our direction." He paused. "Captain, I'm sorry."

Stuermer bent to the speaking tube. "Reverse one-quarter throttle for three seconds, then neutral again." He eyed the U-boat's orientation as his order was executed. "I don't need you to be sorry, Jonas. I need you in control of yourself." His voice was very even. "How many war patrols for you? Seven?"

"Eight," Winkler replied. "One in U-111 before I came to this boat. You remember: the boat the British sank under me off the Channel Islands back in 'forty."

"And you, Otto? How many?"

Dekker frowned up at the treetops for a moment. "Fourteen, some longer than others. Three different boats, including this one, Captain."

Stuermer faced his two senior officers. "Look, neither of you need a lecture from me; we've been through too much, both together and separately. You know that compared to Prien or Schepke, I tolerate a certain amount of free expression aboard my boat—even encourage it. I give myself the privilege of disagreeing privately with the powers that control me, and I extend the same privilege to you. But Jonas, whatever is rotten about Germany's political core right now, we cannot help her—or ourselves—by dwelling on the most disturbing aspects of Nazi policy. We must concentrate on doing our duty and winning the best peace for our homeland that we can . . . or in the end, there may be no Germany to go home to. Accountability for the treatment of displaced people will be assessed after the war is over. First, we must try to win it—or at least not lose too badly."

Winkler nodded slowly. "I know, Captain. We've all discussed it around the galley table when the crew is out of earshot. The momentum of history has caught us, and we're in the maelstrom up to our necks. First we have to fight our way out; then maybe we can change things for the better—put sane men back in charge of Germany."

"And once again, I sympathize with you for the loss of your friend. . . ."

"Yitzhak Pfeiffel," Winkler said. "My *best* friend, since our childhood days at the conservatory. He sat in the flute chair next to me on three orchestra tours of Europe, played with me note for note." He took his glasses off and polished the lenses on his shirtsleeve. "They dragged him out of his house in the middle of the night, herded him and several hundred other Jews onto a cattle car, and hauled them off to the east, toward Poland. I was home that night, right across the street." Winkler's thin face was calm, but his eyes were haunted. "And do you know what I did to help my colleague and best friend? My lifelong friend from childhood?" Stuermer and Dekker stood silently. They'd heard it before. *"Nothing."*

The radio officer held his glasses up to the rising sun, inspected them, and put them back on. "But you're right, Captain. What does that have to do with us, right here and right now? We have to effect repairs and get home. And we can't do that if we allow ourselves to become distracted." He smiled. "Again, I apologize. What I said was not helpful."

Stuermer nodded, his hard-set mouth relaxing slightly. "All right, Jonas. All right."

There was a scraping sound as Dekker shifted his feet on the deck plates. "Let's just get back to Lorient, for God's sake. We'll make our brains bleed if we keep this up."

"Another depressing political discussion, I see," Wolfe said sardonically, his bald head appearing in the bridge hatchway. "Permission to enter the bridge, Captain."

"Granted." Stuermer said. The air cleared quickly as the officers' minds returned to the situation at hand. The *Kapitänleutnant* fixed his gaze on the pirogue carrying Bock as it probed the narrow cutaway in the bank. A small splash kicked up as the young exec heaved the sounding lead yet again.

A few minutes later the pirogue came skimming back across the pond, Bock on one knee amidships. The two Cajuns brought the craft up alongside the U-boat, and he stepped out quickly onto the port saddle tank. As the pirogue backed off, he looked up at the bridge.

"Well?" Stuermer inquired, leaning over the bridge rail. "Too shallow?"

Bock grinned. "Four meters at the extreme inshore end of the inlet, Captain," he reported, "sloping to nine meters at the midpoint, and nearly fourteen at the mouth. And then it gets deeper toward the center of the pond. It's perfect, sir."

Stuermer rapped his knuckles on the rail. "Excellent. Good work, Exec." He turned to Dekker. "I want a deck crew fore and aft, Chief. Break out mooring lines and prepare to back the boat into that cutaway. Let's get under the cover of those trees as quickly as possible."

"Aye, sir," Dekker responded, and turned toward the bridge hatch.

Twenty minutes later, the U-113 was sitting snugly in the narrow cut like a finger in a glove, her stern half surrounded by three-foot-high shoreline and her fore-deck protruding out into the pond. A gang of seamen had rigged a camouflage net along the stabilizing cable that ran from bow to conning tower and were draping it with newly cut branches and brush. Stuermer paced up and down the gunwales of his boat, checking the heavy mooring lines, jumping back and forth across the two-foot water gap between the U-113's afterdeck and the bank. More crewmen were stretching a second camo net above the conning tower, between the two immense cypress trees that bracketed the inlet. A dozen sailors chopped away at the underbrush with axes, hatchets, even galley cleavers, hurriedly collecting the loose foliage that would ultimately conceal the U-boat from air-borne eyes.

Bock jumped across the water gap to the back deck and threw the armful of willow branches he was carrying down near the men who were weaving the foliage into the overhead netting. Sweat was running down his face and throat in a torrent. He took off his peaked officer's cap and passed the shirtsleeve of his upper arm across his forehead and eyes, breathing hard. Stuermer paused

beside him, breaking off his relentless inspection of the
moorage and camouflage procedures.

"And I thought the interior of a U-boat was humid,"
Bock panted. He eyed the half-dozen pirogues full of
curious Cajuns who had paddled down the pond and
were watching the activity from a discreet distance.
"How do these people put up with the heat? It sucks all
the energy out of you."

Stuermer wiped the sweat from his own forehead.
"They're accustomed to it, I guess. And I think we move
too quickly, like Northerners in a cold climate. Have you
noticed? *Les Isolates* never do anything in a hurry. Their
pace matches the environment; they move as fast as the
heat lets them, and no faster."

Dekker, stripped to the waist and dripping, tossed a
bundle of branches onto the back deck and spat noisily.
"The *Bürgermeister* is coming, Captain," he said dryly,
pointing up toward the bow. "By private yacht, it
looks like."

Stuermer and Bock looked forward in time to see a
pirogue slide past the U-113's sharp nose. In its bow,
seated in his spindle-backed chair, was Papa Luc, looking very much like some kind of overdressed white colo-
nial trader being chauffeured around by dugout canoe.
The boat, Bock noticed, was being paddled by the same
slender, pretty girl in the baggy clothes who'd been at
the mouth of Bayou Profond the previous night. She did
a creditable job of handling the pirogue, he thought. She
glanced up and smiled at him shyly, then dropped her
eyes again. She really was very pretty.

Papa Luc raised a hand as the girl halted the canoe
near the bank with a quick reverse-sculling stroke.
"Good mornin', Captain!" he called. "You had no trou-
bles getting in here, *n'est-ce pas?* You see? Just like I
said, plenty water in our bayou."

Stuermer walked along the foredeck, accompanied by
Bock and Dekker, until he was looking directly down at
the gray-haired Cajun. "We slid over one shallow area,"
he said, "but otherwise, everything has gone smoothly."
He paused. "And there were guides waiting for us at

the head of the bay, as agreed. You have your first installment coming, my friend." Stuermer turned to Bock. "Erich? Two bars, if you would. In my cabin safe. You have the combination."

Bock clicked his heels and snapped off a salute for Papa Luc's benefit, then turned and trotted toward the conning tower ladder. Dekker lowered his head and put a grimy hand over his mouth to hide the smile.

"Military discipline," Stuermer said, keeping an admirably straight face. "I sincerely hope that you have similar control over your people, *mon ami.*"

"Are you worried about something, Captain?" Papa Luc countered mildly.

Stuermer glanced off into the cypress. "Well, to be honest, it *has* occurred to me that if anyone in your community—mind you, I'm not suggesting you *personally*—was to suddenly decide that it would be easier to simply try to take our gold and currency rather than work for it, they might be inclined to inform the U.S. military of our presence here—in hopes of, say, snatching the bullion in the confusion following an attack on my boat. This would be a rather costly miscalculation."

"Nothin' like that will happen," Papa Luc said, shaking his head. He peered up from beneath his dark brows. "But just out of interest—why wouldn't it work?"

Stuermer's gray green eyes fixed on the Cajun's. "Because most of the gold and money is no longer aboard this vessel. It is hidden somewhere out there"—he jerked a thumb over his shoulder—"along the coast, underwater." He looked up as Bock reappeared on the conning tower, carrying two bars of gold. "I have enough bullion aboard to fulfill my end of our bargain, *mon ami*, at least for the immediate future. You will be paid as we complete the various stages of the repairs to this boat, and in the end you will get it all. But"—Stuermer smiled—"if my boat should be discovered or attacked, you will get nothing." He paused. "Therefore, I'm sure you will keep your people well under control. Secrecy is critical, don't you agree?"

Papa Luc looked up at the *Kapitänleutnant* with a black stare. Then, slowly, he grinned. "Of course, my friend. My interests are your interests, *n'est-ce pas?*"

"Bien sûr," Stuermer said. "Now, I need to talk to you about retaining the services of a certain type of contractor. . . ."

Chapter
Eleven

"**A**h, the hell with it!" Mike Holt threw down the cards he was holding and slumped back in his chair in disgust. "Not a single damn face card the whole night." He tipped the half-empty bottle of gin to the shot glass in front of him. A generous splash of liquor ended up on the green felt surface of the card table. Holt scowled, raised the shot to his lips, and banged it back.

"That's it, Holt—you're cut off," exclaimed the heavy-set tugboat skipper sitting opposite him. He paused for effect, a smile curling on his lips. "You're *outta hand! Hahahahaha!*"

The other men at the poker table guffawed in unison at the overused, tasteless joke. Holt nodded through his gin haze. "Yup. Out a hand." He held up his left arm with a grin—a grimace—of resignation. At the end of his sinewy forearm was a scarred stump where his hand should have been.

"Hahahaha! Put that ugly damn thing away, bro!" the tugboat skipper roared. "What you tryin' to do? Make us all sick?"

Suddenly it wasn't funny anymore. Not funny at all. Holt felt his insides boil up like lava in an active volcano. He lashed out with his foot and caught the leg of the poker table, kicking it forward and his chair back. Loose silver, bills, and cards flew. The liquored-up chortling of the other four players switched immediately to blank shock.

Holt jerked himself to his feet, weaving unsteadily. "Fuck you," he snarled, and snatched the gin bottle off the table with his one remaining hand. He kicked the chair out of his way and staggered off toward the door of the bar.

The fat tugboat skipper half rose to his feet, his face flushing crimson. "What's your fuckin' problem, Holt? You can't take a goddamn joke no more? What—"

The skinny, weather-beaten fisherman next to him leaned over and pulled him back into his seat. "Let him be, Henri. Just let him be."

The tugboat skipper blew out a long breath and began to sort out his scattered cards and winnings. "I'm tellin' y'all, Mike ain't the same ol' boy he used to be. . . ."

The hot red haze faded gradually from Holt's eyes as he stumbled out of the bar and into the cool night air of Venice. Across the street, between the dirty industrial wharves and the fishing piers lined with shrimp boats, he could see the black water of the Mississippi River as it flowed down from New Orleans like blood in a great muddy vein. In his mind's eye he clenched the hand that was no longer there into a fist. When he did that he could feel every knuckle, every finger, the nails digging into his palm. Phantom sensation, the doctors said. The body's lingering physical memory of something long gone.

He tipped the gin bottle up, took a long swig, then steadied himself and began to trudge down the middle of the deserted street. Tucking the bottle under his left arm, he fumbled in his shirt pocket and came up with a Lucky Strike. Three matches later he had it lit and, ignoring the dull, burning pain that bloomed in the left side of his chest as soon as he inhaled, continued to wend his way along the rain-puddled road. Somewhere upriver, a night-running tug signaled its presence with two long, distant blasts of its horn.

Holt scuffed through the dirt parking lot and onto the rickety wooden dock behind the Lanctot Fish Cannery. Next to the parking lot stood the three immense circular tanks of the Venice fuel depot, each sixty feet high by one hundred in diameter, surrounded by a ten-foot-high chain-link fence topped with barbed wire. Searchlights mounted on tall steel poles kept the depot grounds illuminated constantly. Holt scowled at the glare as he clumped down the dock toward the small trawler tied up at its seaward end.

"Hey, Mike!" The female voice hailed him from the second floor of the gray clapboard ship chandlery next to the fish plant. Holt wobbled to a halt and looked up at the dimly lit window. It was Giselle—the day shift bartender from Murphy's up the street who lived alone in the one-bedroom apartment over the chandlery. On the downslope of her thirties, she was plain to begin with and fast losing what little prettiness she had to late hours, hard liquor, and unfiltered Camels. It depressed Holt to look at her; it was like taking a bath in secondhand loneliness. That he didn't need. He had plenty of his own to go around.

"Hey, Gee," he growled, using her nickname. The dock seemed to be tilting slowly this way and that under his feet. Irritating.

"Couple or three guys were looking for you earlier on this evenin'," she said, her voice husky, alluring. The Marlene Dietrich thing. Like her vocal cords had been marinated in bourbon whiskey and cured by tobacco smoke. Holt shuffled his feet in impatience. Every worn-out barfly in the country was doing that voice thing these days. Movie star crap.

"Oh, yeah?"

"Yeah. They went up to the *Shiloh* and poked around. You weren't there, so they left." Giselle fluffed her tangled brunette hair.

Holt glanced down the dock toward his trawler. "They leave a message?"

"How would I know?" She shrugged. "They didn't talk to nobody that I could see."

"Great," Holt muttered. "Thanks for nothing. It's not like I need the work, right?"

Giselle's sagging features hardened. "Hey, I'm tryin' to do you a favor, smart guy. I don't need you givin' me a load of shit for it."

Holt turned back toward the trawler, rolling his eyes. "Whatever."

"Hey, Mike."

"Whaaat?"

"You wanna come up for a while?"

Holt glanced up at her, focused, and shook his head. "I know I'm drunk," he said, "but do I really look like that much of a loser?"

Giselle jerked herself erect and seized the lower frame of the sliding window. "You're mean when you crawl inside a bottle, Holt," she hissed, and slammed the window shut.

Holt blinked, watching as the curtain was yanked across the opening behind the pane of glass, then grinned and proceeded on down the dock toward his boat. "Actually," he said aloud, "I'm a real sweet peach most of the time." He broke into a drunken chuckle.

The *Shiloh* was seventy-four feet long and had an amidships beam of eighteen feet: a high-bulwarked, slightly tubby working boat with a roomy, functional back deck. Framed and planked with cypress, like most of the shrimpers and fishing trawlers in Louisiana, she was seaworthy and strong with a large fuel capacity, designed to endure long weeks offshore in all kinds of weather. A rounded, cheesebox-style bridge was built onto the front of her short, squarish deckhouse, looking out over the foredeck and bow. A central mast and several booms for handling fishing nets and salvage tackle loomed overhead, creaking as they swayed with the boat's slight motion.

Holt weaved past the name on the bow, *Shiloh*—rendered in peeling blue paint over a fading Confederate battle flag—and past the wooden sign mounted on a dock piling that read HOLT DIVING SERVICES: UNDERWATER SALVAGE, SEARCH, REPAIR. Added underneath in less formally painted script: *Also bottom scrubbing and hull inspection. See Captain Mike Holt, on board the* SHILOH.

He paused at the edge of the dock and looked back at the sign. A bitter smile creased his face; it felt good to have a really first-class wallow in self-pity. Only the third time this week. He let the black mood envelop him like a hair shirt.

"Let the one-handed wonder scrub your hull for peanuts," he muttered. "You're really setting the world on fire, Holt."

He threw a leg drunkenly over the gunwale of the *Shiloh*, climbed aboard, and tottered off toward his cabin.

It was still dark when Holt found himself jarred out of a horrible night's sleep by the sound of pans banging in the galley, just outside his door. The light was on and the aroma of strong coffee and frying bacon thickened the air. It was like a nightmare. He groaned and rolled away from the invading glare, pulling the pillow over his splitting head. Rats were gnawing their way through his skull from the inside out. Maybe if he wished hard enough for death, he'd just expire right then and there. Save a lot of pain.

Bang. Bang, bang. Clang.

It was unendurable.

Holt clapped his hand to his forehead and squeezed his eyes shut. *"Will you keep the goddamn fucking noise down?"* he bellowed raggedly.

There was one more bang for good measure, a pause, and then the door was pushed open all the way, letting light from the galley flood into the cabin. Holt moaned.

"You gots to wake up, Mike," Lucius rumbled, his deep baritone filling the room. "We got us a job."

Holt peered at his first mate through slightly separated fingers. Lucius Dancer's six-foot-five, two-hundred-and-fifty-pound frame filled the doorway, the ebony skin of his bald head and thickly muscled arms gleaming, backlit by the galley light.

"I don't care."

"Yes, you do," Lucius persisted. "Come on now. Coffee's on and bacon 'n' eggs is fryin'."

"Arrrrgh. Give me a minute."

The big man grinned, strong white teeth flashing in his jet-black face. "Okay," he said. "But I ain't lettin' you go back to sleep."

Holt groaned again, rubbing his eyes. "Who's in charge of this boat, anyway?"

Lucius backed out, still grinning. "Why, you is, Mistuh Holt, suh." The Stepin Fetchit exaggeration was letter-perfect. He laughed and turned back toward the stove.

In a little while, the cabin door creaked open all the way and Holt staggered out to the galley table, looking much like a reanimated corpse. He slumped into a wooden chair, the legs of which had been screwed to the deck to keep it from sliding around in heavy weather, and let his head sag into his hand and stump, elbows propped up on the table. Almost immediately a tin plate of scrambled eggs and bacon hit the scarred wood in front of him—*bang*. He jerked up and back, his skull reverberating.

"Coffee's blacker'n my ass," Lucius said. "You want it now or later?"

Holt had to laugh in spite of himself. "You've got no pity in you, Lucius. I'm dyin' over here."

"You done it to yourself." The big man's deep voice held a gentle note. There was a rippling sound and a rich, burned aroma as he poured coffee into a mug and set it down. "Been a long time since you come back from the war. Long time since the hospital. Long time since you been out the service." He paused. "Long time since you been sober more'n two nights runnin'."

Holt put his two arms and one hand straight out, resting on the table on either side of his bacon and eggs, and stared at the steam rising off the food. "You still counting?"

"Yep."

"What the hell for?"

" 'Cause I gives a damn."

Holt looked at his lap for a moment.

"Maybe I oughta quit," he said. "Drinking, that is."

Lucius was silent.

Holt looked at him through bloody eyes. "What do you think?"

Lucius' ebony face was impassive. "When you ready," he said. "You the one gots to do it."

"Yeah," Holt said. "Yeah." He took hold of the coffee mug. "Well, how about now?" Before Lucius could answer, he went on: "Yeah . . . now."

The black man smiled, because for the first time in nearly fourteen months, it sounded like the old Mike Holt. "Okay, Mike." Maybe this time.

"Dreamed I was back in that Kraut prison again," Holt said quietly. An involuntary shiver passed through his body. "Same thing, with that Gestapo bastard kicking me and swearing in German: *'Verdammt! Verdammt!'* Over and over again . . ." A look that was half grin and half horror suddenly contorted his face. He rubbed his eyes. "I don't think I'm ever gonna forget that word."

Lucius nodded his head in silence.

Holt drained the coffee mug and rapped it down on the tabletop. He picked up a fork and began to shovel eggs into his mouth. "Eating kills the pain," he mumbled, chewing, "and I can probably make it to the port rail if I need to throw up."

"That'd be nice," Lucius remarked.

Holt swallowed eggs, grimacing. "Tell me about this job."

"Awright." Lucius sat down opposite him with his own plate of food and coffee mug. "Yesterday, 'bout seven thirty in the evenin', I seen three white men standin' on the dock here, lookin' over the *Shiloh*. Seen 'em from across the ways, from Ma Blackstrap's eatin' house. By the time I got out of there and caught 'em they was halfway up Main Street. We got to talkin' and it turns out they need a boat—a boat that come equipped with divers, dive gear, and riggin' tackle."

"Hell," Holt said, "just like ours."

"Correck," Lucius said. "And they willin' to pay."

Holt nodded. "That'd be a welcome goddamn change. With what? Beads and trinkets?"

"Not exackly," the big man said. "With this." There was a light thump as he dropped a thick wad of bills on the table, folded up and pinned with a steel money clip.

The fork stopped halfway to Holt's open mouth. For a few blessed seconds he didn't even notice his throbbing head. That was a real, genuine, honest-to-God *chunk* of cash. More than he'd seen in a very long time.

Not the kind of money that got handed to a black man by a stranger in Venice, Louisiana, in 1943, in an era of wartime frugality and rationing.

Lucius read his mind, nodding. "Nice young fella did all the talkin'. Sounded like he was from up North somewheres—some kinda Yankee accent. The other two were a little older and didn't say a single word. Just smiled a bit."

"What'd they want?" Holt poked at the wad of bills with his fork. "For this?"

"Young fella said he was a discharged navy survey man, doin' work for some oil companies. Said they wantin' to go look at some ocean bottom about twenty miles out. Dive to the bottom, take some samples. Oil companies think there might be a way to drill offshore, maybe get oil out of the seafloor. He said the U.S. government interested, too. There's a war on, and everything run on oil."

Holt looked incredulous. "Drill for oil offshore?" he exclaimed. "He said that?"

"Yep."

The *Shiloh*'s one-handed skipper set his fork down, threw his head back, and laughed until tears squeezed from the corners of his eyes.

"Lucius," he panted at last, "I'll tell you one thing I know for sure. Ain't nobody *ever* gonna drill for oil out in the Gulf. Not from a boat, not from a barge, not even if they try to set a drill tower on the bottom out there. The sea won't let 'em do it. What won't sink will blow away, and what won't blow away will rust to pieces. It's a pipe dream, Lucius, a pipe dream."

He wiped his eyes on the back of his hand. "So that's where that wad of dough comes from. Oil companies. And these guys represent them. Gettin' paid to chase down crazy fantasies in the name of John D. Rockefeller. No wonder they've got so much moola to throw around."

Lucius shrugged. "Long as they's throwin' it."

"Uh-huh." Holt chewed thoughtfully on a strip of bacon. "When do they want to go?"

"Today. At noon."

Holt looked at him. "You couldn't even get us an extra day to get ready?"

"Boat's ready, Mike," Lucius said. "Has been for months. All she need is her skipper." His gaze was very direct.

Holt locked eyes with him momentarily. Then he simply nodded. "How long?"

"Five days, the young fella said. Maybe a full week."

"And we stay on location offshore twenty-four hours a day, right? We don't run in and out?"

"Correck." Lucius smiled. "I told him it'd cost him."

"And?"

"He didn't 'pear to mind one bit when I told him our regular full-day rate for divin'."

"Hot damn!" Holt slapped the table with his open palm. "A week of full-day rate?"

The big mate held up a callused hand. "Wait. I ain't told you the good part yet. What I quoted him was our full-day rate . . . plus twenty percent."

Holt blinked. "He went for that?"

"Like a crappie for a wiggle-worm," Lucius said, beaming.

Holt shook his head, reached across the table, and clasped hands briefly with the big man. "Just what we need, old buddy. Workin' money. They come through with it, that's enough dough to buy a month's worth of fuel, ice, and provisions for this boat. We can do one long trip for shrimp and snapper, just stay offshore, fishing, and be out of the red in no time." He grinned. "That'll show those damn bankers."

Lucius smiled carefully, forty-seven years of life experience tempering his response. "Sure it will, Mike. Sure it will. But you know, them ol' boys just couldn't see how a one-handed skipper could run a short-handed boat and make it pay. Can't really blame 'em for not writin' you no new loans."

Holt raised his coffee mug. "Fuck 'em," he said shortly. He drained it and banged it down. "Ahhh. I feel almost human. When are these guys showing up again?"

"Noon," Lucius reiterated. "But we's gonna go meet them at the old cargo landing downriver. Pick them all up there."

"What? What for?" Holt lifted an eyebrow, even though it hurt. "That's nearly to the channel mouth, on that little flooded island. What the hell are they doing down there?"

Lucius shrugged once again. "Young fella said that they were gonna have an inshore survey boat take 'em out this morning for a quick check of the shallows, then drop them at the cargo landing. Quicker to meet the *Shiloh* down there, he said, than come all the way back up to Venice."

"Huh," Holt muttered. "That's funny. But hell, it's their nickel. We start the time clock as soon as we leave the dock, whether they're on board or not. Customer's always right. Ain't that so, Lucius?"

The big man grinned at him and purposely thickened his already-dense Mississippi drawl. "Yassuh, Mistuh Holt. That be so, suh."

"You really do speak excellent American English, Erich," Stuermer remarked in German. "I don't believe that large Negro even blinked the whole time you were talking to him."

"Large is right," Wolfe interjected from the amidships seat of the pirogue that cruised alongside the one bearing the U-boat captain and Bock. "I thought *I* had a little size. He made me look like a Black Forest dwarf."

"Well, not quite, Lothar," Bock said, putting a match to one of his Turkish cigarettes. "Aside from skin hue, you actually resemble one another quite closely. For example . . ." He paused and grinned.

Wolfe looked over at him, waiting.

"You're both bald."

Wolfe looked disgusted. "*Thank* you, Lieutenant."

Bock laughed, blowing out smoke. "I'm pulling your leg, Lothar. He's got an inch or two on you, but he's also older. I believe you could take him."

"Maybe he'd just prefer to be friends," cut in Stuermer. "Wouldn't that be nice, gentlemen?"

"I think so," Wolfe grumbled.

"Of course, Captain," Bock said. He examined the end of his cigarette. "You really don't think he caught on at all?"

"I don't believe he did," Stuermer replied. "And it wasn't because he was the least bit slow, either. You simply sounded genuine."

Bock pursed his lips in a quick smile of satisfaction. "Thank you, Captain."

The four Cajuns manning the two pirogues carrying Stuermer, Bock, and Wolfe were now paddling in sync, driving the slender craft along the narrow back bayou at a rapid pace. There were few trees this far down the mouth of the Mississippi, only a network of winding channels, numerous mangrove islands, and a vast prairie of salt-marsh grasses. Every rapid turn around a blind corner sent another flight of egrets or ducks squawking into the air on frantic wings.

After making the long trip out from *les Isolates'* shanty settlement two days earlier and spending the night in a trapper's shack hidden in the swamp just west of Venice, the three U-boat men had been discreetly dropped off by pirogue near the salvage vessel—the *Shiloh*—suggested by Papa Luc. Moving warily through the streets of the waterfront town, feeling dreadfully conspicuous, they'd been disappointed initially at finding no one aboard the boat. The chance meeting on the main street with the *Shiloh*'s huge black mate had put them into better spirits, however. Bock had been smooth and clever, quickly arranging the charter with a minimum of debate, and had even incorporated Papa Luc's last-minute suggestion that rendezvousing with the salvage vessel at an abandoned landing downriver would eliminate the need to risk walking among potentially curious Venice residents a second time.

Now, after a second uncomfortable night in the trapper's shack in the company of their four virtually mute and exceedingly ripe-smelling Cajun escorts, they were being ferried across the wetlands and shallows to the cargo landing for the twelve o'clock meeting with the *Shiloh*. The two pirogues foamed around another bend in the waterway, and a startled school of redfish momentarily turned the surface ahead into a seething pattern of tail swirls and fast-moving Vs.

Wolfe leaned back against the black duffel bag behind him and breathed deeply, luxuriating in the limitless supply of fresh air. "If I close my eyes," he said, "it's almost as if I'm back home in the forest, hunting stag or boar." He was silent for a moment. "I never asked you, Lieutenant: how is it that you speak such good American?"

"My parents," Bock responded simply. "My mother's older brother emigrated to New Jersey before I was born. He's a U.S. citizen. My parents both decided that if they could afford it, I would take a steamship to the United States every summer from the age of twelve on and work with my uncle in his masonry business until the fall. I would learn another trade besides my father's—fishing—and learn English as well. And learn about America."

Wolfe nodded. "Where does your uncle live?"

"In a place called Hoboken."

"Hoboken?" Rendered in Wolfe's guttural German, the name of the New Jersey town came out mangled almost beyond recognition.

Bock laughed. "Yes. Hoboken. Colorful, isn't it?" He drew thoughtfully on his cigarette. "I liked it there. I didn't much care for hauling and cutting stones all day long, but I liked the town. And I liked learning English. American English."

"But you ended up at the Naval Academy in Flensburg," Stuermer interjected, "and emerged a first-class *Ubootwaffe* officer. Who—thank God—speaks flawless American. Remind me someday, when this wartime unpleasantness is over, to send your uncle a bottle of cognac for taking you on all those summers ago. He may be partly responsible for getting us all back home alive."

"If—when—we get back home, Captain," Bock returned, "I'll buy the cognac."

"Hoboken," Wolfe repeated, trying out the word. *"Hoboken."*

The Cajun paddler seated in the bow just forward of

Stuermer stopped stroking, turned in his seat, and pointed ahead. *"Regardez."*

The three Germans raised up as high as they dared in the unstable pirogues and surveyed the watery landscape before them. The narrow bayou they had been following intersected the main Mississippi ship channel some two hundred yards ahead. Just to one side of the confluence was a small island, less than two hundred yards long, slightly higher than the surrounding marshland, with a broad, flat dock of rotting wood built onto its downstream end. Brown river water swirled around the aged pilings on its way to the open Gulf.

"Good," Stuermer said, glancing at his watch. "A full hour early. Let's hope we haven't spent our money foolishly, gentlemen, and that the *Shiloh* shows up."

Chapter
Twelve

The tears of confusion, pain, and rage had long since dried on Jolene's face as she drove the slender pirogue down the twisting bayou with her short paddle. A twelve-foot male alligator napping on the bank in the predawn hours lurched forward, startled, and dove into the black water with a tremendous splash as the pirogue powered around another bend, but the young woman barely noticed him. Her left cheekbone, discolored and swollen, still stung from the blow delivered earlier by Papa Luc's hard open hand.

The moonlight dappled the cypress trees through the sheaves of hanging Spanish moss, the salt-marsh grasses wavered in the slight breeze, but Jolene saw none of it. In her mind's eye the confrontation played itself over and over again, like an interminable visual echo.

She'd been nearly asleep, in her bed, in her room. And then Papa Luc had been there, his hoary face close beside hers in the dark. His hands had wandered over the thin blankets, over her stomach and thighs, and his voice had been trembling, urgent.

"The time has come, Jolene, for you to belong to me. I have decided. You are no longer a child. For years I've waited for you, waited for you to become a woman . . . and now you are. I saw today. You didn't think I would notice, but I saw. The way you looked at that young German officer. You know how to talk with your eyes, your body. You made him look back at you. You thought I wouldn't notice? I did. And I realized that you are a woman now. Ready for me to take as my wife.

"It's my right, Jolene."

She'd clawed the side of his face and spun out of the bed like a wildcat, clutching her loose sleeping shirt around her. With a strangled cry he lost his balance and landed on the floor hard. It gave her enough time to reach over to the low-wicked lantern sitting on the single crude dresser and turn it up.

In the eerie yellow light he'd regained his feet like a gangly spider unfolding itself from a tight curl, all legs and arms. His eyes had been huge.

"I forgive you for that, Jolene. But I won't have you defyin' me. You don't understand: after I get the U-boat captain's gold and cash money, you and I will leave this place. I'll show you things you never even *dreamed* of . . . big cities, fine cars, fancy clothes. You won't want for anything, bein' my wife."

She dodged behind the corner of the dresser. "I don't want to be your wife, Papa Luc!" It was crazy. Her guardian of nearly ten years, the man she'd always looked upon as a surrogate parent and a teacher, was calling her his *wife*.

"That don't make no never mind, girl," Papa Luc said. He opened his arms wide. "Come on over here to me, now."

As he moved forward she tried to feint past him toward the door, but he cut her off with a quick side step. Seizing her roughly by the upper arms, tearing her nightshirt, he tried to kiss her, his breath hot and foul with tobacco. She shrieked and heaved against him with all the frantic strength in her young body. Somehow his clawlike grip loosened and he stumbled heavily against the dresser.

She made it halfway through the door when he flung out a hand and grabbed the hair at the back of her head, nearly yanking her off her feet. As she brought her hands up automatically to relieve the strain, he spun her around.

"You've vexed my spirit for the last time, girl!" he
shouted. "You are beholdin' to me, Lord knows! And
I'll have my rights with you!"

When he swung he put most of his body weight into
it. She never saw the hard, bony hand coming. It cracked
into her cheekbone in the dim light and the room exploded into a whirl of stars. Her ears rang. The blow
fell so hard that the hand in her hair lost its grip.

She reeled back against the dresser once again, her
fingers falling onto the base of the oil lamp. Without
thinking, she grasped it and brought it around in a wide,
flailing arc. Papa Luc's face was right there, looming up
frog-eyed in the darkness.

The lantern glass shattered against the side of his head
and the light went out. The sharp smell of kerosene
pierced the air. Jolene shrugged the dead weight of Papa
Luc's falling body off her shoulder as she twisted out of
the way. He hit the floor with an unconscious grunt and
lay still.

Trembling, she sagged against the doorframe, her
breathing coming in fitful gasps. There was one clear
thought in her mind: *get away*. It took her only a few
seconds to grope for her old clothes and boots on the
floor beside the bed, step over Papa Luc's already stirring legs, and run through the shanty out onto the
front dock.

It had taken only seconds more to throw her clothes
into her small pirogue, yank loose the painter, and hop
into the stern. Kicking the narrow boat away from the
dock, she'd set off across the ink black pond, the blade
of her paddle flashing in the moonlight.

She'd paddled all night, stopping only to slip on her
baggy old shirt and trousers. She was barefoot; her shoes
lay up under the pirogue's bow thwart. But her old wide-
brimmed fedora had been under the stern seat where
she always stowed it, and she'd taken the time to set
it firmly on her head. It made her feel more like the
real Jolene.

Now, her hands blistering on the paddle, her shoulders
burning with sustained exertion, she was surging along
less than two miles west of Venice. *Les Allemands* were

there, following Papa Luc's suggestion to use the *Shiloh*
for a salvage boat. She'd overheard it all, sitting quietly
nearby as the hard-faced captain of the strange gray
black war vessel and his handsome young lieutenant—
Bock, she thought his name was—bargained with Papa
Luc for information. The lieutenant kept glancing over
at her, as if he couldn't control his eyes. That had been
all right. She couldn't control hers either.

She dug the paddle into the water with all her
strength. Papa Luc had told them to use the old
nineteenth-century cargo dock on the small island just
south of Venice as a meeting place. It was less conspicuous. And they had said they would try to arrange to
meet the *Shiloh* at noon on the third day. Today.

Jolene looked up at the sky to the east. It was beginning to lighten. She put every ounce of energy she had
left into driving the paddle through the water.

Whatever unknown thing she was fleeing toward, it
was better than the unthinkable thing she was leaving
behind.

It had been over an hour before Papa Luc's senses
returned sufficiently for him to stagger to his feet and
navigate a wandering path through the darkened shanty
to his own bedroom. By the glow of a large candle he'd
picked most of the glass shards out of the side of his
face and washed the blood out of his tangled beard. The
cuts were numerous, but none were deep.

Now, simmering with a self-righteous, injured rage
that he could barely contain, he drummed his fingers on
one knee as he sat in the center of the pirogue that
Claude was propelling across the pond. The squat Cajun
used a short, powerful stroke, emitting a hoglike grunt
with every dip of the paddle. The narrow boat surged
forward each time as if kicked in the stern. Not very
smooth, but effective.

The leader of *les Isolates* looked up at the dark bulk
of the U-113's conning tower as the pirogue passed the
war vessel's bow. Something in the intensity of his stare
made Jonas Winkler, standing the last hour of the midnight watch on the bridge, lower his flute in the middle

of a quiet rendition of Brahms' "Lullaby" and set a hand on the nine-millimeter Luger pistol in his belt. As the senior radioman looked on, the hair prickling on the back of his neck, the pirogue continued on up the pond, leaving a spreading V behind it on the black water.

Earlier in his watch, after hearing a slight commotion emanate from the main cluster of shanties, Winkler had seen a small pirogue traverse the midnight-still pond at high speed, driven by a slightly built lone paddler. The natives were restless tonight. But as long as they stayed clear of the U-113, their little domestic squabbles were none of his concern. He let go of the Luger's handgrip, raised the flute to his lips, and, softly, resumed playing.

The pirogue emerged from a patch of mist and glided up to the dilapidated dock at the front of Estelle's shanty. Papa Luc was out of the boat before it stopped moving, nearly upsetting it in his haste. Claude caught the dock just in time, swearing under his breath in French. He tied the pirogue off, scrambled out, and followed Papa Luc up to the shack's front door.

The door was ajar. Papa Luc pushed with one hand, and it swung open to reveal the shanty's virtually lightless interior. He strode inside, Claude on his heels.

"Where is she?" he shouted. "Show yourself, you old witch! Where have you hidden the girl?"

He paused for breath. Only the steady *drip* . . . *drip* . . . *drip* of moisture falling from the shanty's corroded roof overhangs disturbed the silence. There was a creaking of floorboards as Claude nervously shifted his feet.

"Maybe she not here," he ventured in an unsteady whisper.

Papa Luc shot a daggerlike glance over his shoulder and seized the back of an old wooden chair. Lifting it high, he flung it with great violence into the room's dark recesses. There was a tremendous crash as the chair collided with something made of glass and thin wood.

"She's *here!*" Papa Luc roared. "She's always here! And so is Jolene!" He kicked at a small side table, sending it clattering across the floorboards.

The noise died away, leaving only the insistent dripping sound, and then a slow, throaty laugh came out of the darkness.

"Heh heh heh. I think you've broke up enough of my furnishin's, Luc."

Claude jumped as though stung. Estelle had appeared suddenly out of the gloom right at his shoulder. The trapper stepped back hurriedly and fell over a small stool. The old woman shuffled forward, her animal-bone charms rattling, and grinned down at him.

"Heh heh. You jumpy tonight, Claude," she rasped. "Maybe your spirit ain't clean, hmmm?" She extended a withered hand and shook a small fetish made of dried bird feet and other mummified remains at him.

Claude cowered, putting a hand up in front of his eyes, and scuffled backward on the seat of his pants. Something resembling a whimper escaped his lips. Estelle pursued him a few more steps, shaking the fetish, then stopped and chuckled again.

"Heh heh heh."

It put the hair up on the back of even Papa Luc's neck. He blinked and shook his head to clear it, refocusing on his rage. "Don't shake your bones at me, old witch," he scowled. "I don't believe in your tricks."

"No?" Estelle said elaborately. "Claude does." She wheeled with surprising speed for a woman so stooped with age and shook her fetish at the trapper again. He flinched, turning his head away in fear.

"*S'il vous plaît,* Papa Luc," he said in a small voice. "Make her stop."

"Make her stop what, *imbécile?*" Papa Luc shouted. "She's doin' nothing to you!"

"I can feel it," Claude whimpered. He scraped backward another couple of feet.

"Feel *what?*" Papa Luc bellowed. "Get up off the floor and stand on your hind legs, fool! She's nothing but an old hag with a handful of animal bones!"

Claude held Papa Luc's eye for a moment, then glanced up fearfully at Estelle. The old woman hovered over him like a hunchbacked troll, then abruptly lurched forward and stamped her foot hard on the plank floor.

"*Yaaaaghhh!*" she hissed, her benevolent expression

contorting into a gargoylelike leer. Her right hand darted out toward Claude's face. There was a sudden flash of blue flame at her fingertips, an eerie foot-high tendril that came and went in an instant. The trapper howled and covered his eyes.

"Claude!" Papa Luc shouted.

If the terrified man heard him, he gave no indication. Clawing his way across the floor in the darkness, he gained his feet and fled out through the shanty's front door in a blind panic. A wooden banging ensued from the dock, followed by the rapid slapping of a paddle thrust into water. The sound faded quickly into the distance, then was gone altogether.

Estelle chuckled deep in her throat, shuffled across the room, and sat down in her rocking chair. *Creak. Creak.*

"You wantin' to see me, Luc?" she asked pleasantly.

The tall Cajun turned and glowered at her with all the Old Testament malevolence he could muster. It was a wasted effort. Estelle's aging eyes couldn't make out his face in the dimness. Even if they could have, she wouldn't have cared.

"Don't think me no fool like Claude, old witch," Papa Luc breathed.

"Oh, I don't, Luc," Estelle said. "You another kind of fool."

"Eh?" No one ever spoke to Papa Luc like that. It took him off guard.

"A fool what thinks he can take a girl like Jolene to his bed. You like her *grand-père*, Luc, not no husband." Estelle grinned like a Cheshire cat. "She don't want no part of you. Best you stick to frightenin' the simple folks with Bible readin's and such. Jolene be too smart a gal for the likes of you."

Papa Luc advanced a step, his hands clenched at his sides. "Where's Jolene?" he asked, his voice tight.

"She gone."

"Where."

"Away."

"Where."

"Away from you, you old fool." Estelle rocked contentedly, gazing up at him. "And she ain't comin' back this time, neither." A black cat appeared out of nowhere and climbed silently up into her lap. She stroked its back. "Come to think of it, neither is Claude, I reckon. Weak will, that boy."

Papa Luc lunged forward, his hands reaching for Estelle's throat. "Where is Jolene?" he roared.

The old woman threw the cat at him. There was an ear-rending feline screech, and then Papa Luc was staggering backward, tearing at the whirling ball of black fur and claws that had fastened itself to his face.

With a shriek he ripped the enraged cat clear and threw it sideways. It landed on its feet, meowed indignantly, and disappeared. In front of Papa Luc, the chair Estelle had been sitting in was empty, moving gently to and fro on its rockers. There was a loud click as the heavy door to one of the rear rooms was latched. From behind it came a low laugh: "Heh heh heh. You gettin' slow in your old age, Luc. Now come on; you try and get through this door the best way you can—without makin' too much of a ruckus and lookin' like a fool in front of everyone in the settlement—and I'll make sure I got a surprise or two for you once you get in here, heh heh."

Papa Luc strode forward and hammered on the door with his fist. It barely rattled. He paused, breathing heavily. "Listen to me, old witch: the Lord's done made a deep pit in hell for pagan tricksters like you. You defy me, one of his servants, you defy *him*. Now, your rotten soul don't concern me, but I ain't about to let you drag Jolene's innocent spirit down to perdition with you. You—"

"You wastin' your breath, Luc," Estelle chuckled through the door. "We in the same line o' work, you an' me: layin' the fear of *that what ain't known* on other folks. Bible fear or voodoo fear, it don't matter. Both get the same result, in the end, *n'est-ce pas?*"

Papa Luc battered on the door with both fists in an uncontrolled burst of rage and frustration. *"Where's Jolene?"* he foamed. *"Tell me where the girl is, damn you!"*

"Heh heh heh. I think I ain't the one gonna be damned, Luc."

Landing one last vicious blow, Papa Luc backed away. He glowered at the unmoving door as if attempting to burn holes through it with his eyes. When he spoke, his voice wasn't quite human. "I'll deal with you, old witch," he croaked. "And I'll have the girl—or no one will."

There was no reply.

Papa Luc turned and walked toward the shanty's open front door. As he passed Estelle's rocking chair, his foot brushed against something lying on the floor. He bent and picked it up. It was the fetish bundle the old woman had shaken at Claude, the apparent source of the sudden flash of blue flame she'd conjured up.

He examined it in the moonlight. It was nothing but a half-dozen desiccated bird feet strung on a leather thong, like keys on a ring. There were also a couple of tiny stones, bits of shell, and a shapeless lump of damp skin tied to the thong with sinew. He raised it to his nose; it gave off a wet, putrid odor, like meat going bad. He turned it in his hands. There was no evidence whatsoever of anything that could produce a foot-long tongue of blue fire.

And yet he'd seen it with his own eyes. To his extreme annoyance, a vague, unformed fear once again prickled the back of his neck. He cursed under his breath, threw the fetish bundle to the floor, and stalked out of the shanty.

There were several other pirogues tied up to the dock. Settling into one, he yanked loose its painter and paddled off into the gauzy, moonlit night mists that hung like damp shrouds over the black-mirror surface of the pond.

After a while, the heavy door inside the shanty opened and Estelle emerged, humming softly. Stopping beside the rocking chair, she bent down slowly, painfully, and picked up the fetish bundle. She looked it over briefly, then chuckled to herself and proceeded out the front door, onto the rickety porch, and around to the side of her stilt house. A single hand-split cypress plank, twelve feet long and no more than six inches wide, extended from the edge of the side porch to the swampy, overgrown shoreline, bridging a water gap of nearly ten feet.

Without a pause, Estelle shuffled onto the narrow plank, humming once again, and began to traverse it, ignoring the alarming bow that developed immediately under her weight—as well as the five-foot drop to the water. The plank bounced and wobbled, but the old woman was completely unaffected by the precarious motion, continuing on at her same unhurried pace until alighting on the soft ground at the far end.

She went about twenty feet into the dense tangle of reeds and vines until she came upon a patch of soft muck about three feet in diameter. Standing upright in the gooey earth were a dozen stalks of dried, hollow reed, each perhaps six inches high. Bound to the end of each was a small, pale bladder of animal skin—the tiny stomachs of muskrat. They glistened in the moonlight with the oil that had been rubbed into them to keep them flexible, waterproof, and airtight.

Estelle untied the small, shapeless lump of hide that dangled from her fetish bundle and raised it to her lips. With a quick puff she inflated it, then bent down to slip the tiny stomach over a reed stalk that bore no bladder. Then she pinched off the neck of another between her thumb and forefinger, plucked it from its reed, and sealed it quickly with a wrap of sinew. As she moved her feet on the soft earth, the smell of escaping swamp vapors—methane from rotting organic material and natural gas from the small oil seep on which she stood—rose around her.

The tiny garden of gas-filled bladders gleamed palely in the moonlight. Estelle smiled as she secured the swollen little stomach to her fetish bundle. On a whim, she palmed it and, using the same hand, caught a small piece of flint and another of rusty steel that dangled from the fetish thong between her thumb and forefinger. Her smile broadened as she envisioned Claude's dim-witted face blanching in the darkness as she stamped her foot. . . .

With a magician's grace she swung her arm out in a smooth arc, keeping her palm down. At the arc's apex she squeezed the bladder with her two middle fingers, simultaneously grinding the little chunks of flint and steel together between her thumb and forefinger. The resultant spark ignited the puff of methane and natural gas forced from the muskrat stomach in the blink of an eye.

With a soft *whoosh* the familiar foot-long tongue of blue flame lapped at the night air, and was gone. A few feet off in the brush, a confused firefly flashed its own luminescence in misguided reply.

Estelle chuckled—*heh heh heh*—and stooped in the moonlight to replace the depleted gas bladder with a fresh one from the little garden of reeds and muskrat stomachs.

Chapter
Thirteen

"Comin' around, Lucius!" Holt yelled through the open window of the wheelhouse. Standing at the starboard bow bitt, with several coils of one-inch hawser draped over his shoulder, and the loop at the end of the mooring line dangling from his right hand, the big mate nodded calmly, waiting. Holt spun the oaken wheel, its spindles becoming a blur just beneath his palm, and gunned the diesel engine.

The *Shiloh*'s exhaust stack, mounted on the back of the wheelhouse, beside the mast, coughed out a dirty smear of black smoke, and the trawler cut across the fast-flowing Mississippi current toward the little island. Holt kept her turning up into the stream, then finished the maneuver by throttling back and allowing the current to crab her sideways up to the dilapidated cargo dock. He eyed the three men standing on it and tried to take their measure.

Serious types. Holt was mildly surprised at their appearance. He'd been expecting three prime examples of the unimpressive subspecies that oil companies, government agencies, and university science departments usually dispatched to the working regions of the Gulf of Mexico: white, doughy creatures with soft hands and weak backs, their plump office bodies encased in stiff new work clothes, immaculately clean. Always trying too hard to give the impression that they were as tough and salty as the lean, rawboned, blue-collar fishermen and mariners among whom they suddenly found themselves—and failing miserably.

The three men on the cargo dock were not of that breed. They stood like seamen, erect, relaxed, legs shoulder-width apart, their stance the unconscious giveaway of the seasoned sailor. Their faces were impassive, but their eyes appraised Holt's handling of the *Shiloh*'s approach with the detached interest of true professionals. All three were clad in dark, heavy clothing and seaboots well suited to offshore use, the buckles and fasteners green with verdigris, the leather and fabric cracked, worn, and salt-stained.

The shortest of the three—every inch of six feet—also appeared to be the one in charge. He looked about Holt's age, somewhere around thirty, and had a lean, hard-eyed face that had been turned leathery by sun and windburn. His sharp, reddish blond beard had traces of gray and white in it, and was in need of a trim. Like his two companions—one dark, slender, and a few years younger, the other bald and built like a two-ton truck—he gave the impression that he'd been through some kind of meat grinder and emerged intact, but changed . . . wary, somewhat weary, and as tough as ten days in jail.

Holt shrugged inwardly as the *Shiloh*'s port side gently bumped the cargo dock. At least it looked like he and Lucius would have more in common with these three than the posturing urbanites who sometimes chartered his boat.

He smiled to himself as the dark-haired young man and the bald heavyweight fanned out on either side of their leader, moving into position—without being asked—to receive the *Shiloh*'s dock lines. More giveaway evidence of experienced seamen. Fat-assed corporate reps and academics would have stood around looking stupid, as if waiting to be fussed over by the maître d' in a five-star restaurant, while right in front of them heavy equipment was in motion and lines needed to be handled. Holt continued to smile as the bald man caught the line Lucius tossed him and effortlessly threw a locking figure eight wrap over one of the dock's rusty cleats.

Moments later, at the stern, the dark young man followed suit.

These guys were all right, Holt decided. He hoped that when they opened their mouths they wouldn't destroy his favorable first impression. That had been known to happen, too.

He stepped out of the port wheelhouse door. "Mornin'," he called, raising his hand. "I believe you gentlemen put money down on a charter."

Bock and Wolfe moved back up behind Stuermer as the captain of the *Shiloh* hailed them. The big torpedoman spoke quietly, barely moving his lips: "My English isn't as good as yours or the lieutenant's, Captain. He's talking about money?"

Stuermer nodded imperceptibly. "Just confirming the charter, Lothar. All right, as of now, we stick to the plan. You don't speak at all—you're mute because of a childhood throat infection—and I speak in monosyllables and grunts because I'm too lofty and important to talk to anyone except Erich." He looked over his shoulder at Bock. "Remember, you've got to do all the talking—jump in anytime either of the Americans wants to pursue conversation. They get one hint of Lothar's or my German accent and the masquerade is over. Are we clear?"

"Yes, Captain."

"Aye."

"Good. Then here we go, gentlemen. Erich?"

Bock stepped forward, putting on a charming smile, and waved a hand at the wheelhouse. "And good morning to you, Captain. You're early. That's good!"

Holt shrugged. "What can I tell you? I'm an early riser. Clean livin', you know?"

"I know," Bock said. "Permission to come aboard?"

"My pleasure," Holt replied. "Watch your step, boys—though it don't look like you need me to tell you that."

The three Germans stepped across the water gap to the *Shiloh*'s gunwales, Wolfe and Stuermer shouldering the two heavy black duffels. Bock jumped lightly to the deck and went forward to greet Holt. As Stuermer fol-

lowed suit, Lucius brushed by Bock coming the other
way. He stopped in front of the *Kapitänleutnant*, unintentionally barring his way, a friendly smile on his
ebony face.

"How 'bout you let me tote them bags for y'all?" he
offered. "And show you gentlemen your quarters."

Stuermer caught the gist of it, even camouflaged as it
was under the Mississippi drawl; Wolfe drew a complete
blank. The U-boat captain quelled his courteous instinct
to smile and respond, and substituted instead a cold,
imperious stare. He stalked past Lucius without uttering
a syllable, Wolfe following his lead and doing the same.
The big mate, quite caught off guard by their frosty demeanor, raised his eyebrows and scratched his head in
puzzlement. You'd have thought he'd just insulted
their mothers.

Up in the wheelhouse, Holt clasped Bock's hand.
"Mike Holt, *el capitán* of this here fine vessel. And
you are . . . ?"

"Eric—Smith," Bock answered, taking in the skipper
of the *Shiloh* at a glance. Thirtyish, sandy hair, compact
medium build. Blue eyes—slightly bloodshot—and a seaman's weathered skin. Two days' worth of stubble on a
strong jaw. "Pleased to meet you. And glad you were
available. We're on a tight schedule and we were afraid
we'd have a little trouble finding the boat we needed.
Management big shots"—he rolled his eyes—"they want
the world delivered to their doorstep, and they want it
done in two days at the cost of a nickel."

"Ha!" Holt grinned. "Ain't it the truth." Nice sort of
fella, this Smith. He looked out the wheelhouse door
and saw Wolfe and Stuermer standing nearby on deck.
"Why don't you gents come on in?"

Stuermer shot him the same aristocratic stare that had
made Lucius take one step back and turned away to gaze
across the Mississippi. Wolfe didn't move. Holt frowned.

Bock cut in smoothly.. "Mr. Stuermer and Mr. Wolfe
don't talk much," he said. He lowered his voice conspiratorially and leaned closer to Holt. "Stuermer's upper
management, out here to see that I do my job. He'd
much rather have been drinking martinis in Dallas for

the past three weeks instead of being stuck out in the field, and it's given him a sour outlook, I'm sorry to say."

Holt pursed his lips. "Really? Too bad—for everyone who has to work with him."

"Precisely," Bock confirmed. "Sad but true. However, if you just don't try to talk to him, he doesn't get too cranky and morose. You understand what I mean?"

"Sure. I'll deal with you, let *you* deal with him. Fine with me." Holt scratched his chin. "What about the other guy? Looks like he could whip Joe Louis."

"Mr. Wolfe. He's a technician. My assistant, and very useful to have around. An unfortunate thing: he suffered a severe throat infection as a child and became mute as a result. He can't speak a word, I'm afraid."

"You don't say. Kind of limits his conversation, don't it?"

Bock smiled. "Pretty much."

"Well, hell." Holt fished in his shirt pocket for a Lucky Strike. "Guess I'll just talk to you, then, Eric."

Bock snapped a match with his fingernail and held it out to Holt. "Probably be best, Mike," he said, grinning broadly.

Lucius excused himself past Stuermer and Wolfe into the wheelhouse, his expression set firmly in neutral. "You've already met my mate," Holt said. "Lucius, my right-hand man and—literally—my *left* hand." He held up his left arm with its scarred stump of a wrist and smiled thinly.

Bock was momentarily taken aback at the sight of the ugly injury. He hadn't noticed the arm until Holt called attention to it. Fleetingly, he was reminded of the dying young sailor in the lifeboat of the freighter they'd torpedoed off Florida, his leg gone from the knee down. He composed himself and turned to Lucius.

"Ah, yes—Mr. Dancer," he acknowledged. "Nice to see you again, of course." He shook the big mate's hand. Lucius nodded with a cautious smile. Cold treatment from many whites was a fact of life for him, and these three already had two strikes against them. Smith seemed decent enough, though.

"Pleasure to see *you*, suh."

There was a sudden bumping noise from somewhere along the trawler's hull, like wood on wood.

"Damn tree trunks, drifting everywhere," Holt growled. "Bust your prop on 'em if you're not careful. You know," he went on conversationally, "it's a bit of a surprise to see a guy your age not in the military these days. There's a big goddamn war on, you know."

Bock was ready for that. "Right. But the government considers the oil business an industry vital to the war effort. It wants some of us left in place to keep it growing and producing. I'm high up enough on the corporate ladder that I was granted a deferment. Same with Stuermer and Wolfe." He grinned. "Just lucky, I guess."

Holt grinned back, his teeth clenched a little too hard, and held up his stump. "Luckier than me."

"War wound?"

"Uh-huh. I'm out, too." Holt lowered his arm and gestured toward the chart table. "Want to tell me where you plan on going? We could get under way. *Shiloh*'s been on your dime since we left the dock in Venice this morning."

"Sure." Bock went to the table, glanced down at the large chart of the northern Gulf of Mexico spread out on it, and pulled a small notebook from his shirt pocket. He flipped through the pages, then picked up a parallel rule from the instrument nook and expertly walked off a latitude and longitude, marking the position with a pencil stub. Once again, Holt was impressed. The guy knew how to plot properly on a marine chart. Looked like he could do it in his sleep.

"There," Bock said, setting the pencil down. "That's where we need to go."

Holt nodded, looking down at the position. "Not very deep, lots of mud bottom and silt. Not much there that I know of." He raised his eyes. "But I guess it's buried treasure we're after, huh? Your company thinks there's oil there, Lucius tells me."

"Yes," Bock replied.

"And they think they can get it out of the seafloor, even if they find any?"

"Yes."

Holt grinned, shaking his head. "That I'd like to see." He thought a moment. "You need to dive to take bottom samples? Can't you just drop a coring tool down there and stab it into the mud? Haul up a pipe full of sediment layers?"

Bock's smile was seamless. "Not the way we're trying it this time. New technique." He let it hang.

And, shrugging, Holt let it be. "Hey, like I said, it's your dime," he chuckled. "Well, let's get going." He turned to Lucius, who'd been standing quietly, leaning against the bulkhead with his massive arms folded. "Let's throw them lines off. Bow first—I'll let the current spring us off the stern."

"Okay, Mike." Lucius moved past Bock like a human mountain and stepped out of the wheelhouse. "'Scuse me, gentlemen," he said to Stuermer and Wolfe in passing.

Thirty seconds later, the bow line came flying over the forward port rail in a neatly thrown open coil. The *Shiloh* began to drift off the dock at an angle as the current caught her. When she had fallen off about thirty degrees Holt stepped to the port door. "Cast off, Lucius!"

At the stern, the big mate flipped the half turn of rope he'd been holding off the rusty cleat and tossed the dock line aboard. Then he climbed onto the aft gunwale, gripping the rigging, as Holt gunned the *Shiloh* out into midstream.

"On our way, boys," Holt exclaimed. He felt better than he'd felt in months. It was good to be working again, like a normal person, earning real money. The hell with the war. The *Shiloh* turned into the main ship channel and headed toward the Gulf under a blue sky cluttered with wheeling gulls.

No one noticed the small, empty pirogue that drifted out from under the old cargo dock in her wake, its rotten tether snapped by the backwash of the trawler's screw. On its side were traces of white paint where, earlier, it had rubbed alongside the *Shiloh*.

Chapter
Fourteen

"**G**onna be a few hours runnin' out to where you want to be," Lucius said. "I'm fixin' to cook up some lunch. If y'all are hungry, come on up and get you a plate." He smiled and closed the door to the cramped stateroom. The three Germans looked around: four bunks racked two on two, dark wood bulkheads that smelled of old varnish, two gimballed, wall-mounted oil lamps, and a single porthole, its bronze safety lid dogged shut.

Stuermer went over to the porthole, twisted free the butterfly nut that secured the lid, and lifted it. A thick shaft of sunlight illuminated the dim quarters. Latching it open, he repeated the procedure with the heavy glass plate behind it. When he swung it back a blast of warm, salty-fresh air sent the dust motes that had collected in the seldom-used cabin swirling through the sunbeam.

"Thank you, Captain," Wolfe growled in German, keeping his voice very low. "For a moment there, I thought I was back in the U-113—in the head."

Stuermer smiled. "A bit close in here. It'll air out."

Bock sat down on one of the lower bunks. A puff of sunlit dust rose around him from the rough wool blanket. "Well, we're on our way. Captain, how long do you plan on maintaining this little deception? One of us could slip at any time and give the game away. Holt could get suspicious."

"Or the Negro," Wolfe interjected.

"Right," Bock continued. "Or the big Negro. He's quiet, but he doesn't miss much, in case you hadn't noticed. Maybe we should just take over the boat now, before they suspect anything. Why risk losing our advantage by waiting?"

"Because then we'd have to spend the next five to seven days watching *them*," Stuermer replied. "Those men are both capable; if we have to lock them in or tie them up for an extended period of time, believe me, it's my estimation that they'll find some way to get free and make trouble for us. No, I'd rather have them helping us for as long as possible, and then have to restrain them closer to the end of the operation."

Bock thought a moment. "There is, of course, another alternative," he said.

Stuermer looked at his young exec silently. Then he nodded. "Of course," he replied. "Of course there is." Reaching into the pocket of the heavy hunting jacket he'd obtained from one of the Cajuns, he produced his Walther automatic pistol and held it out. "Here, Erich. You do it."

Bock blinked. "Now, sir?"

"If you think it best. We can wait until dark to weight the bodies and throw them over the side."

Bock blinked again and looked at the pistol. Then he sat back and shook his head.

"No?" Stuermer swung the handgun over toward Wolfe. "Lothar? Perhaps you?"

The big torpedoman put up a palm. "Not me, sir. I only shoot people who are trying to do the same to me . . . and game animals."

"Ah." Stuermer lowered the pistol and put it back into his pocket. "I assume we've explored this particular option sufficiently, then, gentlemen. So we go with the original idea to keep them cooperating as long as possible. Then, when we anticipate that they're about to find us out—say, just before the first screw and shaft assembly from Schecter's sunken U-boat breaks the surface—we move."

"You're assuming that Holt or the Negro—what's his

name? Lucius—won't want to make a dive as well,"
Bock said. "I'm not trying to be contrary, Captain, just
examining the possibilities."

"I think we can defuse that eventuality on the grounds
that we need to do the diving, with them assisting on
the surface, and we're paying for the charter," Stuermer
replied thoughtfully. "Of course, you're quite correct: we
all have to be on guard for the moment the whole deception breaks down. But until then, cooperation."

Bock and Wolfe nodded in unison. "Aye, sir."

"All right, then." Stuermer blew out a long breath.
"Here's what we'll do: we have at least six hours, at the
cruising speed this old trawler can maintain, before we
reach the position where Schecter's boat is. Or where
we *hope* she is. Let's go and get something to eat. We'll
bring the food back to our quarters, and Lothar and I
will stay in the cabin, both because we're antisocial and
we want to catch up on some sleep. You, Erich, on the
other hand, will circulate freely and give Holt and Lucius
the necessary excuses for our behavior. Don't lay it on
too thick, but try to keep them relaxed and smiling. You
know what I mean."

"A good thing you're fairly oozing natural charm,
Lieutenant," Wolfe remarked. "A lesser mortal probably couldn't pull it off."

"I'd pull *rank* on you, Lothar," Bock replied dryly,
"except that I know it wouldn't do any good."

"Not in this case," Wolfe concurred.

Stuermer cleared his throat. "A question, Erich. Lothar doesn't have to do anything but nod, since he's
mute, but what's the best casual response if Holt or Lucius hands me my food—or anything else, for that matter? One or two words in the American vernacular that
won't reveal my accent. My English is too formal."

Bock shrugged. "Just say 'thanks,' Captain. Make sure
you get the *th* sound right, mumble quickly through your
nose, and you'll sound like any American. Try it."

"Sunkz," Stuermer said, struggling. *"Sanks."*

"No, Captain. Get the *th*."

"Thanks." The U-boat commander lowered his voice.
"Thanks."

"That's it," Bock said. "You've got it."

"I hope so," Stuermer replied. "All right. Let's go."

Lucius ladled a huge serving of Cuban black beans onto Bock's plate, followed by half a dozen slices of pan-fried peameal bacon and a mammoth wedge of hot jalepeño corn bread. He topped it off with half a stick of sweet creamery butter, hard from the icebox.

"Gotta love them beans, gents," he rumbled good-naturedly. "Keep a man regular."

Bock grinned. "Thanks, Lucius. It looks great."

"It sho' is. Next!"

Stuermer held out his plate, looking as aloof and bored as possible. "There, now," Lucius said, filling in the awkward silence as best he could while he served up the food. "There you be, suh."

"Thunkz," Stuermer muttered down into his beans. He winced inwardly at the sound of his own voice. *Verdammt.*

If his response sounded odd, Lucius didn't notice. He smiled again as Wolfe stepped up. "You damn near as big as me," he said. "A two-helpin' man." He dumped a second ladleful of beans on Wolfe's plate. "Got to feed the furnace inside, ain't that so?"

"Mmrgh," the torpedoman grunted. But he smiled back. Lucius was a hard person not to like.

The big mate gestured at the galley table as Stuermer and Wolfe moved toward the door. "Sit you down, gents. Got a few things to drink in the icebox, if you like: water, lemon tea, cold buttermilk, Co'-Cola. . . ."

"Mr. Stuermer and Mr. Wolfe are going to take their food to our cabin, Lucius," Bock said. "They're tired. They want to eat and get some sleep while they can." He paused as his two companions shuffled through the galley door. "I'll take them along something to drink in a little bit. I don't suppose you have any wine? Red, preferably, and not too dry? A good country wine?"

Lucius looked confused. "Wine? At lunch? Ahh, no suh. I'm sorry. Ain't no alcohol of no kind on this boat, neither." Before they'd left the dock, he'd made damn certain of that, ferreting out Holt's little caches of bourbon and scotch and smashing the bottles over the side on the tip of the main anchor.

Bock realized his mistake instantly. Unlike Europeans, Americans rarely drink wine with midday meals; neither is wine a ubiquitous presence on the working-class table. He glanced at Lucius. No harm done. The big man had simply thought that the request was a little eccentric. He'd have to be careful, though. It was far easier to slip than one would imagine.

"Oh, well, the hell with it, then," he said good-naturedly. "They can drink tea or water. I'll cart it along to them after I get a few bites in my stomach." He lowered his voice. "To tell the truth, I was just trying to make Stuermer happy when I asked you for the wine. The guy's a fancy-restaurant nut. And the other thing is, if I feed him wine along with lunch, he tends to go to sleep for the rest of the afternoon. Keeps him out of my hair."

"Mm mm *mm*," Lucius grunted, shaking his head with each syllable. "Ain't nothin' wrong with a man likin' his liquor, but to my way of thinkin' it can't serve him no good to drink himself to sleep halfway through a workin' day."

"Very true, Lucius." Bock set his plate on the galley table and sat down. "What is this?" He touched the bacon with the tip of his knife. "It smells delicious. Some kind of ham?"

"Sho' is," Lucius said. "Peameal bacon. That's corn-meal there on the edges. Real good eatin'. We can't always find it, but it's better than your regular fatback. Lean an' smoky as a fine country ham."

Bock cut off a piece and forked it into his mouth. "That's wonderful," he said, chewing. "And you cooked it just right, too. Tastes a lot like a good Black Forest boar ham . . ." His voice trailed off. Another mistake.

The big mate's brow furrowed. "Black Forest? Don't believe I ever heard of it in these parts. Where you get it?"

"Uh . . . up in Connecticut. Black Forest is the name of the company."

Lucius nodded, smiling, and leaned back against the

stove with his big arms folded as he watched Bock eat.
He liked the young man; he was pleasant and made the
effort to be friendly. Odd that he'd been paired with two
such disagreeable companions. But often a man couldn't
choose who he had to work with—that was a fact.

There was something strange about him, however,
something that Lucius couldn't put a finger on. It was
in the way he talked—a curious throaty quality to some
of his words. It was in his body posture, erect and alert,
belying his relaxed demeanor. It was in his eyes: smiling
one moment and then flickering sharply over everything
nearby the next. Eyes like a cop, taking it all in.

And it was in a dozen other things, almost too incon-
sequential to notice. Like now. Lucius frowned as he
watched the young man eat. The way he held his utensils: the fork in the left hand, tines curving down, and
the knife in the right. It looked funny. Most folks would
cut their food, then set the knife down and spear it or
scoop it up with the fork cradled, tines up, in the right
hand.

Bock glanced over at him and smiled happily, working
on the last slice of peameal. Lucius smiled back.

Nice young fella, even if he did eat funny.

Holt was sitting in a battered wooden armchair behind
the *Shiloh*'s wheel, steering with his feet propped up
between the spindles. He'd extended the legs of the armchair another three feet to give it the height needed for
the helmsman to be able to sit down and still see out the
front windows of the wheelhouse. A plate was balanced
beneath his chin on the back of his crippled forearm
while his remaining hand shoveled beans into his mouth
with a large spoon. Lucius was leaning against the forward console in his preferred stance: arms folded across
his broad chest like intertwined ebony tree trunks.

"They done eatin'?" Holt mumbled, sucking in beans.

"They went along to their cabin," Lucius answered.
"Carried their vittles in there. The young fella—Smith—
he stayed and talked awhile."

"The other two act any friendlier while you were feed-
in' them?"

"Can't claim to have noticed it."

"Huh." Holt folded a piece of peameal bacon on top of a hunk of corn bread and stuffed it into his mouth. "Mmff—wait a minute—" He chewed rapidly. "Maybe they'll warm up a bit as time goes on. They say anything about the diving? They chartered us as a dive boat, so they're gettin' charged for a diving day whether we get wet or not."

"Never mentioned it," Lucius said. He peered at Holt. "You lookin' better, Mike. Not so bloodshot an' wrung out."

Holt burped. "I feel better, buddy." He glanced at Lucius and ran a hand through his tousled hair. "I was thinkin' I might just have a quick taste about a half hour ago, just to take the edge off my headache." He laughed ruefully. "I look high and low, but all my stashes are gone. It seems like somebody went around and got rid of all my bottles." He paused and looked at the big mate again. "I suppose I oughta thank you for that."

Lucius shrugged. "Just tryin' to help."

"Thanks, Lucius."

"Uh-huh."

The *Shiloh* had come onto a converging course with a small freighter that was skirting the very edges of the shoals that lurked along the approaches to the Mississippi's mouth. Holt glanced at the compass, then rotated the wheel slightly to port with his feet, applying the old helmsman's trick of pointing one's bow at a converging vessel's stern, then following it back onto the original compass course. Such a steering tactic precluded the possibility of ramming head-on into an approaching ship, particularly at night when only running lights could be seen.

"She in close, ain't she?" Lucius commented, gauging the freighter's position with an experienced eye. "Right on top o' them shoals."

Holt nodded. "Still scared of U-boats," he said. "The skipper feels safer in shallow water, where they can't operate." He laughed, shaking his head. "I'll tell you, though: he's more likely to lose his ship by runnin' aground, close as he is, than by takin' a torpedo."

"Ain't no call for that," Lucius said. "Been nearly a year since any vessels been attacked in the Gulf."

"Pretty near," Holt nodded. "Still, they were goin' down awful regular there for a while. Put the fear of the devil in most tanker and freighter drivers. Can't say as I blame 'em for that. Goddamn sneaky Nazi subs. Ambush killers, that's what they are, pickin' off unarmed merchantmen that can't fight back."

"Well, most of them boats is carryin' war goods," Lucius observed. "Don't take me wrong—I ain't on their side—but they got to try to stop the supply of bombs and bullets that gets used agin' their troops across the ocean."

"Yeah, but there's fightin' and then there's fightin' *fair*," Holt said. "And gutshooting merchant ships from underwater ain't fair. It's like backstabbing."

Lucius thought for a moment. "Maybe they ain't fightin' to be fair, Mike," he said quietly. "Maybe they gettin' more backed up agin' the wall all the time. Maybe they just fightin' to *win*." His face took on a grim cast, as if he was remembering something from long ago. "When you cornered, fightin' for your life, you don't give a damn about fair."

"You got that right," Holt agreed, glancing down at his stump of a wrist, "and that's a fact. But I still don't like them goddamn U-boats—or the goose-steppers drivin' 'em."

The *Shiloh* had steadily tracked the converging freighter's stern back to starboard until the compass once again indicated the original course. Holt nudged the wheel straight and the bigger vessel slipped on past the trawler's bow with an eighth of a mile to spare. He and Lucius continued to look the freighter over as it presented its full profile.

"Single deck cannon mounted on the bow," Holt mused, "and another on the poop. Gives her a little punch, anyway."

"Got machine guns amidships, too," Lucius added. "Antiaircraft."

"Yeah. I see 'em."

"She look funny with them guns welded on her," the

big mate concluded. "It don't suit her. Like a school-marm wearin' boxin' gloves."

Holt laughed out loud at the image. "It does at that."

"I'd imagine, though," Bock said, as he reached the top step of the companionway ladder leading up from the galley, "that those guns hit a lot harder than a schoolmistress wearing boxing gloves. Particularly if they happen to be aimed at *you*."

Holt and Lucius jumped slightly at the sound of his voice. He'd ascended the short ladder without making a sound. "Didn't hear you come up, Eric," Holt said. "You're light on your feet. Everyone okay down below?"

"Just fine. Did you manage to firm up an ETA for us? Stuermer's bitching at me about it."

Holt looked over his shoulder at the chart. "Just plotted a position a few minutes ago. Estimated time of arrival is four hours, thirty-y-y . . . two minutes."

Bock stuck his head out the port wheelhouse door and peered up. "We'll be on location in time for a nice sunset."

"Yeah, I guess." Holt shot Lucius a quick look. "You gonna want to dive right away? Pretty dark down there at night. Hell, with all the silt in the water from the Big Muddy, it's pretty damn dark during the *day*. But if you're just diggin' up bits of bottom, I guess it don't hardly matter if you can see or not."

"No, no," Bock replied. "We want to see what we're doing. It's part of the new technique."

"Sounds interesting. How's it work?"

"Well . . . it . . . it's rather complicated. A little hard to explain." Holt kept looking at him, so Bock soldiered on: "It involves running small wires and rods into the seabed, and—uh—setting off little pulses of electricity to see what's in the . . . the various layers. Highly experimental. We have to fool around with it quite a bit. Probably move the boat from place to place, too . . . in the same general location."

Holt grunted and turned back to the wheel. "Sounds like a huge pain in the ass."

"It can be," Bock said, hoping the strain of high-speed

lying wouldn't show in his voice. "Working the bugs out of new technology always is."

"Glad it ain't me," Holt muttered. He looked over at Lucius—once again standing silently, his arms folded—with a wry twinkle in his eye. "I like things simple."

The *Shiloh* bucked gently up and down as the wake from the passing freighter reached her, her overhead rigging and spars creaking as they flexed. A gull that had been sitting like a hood ornament on the very tip of the bow was dislodged by the motion. Hurriedly spreading its wings, it soared off past the starboard side of the wheelhouse, screaming its annoyance. Lucius watched it idly, then shifted his attention back to Eric Smith.

There it was again. Something odd about him as he stood watching the stern of the freighter recede into the distance.

Once more, it was in the eyes. Lucius had seen those same eyes on a cat stalking a bird, on a dog tracking wounded game. On another young soldier like himself, prowling the midnight trenches of no-man's-land in 1918 with a bayonet clenched in one fist, in the midst of a hell on earth called the Argonne Forest.

The eyes of a hunter.

Chapter
Fifteen

Dekker was leaning on the bridge rail of the U-113's conning tower, sweating profusely through his undershirt as the afternoon sun hammered down on the camouflage netting over his head. The humidity was unbelievable. Chewing contemplatively on the stub of a dead cigar, he inspected the barked and scabbing knuckles of his work-worn hands with idle curiosity. Nine hours in the after section of the engine room with a rotating crew of four men—all that could work effectively in the cramped space—doing everything possible to prep the damaged through-hull glands to receive the replacement shafts that Stuermer would, hopefully, provide. Sweat trickled into his eye, stinging it, and he blinked it away.

He turned and looked toward the stern. With the exception of a skeleton duty crew below, all the men were stretched out on the back deck beneath the camo netting, talking quietly, smoking, or dozing. Over their heads, tensioned between two massive trees on opposite sides of the little inlet, was a cobweb of block-and-tackle rigging, ready to handle the heavy lifting of shafts and screws. There was little to be done now until the captain returned.

Dekker watched casually as a pirogue paddled by two black-bearded Cajuns in floppy, wide-brimmed hats slid by the U-boat's bow. Between the paddlers was a dead alligator lying on its back, yellow white belly skin upturned, the thick, saurian tail dragging limply in the water alongside. Neither Cajun looked up as they passed by; the presence of the U-113 had long since ceased to be a novelty and was now merely a fact of life. *Les Isolates* had resumed their hunting-and-gathering existence after only a couple of days, accepting the great war boat as part of the landscape.

There was a light footfall on the steel plating behind Dekker. Winkler had emerged from the bridge hatch. He moved up beside the chief and squinted at the pirogue from behind his wire-rimmed glasses.

"What part is it they eat again?" he inquired.

"The tail," Dekker replied. "They eat the tail."

Winkler shook his head. "How utterly bizarre." He looked at the chief. "I just don't think I could eat any part of a reptile. They'd have to lie to me about what it was before I could get it past my lips."

"Wouldn't you be embarrassed if you actually liked it?" the chief commented. "To them, it's a delicacy."

"They can have it." The radioman took off his glasses and began to clean the lenses on his shirtsleeve. Dekker regarded him idly for a moment.

"Don't you ever sweat, Jonas?" he asked finally. "It's hotter than blazes out here."

"No," Winkler said.

"Why the hell not?" the chief demanded.

Winkler put his glasses back on and adjusted them carefully on his nose. "Sweating is vulgar," he said, "a habit characteristic only of troglodytes such as yourself, Otto. I, on the other hand, endeavor to abstain and therefore remain . . . nonodoriferous." He smiled slyly at Dekker. "You should be grateful for one less stinking body in this sardine can."

The chief laughed. "Oh, I am. I'm not sure, though, if it makes up for the stench you spread when you put on that highborn attitude, *von* Winkler. As for not sweating, it must be that thin blue blood of yours keeping you cool."

"Undoubtedly." Winkler touched Dekker's sleeve. "Look, let's be serious for a minute, Otto. I have something to tell you."

"Oh?" The chief chewed on his cigar. "Tell me only if it's good news. Anything bad, don't bother."

Winkler smiled. "I think I've fixed the radio."

"You what?" Dekker's jaw slackened, nearly causing him to drop the cigar stub.

"The radio. I think I've fixed it." Winkler sounded amused at himself. "Don't ask me how; it was nothing but a pile of wire, glass, and dials. But I found some old replacement tubes and a few switches, and I've been trying to jury-rig something for the past week. Just now I hit the power switch and the damn tubes started to glow! Again, don't ask me how I did it, but I think we've got a viable Morse transmitter and receiver."

Dekker clapped Winkler on the shoulder. "Good work, Jonas! But . . ." He paused, his brow furrowing in thought. "Well, this actually presents a number of problems, doesn't it?" The question was rhetorical.

Winkler nodded. "Yes, it does. That's why we need to discuss it."

The chief stood up straight. "Let's go have a look at your Frankenstein contraption while we're talking."

The slender radioman stepped aside. "After you, my friend."

They proceeded through the bridge hatch and down the conning tower ladder to the radio room below. Once there, Winkler slid onto the small operator's seat and tapped a long finger on the top casing of what looked like a child's science experiment—a mass of interconnected tubes, wires, dials, and switches that covered the entire surface of the radio room's small folding table.

"A thing of beauty, isn't it?" Winkler remarked dryly.

"It's hideous," Dekker said. "But you're a genius for putting it together, Jonas. And you feel sure it's operable?"

The radioman hit a switch on the side of the main casing. There was a light hum and filaments in a bank of smoked-glass tubes began to glow. "Almost certain, Otto."

"Hmm." The chief slipped into a small folding seat near the doorway. "But how can it help us? That's the big question now."

"Shall I list the pros and cons?" Winkler said. "I've been sifting through them for a couple of hours now."

"Go ahead."

"All right. Even assuming the radio works, we'll never get a message across the Atlantic to BdU from this far away. There is a chance, however, that we might have our transmission picked up by another U-boat operating off the east coast of Florida, Georgia, or the Carolinas, or south of here in the Caribbean. They could relay news of us back to Lorient. What the Lion might decide to do for us, of course—if he can do anything—remains to be seen."

"True enough," Dekker muttered gloomily. "We're slightly out of pocket, I'd say, parked over here within spitting distance of New Orleans."

"Anyway," Winkler continued, "there's another complication. The *Schlüssel* machine. It's broken beyond repair. I have the HYDRA notebook with the settings, of course, but without a workable *Schlüssel* to encrypt the body of a message, it's worthless. So, the question is, do we try to send an unencrypted transmission out into American-monitored radio space? Do we send it in German? English? Do we try to phrase it in some way that makes it less obvious?"

"I can think of a dozen other stumbling points in addition to those you just came up with," Dekker grumbled.

"Of course you can," Winkler sighed. "Maybe I should just have left the damn thing broken. Now that it's fixed, we're rather obliged to figure out some way to use it."

"I know what Stuermer would say," Dekker said. "Our obligation is to use every means at our disposal to ensure the safety of the crew and the preservation of this boat as a viable German war asset—in that order." He shrugged. "If we try to send a message and the Americans home in on the source of the transmission with multiple directional antennae, they'll be able to triangulate us. They'll find us, Jonas, and I hardly need to point out that we can't move around and dive as if we were at sea. They locate us once—we're dead."

"I know, I know," Winkler said, "but do we pass up an opportunity to stack the deck in our favor? Supposing if, by waiting, we miss an opportunity to catch the ear of the last passing U-boat heading north out of the Caribbean? Then we've lost all hope of letting BdU know our situation, and must continue to rely solely on Stuermer's plan to salvage the shafts and screws from Schecter's boat." The radioman blew out a long breath. "You know I have nothing but respect for the captain's judgment and ability, Otto, but even he is going to be very lucky to pull this off. Look at it another way: if he were here, wouldn't he decide to take the calculated risk to transmit a brief message, on the chance that it might bring us some extra help?"

Dekker rubbed his eyes. "You're right, of course. On the one hand, it might be better to sit tight and keep quiet. On the other, we might be fools to let an opportunity to signal for help pass us by. And Stuermer left us in charge, so basically, it's our call. He knew that the other day when he handed command over to us and went after the shafts."

"So, then. What do we do?"

Dekker looked at him. "We transmit. You and I bang our heads together until we come up with a short message that will let BdU know we're still in one piece and need some form of assistance—rendezvous, rescue, whatever—and then you tap it out on the Morse key.

"And then," he continued, "we sit here in this mud-hole and hope that a squadron of Catalinas doesn't suddenly appear over our heads and bomb us into bratwurst."

"You have a rare gift for imagery, Otto," Winkler commented. "Try to contain yourself, for my sake."

He dug into his shirt pocket and extracted a dark-papered cigarette. "Courtesy of Executive Officer Bock," he told Dekker. "Let's go up on the bridge, have a smoke, and see what kind of message we can come up with." He picked up a pencil and a piece of notepaper from the tabletop. "For starters, I'd suggest phrasing it in English. We'll attract less attention."

"I thought you quit," the chief said.

"I started again," Winkler replied.

"When?"

The radioman stuck the cigarette between his thin lips. "Now."

British Royal Navy Lieutenant Commander Trevor Fetherstone-Pugh, immaculate as usual in his dark blue Savile Row–tailored uniform, entered the primary tracking room of the Central Gulf Coast Defense Grid, carrying his midafternoon tea in a bone china cup and saucer. Downtown New Orleans was barely visible through the grime-caked windows of the second-floor office, which was located in a plain brownstone building in a heavily guarded U.S. Navy yard on the east bank of the Mississippi River. The yard was, unfortunately, downwind of a veritable battery of petroleum- and chemical-refining plants that belched greasy, noxious smoke from their towering stacks twenty-four hours a day. In calm weather, the bad air would hang in a yellow brown pall over the industrial sector of the river, coating vehicles, buildings, and inhabitants with a thin layer of toxic grit. Few people seemed to notice.

Fetherstone-Pugh noticed, however. The atmosphere here was a far cry from the breezy green vales of his family's estate on the northwestern coast of England, just south of the Scottish border in the scenic, pristine area known as the Lake District. A chap could barely bloody breathe in this damnable Yank city, let alone function with any degree of comfort. But the lieutenant commander was of that singular breed of landed English aristocrat for whom duty, conduct, and—above all—an unflappable demeanor were bred into the bone. So he ignored the perspiration prickling his neck beneath his neatly buttoned collar, nodded politely to the marine corporal standing guard at the tracking-room door, and sat down at one of the central desks to sip his tea.

Along the pastel pea green walls of the room, at six

separate locations, radio technicians were monitoring wireless traffic through all bandwidths known to be in use by Allied and Axis militaries. In the center of the room, facing the door, was a six-by-six-foot square of inch-thick plate glass mounted vertically between two aluminum uprights. On the glass was scribed a detailed map of the northern Gulf of Mexico, and over this was a close grid of vertical and horizontal lines. A chrome-silver button about the size of a quarter had been affixed to the glass on the location of New Orleans; similar buttons half as big denoted Biloxi, Pensacola, Tampa, and Jupiter Inlet to the east, and Lafayette, Beaumont, Galveston, and Corpus Christi to the west.

The Central Gulf Coast Defense Grid was Fetherstone-Pugh's baby. On the day he had stepped off the transatlantic military transport from London into the sweltering heat of early-summer New Orleans, on loan from the Royal Navy to its U.S. counterpart as a technical expert in the detection of U-boats by HF/DF—high-frequency direction finding or Huff-Duff—he had set to work cobbling together an interlocking chain of wireless-monitoring shore stations equipped with high-powered directional antennae—the first such system in the southern United States.

It had not always been easy. He was a lone British officer transplanted into a sea of Americans, charged with instructing them how best to protect their own coastline. As would have been the case in dealing with any established military hierarchy, he had anticipated a certain amount of resistance to new ideas from an outside source, a certain amount of institutional inertia. What he hadn't expected was the blatant lack of cooperation he had encountered at some, though not all, mid-range levels of U.S. Navy bureaucracy, coupled with what seemed to be a sulky, Anglophobic resentment on the part of a number of American officers. He'd been rather put off by their attitude at first—weren't they all on the same side? It was their bloody shipping that ace U-boat captains like Reinhard Hardegen, Richard Zapp, and Ulrich Folkers had been sinking at will virtually under the lights of the big U.S. east-coast cities, particularly during the highly successful Operation Drumbeat of the previous year.

But a considerable number of British ships had gone down, too, and *all* ships were bound for England or the Arctic coast of Russia laden with desperately needed war materials. In the months following Drumbeat, the Gulf of Mexico had become a veritable shooting gallery for prowling Nazi subs. So Fetherstone-Pugh had stiffened his already immobile upper lip and proceeded to charm, barter, threaten, plead, and cajole the Central Gulf Coast Defense Grid into existence.

Just in time for *Grossadmiral* Karl Dönitz to pull virtually all of his U-boats out of the Gulf of Mexico and away from the U.S. east coast, and throw them into pitched battle with American, British, and Canadian destroyer escorts riding herd on massive convoys in the North Atlantic just south of Iceland.

So, after all his well-intentioned labor, Fetherstone-Pugh found himself sitting on top of a well-organized, state-of-the-art, wireless-tracking network that had yet to justify its existence by identifying and triangulating a single enemy submarine.

Galling.

The Royal Navy lieutenant commander sipped at his Earl Grey, holding the saucer up high near his chin, and listened to the humming of radio tubes and the scratching of pencils on paper as the half-dozen radio techs copied down any potentially interesting signal fragments that came through their headphones. It was dry work, and several of them looked half asleep. Fetherstone-Pugh sighed inwardly. It was difficult to keep people motivated when their labor yielded no results. *Ours not to reason why,* he reminded himself, *ours but to do or—*

"Well, how-dee-do, Feathers!"

Oh, *God.* Blodgett.

And the day had—until now—been so blissfully devoid of loud noises.

Fetherstone-Pugh looked up from his tea. "Good afternoon," he said, purposely unleashing a full dose of the arid English superiority that seemed, instantaneously and without fail, to drive all Americans into a state of near violence. It came naturally to him; he was the son of an earl, and an Oxford man.

Lieutenant Commander Hiram Blodgett had never been to Oxford. Or any other university, for that matter. His formal education—interrupted by long seasonal absences spent harvesting snap beans and pecans on his sharecropper father's Alabama farm—had ended at the tenth grade. At age seventeen, in the first year of the Great Depression, his career options had been (a) the continuation of a life sentence of dirt-scratch sharecropping, or (b) the United States military. Blodgett had literally run to the navy.

And had done well in his own right, rising slowly and steadily through the ranks to his current level of lieutenant commander. Always keeping to the administrative, noncombatant side of things—the navy was a career and home for him, not some get-killed-quick, glory-hounding diversion of youth. He functioned well in military middle management, mildly bullying those below him and artfully kissing the asses of (and, on occasion, humbly taking an ass-chewing from) those above. After thirteen years of maneuvering, he'd developed an undeniable expertise: a certain bureaucratic cunning that kept him contented, relatively secure, and out of the line of fire.

All of which did nothing to dispel the essential truth that he was, fundamentally, a fat, ignorant redneck with a mean streak as wide as the strap his father had laid across his back whenever he'd ingested a jug too much of rotgut corn liquor.

Fetherstone-Pugh, the slender, immaculate product of English boarding schools and Very Olde English money, and imbued with the certain knowledge that he *was*, in actual fact, superior in every way to at least ninety-nine percent of the Earth's population, was well nigh Hiram Blodgett's polar opposite.

The two men had detested each other on sight.

The year they had spent working together, ordered onto the same project by Admiralty-level brass, had not ameliorated their mutual detestation. If anything, it had enhanced it. The two officers smiled at each other, aware of the darting glances of the radio techs and the other lower ranks in the room.

Blodgett drew up a chair, reversed it, and sat down heavily, his forearms dangling across the wooden back. He was chewing something. Fetherstone-Pugh regarded him down the bridge of his long nose. The American's bulldog face, wide and jowly with smallish blue eyes close-set beneath a sandy crewcut, sported a permanent flush like an overripe berry. There was egg on his khaki-colored tie, more on his khaki-colored shirt. Fetherstone-Pugh kept his lip from curling in distaste by act of will.

Blodgett finished chewing, grinned, and looked over his shoulder at the nearest radio tech. "Hear anything worth a damn, Carson?"

The radio tech lifted one of the headphone speakers from an ear. "What say, sir?"

"I said, have you heard one worthwhile goddamn thing on them phones this mornin'?"

"Nope." The tech shrugged. "Lots of static, sir."

Blodgett set his flat gaze back on Fetherstone-Pugh, still grinning. "Probably some kind of top secret German code, eh, Carson? Better keep listenin', son."

Carson gave a short laugh. "Yes, sir. They ain't gettin' nothin' by me."

"Well, that'd be a relief to know, son, if there was actually anybody out there tryin' to get something past you."

Fetherstone-Pugh felt the burn rise to his cheeks. He quelled it, as he always did, before any trace of discomfiture could manifest itself. "Come to check the day's intercepts, have you, Mr. Blodgett?" he asked smoothly.

Blodgett burped. "What the hell for, Feathers? You know there ain't nothin' there." He reached over and slapped Carson on the back with a meaty hand. "My boy Carson here woulda already informed us of any soo-rep-titious activity. Ain't that so, Carson? Haw-haw-haw!"

"Haw-haw-haw!" replied Carson immediately.

Fetherstone-Pugh redirected his eyes to the ceiling and hid the tightening of his mouth by taking a sip of tea. It was absolutely unbearable—like being locked in a closet with a pair of bipedal jackasses. Fleetingly, he hoped that the recent letter he'd written to his Uncle Bindley, a member of the British War Cabinet, had been taken seriously and would result in his being reassigned back to England posthaste. If not, he could look forward to another long, dreary winter in New Orleans in the company of Blodgett and his innumerable sycophants. An atrocity not to be contemplated.

"Ahem. I take it you don't intend to check the day's intercepts, then, Mr. Blodgett?" he queried.

"Don't see the point," Blodgett responded, leaning back, still grinning.

Fetherstone-Pugh got to his feet. "Then I'll do it." He set the teacup and saucer down on Carson's desk and blithely stepped past the beefy American without looking at him. Carson snickered something that sounded vaguely mocking and Fetherstone-Pugh stopped. Blodgett was an officer of equivalent rank, and nothing could be done about that, but the Englishman didn't have to absorb any insolence from a mere radio tech.

He spun around and fixed Carson with an icy stare. "Get on your feet, Petty Officer!"

Carson blanched, then pulled off the headphones and stood up sullenly. In two quick strides, Fetherstone-Pugh was in his face. "Get those heels together, *now!*"

The young petty officer snapped to attention, realizing at last that the joke was over. Fetherstone-Pugh looked him up and down, then stepped back. "I expect the duty personnel in this room to have their minds fully on their work, Carson. *And on nothing else!* Do I make myself perfectly clear? Or shall I make myself even clearer by filing a report charging you with insubordination and dereliction of duty?"

Carson became paler. "No, sir."

"I beg your pardon?"

"Uh—yes, sir."

"What, man?"

"I mean—no, sir. . . . I mean, *yes,* sir. . . ."

Fetherstone-Pugh looked disgusted. "Sit down, Carson. Put your headphones back on and keep your mouth shut."

Blodgett just sat there, grinning like a fat idiot.

Fetherstone-Pugh turned away and went across the room to the farthest receiving desk. It was manned by a young tech named Knowles. Wearily, the British officer pulled up a chair, sat down, and began to sort through the loose pile of paper that Knowles had generated on his shift. Scrawled on the paper were fragments of wireless transmissions, instantly translated by the tech from Morse code to letters and words.

"Anything today, Knowles?" Fetherstone-Pugh sighed.

Knowles half turned, writing fast on his tablet as he listened to another fragment, and smiled. "Not much, sir. Merchant traffic, mostly. English, some Dutch, a little Spanish. Nothing in Enigma code, sir. Nothing that sounds like a U-boat."

"Mm." Fetherstone-Pugh flipped through the scrawled intercepts. "Merchant traffic, merchant traffic, routine navy air patrol reports, more merchant traffic . . ." He stopped and held up one of the sheets. "What's this?"

Knowles glanced over. "Oh, that. It caught my ear, sir. It's been coming through on one of the ultrahigh bandwidths every forty minutes or so since early this afternoon. When I realized it was being repeated, I just kept transcribing it onto the same piece of paper." He laughed. "Looks like some kind of illegal ham radio operator, maybe. Or one of the communications guys trying to set up a stag party on the sly."

Fetherstone-Pugh smiled. "It won't be much of a party if he gets caught." He studied the paper. "Four times this has come through in under three hours, you say?"

"Yes, sir."

The British officer read over the pencil scrawl again:

To Mr. Kaleu: Celebration hosted by fifty-two of your fleet brethren. Marooned here waiting for company to arrive. Address 113 Undersea Blvd. Hydra broken, our car won't go. Come join the party. Rescue us with repair. Tell the Lion he's invited, too.

*RSVP, Mr. Kaleu. RSVP, Mr. Kaleu. Regards, K.
Storm.*

Fetherstone-Pugh frowned. "Doesn't make much
bloody sense, does it?"

"No, sir," Knowles replied. "But like I said, it just
keeps coming through every forty minutes or so."

"Hm." Fetherstone-Pugh glanced at his watch. "When
was the last time you heard it?"

"About ten minutes ago, sir."

"All right." The natty Englishman got to his feet. "I'll
sit in on your receiver in about twenty minutes, Knowles.
I want to hear this."

"Sure, sir."

"Carry on, Knowles. Good work."

"Much obliged, sir."

As he walked away, Fetherstone-Pugh folded the
sheet of notepaper and put it into his pocket, thinking
hard.

Kaleu. Mr. Kaleu.

Odd name.

And one he'd heard before.

Chapter
Sixteen

"How many more times do you think we should send this today?" Winkler asked. He fingered the heavy black Morse key that was screwed to the radio-room table. The dank interior of the U-113 echoed with muted laughter. Most of the men were aft in the engine room, playing dice.

Dekker looked at his watch. "I'd say once more. That makes an even ten transmissions. Then we wait a day and repeat, as agreed. All right?"

Winkler shrugged. "Best we can do, Otto. Here we go again. . . ."

With the index, middle, and ring fingers of his right hand held rigidly together, he began to depress the Morse key at high speed, reading the text of the message from a piece of paper. His level of skill was such that the task was completed in seconds.

"That's it," said the radioman. "Now we wait, for Stuermer or a reply. Whichever comes first."

Dekker nodded. "Like I said, let's hope the reply isn't in the form of surface bombs from a squadron of Catalinas."

Winkler smiled at him. "Let's hope."

Stuermer woke abruptly from his light doze, Bock's hand on his shoulder. It took a few seconds for him to get his bearings. Bunk, varnished wood . . . the cabin aboard the *Shiloh*. He rubbed his eyes briefly and looked up at his young exec.

"We're just coming onto location now, Captain," Bock said softly in German. "Holt took an early-evening star shot with his sextant a few minutes ago to check his navigation, and I took three more with ours to confirm it. Told him it was oil company procedure to have triple redundancy on the position."

"And he bought that?" Stuermer replied, lifting an eyebrow.

"Never questioned it, sir."

"Hm." The *Kapitänleutnant* swung his feet to the deck. "Either you're doing a world-class job of pretending to be an American oilman, Erich, or Holt isn't as bright as I gave him credit for."

"No reason for him to doubt me, I guess, sir." Bock grinned.

"I told you, Lieutenant," Wolfe growled from the opposite bunk, "you're fairly oozing natural charm."

"Thank you, Lothar."

Stuermer and Wolfe pulled on their seaboots, and the three of them made their way forward along the narrow passageway to the wheelhouse. Holt was leaning out of the port door, smoking a Lucky Strike, the warm wind ruffling his hair. There was a becket on the *Shiloh*'s wheel, and the engine was idled down. The trawler rose and fell gently on a coppery pink sea of two-foot swells, lit from the west by a classic Gulf sunset. With the exception of a few galleon clouds set aflame along the far horizon, the sky was clear, a rich, deepening blue.

"As soon as you got done plottin' your third fix," Holt said, "I dead reckoned back through the position and had Lucius drop a buoy over the side. We're circling it now." He grinned, the cigarette poised between his teeth. "Close as I can get you, gents."

"That'll do fine," Bock said. He squinted through the wheelhouse windshield, looking for the buoy.

"Over there," Holt said, pointing. A small, yellow-painted wooden float about the size and shape of a milk bottle bobbed on the light swells off the starboard bow.

"Good. That gives us an initial point of reference. A

good starting point." Bock paused to nod at Lucius as he entered the wheelhouse. "All right, Mike. What we need to do is anchor right next to the buoy, then prepare to send down a diver."

Holt glanced at the setting sun. "Now? You sure?"

"Yes."

Holt took a last drag on his cigarette and snapped it deftly out the wheelhouse door and over the side. "Gonna be blacker'n the ace of spades down there," he said. "Visibility is always bad on the bottom in this area, but at least you'd have some ambient light in the daytime."

Bock looked briefly at Stuermer, then smiled. "Well, it doesn't really matter about the visibility at this stage. What we need to do is make a number of circular sweeps in this area—each one with at least a hundred-foot radius—and have a look at the bottom features. Later on, perhaps we'll take a selection of sediment samples." He leaned in closer. "To tell you the truth, we're on a bit of a schedule here. We took a few extra days to finish the inshore surveys, and now we're running late. Doing these sweeps tonight, even if we have to work past midnight, will help us get caught up again. The actual testing will only take a couple of days."

"Huh. Sounds like the oil company's got you boys doin' things the hard way," Holt said. "Whatever. Your dime, your dance. I'll drop the hook upwind of the buoy and back down until the stern's right on top of it. That okay?"

"Perfect." Bock smiled.

Holt shifted his eyes suddenly to Stuermer. "That okay with you, too?" he demanded. There was a belligerent jut to his jaw.

Stuermer returned his gaze with icy disdain, then nodded slightly and stepped out through the port door of the wheelhouse. Holt watched him walk slowly up the port rail to the bow, his hands in his coat pockets, looking out over the darkening sea.

"I hate to tell you this, Eric," Holt muttered, sticking another Lucky Strike into his mouth, "but your friend Stuermer's starting to get on my nerves."

"Ahh—he can do that," Bock said quickly.

Holt flicked his Zippo and flamed the end of the cigarette. "World-class corporate prick, if you ask me." He puffed and scowled. "What the hell kind of name is *Stuermer* anyway? Sounds like some kind of overpriced vacuum cleaner."

"I think it's Dutch," Bock said. "His family's from Pennsylvania. Old American money. Been here for hundreds of years."

"Nice for him. But I tell you what: he better lose the goddamn airs." Holt's face was getting redder by the second, and he puffed vigorously on his cigarette. "I don't put up with nobody throwin' big-shot goddamn airs at me on my own boat."

Lucius reached out and put a hand on Holt's elbow. "Easy, now, Mike."

Holt snapped his head around, his eyes blazing, and started to say something. But as he met the big mate's eyes, he hesitated, then cleared his throat and looked back out the forward windshield. Lucius kept his hand on his elbow for another few seconds, then let it fall away.

"Just don't like nobody around me puttin' on airs," Holt muttered.

Bock's tones were careful, measured: "I'll mention it to him, Mike. Don't let him bother you. He does that to everybody, even me." He looked at Lucius. "Tell you what: I'll throw in another hundred bucks for your trouble. Hell, the oil company's got lots of money."

Holt was cooling off as fast as he'd heated up. "I just don't like people puttin' on airs," he reiterated. Then he turned and flashed a thin smile. "But for an extra hundred bucks, I guess I can deal with him."

Lucius grinned, strong white teeth gleaming in his ebony face. "Put up with the ten plagues of Egypt for that kinda dough, eh, Mike?"

"Yeah," Holt said. "Yeah, I guess." He spun the wheel. "Wanna stand by on the hook now, Lucius?"

"Sho'," the big mate replied, and ducked through the door.

Bock and Wolfe—who'd been standing quietly to one side—watched him move up past Stuermer to the bow and take up position beside the anchor winch. Lucius turned and looked back through the windshield glass at them. Right at them. Bock's pulse quickened. There was something unnerving about the black man's stare, a penetrating quality that was in direct contrast with his usual geniality. Bock dropped his eyes and turned to Wolfe.

"Bring up our equipment for checkout, please, Mr. Wolfe. We'll stage everything on the stern and prepare to dive using the boat's heavy gear when Captain Holt is ready. Is that all right with you, Mike?"

"Fine with me," Holt replied, exhaling smoke. "As soon as we get the hook down and set, Lucius and I'll come back and lay out the Mark Five equipment. Rig up the compressor and hoses."

"Good," Bock said, glancing out at the big mate one more time. "We'll be ready."

"When was the last time you dove in a brass hat and full suit?" Wolfe asked quietly as he rummaged through one of the duffel bags on his bunk. The gimballed oil lantern mounted on the bulkhead swayed slightly, casting long shadows around the stateroom as the *Shiloh* rode gently at anchor.

Bock pulled the moth-eaten wool turtleneck sweater down over his head and brushed his dark hair back with both hands. "Hmm. I guess it must be five years ago, just before the invasion of Poland. I was home on leave from the Naval Academy. One of my uncles snagged an expensive fishing net on the wreck of an old barge and my father decided he wanted it back. We found an old British dive helmet, a suit, and a compressor in a waterfront pawnshop and ran our own little salvage operation. I did all the diving, cutting the net free of the barge over three days."

"How was it?"

Bock pulled on a pair of heavy wool socks. "Cold, black, and dangerous. It was February in the Baltic, the suit leaked, and the bottom was eighteen meters down. I thought I was going to freeze to death. And I must have gotten wrapped in that damned net twenty times. Whenever the wind changed up on the surface, the compressor would suck in diesel fumes from the boat's stack. Every time I came up I was poisoned green in the face and had a splitting headache."

"You make it sound truly irresistible," Wolfe muttered. "An experience not to be missed."

Bock stood up, fully clad now in long johns, thick sweater, and bulky socks. "Well, that was the Baltic Sea in winter," he said. "This is the Gulf of Mexico." He smiled ruefully. "I'm hoping for better conditions this time, Lothar."

"So am I," the big torpedoman replied glumly, "since I'm diving next."

He pulled a gray canvas satchel about the size of a shoe box out of the duffel bag and held it out to Bock. "Here. This is your mysterious electronic bottom-testing device. You should be able to sling it through the suit harness and let it hang behind you, out of the way. That is, whenever you decide you need to look like you're actually using it."

Bock took it. "What's really in here?"

"A tin first-aid box filled with rusty chain."

The exec rolled his eyes. "I guess we won't be letting Holt or Lucius have a look at this sophisticated new piece of equipment."

"Absolutely not," Wolfe said. "Military secret." He grinned. "At least the satchel looks convincing enough."

"Let's hope. Are you ready?"

"When you are, Lieutenant."

They exited the stateroom and proceeded up the companionway stairs to the *Shiloh*'s back deck. Holt and Lucius were standing near the base of the heavy mast that supported the twin trawling outriggers, inspecting the Mark Five dive gear they'd laid out on top of a large rope chest. Stuermer stood off to one side, looking out at the remnants of the sunset and smoking. The upright outriggers flexed and creaked as the boat wallowed easily in the light swell. The soft purr of the idling main engine vibrated up through the deck planks underfoot.

Bock went directly over to Stuermer and handed him the satchel. "The electronic testing unit," he said.

"Mm." The *Kapitänleutnant* nodded and slung the satchel over his shoulder.

Grinning, Bock turned and walked back up the deck. "Are we ready, Mike?" He prodded the dive suit that lay across the rope chest with his finger. "The gear looks a little worn, but not worn out."

"Hey, it'll do the job for ya," Holt responded. "Just a little chafin' here and there, mostly on the knees. She's watertight—unless you poke a hole in it down there. Good seal on the hat, too. Lotsa air." He smiled around his Lucky Strike.

"What about the compressor?"

"Here," Holt said, "lemme show you." He glanced over his shoulder at Lucius. "Turn the aft spotlights on, will ya? It's gettin' dark."

As the big mate went forward to the deckhouse, Holt slapped a hand onto the rectangular wooden housing of what appeared to be an antique steam engine, about six feet long and four high, with two bronze flywheels three feet in diameter mounted on either side. Between the flywheels, in the heart of the contraption, were two large cylinders with piston arms protruding from their heads. The arms were coupled in turn to a single long camshaft that connected the two flywheels. Bock frowned, then shaded his eyes as the aft spotlights snapped on and flooded the back deck with a yellowish glare.

"This is an old hand-driven compressor," he said. He looked at Holt. "You're not going to tell me that you need two men to stand here cranking on these flywheels to push air to the diver, are you?"

"Nope," Holt replied. "The flywheels are only for backup, in case the mechanical drive fails." He grinned. "Look here."

He bent down and removed a three-foot section of four-inch-wide deck plank, then reached into the void and pulled up a loop of heavy drive belt, which he fed up into the compressor housing and slipped over a drum below the camshaft.

"Power takeoff from the main engine," Holt explained. "I reconditioned that old compressor—new seals, valves, the works—and then installed this here drum and gear system. This belt runs off the front of the drive shaft on a slip drum down below. All I gotta do is tighten it up and she drives the compressor. Watch."

He pulled back on a yard-long wooden lever protruding from the deck nearby. Instantly, the drive belt tensioned and began to turn the camshaft and the flywheels rapidly, the cylinders rocking back and forth on their carriages, the head valves chuffing out air.

"See?" Holt called over the noise. "Plenty of volume." He disengaged the belt, and the old compressor's mechanism slowed to a halt once again.

Bock shrugged. "All right. You've convinced me. Let's get me suited up."

"Sure."

Donning the navy surplus hard-hat gear was no easy task. First came the thick rubberized twill suit, stiff with age and smelling like the inside of a fisherman's boot. Next was the heavy metal chest plate, the shoulder-supported yoke onto which the brass hat would lock. Before the hard hat itself was lowered into place, a lead-weight belt was buckled onto Bock's hips, and support straps were run up over the chest plate. Clumsy bronze-weighted boots were laced onto his rubber-encased feet, and additional weights clipped onto his harness until he could barely sit upright without being steadied by one of his companions.

"How are ya?" Holt grunted as he fiddled with an uncooperative harness buckle.

Bock wiped a trickle of sweat away from his eyebrow with one gloved hand. "Hot." He smiled.

"Huh. You won't be in a few minutes," the *Shiloh*'s captain commented. "Cool on bottom this time of year." He finished with the buckle, gave it a slap, and turned to Lucius. "Got them hoses all hooked up?"

"All set," the big mate replied. He hefted the bulky sphere of brass and glass in the crook of one arm. "Hose fittin's is tight. View port seals look good, too." He spun the hat so that Bock could see. "This here's your free flow, Mr. Smith, just to remind you. And this is your main vent valve." He spun the two bronze knobs a few times. "You need more air, open the free flow a little more. Shut down the exhaust vent until the suit fills out with enough air to make you neutral, but don't be closin' the vent right off, or you might blow up to the surface. Get the bends." He smiled at Bock. "You don't want none o' that."

"Right," Holt interjected. "And just before we lock the hat on, let's make sure we got the line pull signals straight. We'll keep it simple for now: one pull means stop, two pulls means you want slack, three pulls means you want us to come up on you, and a whole mess of fast pulls means 'Get me the hell out of here.' Okay?"

"Okay," Bock said.

"One more thing." Holt held up several three-foot-long, one-inch diameter cylinders wrapped in brown waxed paper. "I'm gonna give you these phosphorus torches. Each one'll burn for about twelve minutes. I'll hang three off your belt right now, then fire up the fourth and hand it to you just before you go in. When one torch starts to die, light the next one right off it. You understand?"

"Got it. Let's go."

Carefully, Lucius lowered the hard hat over Bock's head, threaded it onto the chest plate, and rotated it until the thick glass of the main view port was positioned directly in front of his eyes. Then, with a final twist, he locked it into place. As he did so, Holt threw the tensioning lever on the drive belt and the compressor chugged into life. Air began to hiss from the vent valve on the side of the hat.

Holt walked around and peered into the view port. "Okay?" he yelled.

Bock nodded and gave the aviator's thumbs-up sign. *A nice little Americanism,* he thought. You rarely saw *Luftwaffe* pilots use it.

He felt hands clap him on both shoulders, and with a heave, he stood up. Fully rigged, the hard hat and the suit weighed over 180 pounds. Leaning on Wolfe and Lucius, he wobbled over to the wooden steps that led up to the top of the port rail, his bronze-weight boots clumping hollowly on the deck. Gathering his hoses and

safety rope in the crook of one arm, he negotiated the
steps with difficulty and paused on top of the rail.

Six feet below, the black waters of the Gulf lapped
against the *Shiloh*'s drab white sides. There was a brilliant flash through the side view port of the hat, and
then Holt was guiding his glove to the handle of the
phosphorus underwater torch he'd just lit. A last clap
on the shoulder, and it was time.

Bock cracked open the hat's free-flow valve, holding
the spitting, white-hot torch well away from his body,
and stepped out into empty space.

As his weighted boots hit the water, a twisted bight
of the safety rope trailing behind him locked off momentarily on the little finger of Wolfe's left hand. The torpedoman instinctively snatched his hand away, cursing as
the rough hemp barked his skin raw. At the same time,
he stumbled against Holt, who was standing beside him
tending the air hoses.

Unfortunately, his unthinking exclamation came out—
loud and clear—in German.

"Verdammt!"

Chapter
Seventeen

At the sound of the guttural oath Holt went rigid, the air hoses slipping from his fingers. Regaining balance, Wolfe whirled to face him, his own hands tightening on Bock's safety rope. The two men stared at each other for a frozen moment.

"Son of a bitch," Holt whispered in a choked voice. *"Son of a bitch!"* The ruddy color drained from his face, and his lips twitched uncontrollably.

Unsure of what to do, Wolfe let his eyes flicker over toward Stuermer, standing on the opposite side of the back deck. In that instant Holt stepped forward and hit him, a short, driving right to the jaw that traveled less than a foot, but had every ounce of the wiry captain's body weight behind it.

Wolfe's eyes rolled back white and he went out on his feet momentarily, slumping over against the wooden stairs. The safety rope slid free between his slack fingers, the air hoses flopping over the rail along with it. Holt ran, heading for the wheelhouse.

Stuermer whipped up his Walther and snapped off a shot at him between the outriggers. The slug missed, splintering the greasy wood of the mast as Holt ducked by. At the rail stairs, Lucius lunged over Wolfe's dazed bulk and seized the fast-running safety rope.

Twenty-five feet below, frantically trying to close off the hat's vent valve and halt his free fall toward the bottom, Bock felt a sudden stabbing pain deep in his left ear. It was as if someone had just lanced it with a knitting needle. He let out an involuntary cry of agony as his sense of balance went haywire, his inner ear reacting to the sudden influx of cold air through his ruptured eardrum. Dropping the phosphorus torch, he wrenched the vent completely shut, clasped the hard hat in both hands, and sagged over sideways in the open water.

On the deck above, Stuermer vaulted over Lucius in hot pursuit of Holt as the black mate squeezed the rope in a desperate attempt to halt Bock's descent, the coarse hemp burning his hands bloody. Groggily, Wolfe's eyes refocused and he rolled forward against Lucius, getting his own hand on the slipping line. Under the combined strength of the two big men, it stopped.

Thirty-five feet below the *Shiloh*, dangling in a black void, completely disoriented, nauseated, his head pierced by knifelike pains, Bock was barely conscious of the fact that his suit was filling rapidly with air. Without the hat vent open to bleed off the surplus pressure, the thick rubberized canvas garment began to balloon.

In a matter of seconds the arms and the legs snapped straight out, imprisoning Bock in a spread-eagled position, rendering him unable to bend his elbow and reach the vent valve. Excess air began to stream from the cuffs of the suit. The weight of the sixty-eight-pound hard hat made him top-heavy, and he flipped upside down as the dive suit began to rise toward the surface, gaining speed with every foot. His sinuses squeaked and popped as they equalized in response to the decreasing pressure. His ear felt like it was full of molten lead.

You're blowing up, he told himself. His own calm surprised him. *Don't hold your breath. Do not hold your breath. . . .*

On the deck above, Wolfe and Lucius looked at each other as the safety rope went slack in their hands. The sound of another shot came from the wheelhouse. As if prompted by a starter's pistol they lunged at each other, colliding like a pair of rutting bulls. Arms locked, grappling for a choke hold, they reeled against the *Shiloh*'s gunwale, kicking and twisting in an attempt to heel-hook each other's feet. They fought in tooth-gritting, vein-popping silence, eye to eye, powerful muscles creaking under the strain.

All of a sudden, in a seething boil of foam and bubbles, Bock popped to the surface less than thirty feet away. Suit sleeves and legs fully inflated and rigid, he bobbed stiffly like a wooden mannequin, turning over once. He stabilized in a face-down position with his arms locked out wide, crucified against the black water.

Wolfe and Lucius glanced at him, then back at each other. Simultaneously, they both let go and seized the stricken diver's trailing lines, Wolfe on the safety rope and Lucius taking in air hose. Breathing hard, sweat pouring down their faces, they reeled Bock in closer to the side of the boat.

In the wheelhouse, Stuermer ducked back behind the jamb of the main companionway as Holt emerged from his cabin on the opposite side of the galley, swinging up a sawed-off double-barreled shotgun. There was a deafening blast, and the doorframe near the *Kapitänleutnant*'s head exploded in a spray of wood splinters. Stuermer dropped to one knee and returned fire across the galley, keeping his head low.

A string of epithets turned the air blue as Holt dodged back into his cabin, breaking open the shotgun and ejecting the two spent shells. Stuermer took his chance. In three running strides he was across the galley and up against the far bulkhead. Without hesitating, he brought his gun hand around and leveled the Walther into the captain's quarters.

The second door that led out onto the starboard side banged once, swinging on its hinges. Stuermer swore under his breath, made a fast choice, and ran back through the galley, heading toward the *Shiloh*'s helm. As he ducked through the companionway he saw the top of Holt's sandy crewcut head moving quickly along the bottom sill of the forward windows in the direction of the port side. The business end of the double-barreled shotgun was clearly visible just ahead of him.

Stuermer brought the Walther up, took an extra second to track Holt in the pistol's sights, and fired just as he reached the lower left corner of the portmost window. The thick glass pane shattered, and the sandy head disappeared.

Letting out a tight breath, the *Kapitänleutnant* leaped to the port wheelhouse door and looked out quickly over the barrel of his weapon. Holt lay on his side up against the port rail, groaning, covered in shards of broken glass. He was rocking back and forth with his hand and stump clasped to his profusely bleeding head. His dropped shotgun had skidded into the scuppers. Stuermer stepped out, keeping the Walther trained on him.

Holt blinked away the blood running into his eyes and tried to focus on his opponent. His vision was slow to clear, and as it did the expression of pain on his face was replaced by one of undisguised hatred.

"You better finish it," he croaked through clenched teeth.

Stuermer, who had no intention of shooting the wounded man again, nevertheless kept his pistol raised. His cautious approach was misread by Jolene, who appeared suddenly from behind a foredeck locker and stepped directly into the line of fire.

"Don't shoot him!" she pleaded, holding up her hands. "Please . . ."

Stuermer blinked. The young Creole girl from *les Isolates'* camp. *What—*

Even with a deep, bleeding furrow in his scalp, Holt was not slow. He sprawled sideways for the shotgun, reaching out with his single hand. Stuermer aimed the pistol, saw Jolene's baggy shirt in the way, hesitated— and then Holt had the short scattergun up.

Jolene spun and backed up hard against Stuermer, crowding him along the port rail and pinning his gun hand between them. Now it was Holt who had no clear shot.

"He'll kill me!" Jolene shouted, keeping herself pressed up against the utterly confused U-boat commander. "I'm beggin' you, Cap'n, do like he says! Please—Lord knows I don't want to die!"

Briefly, Holt considered shooting directly through the

girl to get at the man behind. Twelve-gauge triple-aught buckshot had enough punch to do the job nicely. But even in his pain-driven rage he could not quite bring himself to pull the trigger. Neither, however, was he inclined to lower the shotgun.

Stuermer had stopped trying to get clear of the girl and now stood still, letting her lean back against his chest. He was catching on. Extracting the Walther from between them, he thumbed the hammer down to a safe position and touched the barrel to Jolene's temple. She didn't move, didn't even tense up.

"Drop the weapon, Captain Holt," he called. "Whoever this girl is, she means less than nothing to me."

Holt blinked blood from his eye, looking down the shotgun. "I don't know her, either," he said.

Stuermer smiled, and he tried to make it a cold, evil smile. He'd judged his man. "Then shoot," he replied, "and if you don't kill us both, I'll shoot back. Or"—he moved back toward the wheelhouse door, pulling Jolene with him—"perhaps I'll step in here, shoot the girl in the head, and we'll continue where we left off . . . that is, of course, unless you drop your weapon and lie still."

A faint smile played on Jolene's lips. Holt didn't notice. His attention was fully on Stuermer, on the Walther, and on his guttural, unmistakably German accent.

"You Kraut bastard," he rasped. Blood was running down his face in rivulets, onto his lips. He licked them once, spat red, and then slid the shotgun into the scuppers.

Stuermer reached inside the wheelhouse door and plucked a clean towel off a bulkhead shelf. "Direct pressure," he whispered in Jolene's ear. "Right on the wound. Carefully."

She took the towel and moved forward. Keeping the Walther leveled at Holt, Stuermer bent down and retrieved the shotgun. It was an ugly thing: the butt sawed off so that only the scarred pistol grip remained, the twin barrels cut back to no more than sixteen inches in length. Terribly effective at close range.

Stuermer flicked the thumb lever that broke open the shotgun, saw that it contained two unspent shells, and closed it with a snap of his wrist. *Clack.* In the scuppers, Jolene had helped Holt to a sitting position against the bulwark and was attempting to secure the towel around his head. The injured American, his face pale and blood-streaked, was staring daggers at Stuermer. The *Kapitän-leutnant* waggled the pistol barrel at him, glanced toward the back deck, and moved aft along the port side of the wheelhouse.

Wolfe and Lucius had recovered Bock to the foot of the short ladder that extended over the *Shiloh*'s side. The torpedoman took a fast half turn around a gunwale cleat with the taut safety rope, passed the tail end to Lucius, and clambered down the ladder. With the water lapping up past his knees, he reached around Bock's hard hat, located the vent valve, and opened it.

A miniature geyser of air bubbles foamed up around the hat as the excess pressure within the dive suit bled off. The rigidly inflated arms, legs, and trunk of the garment collapsed, and Bock immediately began to sink. Lucius took up slack on the safety rope, holding him at the surface.

Gripping the ladder with one hand, waist-deep in salt water, Wolfe attempted to guide Bock to the lower rungs. The young exec floundered helplessly, too disoriented to respond. Wolfe wasted no time. Pulling Bock close, he ducked underwater and came up beneath him, bearing his entire weight across his broad shoulders in a fireman's carry.

Grunting with the strain, Wolfe heaved his way up the ladder, shedding cascades of water. Lucius reached down and grabbed the straps of Bock's harness, and together the two men maneuvered him over the rail and down onto the deck. He lay motionless on his back, a sodden heap of brass, canvas, lead, and black rubber hose.

"Up!" Wolfe gasped in his broken English. "Sit him up!"

Lucius pulled Bock upright and propped him there with a knee between his shoulder blades. Working quickly, Wolfe loosened the dive helmet and unscrewed it from the chest plate. As he lifted it clear, Bock's head lolled over to one side. His eyes were fluttering and there was a trickle of blood from his left ear.

"Po' boy done blowed up to the surface," Lucius said quietly, supporting Bock's head with one large ebony hand. "He ain't coughin' up no blood, though. That's one good thing."

"He is an experienced diver," Stuermer called, "and has deep-water emergency ascent training. It is unlikely that he held his breath and ruptured his lungs."

Lucius turned and looked over his shoulder. The man he knew only as Mr. Stuermer was standing a few feet up the deck, leaning against the port rail. He was pointing a pistol back up toward the bow with one hand and carrying Mike Holt's sawed-off shotgun in the other. Very deliberately, Lucius passed Bock's weight over to Wolfe, rose to his feet, and picked up a short boat hook that was secured just beneath the gunwale.

He advanced toward Stuermer, his face set. The U-boat commander brought up the shotgun and pointed it at Lucius' chest. The big mate seemed not to notice.

Something that might have been sadness came and went in Stuermer's eyes. "Stop, Lucius," he ordered.

The tall black man halted only a few feet from Stuermer and pointed the boat hook at him, looking as immovable as an obsidian statue.

"Where Mike at?" he demanded.

Stuermer made a slight motion with his head. "On the bow."

"You shoot him?" The boat hook rose slightly.

"He was grazed," Stuermer answered, his voice measured. "He will be all right once the bleeding stops."

"I'm goin' up there, Mr. Stuermer. Git outta my way, now."

The *Kapitänleutnant* considered, then lowered the shotgun halfway. "I will be behind you," he said. "I want you to bring Captain Holt astern, quietly. Do you understand me?"

For a long moment Lucius didn't move. Then he dropped the boat hook into the scuppers and nodded. "Okay."

Stuermer stepped aside and let him pass, keeping the pistol at the ready. As he turned to follow the big mate, he glanced down at Bock, who was sitting on the deck in his drenched dive suit, holding one hand over his ear and wincing. Wolfe was tugging at the straps of the weight belt harness, trying to loosen them.

"All right, Lieutenant?" Stuermer inquired in German.

Bock lifted the hand from his ear. "What?"

Stuermer half smiled. Perforated eardrum. Uncomfortable, but not fatal. "Are you all right, Erich?"

Bock returned the half smile through his pain. "I've been better, sir," he replied.

The *Kapitänleutnant* nodded. "Easy. Let Lothar help you." He glanced up at the bow just as Lucius knelt down beside Holt and Jolene. "I'll bring these three back here where we can keep an eye on them."

As he walked up the port side, Bock, still holding his throbbing ear, turned and looked at Wolfe. "I must not have heard right," he said. "Did he say 'three'?"

Chapter
Eighteen

In the tracking room of the Central Gulf Coast Defense Grid, Fetherstone-Pugh stirred a splash of milk into his ninth cup of Earl Grey and adjusted the headphones on his ears. He winced in distaste as he sipped the tea. The damned orderly never brought the water to a proper boil before steeping the leaves. One of the more intolerable torments associated with his tenure in New Orleans. Fetherstone-Pugh reflected that in a perfect world such thuggish mishandling of a British officer's tea would be a hanging—or at least a flogging—offense.

Dit dah ditditdit dah dit . . . the lieutenant commander set his cup down hurriedly as a burst of Morse signals came through his headset. Seizing a pencil, he began to write on a sheet of notepaper.

"To Mr. Kaleu: Celebration hosted by fifty-two of your fleet brethren . . ."

Fetherstone-Pugh raised his free hand as he wrote, pointing at the technician who stood juggling pieces of colored chalk in his hand behind the glass chart of the Gulf of Mexico. "Plot!" he ordered loudly. "Frequency zero-six-nine-six . . ."

The tech began to write rapidly on the transparent panel with the colored chalk. He wrote backward so that those on the opposite side could read the frequency and bearing details easily. Completing the figures, he pulled down a parallel rule that was mounted by a swing arm to the support frame of the chart. Positioning it carefully on the glass, using a contrasting color of chalk, he drew a line diagonally to the south-southwest from the silver button that designated New Orleans.

As Fetherstone-Pugh listened intently to the stuttering pulses coming through his headphones, something stirred in his memory. Like a word or name on the tip of one's tongue, lurking just out of reach.

. . . *Regards, K. Storm.*

The transmission ceased. Fetherstone-Pugh wrote down the last of it and compared his text with Knowles' earlier translation. They were identical. Same words, same frequency.

He looked up at the glass chart. The bearing line of bright blue chalk glowed faintly in the subdued light. From New Orleans it cut down through the deep swamp west of the Mississippi ship channel and on out into the Gulf.

He turned and directed his gaze at the junior officer in charge of coordinating the secondary relay stations. "Jones, check with Biloxi, Lafayette, and Beaumont. See if any of them picked up on this and got a bearing. I want a triangulation. Inform all stations that this signal has been transmitted repetitively on the same frequency over the past four hours. They are to listen for it and determine its bearing."

"Yes, sir." Jones adjusted his headset, leaned forward, and began to speak quietly and rapidly into the microphone at his radio desk.

Fetherstone-Pugh gazed down at the scrawled message and drummed his fingers on his knee, his brow furrowing in thought. *Kaleu.* An odd name. Why the devil was it so familiar?

"Negative on the other tracking stations, sir," Jones reported from across the room. "Nobody picked up on it. One of the techs in Biloxi remembers the transmission, but he didn't lock in on it. It sounded like local traffic to him."

"Unfortunate," Fetherstone-Pugh mused in his arid tone. "I assume they're looking for it as of now?"

"That's affirmative, sir," Jones replied. "All six secondaries are listening for the next repeat, ready to take a bearing."

"Good. Carry on."

Jones bent back over his work and Fetherstone-Pugh picked up his teacup. As he took a sip, Knowles, the tech whose station he'd commandeered, returned and slid into a chair beside him.

"Did you hear it, sir?"

Fetherstone-Pugh nodded. "Yes. I monitored the entire thing." He pushed the sheet of notepaper over to Knowles. "Identical to what you heard. Eight-second duration, standard Morse, in English. High bandwidth."

The tech chewed his lip. "You think it's anything, sir?"

"I'm not sure." The Englishman set the teacup down carefully in its saucer. "Two things about it bother me. One is the name *Kaleu*. Damned if I haven't heard it before someplace. The other is, well, something I can't really explain. More of a feeling, really. It's . . . it's . . ." His voice trailed off in frustration.

"A hunch?" Knowles suggested.

"Rather," Fetherstone-Pugh replied. He thought for a moment. "Have you ever answered the telephone and instantly recognized the voice, but then just as quickly realized that you haven't the slightest idea who it is?"

"Sure, sir."

"Like that," the lieutenant commander said. "It's like that."

"Well, hell, Feathers!" Blodgett exclaimed, coming up from behind unseen. "That don't make much sense. You actually got to hear a person talk at you to recollect his accent or tone." He stuck his thumbs into the belt beneath his whiskey paunch and winked at Knowles. "Now, how do you figure you might know somebody who's sendin' a message when all you can hear is a mess of dots and dashes?"

Knowles, who was no admirer of Blodgett's, kept his face expressionless and strategically lowered his eyes to the desktop. *Good lad,* thought Fetherstone-Pugh, *you'll rise fast and far by not taking sides in a useless argument.* He turned unhurriedly enough to communicate the sheer disdain he felt for his U.S. Navy counterpart and managed to look down his nose at him, even though he was sitting and Blodgett was standing.

"It always amazed me, Hiram," Fetherstone-Pugh said, breaking precedent by using Blodgett's given name, "that the Admiralty would assign an officer who was a nonspecialist in radio and communications, such as yourself, to be my co-coordinator on this project. Your lack of appreciation for the finer points—and very often the fundamentals—of radio technique has been a considerable hindrance to the operation of this defense grid."

Everyone in the room was looking over their sets at the two officers, but for the first time ever, Fetherstone-Pugh did not seem to care.

Blodgett's gum-cracking grin lost some of its assuredness. "I'm mainly an administrator, Feathers," he countered. "I keep the boys in motion—you know that. The fancy radio gear and such, that's always been your department."

"My point exactly," Fetherstone-Pugh said, rising to his feet. "That's why when I tell you that I hear something familiar in a Morse transmission, I expect you to do me the courtesy of taking my statement at face value."

Blodgett reddened slightly, aware of the eyes on them. "So how *can* you tell the difference between one group of Morse signals and another? Crystal ball?"

Fetherstone-Pugh swept the notepaper off Knowles' radio desk and turned to leave. "No, Hiram, you poor, uneducated bumpkin. I can tell by listening to the *fist*."

With that, he stalked across the tracking room and exited through the hall door.

Blodgett stood there, cracking his gum, his face beet red. He glanced down at Knowles, who was trying not to smile.

"Fist?" the corpulent officer muttered. "What's *fist*?"

In the radio room of the U-113, Winkler leaned back from the Morse key with a sigh. Pushing his steel-rimmed glasses up on his forehead and rubbing his eyes, he regarded the metal ceiling above him blankly. There was a light footfall as Dekker entered the cramped compartment.

"Is that the last transmission?" the chief inquired, glancing at his watch.

Winkler nodded. "Yes. For now, at least." He resettled his glasses on the bridge of his nose. "We'll stick to the twenty-four hours of silence now, as agreed, and monitor for replies. If none come, we'll try again the day after tomorrow."

"Best we can do," Dekker grumbled. "Maybe next time someone will have cruised within range. Or be alert enough to decipher our little riddle. Not every U-boat radio operator can understand English, you know."

"The message is a bit oblique, I'll admit," Winkler said, "but there are enough catchwords in it to make it stand out to another *Ubootwaffe* radioman. Maybe we'll be lucky, Otto."

"That would be a welcome change," the chief commented. He extracted half a cigar from his shirt pocket and tapped Winkler on the shoulder. "What about a smoke up on the bridge? The air has cooled off and the mosquitoes aren't too bloodthirsty tonight, for some reason."

"All right."

The senior radioman pushed himself out of his chair with a sigh. The two of them proceeded to the control room and ascended the conning tower ladders to the bridge. To Winkler's surprise, he could see his breath in the chilly night air.

"Just when I was getting used to hundred-degree heat and perpetual humidity," he said, lighting a cigarette. He held out the match to Dekker. "These climatic changes can cause rheumatism, you know."

"If any of us live long enough to get rheumatism," Dekker scowled, drawing on his cigar, "I, for one, will be eternally grateful." He leaned over the edge of the armored wind baffle, squinted into the night, and focused on the crewman on watch. The man was strolling slowly along the foredeck of the U-113 with a *Schmeisser* machine pistol cradled under one arm. He, too, was smoking.

"All well, Mohler?" the chief called out.

Mohler turned, plucked the cigarette from his mouth, and waved. The glowing coal traced a momentary orange streak in the darkness. "All clear, Mr. Dekker," he reported. "Not even a raccoon moving tonight. Too cold, maybe."

"Good," Dekker said. "You need a coat?"

"I've got one, sir. I'm fine."

"All right, carry on." The chief turned back to Winkler. "Good man, that Mohler. Reliable. He hasn't seen a—"

He stopped in midsentence. Standing next to Winkler, just behind his right shoulder, was a hunchedbacked old woman not more than five feet tall. She wore a ratty, capelike garment from which small ornaments dangled. In the darkness, her face was broad and shapeless like a mass of putty, punctuated by two glittering eyes that seemed to catch the starlight and reflect it outward. The immediate impression was that of some kind of hideous oversized dwarf.

It took Winkler a second to realize that something was at his shoulder. He looked down, came eyeball to eyeball with Estelle staring luminously up at him, and jerked away as if he'd been electrocuted, coughing out his cigarette. Losing his balance, he stumbled along the bridge rail into Dekker.

"Heh heh heh," the old woman chuckled.

"What—" Winkler stuttered in English, "where did *you* come from?"

"Been standin' here quite a while," Estelle replied. "Nice evenin', don't you think?"

"How did you get up here?" Dekker demanded in his own heavy accent. He glanced down at Mohler, who was standing on the bow. "How did you get past the watch?"

"Heh heh heh."

Winkler regarded her incredulously. She was so bent with age that it appeared impossible for her to stand without the support of the wooden cane on which she was leaning. She could not have climbed the external conning tower ladder to the bridge . . . and yet here she was.

"She must have been on the other side of the periscope housing," Dekker said. "That's why we didn't see her when we came up."

"That doesn't explain how she got up here past Mohler," Winkler replied. He spread his hands. "We're not going to hurt you, old mother."

"Oh, I know you ain't," Estelle said. She grinned, showing a few blackened teeth.

Winkler glanced quickly at Dekker. "Is there something you want?"

"Who the devil are you, anyway?" Dekker said irritably. "You shouldn't be up here."

Estelle shuffled forward. "I'll be leavin' soon enough. But I come up here to do you boys a favor." She grinned again. "You know Papa Luc, I expect?"

Winkler nodded. "Mm."

The old woman beckoned conspiratorially. "Thought so. Now look here: me an' Luc, we ain't exactly on speakin' terms these days. So I'm tellin' you, he's fixin' to show up here and try to take your *bateau*. Got a few fellas with him, too. Figgers he can get the jump on the boy walkin' the deck when everyone else is inside asleep. Lock y'all in." She looked pointedly at the lines and the rigging that secured the U-113 to the shore. "He knows you can't do nothin' from inside as long as the boat's tied up to the trees."

Dekker frowned. "Why would he do that? We're going to pay him."

Estelle shrugged. "He wants more. More money, more gold. He thinks you got it. Me, I figger we should let you fix the boat, pay us, and go on your way. Less trouble. But not Luc."

She turned and stepped out through the opening in the rear baffle onto the external conning tower ladder. "You don't have to believe me," she croaked, "but I'd keep an eye peeled for Luc, if I was you."

As Winkler and Dekker watched, she clambered down the metal ladder with apparent ease and quickly reached the deck. Mohler still stood on the bow, looking off across the misty surface of the pond. The old woman shuffled onto the gangplank, across the water gap to shore, and disappeared into the dark foliage.

As if a spell had been broken, Winkler and Dekker shook their heads and looked at each other. Dekker whirled and faced the bow.

"Mohler!" he barked. "Come here!"

Startled, the seaman turned, tossed the butt of his cigarette, and came back down the foredeck at a trot. "Sir?"

"How did you let that old woman get aboard?" the chief demanded. "You're supposed to be on watch, man!"

Mohler looked confused. "Old woman? What old woman, sir?"

"The one that just left, for God's sake!"

"Left?"

Winkler leaned forward. "You didn't see an old woman just get off this boat, crewman?"

"No, sir," Mohler said helplessly. "I swear to you, nobody has come aboard or left since I've been on watch."

Dekker glowered at him. "You're relieved, Mohler. Obviously you need sleep. Tell the next man on the watch schedule that he's due on deck early."

"Aye, sir." Too much of a veteran to protest further, the seaman turned and walked quickly up the deck toward the forward hatch.

Dekker looked back at Winkler, who was staring off into the foliage where the old woman had disappeared. A shred of night mist drifted past the conning tower.

"Ridiculous," the chief muttered. "Ridiculous for Mohler not to have seen her when she came aboard."

"Yes," Winkler agreed, nodding slowly. "Ridiculous." He paused to clear his throat. "I want to triple the watch, Otto. A man on the foredeck, one on the stern, and a third up here on the bridge."

Dekker looked at him again.

"All right," he said.

Chapter
Nineteen

Holt sat on one of the rigging chests, his head bandaged with a torn towel, and glowered silently at Stuermer. Lucius hovered beside him, steadying him with a hand on his shoulder. A few feet away, Jolene was helping Wolfe get Bock out of the cumbersome dive suit. A thin line of blood still trickled persistently from the young exec's ear, and he was having trouble keeping his balance. Stuermer stood against the rail, his arms crossed, the Walther ready in one hand, its muzzle directed off to the side. His eyes were shifting rapidly from person to person.

"Captain Holt," he said finally, "I am sorry about your head. You gave me no choice. Even though the wound is superficial, you should have it properly attended to. You may have a concussion." His formal, heavily German-accented English hung in the air.

Holt continued to stare, saying nothing.

The *Kapitänleutnant* went on: "The quickest way for you to get back to shore and into a doctor's care is to cooperate with us. We need your help to salvage something from the ocean floor. And I said *cooperate,* not *collaborate.* There is a difference. It is also the quickest way for you and Lucius to be rid of us. Once we have what we need, we will release the *Shiloh*—and the two of you—unharmed."

"Sure you will," Holt growled.

"I give you my word."

The one-handed captain snorted and looked off into the night. "Your word ain't worth spit to me, goose-stepper." He dug in his shirt pocket, extracted a battered Lucky Strike, and jammed it between his lips.

As he was searching his trouser pockets for a light, he appeared to lose his balance, sagging off to one side. Lucius caught him immediately, straightened him up, and flicked open his own Zippo.

"Easy, now, Mike," he rumbled gently, his ebony face creased with concern. "Got you a light right here."

Stuermer watched the interaction between the black mate and his captain for a moment, then changed tack: "Lucius, you want to see Captain Holt get the medical attention he needs, don't you?"

Lucius looked at him. "Uh-huh."

"Well," Stuermer continued, "the sooner we locate what we're looking for and recover it from the bottom, the sooner you'll have him into a hospital. If you help us, everything will go much faster. That's what you want, isn't it?"

Lucius regarded Stuermer evenly. "I know you prob'ly thinkin' all us colored folks got a hard head bone, but let me tell you: it ain't so. You wastin' your time tryin' to play me off against Mike."

"I am simply giving you an opportunity to end this situation quickly and help Captain Holt," Stuermer said. "Look at him. I suggest you take it."

"Don't listen to this piece of shit, Lucius," Holt snarled, exhaling smoke. "I don't know where these Krauts came from, but they ain't here for Mardi Gras. If they want something off the bottom out here, they can get it themselves."

Holt's face grew increasingly purple as he worked himself up, and he looked none too steady. Then, without warning, he sagged sideways into Lucius again. Stuermer watched silently, eyeing the black mate.

"You gots to lie down, Mike," Lucius said. He kept one huge arm around Holt's shoulders, supporting him. Then his eyes came up and met Stuermer's.

"I help you an' you take the *Shiloh* in?" It was more of a statement than a question.

"Yes," the *Kapitänleutnant* replied. "We need time to get clear, but we will release you. And in the meantime, we'll see that Captain Holt's wound is properly tended. You have my word."

Lucius considered. "What you gonna need?"

"Just your assistance with the diving and rigging lines. The items we need to salvage are quite heavy. Lieutenant Bock has a perforated eardrum and can no longer dive. We are shorthanded."

"Who's Lieutenant Bock?" Lucius inquired.

Stuermer half smiled at his own mistake. He'd never been a particularly skilled liar. Well, it made little difference now. "Mr. Smith's real name is Erich Bock."

Having shed the bulky dive suit, now sitting on the edge of a winch and dabbing at his ear with a towel, Bock nodded across the deck at the mate.

"I'm tellin' you, Lucius," Holt cut in, "don't trust these bastards. They—they—" Once again dizziness overwhelmed him and he reeled in the black man's arms.

Lucius looked at him. "What I'm supposed to do, Mike? Let you die?" He turned back to Stuermer. "All right. I'll help you."

The U-boat commander smiled. "Good, Lucius. That's good." He waved the Walther gently at Holt. "On your feet, please, Captain. You're going to your quarters. Lothar!"

"Yes, sir," Wolfe replied.

"I want Captain Holt tied to his bunk so that he stays there. Can you do it without making him too uncomfortable?"

Wolfe smiled. "Not too uncomfortable, sir." He pulled a coil of line out of the nearby rope chest.

"Fine. Let's go, gentlemen." Stuermer motioned again with the pistol, and he, Lucius, Holt, and Wolfe headed for the wheelhouse.

Jolene and Bock were left alone on the back deck. Bock dabbed once more at his ear, wincing, and then examined the lightly bloodstained towel. He dropped it to the deck and put his face in his hands, rubbing his eyes. "Ahhh," he sighed. "What a mess."

Jolene hesitated, then came over and sat down on the other end of the winch. "What's a mess?"

Bock looked over at her. "This. This whole thing." He waved his hand in exasperation. "It's gotten way out of control." A strained laugh broke from his lips. Shyly, Jolene laughed as well, and as she did so it suddenly struck Bock that he was looking into the dark, almond-shaped eyes of a very pretty girl. The same very pretty girl who'd caught his attention several times at *les Isolates'* shanty settlement. And who had absolutely no business being where she was now.

"What in God's name are you doing aboard this boat?" he asked. "You shouldn't be here."

Jolene's eyes stayed on his. "I stowed away. Snuck up by pirogue when you were at the old cargo landin' in the mouth of the river. Y'all were too busy to notice me, I guess." She smiled. "I seen you lookin' at me back at the shack town, you know."

Bock lifted an eyebrow. "Is that so?"

"Yup." Jolene cocked her head assertively and stuck out her lower lip. "That's so. You know it, an' I know you know it."

Bock grinned. "Is there anything you don't know?"

The color of her cheeks deepened slightly. She lowered her eyes, smiling ear to ear, then brought her gaze back up to his. "Nothin' I can't learn," she said.

"Huh." Bock suddenly became aware that he had been leaning forward and was starting to slip off the winch. You could almost fall right into eyes that deep and dark. Collecting himself, he straightened up.

"My name's—"

"Erich Bock," Jolene interrupted. "I heard your friend say it."

Bock smiled. "Well, that puts me at a disadvantage, then."

"Yeah? Why?"

"Because you know my name and I don't know yours." He peered at her. "Hardly seems fair."

Jolene's jaw stuck out slightly. "Maybe I'll tell you and maybe I won't."

"Hm." Bock bent down, picked up the towel, and got to his feet. "Well, in that case, I guess we're through talking to each other. I don't have conversations with people who won't tell me their names." He began to step past her, keeping an admirably straight face. "Excuse me, please."

"Jolene," she declared quickly. "My name's Jolene." She looked up at him.

Bock stopped, toweling his damp hair. "That's a pretty name," he said, and when he saw her smile, he matched it with one of his own.

In the captain's quarters, Wolfe pulled tight a final seaman's knot and stepped back to check his handiwork. Holt was lying on his back. His ankles and one wrist had been lashed to three corners of the bunk. His missing hand had presented a problem. Wolfe had finally elected to lash his disabled left arm to the side of the bunk with wraps of line above and below the elbow.

"I am sorry about this, Herr Captain," he had muttered in his broken English as he worked. "I will try not to make the ropes too tight."

To which Holt had replied that he could go fuck himself. The big torpedoman had finished the job in silence.

"I don't think he's going anywhere too soon, sir," he said to Stuermer in German.

"All right, Lothar." Stuermer switched back to English. "Captain Holt, are you comfortable?"

"What the hell do you think?" Holt snarled.

Stuermer sighed. "Just lie back and rest. If you struggle, you will make your head wound bleed again. I'm sorry this is necessary, but again, you give me no choice."

Lucius stood at the foot of the bunk, looking down unhappily at Holt. "I don't like it. What if them ropes is too tight? Cut off his circulation."

The *Kapitänleutnant* shook his head. "They are snug, not cinched down. If he refrains from tugging on them, the captain should be fine."

"Mike," Lucius said. "Mike, I gotta do this. I gotta help them so we can get the *Shiloh* in, get you to a doctor. That's why I'm doin' this, Mike."

Holt didn't say anything, but he nodded. Lucius put a hand on his shin for a moment, then turned to Stuermer. "Remember, we got us a deal."

"Yes, we do." Stuermer put the Walther into his pocket. "Let's go to work, gentlemen."

They exited Holt's quarters, leaving him swearing under his breath, and made their way astern. Bock was rearranging the Mark Five gear on top of the rope chest, assisted by Jolene. At Stuermer's approach he turned and straightened.

"No damage to the diving equipment, sir," he said in German. "If we can just get lucky enough to hit Schecter's boat with our first bottom sweeps, we should be able to recover the shafts and propellers."

Lucius looked at him blankly. "Ain't heard talk like that since I was in France in 1918."

Bock's eyebrow went up again. "You were in France during the Great War?" he asked, switching to English.

"Yeah. Colored regiment." Lucius said, matter-of-factly. "Heard a lot of German folks speakin' their own tongue." He smiled. "Thought I done heard the accent from you a couple of times when we was comin' out here. You talk American so good it was hard to be sure."

Bock shrugged. "I thought you seemed suspicious up in the wheelhouse. You were right." He put a hand on top of the diving helmet. "You must have met a lot of Germans over there."

"I did," Lucius agreed. "'Course, for a while there, I done killed most of 'em I met. 'Specially in a place called the Argonne Forest." He paused and looked out into the night. "Lot of killin' in that place. You know, they give me a medal for it. The Frenchies. Nice folks. Pretty little piece of metal they called the Croix de Guerre."

Stuermer looked up from his examination of the dive helmet. "You won the Croix de Guerre?" he exclaimed. "For what?"

"Well, there was this machine gun nest been holdin'

up our advance for days," Lucius recalled. "One night, me an' another ol' boy just got tired of sittin' in the mud gettin' shot at, so we done snuck over there and took it out. That's what they give me the medal for."

"How many men in the nest?" Wolfe inquired, coiling air hose.

"Seven," Lucius replied. "But there was about thirty more foot soldiers all around it."

"You got all those men?"

"No, suh. We killed the men in the nest, busted off the firing pin in the machine gun, an' snuck back outta there. Next mornin', without that gun workin', our regiment was able to charge right through that position. Didn't lose a man, neither."

"How were you able to kill seven men in a machine gun nest without making any noise?" Stuermer asked.

Lucius' smile was feral. "Knife work," he said simply.

The three Germans looked at each other, then at the black mate's empty hands, and shifted on their feet uncomfortably.

"Pretty little piece of metal, that Croix de Guerre," Lucius mused. "Made a hell of a nice fishin' lure once I hung a treble hook off it."

"You still have it?" Bock asked.

"No, suh."

"Where is it now?"

Lucius smiled again. "Inside the big-ass fish that broke the line it was tied to."

Stuermer cleared his throat. "All right, let's get to work. First of all, we'll speak only English so that Lucius and"— he glanced over at Jolene—"this young lady can understand what we're doing. We'll need them both. Secondly, we need to check on Captain Holt fairly often. He's too resourceful for his own good, or ours. And last of all, Lothar—I believe it is your turn to wear the dive suit."

Wolfe nodded. "Yes, sir."

"Then let's get started," the *Kapitänleutnant* said briskly. "We've wasted too much time as it is."

A half hour later it was Wolfe, brandishing a freshly lit phosphorus torch, who stepped off the port rail of the

Shiloh, with Bock and Lucius closely tending his air hose and safety line. The big torpedoman filled out the canvas suit more fully than the slender Bock, and he kept a cautious hand on the helmet's vent valve to regulate his buoyancy. With the elbow of his torch arm hooked around the tethering line of the marker buoy Holt had dropped earlier, he opened the valve a little more, vented some of the suit's internal air volume, and began a controlled sink into the pitch blackness beneath him.

He could feel the air hose and the safety line tugging at his harness as they were fed out. A sediment layer rose up past the helmet view ports, and he felt the chill of a thermocline travel up his legs and envelop his entire body. The suspended particles in the water caught the torch's brilliant white glare and reflected it back at him, creating an effect that resembled an undersea snowstorm and reduced visibility to less than arm's length. Still he sank, the water temperature dropping by the second.

And then his weighted boots encountered a sudden resistance and he found himself buried to the knees in cold, viscous goo. A cloud of mud boiled up in front of his main view port, temporarily blacking out even the incandescent whiteness of the phosphorus torch. He was on the bottom—or, more correctly, *in* the bottom.

"*Verdammt*," Wolfe swore aloud, struggling to move. The word was lost to his own ears, drowned out by the constant hiss of compressed air into the hat. Perhaps a little more buoyancy. He closed down the helmet vent carefully, and the suit's internal air volume began to increase.

Just shy of positive buoyancy he regulated the valve again and stabilized himself. Now he and the 180 pound suit were virtually weightless, and he was able to toe his way along the surface of a semifluid mud bottom that would have qualified as quicksand had it been found on land. Tying a thin search line to the buoy tether, he moved outward in one direction, holding the torch high and paying out the line behind him.

After a couple of minutes of churning along in a boil of cold mud, he reached the end of the search line. Slipping his gloved hand through the loop at its end, he pulled it tight, looked in both directions at murky black water, and set off to his right in a counterclockwise sweep.

He'd taken two steps when the bottom erupted under him as if someone had yanked a carpet from beneath his feet. Something flexible, powerful, and very much alive flapped against his legs and hips, upending him. For a split second he seemed clear of it, fighting to stay vertical, and then a huge gray shape whirled out of the darkness into the torchlight and hit him in the chest with tremendous force. He went over onto his back in the cold ooze as the air came out of his lungs in a harsh gasp. Mud billowed up over the helmet view ports, and Lothar Wolfe's world went black.

Chapter
Twenty

Rear Admiral Richard "Zack" Zacharias, U.S. Navy Commander-in-Chief of Coastal Defense Operations, Gulf of Mexico (CIC/CDOG), looked up from his paperwork as Fetherstone-Pugh entered his office. He took from his mouth the stem of the briar pipe he'd been smoking and nodded pleasantly. Fetherstone-Pugh removed his cap and tucked it under his arm in one brisk motion, came to attention, and executed a crisp Royal Navy salute.

"Thank you for seeing me, Admiral," he said.

"Of course, Trevor. Relax, have a seat." The square-jawed, gray-haired Zacharias leaned back in his leather office chair and drew on his pipe. Unlike many U.S. Navy officers on the base, he liked the lanky young lieutenant commander. Fetherstone-Pugh exhibited an old-school pride in traditional military deportment that Zacharias felt was lacking in many of his more junior officers. And he was good at his job, another reason the admiral found it relatively easy to overlook the Englishman's somewhat arrogant demeanor.

Zacharias puffed out a cloud of cherry-bourbon tobacco smoke and rapped his knuckles on the papers covering his desk. "Sometimes this job requires me to pay attention to the most ludicrous things," he said. "Do you know what this is?"

"I have no idea, sir," Fetherstone-Pugh replied in his sere tone.

"This is a personal letter to Admiral King requesting that the official terminology designating my current rank and position be changed for reasons pertaining to morale. As you are no doubt aware, some of the more bored personnel around here have taken to referring to me privately—using a creative pronunciation of the acronym CIC/CDOG—as 'Sick Sea Dog.'" Zacharias shook his head. "Not exactly the way I'd like to be remembered in military history books down through the ages."

"I would think not, sir."

"But of course, the more immediate concern is that soldiers don't need a built-in reason to disrespect their commanding officer. It's a morale killer. So I want it changed." Zacharias smiled. "It's not as if Admiral King doesn't have other things on his mind, but the hell with it."

"I see your point, sir," Fetherstone-Pugh said. He leaned forward. "Admiral, you asked me to inform you if I ever found anything unusual occurring within the Gulf Coast Defense Grid."

"That's right," Zacharias replied. "It'd make us all look a bit less like we're sleepwalking through the war down here if we could get a little action in this sector. Hell, it wasn't our fault that Dönitz pulled his U-boats out of the Gulf and sent them off to the North Atlantic. But we have to keep watch, just in case, so here we sit."

"Quite, sir," Fetherstone-Pugh said through his long nose. "It was with that in mind that I wanted to stop by your office for a few minutes. I think I may be on to something. In fact, I'm almost certain."

"How so? You find a sub?"

"I couldn't say that definitively at this point, sir," Fetherstone-Pugh continued, "but I've isolated an unusual Morse transmission that I simply can't get out of my head. You see, even though it's in English and unencrypted, I'm sure I recognize the fist."

Zacharias puffed out a cherry-cognac cumulus. "Fist?"

"Yes, sir. Let me explain." The Royal Navy officer

crossed his legs. "All Morse key operators of long experience develop their own personal sending style. The way they group the dots and dashes of code, the speed at which they key, the way they phrase messages—all these things combine to give them their own identifiable accent, or fist. A person experienced at reading Morse code can recognize a particular sender within the first few seconds of transmission."

"Mm. Interesting," Zacharias mused. "Could prove handy."

"Yes, sir, well, it *did* prove handy, as you put it, when I was attached to the Royal Navy's Operational Intelligence Center in England back in 'forty-one. One of my duties was to coordinate the smooth flow of deciphered intercepts from our Huff-Duff listening stations to the main Submarine Tracking Room. I spent a lot of time actually sitting in and listening to the transmissions.

"The intercept technicians—mostly Wrens—had gotten to know many of the individual German Morse senders by their keying style. The messages were all encrypted in Enigma cipher, of course, so they couldn't tell what the content was, but they knew instantly who was doing the sending. 'Oh, that's Fritzie!' they'd say, or 'There's Munchen—he's in a hurry today!' Or 'Oktoberfest', or 'Lederhosen,' or any one of a dozen other nicknames. I was fascinated by this, and listened in enough to become familiar with the styles of a number of U-boat radiomen. They stuck in my memory."

"Impressive," Zacharias said. "Could be some intelligence applications, there."

Fetherstone-Pugh nodded. "In Britain we used this specific knowledge on at least one occasion. Early one month we had detected a large sortie of U-boats from bases in Brest, Lorient, and Saint-Nazaire heading out into the Atlantic in a wolf pack. They dispersed, of course, and maintained virtual radio silence until they were far from land, which made the individual boats difficult to track. For the next two weeks, predictably, Allied shipping sustained heavy losses along the North Atlantic convoy routes. Dönitz's wolf pack of U-boats was just prowling the sea-lanes in midocean, waiting for the next flotilla of victims to come along so they could slip in close at night and wreak havoc.

"But we knew the U-boats had operational limits, so we expected to see them coming in to base for repairs and refueling after fourteen days or so. But they didn't. Instead, our tracking showed them converging on an area of ocean just southwest of Iceland. At the same time, aerial reconnaissance confirmed that a large *Milchkuh* refueling U-boat had departed the Nazi base at Bordeaux, and was heading northward up the Channel in the company of two other conventional U-boats. As far as we could tell by triangulating their infrequent Morse transmissions, they were all making way toward Iceland."

Zacharias laughed. "Don't tell me. Once they were somewhere north of the Faeroe Islands, they suddenly split up and headed in three different directions. And the wolf pack was nowhere to be found. Am I right?"

"Exactly right, sir," Fetherstone-Pugh confirmed. "And intermittently, each boat in the *Milchkuh* group, as it headed away from the other two, was transmitting a partly encrypted message containing the words *Milchkuh* and *rendezvous.*"

"Decoy tactic," Zacharias said. "You don't know which boat of the three is the genuine resupply sub, so you don't know where to send the patrol bombers and destroyers to intercept the wolf pack—or, at the very least, the vessel that carries the juice they need to stay offshore and on the hunt."

"Correct," the Englishman said, "and it would have had us chasing all over the North Atlantic after shadows, and us without enough long-range planes as it was—except that the Germans hadn't counted on Mrs. Veronica Cowperthwaite."

"*Who?*" exclaimed the admiral.

"Mrs. Veronica Cowperthwaite. A Wren who was our best radio technician. Widow of an RAF pilot whose Spitfire was shot down during the Battle of Britain. She'd memorized the fist of the real *Milchkuh* U-boat's radio operator. Because of her, we always knew which of the three boats was the actual resupply vessel for the wolf pack."

"What happened?"

"We triangulated the *Milchkuh* when it went into a holding position to the southeast of Iceland, waited until we intercepted a cluster of other signals nearby, and then dispatched a squadron of patrol bombers to that general location. They caught the *Milchkuh* and four other U-boats on the surface while they were refueling, and sank them all. The remaining members of that particular wolf pack were detected returning to their bases in France immediately afterward, nearly out of fuel. There was no U-boat activity along the convoy routes for a full week after the *Milchkuh* was sunk. No fuel, no fresh torpedoes—no means of staying on the hunt. All thanks to Veronica Cowperthwaite and her sharp ear for a radio operator's identifying *fist*."

Zacharias leaned forward and tapped the inverted bowl of his spent pipe into a large black ashtray. "I hope that woman was officially commended for outstanding performance of duty," he remarked. "Superb."

Fetherstone-Pugh's face was expressionless. "Actually, sir, she was killed the following week in a Stuka attack on the radio receiving station."

There was a pause as Zacharias refilled his pipe bowl, looking down. Tamping it to his satisfaction, he lit it with a wooden match and regarded Fetherstone-Pugh again. "I'm sorry to hear that," he said. There was another pause as he drew on the briar and got it going. "All right, Trevor, you've convinced me of the value of recognizing 'fist,' as you call it. Where do you want to go with this?"

"The transmission I'm concerned about came in one last time a few hours ago," the Royal Navy officer said, "and then stopped. I heard it only once, and the other stations weren't attentive enough to get a bearing on it so we could triangulate. What I'd like to do is formulate a response, send it out on the same bandwidth, and see if it generates a recognizable reply. I'll make sure the other stations are listening for it specifically, and if anything comes through, we'll be able to take multiple bearings and get a point of origin. I need your permission, however, to send out a false message as bait."

Zacharias chewed his pipe stem. "What do you really think you're going to find? You don't seem at all certain that this message fragment you're talking about indicates a U-boat in the area."

"I'm not, sir," Fetherstone-Pugh said. "For one thing, as I said, I can't see why a U-boat would transmit an unencrypted message in English. I might end up getting a triangulation on an officer's stag party in Houma or Morgan City. But I just can't shake the feeling that there's something more to this than seems apparent."

"You've been listening to a lot of local transmissions over the past year and a half," Zacharias said. "Are you sure you aren't just recognizing the fist of one of our own Morse operators? Maybe someone from one of the navy yards?"

"I don't think I am, sir. Any memories I have of individual sending styles come exclusively from my experiences tracking U-boats in the Channel and North Sea."

The admiral drew on his pipe. "All right. Go ahead and do it." Fetherstone-Pugh smiled and got to his feet. "And Trevor"—the Royal Navy officer paused, lifting a questioning eyebrow—"you haven't been having too much trouble with Blodgett lately, have you?"

Fetherstone-Pugh smiled as he set his cap back on his head. "None at all, sir."

Zacharias nodded. "Very well. Let me know if you do."

"I will, sir," Fetherstone-Pugh said, saluted, and left the room.

The trapper Claude had spent the day poling through the deep swamp in his leaky pirogue, checking his snares and traplines. Pickings had been slim: the twenty-four traps he'd set had yielded one juvenile muskrat and one nutria—or more precisely, the head of one nutria. The animal's body had been ripped away by an alligator that had apparently been attracted to its thrashing as it attempted to escape.

The day hadn't been a complete loss, however. On the return trip, just before dusk, he'd spotted a female raccoon crossing a deadfall tree trunk, accompanied by two half-grown kits. Taking up his light .22-caliber rifle, he'd knocked her off the tree with a head shot. The kits had milled back and forth above their mother's floating body, too confused to flee, and it had been easy to ghost forward in the pirogue and pick them off as well.

Now Claude was standing on the side porch of his shanty, busily skinning his coons. The two young ones were especially tender. It was near suppertime, and he had a taste for raccoon stew. He gutted and ripped the hides off the two kits, set them aside in two bloody lumps, and turned to lift the large female onto the cutting plank.

"*Bonsoir*, Claude!" Estelle cackled.

The apish trapper nearly fell over backward. The old woman had appeared at the corner of the dilapidated shanty without a sound. There was a thump as the dropped raccoon carcass hit the wooden porch.

"Heh heh heh." Estelle drew her shawl around her, its dangling bones making a light clattering sound. "Got you a good supper here, boy. Fresh coon!" She grinned in the light of the rising moon, showing snaggled teeth. "Young, too, *n'est-ce pas*?"

Gripping the porch railing, his dull eyes wide with fear, Claude could only nod. He cringed slightly as Estelle stepped closer, her crooked grin widening.

"*Voulez-vous voir quelque magie noire?*" she asked, putting the hand that wasn't on her cane behind her back. "Eh?"

Claude began to shake. "*Non, non!* Don't show me nothin', *sorcière! Laissez-moi tranquille!* Let me alone!"

Estelle reared back in mock astonishment. "You sure? Not even a little magic?" The trapper shook his head vigorously. "All right, then. If you're sure."

She prodded the dead raccoon with the end of her cane. "You know, Claude, my boy, I'm sure you'd enjoy to have me stay on for supper, but I just ain't got the time." She smiled at him, her black garnet eyes glinting. "Maybe another night, eh?"

Claude nodded.

"Heh heh heh. Well, I just thought I'd look in on you this evenin', seein' as Jolene ain't around to keep me company no more. Guess she done took up with someone on that big black war boat over yonder." Estelle pointed with her cane across the misty pond at the U-113's dark silhouette. "Seen her walkin' on top of it today, then goin' inside, too." She showed Claude her teeth again. "Guess she likin' it in there, heh heh."

The animal-bone charms on her shawl rattled as she turned and shuffled slowly around the corner of the shack. "*Bonne nuit*, boy. Don't have no bad dreams, now."

Still clutching the handrail, his mouth slack, Claude watched as she disappeared, his slow-motion brain racing.

Chapter
Twenty-one

Blinded by the cloud of mud that enveloped him, Wolfe fought his way to a semivertical position, still clutching the phosphorus torch, and regained his feet. When he stood up, his view ports rose out of the murk into clear, black water. He looked around wildly, squinting as the brilliant incandescence of the torch invaded the helmet and hurt his eyes.

The five-foot-wide Southern stingray that had exploded from the muck under his boots made a rapid, graceful pass through the torchlight, winglike pectoral fins flapping, and departed into the black void, trailing its long whip of a tail. Wolfe bent forward, put his hands on his knees, and stayed like that for a full thirty seconds, willing his ragged, shallow breathing to slow down.

When at last he straightened up, he noticed that the phosphorus torch had consumed itself to within a half inch of the burnout mark. Unclipping a second torch from his weight belt, he touched its head to the fizzling stub of the first, fired it off, and set out once more to complete his bottom sweep.

If I ever get home to the Black Forest, I swear to God I'm never leaving again. . . .

He moved along the bottom through relatively clear water, the torch casting a pool of cold, flickering light about eight feet ahead and around. Beyond the little cocoon of illumination, nothing but empty, endless blackness. Mud. More mud. A small, lizard-like fish propped up on spiny pectoral fins, gaping upward at the noisy, bubbling intruder. Still more mud. And then . . .

A steel hatch cover with a torn hinge, half buried in the bottom. The foredeck escape hatch of a Type VII U-boat. Wolfe lifted the torch high, peering ahead into the gloom.

The great curving side of a U-boat saddle tank rose up in front of him. At the right-hand limit of visibility, Wolfe could make out a huge vertical fracture in the steel plate, as if the tank had been split by a giant ax. A school of small jacks cruised into the light, silver sides flashing, black eyes staring, and quickly vanished into the darkness.

The big torpedoman stood there on the bottom of the midnight ocean for a long moment, unmoving, the air bubbling quietly out of his helmet. The pale gleam of the torch flickered over the immense, shattered side of the U-115—there was no doubt in Wolfe's mind that this was indeed Rolf Schecter's boat—creating the impression of a great sunken cathedral bathed in moonlight and shadow.

A sudden chill gripped him as his mind flashed on a vivid memory of the U-115 berthed beside the U-113 in Lorient, tonnage pennants proclaiming multiple kills of Allied shipping waving proudly from the periscopes of both vessels, their crews celebrating on deck, laughing and passing around bottles of wine while a military band played on the dock nearby. . . .

And now, here, far from the laughter, brass bands, and glory, the dead U-boat lay in cold mud and darkness, an iron coffin for Captain Rolf Schecter and his fifty-one men.

Wolfe shook his head, refocusing on the task at hand. Pulling twice on the safety line for more slack, venting some air out of his suit to increase his negative buoyancy, he dug in with his weighted boots and moved off to the right, following the U-115's hull. Tendrils of sediment drifted through his field of vision on the slight current as he struggled along, legs pumping.

He'd chosen the correct direction. Within sixty feet,

he'd passed the aft end of the saddle tank and found himself standing directly beneath the U-boat's twin propellers. The main pressure hull had been fractured just forward of the engine room, and this devastating damage had, fortuitously, resulted in the U-115's stern twisting upward as she'd come to rest on the bottom. Both her screws, apparently undamaged, were suspended fully eight feet above the mud. Wolfe reached up with a gloved hand and touched the end of one bronze blade that extended down to eye level. Not a scratch on it.

He looked back along the torn, ruined pressure hull. The screws appeared to be the *only* thing on the boat that hadn't been hit by enemy fire. The damage inflicted on the U-115 had been catastrophic. Wolfe swallowed unconsciously. In a boat battered by depth charges or bombs, and flooding at a steady but gradual rate, there was time to muster the men in their Dräger escape gear and evacuate them through the hatches. But in a U-boat literally cracked open like a walnut, no one had a chance. The massive force of the initial influx of water almost always killed the entire crew outright. It was a miracle that *Puster* Hufnagel had been able to get out any message at all in the final seconds.

Wolfe inspected the shafts. From the screws to the through-hull glands they looked fine. Inside, things could be different. He backtracked fifteen feet along the hull to the three-foot-wide vertical fracture just forward of the engine room.

The torn edges of the gaping split were sharp. Wolfe signaled for more rope and hose slack, pulled down an extra twenty feet, and located a relatively smooth section of the fracture. Lashing the safety line and the air hose across it with a short length of cord, he picked up his slack, looped it over his free arm, and squeezed gingerly through the opening.

The slivered edges of the torn metal plucked at his dive suit as he passed into the interior of the U-boat, but did not rip it open. His helmet clunked against something overhead. Stooping over to avoid hitting it again, he began to move carefully toward the stern through a jumble of equipment, cables, twisted steel, and mud.

The exhaust bubbles from his helmet and the gases

produced by the torch streamed upward and along the overhead plating, disturbing several small snapper that had taken up residence there. They swam in an inverted position, orienting to the nearest flat surface. Just to Wolfe's left, a large conger eel slipped around a crumpled circuit box and disappeared, kicking up a little puff of sediment.

The torch was burning low. He plucked another from his belt and lit it, dropping the stub of the first into the mud. Moving astern another half-dozen steps, he came up against a large metallic block that he recognized instantly as the forward end of a MAN engine. Beside it was a second, identical diesel. And attached to the rear of these would be the two propeller shafts, extending sternward past the twin electric motors to which they were clutched when submerged for silent running.

Wolfe took a deep breath, checked his hose and rope slack, and began to pull himself hand over hand along the side of the nearer engine.

"He been down awhile," Lucius mused, flexing his fingers on Wolfe's air hose. "'Bout time to call him back, or he takin' a chance on gettin' bent."

Stuermer glanced at his watch. "An hour." He looked over at Bock. "How deep, again? Twenty meters?"

"Twenty-two," Bock said. "Lucius is right. We're pushing it. He's certainly found Schecter's boat, or he would have continued to sweep."

The black man nodded. "Better'n seventy feet. Long enough, and best we hang him under the boat for five minutes or so—let him breathe out all that bad air."

"Nitrogen," Bock commented. "Nitrogen builds up in your tissues."

"Whatever," Lucius said.

Suddenly Jolene, who'd been leaning on the rail, straightened up and pointed. "Look!"

The small inflatable buoy that Wolfe had been carrying on his harness had popped to the surface some forty feet from the port side.

"He's marked it," Stuermer said. "He must be coming back."

As if in confirmation, Bock felt three sharp pulls on the safety rope. Bracing his knees against the bulwark, he began to take in slack. Beside him, Lucius followed suit on the air hose.

When the rope and the hose were hanging vertically, Bock took a strain and waited for Wolfe, seventy feet below, to adjust his buoyancy. As the dive suit filled with air and the dead weight eased, Bock began to recover him slowly to the surface.

Exhaust bubbles foamed on the black water beneath the rail as Wolfe rose steadily. Lucius was counting hash marks on the air hose, watching his depth. As the ten-foot mark came into his hand, he reached over and tapped Bock on the shoulder. "Stop him there," he said.

Bock took a couple of wraps around a large iron cleat and peered over the side. Through the hissing bubbles he could vaguely see the light-colored dive suit suspended in the dark water a few feet down.

"Five minutes be good," Lucius repeated, looking off into the night.

Bock nodded. He started to say something to the mate, but then changed his mind. Things were different now.

"Five minutes," he said.

Jolene moved up beside him. "Your ear hurtin' you pretty bad?" she asked.

Bock looked at her, and as he did some of the deep creases in his brow softened. "I notice it," he said, managing a half smile.

She dropped her eyes and leaned closer until her shoulder was resting lightly against his arm. "I hope you feel better real soon."

Bock felt no inclination to move away, and waited until she'd raised her dark eyes to his once more before he answered. "Thank you," he said.

Behind them, leaning against the mast, Stuermer watched silently. Interesting development. But Bock was too professional to allow himself to be seriously distracted from the task at hand. There wouldn't be a problem.

Lucius he was keeping an eye on. The big Negro mate

had agreed to help them, but a man could change his mind very quickly given the appropriate opportunity. Stuermer reached into his jacket pocket and felt the reassuring bulk of the Walther under his hand.

Another couple of minutes passed, and then Lucius took in a small amount of hose slack. "Okay," he said, "let's pick him up."

Throwing the wraps off the cleat, Bock slowly retrieved the safety rope until Wolfe's dive helmet broke through the foaming surface at the foot of the ladder. The big torpedoman climbed the rungs awkwardly, shedding water, got a leg over the rail, and gained the deck with a heavy *clump-clump* of weighted boots. A hand on each shoulder, Bock and Lucius walked him over to the rope chest and sat him down on the lid.

With a quick twist, Lucius loosened the helmet and unscrewed it from the chest plate threads. As he lifted it off, Wolfe reached up immediately and scratched the bridge of his nose.

"Damned tin hat!" he panted, breathing in great drafts of fresh air. "My nose has been itching for the past hour!"

"With a nose that size, it must have been excruciating," Bock said. Wolfe gave him a withering look. "Are you all right? No aches or pains?"

The torpedoman moved first one, then the other arm through a circular motion. "Not so far." He tucked his chin in as Lucius lifted off the chest plate.

Stuermer stepped warily around the big mate and put one of Bock's Turkish cigarettes to his lips. "So, Lothar, what's the situation down there? You found Schecter's boat, obviously."

Wolfe nodded. "Yes, Captain. She's down there, pretty badly broken up. The stern section has been cracked off and twisted upward."

"Is that good or bad for us?"

"Good, as it turns out." Wolfe coughed and wiped his forehead with the towel Jolene passed him. "Instead of being buried in the mud, the screws are both suspended above the bottom. It's easy to get into the interior through the big crack just forward of the engine room.

I followed both shafts aft from the MAN diesels, past the electric motors, and right to the through-hull glands. I didn't see any damage. Except for a little rust and mud, they look brand-new."

Stuermer shook his head slightly and blew out a stream of smoke. "Unbelievable luck. No distortions in either shaft, you're sure? They're not bent?"

"No, sir."

"The screws? Any damage?"

"None that I could see, sir," Wolfe said. He passed the towel over his eyes. "It was the pressure hull and superstructure that took the beating. The whole boat must have flooded in seconds. Some equipment has been torn up and thrown around, of course, but the heavy machinery—diesels, electric motors, clutches, mountings, and shafts—is all intact."

"What about removal?" Bock interjected. "Can we drop the shafts from the engines? And can we rig lifting lines from the *Shiloh* to pull them out of the through-hull glands?"

"Dropping the shafts will be no problem," Wolfe responded. "A pair of large wrenches and a strong back, and the couplings can be broken in no time. All the bolts are exposed and undamaged. As far as sliding them out of the hull, I think we may be able to rig a block off the rudder posts to get the angle of pull we need. We could support the screw with one line while we back the shaft out with the other."

He smiled wearily up at Stuermer and Bock, his tough face seamed with strain and fatigue. The *Kapitänleutnant* considered for a moment, weighing what he'd just been told, then stepped forward.

"Good job, Lothar," he said, putting a hand on Wolfe's shoulder. He drew on his cigarette and left the hand there for an extra second. "Good job."

Chapter
Twenty-two

Papa Luc scowled up at Claude from beneath his bushy eyebrows. "You sure about this?" His deep voice echoed through the interior of the little shanty church, and he set down the glass of whiskey he'd been drinking—*bang*—on the wooden altar. "*Pas d'erreur?*"

"*Non, c'est vrai, Papa Luc!*" Claude insisted eagerly. "Jolene, she up on *les Allemands*' boat. I seen her myself!"

The whiskey glass jumped as Papa Luc's fist hit the top of the altar, the loud crash reverberating off the walls. Bloodshot eyes ablaze, he lurched out of the chair in which he'd been sitting and began to stalk back and forth, muttering angrily: "The little tramp thanks me like this! I should have laid a heavier hand on her before she came of age, but I was indulgent. I spared the rod and spoiled the child." He swept the whiskey glass off the altar and drained it in one angry gulp. "Now she thinks she can turn her back on me an' take up with these . . . *outsiders*."

"She gone and done it," Claude insisted. "She on that boat."

Papa Luc stopped pacing and stared at him.

"Not for long," he said. "Not for long. Go an' get Alain, Serge, and Jacques. I'm holdin' a meetin' here in one hour."

Claude grinned. "We gonna go get her, Papa Luc?"

The tall Cajun wheeled and swung at him with a hard, bony hand. The blow glanced off the trapper's temple and he cowered back. "Of course we're going to go get her, *imbécile*!" he shouted. "But not like you think! Now go an' do as I told you, *tabernac*!"

The pink-and-silver light of dawn was driving back the darkness on the eastern horizon as Stuermer finished his decompression stop beneath the *Shiloh*'s hull and ascended to the foot of the boarding ladder. Two of the boat's net booms had been angled over the port side at forty-five degrees, three heavy manila lines trailing into the water from suspended blocks. The shipboard ends of the lifting lines had been passed through fairleads that led to the twin drums of the back deck's main winch. The *Kapitänleutnant* had been working feverishly both inside and outside the sunken U-115 for nearly two hours. Even so, dangerously pressing known safe diving limits, he'd been reluctant to come up.

His boots thumped onto the deck, water sluicing from his dive suit, and he gripped Lucius and Bock for balance as the *Shiloh* heaved gently on the slight swell. Even through the fogged glass of the helmet's main view port, the young exec could see the grim impatience on Stuermer's lean face.

They sat him down, and the U-boat commander helped them twist the helmet free of the chest plate. He ducked his head out of the heavy sphere, passed it off to Lucius, and ran a hand back through his damp hair.

"*Verdammt*! If you'd left me down there for another five minutes, we'd have had one of the shafts pulled!" He slapped the wet knee of his dive suit in a rare display of frustration. It was a true indication of the stress he was under, Bock thought. Stuermer was renowned throughout the *Ubootwaffe* for his cool, collected demeanor.

"You were down far too long is it was, sir," Bock replied. He lit a Turkish cigarette and held it out. "Pardon me for speaking directly, but you'll be no use to us crumpled up on the deck in a heap with the bends."

"*Ach*!" Stuermer managed a thin smile as he took the

cigarette. "I should have worked faster. I wasted too much time getting into position before I uncoupled the second shaft." He drew in a lungful of smoke. "Well, anyway, they're both free, and the port shaft is rigged and ready to slide out."

"But we need to put someone back down to oversee the extraction," Bock said. He paused. "I could give it another try, sir, even with this popped eardrum."

Stuermer shook his head, exhaling smoke. "No, Erich. Your equilibrium will be ruined as soon as you start clearing your ears on descent. You'll be incapacitated and we'll be wasting time." He looked over at Wolfe. "We'll have to wait until you've had enough time on the surface to make a second dive, Lothar."

Wolfe shrugged. "I could try now, Captain. I feel fine."

"No," Bock said. "You'll get bent. It's too soon."

Stuermer lowered his head and rubbed his eyes. *"Verdammt!"* he muttered again. "So much lost time."

Lucius leaned back against the port rail and crossed his massive black arms. "How 'bout if I go?"

The three Germans looked at him in surprise.

"You'd be willing?" Stuermer ventured.

"Uh-huh."

Bock rubbed his chin. "Why?"

"Same reason I been helpin' you rig lines and tend the diver," Lucius said with a shrug. "The quicker you get what you want, the quicker the *Shiloh* gets in, and the sooner I get Mike to a doctor. Simple."

"Do you really think he can find his way around the engine room of a wrecked U-boat?" Wolfe asked Stuermer quietly. "It's hard enough for us, and we've been living on them for years."

Stuermer looked the big mate up and down. "I don't see why not," he mused. "Everything is rigged. All he has to do is signal us to winch the first shaft out, set it on the bottom, attach the third lifting rope to it, then transfer the first two lines to the second shaft and repeat."

"And we just pick them up off the bottom," Bock said. "By then, Lothar would be able to dive again if

Lucius doesn't have time to finish the job." He glanced
at Stuermer. "No more lost time, sir."

The *Kapitänleutnant* hesitated, then made his decision:
"All right, Lucius. If you're willing, you dive next. We'll
work out some line pull signals for handling the winch
up here. You know what we need to do."

The big mate nodded. "Just one thing: if he feels up
to it, I want Mike untied and out here on deck, su-
pervisin' my dive."

Stuermer's eyes narrowed. "Captain Holt is no longer
in charge here."

"He is if *I'm* divin'," Lucius stated.

"Why do you need Holt?" Bock asked. "He's hurt,
and we can take care of the compressor and lines."

Lucius' ebony face was impassive. "Because I trust
him."

For what seemed like a very long time to Jolene,
watching quietly from her seat on a roll of fishing net,
the four men stood in silence, at an apparent impasse.

It was Stuermer who finally spoke: "All right. Lothar,
Erich, go untie Captain Holt and tell him that his presence is required on the back deck, if he's able."

Jolene finished adjusting the fresh bandage on Holt's
head as he leaned against the gunwale, eyeballing
Stuermer. In front of him, Lucius stood sealed inside the
dive helmet and suit, a phosphorus torch in his right
hand, his air hose and safety line in the other. An extra
cord for signaling the topside winch operator trailed
from his weight belt. Wolfe steadied him as he prepared
to mount the four stairs to the port rail.

"Sun's up, but it's still gonna be dark in that murk
down there," Holt shouted through the view port glass.
"Lemme light you up."

He pulled away from Jolene and flicked his Zippo
under the end of the torch. It fired off with a white-hot
flash, spitting bits of smoking phosphorus. Shielding his
eyes, he clapped Lucius on the shoulder and gave him
the thumbs-up.

The big mate clumped up the wooden stairs in his
lead boots, paused at the rail to grasp his vent valve,

and stepped off. He hit the water beside the *Shiloh* with a loud splash and disappeared beneath a roiling patch of bubbles. On either side of the stairs, Bock and Wolfe fed air hose and safety line swiftly after him, trying to keep up with his rapid descent. The thin signaling cord whipped over the rail unattended.

"He's dropping pretty fast," Bock panted, literally tossing over loops of air hose.

"Lucius don't fool around," Holt growled, his ever-present Lucky Strike bobbing between his lips. "He gets on the bottom an' gets the job done." He wobbled slightly, his face pale and gleaming with a thin sheen of sweat.

"Why don't you sit down," Bock suggested. "Before you fall down."

Holt's expression twisted. "Don't worry about me, Kraut," he snarled. "I'm a long way from done. You might find that out yet."

Stuermer, leaning on the port rail near Wolfe, slipped a hand into his pocket and onto the butt of the Walther. By now it had become clear to him that Holt was a damaged human being, both physically and mentally. It made him unpredictable and dangerous, more so because his handicap did little to slow him down. During the chase through the wheelhouse, he'd moved with the speed and agility of a panther, and Stuermer wasn't at all sure that a minor annoyance like a bullet wound in the head would make him any less likely to bolt for a hidden weapon again.

Seventy feet beneath the *Shiloh*, Lucius began to follow the deep footprints Wolfe and Stuermer had left in the mud as they'd moved to and from the wrecked U-boat. They led him directly to the stern, where the two bronze propellers hung suspended above the bottom as if on display. Lucius took a minute to run his eyes over the huge, black, broken hull of the U-115, and moved forward to inspect Stuermer's rigging.

A vertical wall of large red snapper was hanging just in front of the screws. It parted like a curtain as Lucius and his rising column of exhaust bubbles approached, the two living halves retreating to opposite sides of the

wreck. There was now enough ambient light to see fifteen or twenty feet through the murky green water without the torch. Lucius jammed it into a tear in one of the
damaged stern planes, where it still cast some of its pale
white glow onto the screws, and maneuvered himself up
underneath the port through-hull gland.

He saw at once what Stuermer had done: one of the
lines hanging down from the *Shiloh*'s net booms had
been hitched around the hub of the port screw and secured with a slipknot. The second line had been pulled
down and through a shackle attached to a chain plate
eye at the very stern of the U-boat, some ten feet back
from the screw, and then led forward, parallel to the
shaft. Its running end had been timber-hitched around
the shaft with multiple wraps just abaft the through-hull
gland. The third lifting line had been temporarily hitched
to a torn section of steel plate, out of the way.

Inside the dive helmet, Lucius nodded appreciatively
at the ropework. With the weight of the propeller supported by the first line, tightening up on the second
should pull the shaft straight back and out of the gland,
providing the timber hitch didn't slip. Stuermer knew
his business, he had to admit. He couldn't have done it
better himself.

Stepping out from under the shaft and moving to a
safe vantage point about six feet to the side, Lucius felt
for the thin winch-signaling cord at his waist. Pulling the
slack out of it, he immediately gave a series of quick
tugs to confirm the communication, and received a like
response.

The line supporting the propeller had been designated
Number One, and the line hitched to the shaft, Number
Two. Lucius gave two fast tugs—"Number Two"—fol-
lowed by a single tug—"Pull"—and watched closely.

On the deck above, Holt felt the signal come through
the cord in his right hand and pointed the stump of his
left at Wolfe, who was manning the winch. There was a
clanking noise as the big German engaged the clutch
and began to tail the rope off the rotating drum. The
line went taut, yanking hard on the snatch blocks it
passed through and bending the end of the net boom

down with a loud creak. The *Shiloh* took on a soft list to port.

For a moment she stayed there. Then a long, gentle swell moved beneath her, lifted her . . . and with an abrupt lurch and clattering of rigging, the great strain on the Number Two line suddenly lessened. *Shiloh* rocked back onto an even keel, net booms swaying and blocks banging, the two loaded lifting ropes hissing back and forth in the salt water like vertical violin strings.

On the bottom, Lucius had been watching the Number Two line go tight along the shaft. The timber hitch had slipped only very slightly, then held. Nothing had happened for a few seconds. Then, just as he'd decided that something was hung up and the line would break before anything gave, the shaft, with a metallic screech, had shot backward out of the stern gland like a bolt from a crossbow.

Startled, and with an experienced working diver's hyper-awareness of his own vulnerability, Lucius had instinctively lunged away from the fast-moving mass of heavy steel and bronze, falling on his side in the mud. He stayed low for a few seconds, then struggled up onto one elbow and looked back toward the U-boat.

The propeller and the shaft were suspended diagonally from the Number One line, the coupling end of the shaft down in the mud. The whole assembly swayed back and forth slightly on the supporting rope, looking like a giant steel-stemmed, bronze-petaled flower. It had come to rest more than ten feet back from the stern, clear for a lift to the surface.

Lucius scrambled to his feet and tugged once, then three times more on the signal cord—"Number One, slack off." On the deck above, Bock let the line he'd been tailing slip over the winch drum. The propeller and the shaft descended slowly to the bottom. Kicking up billows of mud behind him, Lucius bounded forward to de-rig the two ropes.

In five minutes, he'd duplicated Stuermer's salvage rigging on the second shaft, and attached the third lifting rope to the first propeller-shaft assembly. Clearance was a little tighter on the starboard side, but Lucius was satisfied with the angle of pull. The signal cord danced in his hand as he had the slack taken out of the lines and the load properly supported. Then, with the same two-one tugs, he signaled Wolfe to take a strain on the shaft extraction rope.

The timber hitch stretched and bound down. The Number Two line began to vibrate, miniscule bubbles like little tendrils of steam rising from it all along its length as the fibers compressed under the load. Then, with a high-pitched scraping sound, the shaft slid backward out of the gland.

And stopped with a loud *CLANG* after moving four feet. The entire up-canted stern of the U-115 slowly rotated twenty degrees, accompanied by the fingernail-on-slate sound of tearing metal. The massive vertical fracture facing Lucius opened another foot. Yanking the cord frantically, he signaled for all lifting to stop.

The favorable rotation of the broken-off stern section had resulted in the propeller now resting even higher above the ocean bottom, with greatly improved clearance. Lucius watched closely as everything seemed to stabilize once more. By appearances, it should now be even easier to pull the shaft and the screw clear.

He signaled for a strain to be taken on the Number Two line again. Once more, the thick manila rope tightened, trembled, and emitted its tiny bubble tendrils. The shaft did not budge. Lucius let the rope tighten almost to the breaking point, then signaled "Stop."

The Number Two line vibrated rhythmically as the motion of the *Shiloh*, listing to port and riding the gentle swell, increased and decreased the tremendous load. Lucius frowned. Something was hung up on the inside. *Shit*. He'd known that the first assembly had come free too easily.

Only one thing to do: climb inside and see if he could knock loose whatever was binding the shaft. Oh, and don't get caught in there and killed. That was the other thing.

Hovering red snapper scattered as Lucius moved toward the hull fracture. It was a full four feet wide now, easy to get through. Mindful of the position of his air hose against the sharp edges, he stepped cautiously into the U-boat's interior.

There was sufficient ambient light filtering in through the widened crack to dimly illuminate the engine room. The same resident conger eel that Wolfe had seen was spooked by Lucius' exhaust bubbles and undulated rapidly across the tops of the MAN diesels, a fat six-foot ribbon of gray-and-black-banded muscle. It disappeared into a tangle of ruined conduit.

Lucius gingerly worked his way toward the extreme stern, pausing to pick up a heavy steel mallet with a three-foot handle that had fallen into the bilge. He smiled to himself. When all else fails—hit it with a hammer. Sometimes it was that easy.

Straining his eyes in the dim light, he picked out the coupling end of the starboard shaft. It was a mere eighteen inches from the through-hull gland. Stooping over in the cramped space, he positioned himself beside it and checked for obstructions. There were none. He felt around the entire circumference of the shaft. Nothing.

He sat back on his haunches for a moment, bubbling exhaust and looking at it. The shaft had to be binding on the inside of the through-hull gland; nothing else was holding it. In that case, the answer was to hammer it on through. Lucius got to his feet, steadied himself, and swung at the end of the shaft with the mallet.

Clunk. It moved an inch.

Lucius swung again.

Clunk. Another inch. A low, grinding moan echoed through the stern's interior. Lucius paused, listening, and licked his lips. The sound stopped, and he raised the mallet once more.

Clunk-Thunnggg!

The shaft snapped forward and disappeared through the gland. As it did, there was a high-pitched screeching of metal on metal and the entire broken-off stern rotated 180 degrees. Lucius was thrown backward as the flooded interior became filled with metallic junk—tools, conduit, boxes, broken steel—shifting to the opposite side of the engine-room space.

The MAN diesels moved overhead as the stern inverted. Then, with a cracking sound, one of them broke loose from its mounts. The massive engine block fell through the water and landed directly on Lucius, lying on his back thrashing in a mesh of cable.

There was a crunching sound as the two tons of cast iron pinned his head to the hull plates. The glass view ports of the dive helmet all ruptured simultaneously, and the top half of the brass shell crumpled like a tin can, tearing completely through in several places. The violent distortion halted a mere quarter inch short of crushing Lucius' skull like an egg.

On his back, semi-inverted across a pile of sharp metallic junk with his arms, legs, and body unencumbered, Lucius kicked wildly to free his trapped head. Air was still hissing into the ruined helmet, but it was flooding rapidly, the salt water rising over his forehead and eyes, working up the bridge of his nose. . . .

Fumbling with his right hand, he found the vent valve and shut it off. Immediately, the air pressure inside the helmet increased. Brine rose toward his nostrils, lapped at his mouth. . . .

And then the air and water pressure equalized. The water level stopped rising halfway up the bridge of his nose, his forehead and eyes remaining submerged, his nose and mouth just barely clear to gasp in air.

With all the great strength in his body, he twisted, turned, and wrenched himself back and forth, to no avail. The huge engine block had him, like a brick on top of an ant. He coughed and spat, choking on the salt water that sloshed into his mouth as he struggled.

The deep, grinding screech of metal moving on metal echoed ominously through the stern again. . . .

On the surface, the *Shiloh* rocked back on an even keel as the starboard shaft popped free, her spars and rigging jangling. Holt, caught up in the moment despite the circumstances, punched his stump into his open hand like a fist.

"Hot *damn!*" he exclaimed, watching the twin lifting

lines settle into a free-hanging position. "That's it! She's
come loose!" He glanced at Stuermer, standing beside
him, and almost grinned before he caught himself.
Stuermer nodded. Holt threw him an angry scowl instead, snatched the Lucky Strike from the corner of his
mouth, and turned to Wolfe and Bock at the winch
drums.

"Come on up on both them lines!" he shouted. "All
the way! Stop just as you see the load break the surface,
and we'll swing it around and set it on deck!"

"Perhaps we should recover Lucius to the surface,
Captain," Stuermer said quietly. "To avoid having to lift
all that steel and bronze over his head."

Holt looked sideways at him as the winch revved up.
"Awful concerned about your fellow man for a Kraut,
ain'tcha? Don't make me laugh." He spat over the side.
"Lucius has himself well out from under the load by
now. Me and him's done this kind of work so many
times, we don't even have to check anymore."

Stuermer's eyes narrowed and his expression went
several degrees cooler. "Your man, Captain," he said
simply.

"Goddamn right."

The propeller broke the surface and there was a sputtering sound as Wolfe idled down the winch. Stuermer
glanced across the deck at the two other U-boatmen.
The *Kapitänleutnant*, his young executive officer, and the
hulking torpedoman were unable to keep smiles of mutual satisfaction off their faces. Even Jolene, sitting on
the net roll near Bock, broke into a grin.

It took them only a couple of minutes to swing the
first net boom inboard, winch the dangling propeller and
shaft over the rail, and set it down on the back deck.
Wolfe was already coming up on the third lifting line as
Stuermer and Bock de-rigged the recovered assembly.
The second net boom bounced under the strain as the
starboard propeller and shaft appeared, awash in the
gentle surge beside the *Shiloh*. It, too, was on board in
a matter of minutes.

Bock beamed at Stuermer as he watched Wolfe finish

binding the shafts and the propellers to the deck with lengths of chain. "We did it, Captain," he said. "We did it."

Stuermer put a Turkish cigarette between his lips. "Yes, Erich. We did. All of us."

"Hey!" Holt barked. "You gonna help get Lucius off the bottom?"

With a weary roll of his eyes the *Kapitänleutnant* stepped aside, letting Wolfe and Bock pass on their way to the port rail. Seizing the air hose and the safety line, they began to reel them both in. Holt braced himself against the gunwale, still holding the end of the signaling cord, puffing out smoke and looking angry, unsteady, and ill. Jolene was certain that a light gust of wind stood a good chance of tipping him over the side.

Wolfe grunted and put a foot up on the rail, as the air hose became increasingly difficult to pull in. After recovering no more than twenty feet, he was stopped cold, as was Bock on the safety rope. The exec and the torpedoman glanced at each other, attempted several more backbreaking heaves, and paused again, breathing hard.

"What the hell's wrong with you guys?" Holt growled. "Pull him outta there!"

Bock shook his head. "Can't. His lines are wrapped on something. It's like trying to lift the bottom of the sea."

"Aw, bullshit!" Holt snapped. "Gimme that rope, you goddamn pantywaist!"

He snatched the manila line from Bock's grip with his lone hand, deftly wrapped it around his shoulders by twisting his torso, put a foot up against the gunwale, and hauled with all his might. His body shook with the strain, his face dripping sweat.

"*Arrrgggghh!*" Holt grimaced, and bit clean through his Lucky Strike.

Somewhere far below, the safety line cut over a sharp edge. Holt went headfirst into the roll of fishing net that Jolene had been sitting on. He thrashed for a moment, cursing a blue streak, then came up clumsily with the bandage askew on his freshly bleeding scalp. As the Creole girl stepped in quickly to help him, he sagged sideways, his face purple with rage.

"Get—get him up!" he gasped. Jolene half caught him as he collapsed to his knees. "Something's wrong, goddammit!"

Chapter Twenty-three

Wolfe redoubled his efforts to retrieve the air hose, his muscles bulging with the strain. Bock seized the slack safety rope and reeled it in rapidly hand over hand. When the end flipped up over the rail, he held it up and examined it. It had only a few torn, irregular fibers. Most of them had been cut cleanly, as if by a razor.

He put a hand out and caught Wolfe by the shoulder. "Stop pulling, Lothar!" The big man eased up immediately. "Both lines run almost parallel. Whatever cut through this safety rope could also cut the air hose."

Stuermer moved to the rail and frowned down into the green water, squinting against the midmorning sun. His eyes traveled outboard gradually and then stopped. He pointed. "His bubbles are over there," he said. "Right where the boat is."

Holt staggered up beside him and stared at the simmering circular patch some fifty feet from the *Shiloh*'s side. "You satisfied now, you bastard?" he said bitterly. "You got what you wanted." He gripped the rail for support, weaving. "Goddamn Kraut sonsabitches . . ." He glanced up and saw Stuermer looking the other way, at the two gleaming U-boat propellers and shafts secured to the back deck.

Holt exploded. "You're just gonna *leave* him, ain't you? You got what you came for and—"

Stuermer cut him off. "I am responsible for the lives

of nearly fifty men, Captain. Every minute I waste out here may be the minute that causes those lives to be lost. Therefore, I do not have time—"

Enraged, Holt lunged at him, swinging. "You fuckin' dirty Kraut bastard!" he yelled. "I'll *kill* you!"

The lean U-boat commander easily parried the clumsy attack and sidestepped, letting Holt's momentum carry him into the gunwale next to Bock, who gently but firmly pinned the weakened man against the rail. Stuermer stood by silently until Holt stopped struggling and had gasped in enough air to ease the color of his face from purple to red.

The *Kapitänleutnant* leaned in closer. "One of your overriding flaws, Captain Holt, is that you jump to conclusions. When a man starts to speak, you should let him finish. Not only is it more informative for you, but it is also common courtesy."

Holt twisted his head under Bock's weight and glared up at him, shaking.

"What I was going to say," Stuermer continued, "was that I do not have time to waste exchanging pointless insults with you. It is imperative that we get Lucius off the bottom as quickly as possible and proceed inshore." He nodded to Bock, who took his weight off Holt's back and shoulders. "So if you do not intend to help, at least stay out of the way."

As Holt blinked up at him, Stuermer turned to Wolfe. "Lothar, the Dräger gear. As quickly as you can."

"Yes, Captain," Wolfe responded smartly, and trotted over to the black duffel bags sitting on the deck next to the rope chest. He began to dig through them, extracting the full-face rubber diving mask, fabric belt, coil of thin air hose, and canvas shoes they had brought from the U-113.

Bock tended the slack air hose, keeping an eye on Holt. The American's agitated breathing had slowed and he was leaning back on the rail, keeping quiet for once. Stuermer looked him up and down. The man was mistrustful—not that he could blame him—and notoriously unpredictable. But clearly, he had a powerful loyalty to his Negro mate. Stuermer thought about it for a moment. They could not afford to have Holt go off half-cocked again while Wolfe was in the water. There was a short fire ax hooked underneath the gunwale's cap rail. He grasped the handle and brandished it.

"Listen to me, Captain," Stuermer said. "It seems certain that Lucius is trapped down there, and we are going to try to help him, at considerable risk to ourselves. But I promise you, if you attempt to interfere with us again, I will bring Wolfe back to the boat, cut the air hose, and depart for land without a second thought." He drove the ax into the cap rail with a dull *thunk*. "Whether your friend lives or dies is entirely up to you."

He turned and walked away, over to the rope chest where Wolfe, stripped to his Skivvies, was just buckling on the fabric dive belt.

"Almost ready, Captain," he said. "One problem, though: I can't tap the threaded nipple at the end of the Dräger air hose into any of the fittings on the compressor. It's the wrong bloody size."

Stuermer examined the brass fitting, then turned and held it up toward Holt. "Make a choice, Captain," he called. "Help us to help your friend now, or we save ourselves the trouble, cut the hose, and leave. We need to attach this air line to your compressor."

Holt didn't move for several seconds. Then he lurched off the rail and strode across the deck. Grabbing the end of the Dräger hose from Stuermer, he blew on the fitting, stepped over to the chugging compressor, and tried to couple it to an air valve of similar size. Almost immediately he stood up, cursing.

"Metric threads," he shouted over the chuffing of the cylinder pistons. "Goddammit, why can't you Krauts build things the right way, like us Americans? Pain in the ass."

He rummaged quickly in a small bin attached to the compressor frame, coming up with a roll of cloth tape. With amazing dexterity for a man with only one hand, he tore off a short length with his teeth and wrapped it around the Dräger fitting. Then he jammed the taped nipple into one of the air valves and torqued it tight with a small wrench.

"If it don't fit, force it," he declared. "That's it. It'll leak, and it might blow out, but it's the best I can do."

Stuermer looked at Wolfe. "Your choice, Lothar. Do you want to chance it?"

The big torpedoman's answer was to get to his feet and slip the partly buckled Dräger mask onto the top of his head. "Let's go, Captain."

Stuermer's familiar tight smile came and went, and after Wolfe positioned the breathing mask over his face, he reached up and buckled the remaining straps that held it in place.

"Air," he called to Holt.

The American opened the valve and Wolfe felt a gust of warm air around his eyes, nose, and mouth. Jolene was standing nearby, and as Stuermer walked with the torpedoman to the port rail, he caught her eye and spoke softly, nodding over his shoulder in Holt's direction: "Watch him. The air valve stays open." Anxiously, Jolene bobbed her head, her dark eyes flickering toward the compressor.

Wolfe paused at the top of the rail stairs while Bock did a quick visual check of his lightweight dive gear. After making sure that the retaining strap on his belt knife was snapped shut, the exec handed him a pair of cotton gloves and a short crowbar. "All I can think of," he called, shrugging helplessly.

The big man nodded, donning the gloves, then put a hand over the faceplate of his Dräger mask and leaped. He hit the water with a loud splash and disappeared, his slender air line trailing after him. Bock fed it out rapidly, at the same time holding Lucius' breathing hose. Immediately, he felt Wolfe grasp the hose and begin to pull himself along hand over hand.

Wolfe followed Lucius' air hose down through the murky green water until the dark bulk of the U-115 materialized just below him. Ten feet above it, he paused and assessed the situation. The orientation of the broken-off stern section was not as he remembered; in fact, it seemed to have inverted and separated even more from the main hull. Lucius' air hose led down into the wide, dark fracture that gaped like a ragged mouth, exhaust bubbles streaming up from it. More bubbles were escaping the stern section through cracked weld seams and buckled plates.

Pulling himself down to the fracture, Wolfe eased his nearly naked body through sideways, guarding against the lethally sharp metal edges. He squinted, a hand on Lucius' air hose, trying to trace it back through the ruined interior. It took a minute for his eyes to become accustomed to the dimness.

The hose lay across the top—or more correctly the *bottom*—of one of the MAN diesels. The severed safety rope lay beside it. Wolfe glanced up through his exhaust bubbles. The second MAN was suspended overhead, still attached to its mounts. On the far side of the fallen engine a dense column of air billowed upward, and every few seconds, one of Lucius' legs kicked through it feebly.

Wolfe pulled himself over the top of the engine and looked down. His first impression was that Lucius had been decapitated—that his dead limbs were simply flailing around in the air column. But closer inspection revealed that the dive helmet had not been completely crushed by the engine block, and the black mate was still very much alive. He gripped Lucius' knee, squeezing it to let him know he was there. The trapped man stiffened in alarm at the contact, then relaxed as he realized what was touching him.

Jamming his short crowbar under the MAN diesel, Wolfe braced his powerful legs and heaved with all his might. The massive engine didn't budge. With the strength of desperation, he tried again. The forged-steel crowbar bent under the strain, but again, the MAN refused to shift.

Dropping the crowbar in frustration, Wolfe leaned down to reexamine the crushed helmet. It was pinned beyond hope of extraction, the top half of it so badly mutilated that it was a miracle Lucius was still getting enough air to stay alive. The torpedoman ran his hands around the seam where the helmet screwed onto the chest plate. Here, at least, there was no distortion.

There was only one thing to do: Lucius would have to leave the helmet behind. Wolfe drew his belt knife

and cut the bronze weights off the mate's booted feet.
Then he turned his attention to the weight belt and
within minutes had sawed free the lead pigs attached to
it. Finally, he cut the useless length of safety rope from
the harness, as well as the lashing that strain-relieved
the air hose and prevented it from yanking directly on the
helmet fittings.

Lucius was now relatively weightless and detached
from the jammed diving equipment. All that remained
was to help him withdraw his head from the crushed
helmet. Wolfe wondered fleetingly if the black mate
would have the presence of mind to understand instinctively what he had to do in order to stay alive, or if he
would panic, flail, and most certainly wind up dead in
under a minute. The big torpedoman dismissed the
thought as quickly as it had come: it didn't matter now,
because there was no choice of what had to be done.

Releasing the catches on the helmet, he laid his hands
firmly on Lucius' shoulders and twisted him in the correct unthreading direction. Understanding instantly what
was going to happen, the mate's hands came up and
seized the edges of the chest plate, stabilizing it. Both
men paused, and then Lucius braced his feet against the
metal junk pile and twisted his body forcefully along its
axis, Wolfe assisting by exerting pressure on his
shoulders.

There was a sudden blast of air as the chest plate
unscrewed and separated from the helmet. Lucius' suit
flooded instantly through its open neck. Wolfe pulled
back hard, watching as the mate's ebony face, wreathed
in bubbles, emerged from the ruined helmet. His lips
were pressed tight together, his eyes open but unseeing,
blind in the underwater dimness. He reached out and
clasped Wolfe's upper arms firmly as the torpedoman
pulled him upright, and his grip was that of a man who
would not slip into the grave without a fight.

But he was calm. He waited, looking straight at Wolfe
with his sightless eyes, blinking. The German bent down,
pulled up a loop of air hose, and slashed it free of the
crushed dive helmet with his knife. The cut end in his

hand billowed free-flowing compressed air. He jammed
it up against Lucius' chin, praying that the black mate
had the experience to know what to do with it.

Without hesitation, Lucius let go of Wolfe and seized
the hose. The high volume of air pounded out of it like
a water hammer, jerking his head back and forth. Wolfe
watched helplessly. If Lucius attempted to stick it directly into his mouth and inhale, as a desperate man
might, the instantaneous result would be ruptured
lungs—fatal embolism.

But there was another way, and Lucius knew it. Facing
downward and cupping his fingers around his mouth, the
hose end caught between the heels of his hands, he cre-
ated a small pocket of depressurized air. A tiny, imper-
fect reservoir from which he could breathe.

Starving for oxygen, he inhaled, taking in nearly as much
salt water as air. The stinging brine made him lift his face
from the hose and cough uncontrollably. But at least,
Wolfe observed, he'd taken in enough air to be able to
cough at all. Controlling his urge to inhale by force of will,
Lucius re-flexed his fingers and bent over the hose end
again. This time his cupped hands were more watertight,
and he remained in the hunched-over position as the seconds ticked by. Wolfe watched as his broad back and
shoulders rose and fell with his rhythmic breathing.

Finally, Lucius looked up at him. Not seeing, but acknowledging. His fingers remained locked around his
mouth, the hose clasped between the heels of his hands,
his breathing under control. Wolfe squeezed his shoulder, then shifted his hand to the mate's harness, cleared
both air hoses, and began to lead him gently toward the
fracture in the hull.

They drifted over the MAN diesel and through the
treacherous tangle of steel, wire, and assorted equipment, Wolfe keeping their air lines away from snags and
sharp edges. Lucius paused only once—coughing out an
inadvertent gulp of salt water, then repositioning his
fingers and regaining control of his breathing. Wolfe
waited, and when the black man looked up and nodded,
his face almost completely obscured by the air bubbles

billowing around it, he proceeded to guide Lucius through the opening in the hull and out into open water.

Still wearing the bulky canvas dive suit, metal chest plate, boots, and harness, Lucius was too heavy to simply drop the hose after a deep breath and swim upward. And even without a great amount of negative buoyancy, Wolfe knew, seventy feet was too deep for an exhausted man to make a successful breath-hold ascent without supplemental escape gear like Dräger *Tauchretter*. They would have to be pulled back to the *Shiloh*, Lucius' breathing supply maintained the whole way.

The slender air line to Wolfe's mask was not substantial enough to take hauling strain. Dräger diving gear was designed for use by a mobile swimmer who did not need to be lifted by his umbilical line. The Mark Five hose, on the other hand, was much heavier. Wolfe tightened his one-handed grip on Lucius' harness, yanked hard several times on the air hose, and then locked his legs around the mate's waist. The hose moved upward rapidly, plucking them both out of the mud.

The green water lightened as they rose, Wolfe squeezing the air hose with all the strength he had left. He felt the sudden glossiness of warmer water on his bare skin as they ascended through a thermocline, and he realized for the first time how cold he was, almost shaking. And then the stained white side of the *Shiloh* appeared, and they were on the surface.

Lucius climbed laboriously up the boarding ladder, his dive suit distended by the water it contained, and paused at the top to drape himself over the rail. Seawater gushed out of the neck opening and onto the deck, immediately reducing the unwanted extra weight he was carrying by a hundred pounds. Spluttering and blowing, he pulled himself the rest of the way over the rail and collapsed in a wet heap, totally spent.

Holt knelt by his side and got his hand under Lucius' head. The black man continued to gasp in air, his chest rising and falling like a bellows. Jolene dropped to her knees opposite Holt and gently pressed a towel to his temples. She had never heard a human being breathe so raggedly.

Wolfe sat down on the topmost gunwale stair and peeled the black rubber Dräger mask from his face, assisted by Bock. The big torpedoman was pale and shaking with cold. Stuermer walked up the deck, stepped inside the deckhouse momentarily, and reemerged with two gray army blankets. He passed one to Bock, who draped it over Wolfe's shivering shoulders, and held the other out to Jolene.

"He will want this once we get him out of the suit," he said quietly. Holt looked up at the *Kapitänleutnant*, the expression on his face an unreadable mix of emotions, then back down at Lucius. The black man's breathing eased, and his eyes fluttered and focused. Slowly, his open hand came up and grasped Holt's forearm.

"What say, Mike?" he croaked, grinning weakly.

Stuermer was sure he could see Holt's eyes glisten as he gently rocked the hand that supported his big mate's head. "Hey, Lucius," he said simply. "Hey."

Lucius turned his head and located Wolfe gazing down at him from the top stair, his tough prizefighter's face wet, pallid, and streaked with red pressure marks where the Dräger mask had sealed against his skin. The German grinned and nodded.

The lines in Lucius' ebony face creased into a smile.

"*Danke*," he said.

Chapter
Twenty-four

The *Shiloh* had been running inshore for nearly an hour when Holt, at the wheel, finally broke the silence he'd maintained since Lucius had recovered enough strength to shed his dive suit. He addressed no one in particular, simply gazed straight out over the bow of the trawler and began to speak in a low monotone.

"Just after Pearl Harbor, right when America got into the war a couple of years back, I joined the air force. Wanted to get in on the action, try somethin' different, and get out of Louisiana for a spell. The boys in charge found out I could hit a movin' target with a fifty-caliber machine gun, so they made me a tail gunner in a B-17. You know the plane?"

Stuermer, Bock, and Wolfe, standing on the bridge behind Holt, looked briefly at each other. All of them had lost at least one relative to the relentless daytime saturation bombing of German industrial centers by American B-17 Flying Fortresses. At night, it was the British in their Lancasters, dropping death from the sky and turning cities like Dresden and Bremen into raging firestorms.

Stuermer cleared his throat. "We know about the B-17, Captain," he said quietly.

"Mm." Holt lit his sixth Lucky Strike of the hour off the coal of his fifth before continuing. "I was a good shot when I had two hands."

"You are a good shot with *one* hand," Stuermer observed. "I can attest to it."

Holt blew out a stream of smoke. "Not with a fifty. Not anymore." He held up his stump without looking back at the Germans. "Let me tell you how I lost this."

From his seat on the port end of the bridge console, Lucius stirred, unfolding his big arms. "You ain't gotta run through all that again, Mike," he said, his voice a deep rumble. "Ain't no need."

"Maybe this'll be the last time I ever tell it, Lucius," Holt replied. He looked over at his mate. "Maybe, after this time, I won't have to."

He gazed back out at the horizon where the hazy blue sky met the silt-brown Gulf waters. "The third mission we flew took us over the Ruhr valley. Our ship was always 'Tail End Charlie' for our formation, on account of me and the two waist gunners on board were such good shots. We covered everyone else's rear ends. It was like shootin' fish in a barrel to me. By the time that third mission rolled around, I'd knocked down three Messerschmitt 109 and two Focke-Wulf 190 fighters by myself, and shared a kill on a Junkers 88 bomber with Sid, our starboard waist gunner.

"That day, we got jumped by a swarm of Focke-Wulfs before we even made it across the Rhine. I never seen anything like it. The sky was black with 'em, buzzin' through the formation like angry hornets. And of course, they were concentratin' on Tail End Charlie—us. I shot so long and hard my gun barrels turned red-hot and distorted. Jammed the weapon so it wouldn't fire anymore.

"Sid had been cut in two by a burst of cannon fire that hit amidships, and the other gunner, Frank, was dying with a big hole in his belly. So I unbuckled and crawled forward to man one of the waist fifties. I couldn't believe we were still in the air—we were so shot up. I got to the gun, didn't even take time to harness myself in, and racked up a fresh belt just as another three Focke-Wulfs came bankin' in. I started firing, cannon shells started smashin' all around me—and then the starboard wing broke off between the inboard and outboard engines. The plane pitched and rolled, and I got sucked out the waist window.

"I musta fallen over a mile. I liked it. The wind was loud, but there was no other sound. No gunfire, no explosions, no buddies screamin'. It was as if I'd suddenly just . . . checked out, you know?"

Holt paused to draw on his Lucky Strike. "Some nights, I think I should have just kept on fallin'. Never opened that parachute." He waved his stump. "Would have missed everything that happened after that." A terrible look passed over his face, and he laughed quietly, bitterly. "Shoulda, woulda."

"What'd I tell you 'bout talkin' like that, Mike," Lucius cautioned. "You gonna give yourself the blues again. Get too melancholy an' wake up hollerin' at three in the mornin'."

An involuntary shudder gripped Holt. He appeared to quell it by staring out at the horizon and squeezing the spindle of the *Shiloh*'s wheel until the wood creaked. When the cigarette between his lips stopped trembling, he glanced over at Lucius, nodded, and went on with his story: "I pulled the rip cord and my chute opened. I saw my B-17 fall right past me in flames. I was the only guy that made it out, and I was *thrown* out by accident—just dumb goddamn luck. The plane fell into the forest below me and exploded.

"When I hit the ground in a small clearing, I twisted my ankle. The first thing I wanted to do was get the hell away from there and hide my chute, so I bundled it up and limped into the trees. I stuffed the chute into a hollow log and went about three miles through the woods before I came to a farmer's field. There were haystacks everywhere, and I burrowed into one and went to sleep.

"When I woke up I was being yanked out of the hay by six *Waffen SS* troops—I recognized that nasty little double-lightning-bolt insignia on their collars from pictures I'd seen in England. They had a good time stompin' the living shit out of me, and then hauled me off to what looked like an old castle or manor house in one

of the nearby towns. Turns out I was still in France—
we didn't even make it over Germany before we were
shot down."

Good, Bock thought, *that was one less planeload of
bombs that could have been dropped on my mother
and father.*

"They threw me into a cell in the basement of this
place. Like a goddamn dungeon—dirt floor, no light, no
fresh air. I was in there for three days without any food
or water. I know because I still had my watch. Three
full days."

Holt drew a ragged breath, as if trying to calm himself
before continuing: "On the morning of the fourth day,
I got a visitor. Black uniform, real sharp, red armband
with that fuckin' swastika on it."

Stuermer and Bock glanced at each other. *"Gestapo,"*
the *Kapitänleutnant* said. The word came off his tongue
as if it tasted bad. Wolfe, leaning back against the rear
bulkhead, scowled darkly.

"Yeah," Holt said, nodding slowly as he stared out
across the Gulf. "Gestapo. A Major Fuhrmann . . ."

"Mike," Lucius cautioned again.

"I'm gonna tell it, Lucius." Holt's voice was raw,
barely above a whisper. "I got to."

Lucius' sharp eyes flickered over the three Germans,
then back to Holt. With a long sigh, shaking his head,
he folded his arms and leaned back against the port
bulkhead. "Do what you gotta do," he said.

Holt took a deep drag on his cigarette, and when he
spoke, his voice had a slight tremor: "Three SS soldiers
hauled me out of my cell and down this basement passageway to another room. Major Fuhrmann was in there.
He was sitting at a wooden table with nothing on it but
a white silk handkerchief. Something was underneath it.
There was one bare light bulb overhead and a second
chair in front of the table . . . a wooden armchair fitted
with leather straps.

"They sat me in the armchair and buckled me in.
There were straps everywhere, around my chest, my
wrists, my knees, my ankles—I mean, I couldn't move

an inch. Then the SS soldiers left and it was just me and
Fuhrmann in the room.

"He sat there for a long time, just looking at me. He
was about my age, in pretty good shape, with real clean,
square features, like he'd been chiseled out of marble.
The thing I remember most about him, though, was that
he didn't seem to have any human *color* to him. His
skin, his hair—they were all the same shade. It wasn't
even white; it was just pale, like the underside of a
snake. Even his eyes were like that—flat and pale like
a dead animal's.

" 'You are a spy,' he said. 'I want to know who your
contacts are in the French Resistance.'" Holt glanced
back at Stuermer. "His English sounded a lot like yours.

" 'I'm an American soldier,' I told him. 'U.S. Air
Force. I'm no spy. Look at my flight suit. I'm in
uniform.'

"He smiled and shook his head. 'I see no uniform,'
he said. 'And I want names.'

" '*What* names?' I shouted at him, because he was
pissing me off.

"He didn't say anything, just kept smiling and reached
over and lifted the silk handkerchief with two fingers,
real delicate, like it was dirty or something. Underneath
it was a small pair of bolt cutters.

"He leaned back in the chair, lookin' at me with them
snake eyes, and put on a pair of black leather gloves.
Took his time about it, too. Then he got up, picked up
the bolt cutters, and walked around the table beside me.

"I figured what he was gonna do, and I started talkin'
fast, about anything I could think of, but it didn't matter." Holt paused, swallowing. "By the time he set the
business end of those bolt cutters down over the little
finger of my left hand, I was beggin' him not to do it.

"He clipped it off right at the first knuckle, real calm,
as if he was trimmin' roses. He never stopped smiling.
Just stood back and watched me scream, foam at the
mouth, and jerk around against them straps."

Holt's face contorted as his voice faltered and broke.
"Not exactly John Wayne."

"I done told you, Mike," Lucius cut in, "*John Wayne* wouldn't be John Wayne if someone did him like that."

The bridge fell silent as Holt slowly regained his composure, then continued: "After about five minutes I wore myself out, and he leaned down, picked up my little finger, and set it on the table in front of me. 'When I ask you a question,' he said, 'I want an honest answer. You can choose to lie, but you will pay for your lies. In fingers.' He put down the bolt cutters, picked up the silk handkerchief, and wiped some of my blood from the tips of his black leather gloves. I remember he looked a little annoyed, like a woman who's just found a dirty mark on a freshly cleaned dress."

Behind Holt, Stuermer's lean face was set in granite, his mouth a grim line above his chin. Wolfe was scowling at the deck plates, and Bock was staring out at the waters of the Gulf, his eyes haunted, incredulous. In the starboard corner of the bridge, sitting on the console and hugging her drawn-up legs, Jolene had buried her face in her knees. At the opposite end of the console, Lucius stood with his arms folded and watched the others stolidly.

"I was in there for hours with that fuckin' *Gestapo* animal," Holt went on. "I screamed myself hoarse, gave him my commanding officer's name, my friends' names, Churchill's name, Ike's name, my mother's name. It didn't matter. He kept clipping. I threw up all over myself, pissed myself, shit myself. I begged him to stop, begged him to shoot me. He didn't. He clipped three fingers from my left hand, about an hour apart. When he wasn't using the bolt cutters he was kicking me and swearing '*Verdammt! Verdammt!*' over and over. That word is tattooed on my brain. Then he left the index finger and took my thumb. When the shears crunched through the bone, I passed out."

A sob of horror came from Jolene. Bock felt as though he was going to vomit.

"When I woke up, I was back in my cell. A dirty rag had been wrapped around the lump of chopped meat that used to be my hand, and I was covered in my own filth. I didn't think a man could be in that much pain and still

live. After a while, the door opened; it was Major Fuhrmann, dressed for dinner. 'I left you one finger,' he said,
'since an unconscious man can't feel anything. Tomorrow,
we'll finish up on that left hand, and get started on the
right. Sleep well.' And he laughed and shut the door.

"That night, the Lancasters came. The RAF had targeted a fuel depot that happened to be located on the
other side of town. Some of the bombs missed their target and fell real close to the manor house. I thought the
whole place was gonna cave in, and the way I felt, I was
prayin' for it.

"Turns out the manor was bein' used as a *Gestapo*
prison, and there were other folks in there besides me.
Captured French Resistance leaders. While the bombing
raid was under way, the Resistance attacked the prison,
tryin' to get their people out. All of a sudden there's a
lot of yelling outside my cell, and then a burst of machine gun fire blows the lock open. Next thing I know,
these two guys in dark street clothes with blacked-out
faces are draggin' me up the stairs and out the front
door. Bombs still goin' off everywhere.

"Some kind of formal dinner had been happening in
the main dining room. There were dead Germans in
dress uniforms and tux tails lying all over the place.
Women, too, and some of them looked like French gals.
Didn't matter to the Resistance boys—they were walking around the bodies, shooting everyone who'd been at
the dinner in the head with captured German machine
pistols. Wounded or dead, male or female, it didn't matter. If you were at the dinner, you got a burst in the
head." Holt smiled for the first time since he'd started
telling his story. "Them fellas in the French Resistance,
they don't mess around."

Stuermer shook his head slightly, as if coming out of
a trance. Very slowly, he pulled a dark-papered cigarette
from his pocket, put it between his lips, and lit it. "What
happened then?" he asked, his voice low.

Holt grimaced. "My hand got infected," he said. "The
Resistance evacuated me to England as fast as they
could—they arranged a midnight pickup by Blenheim
bomber in less than a week—but it was too late. Gan-

grene was starting to travel up my arm. The doctors worked on it in London, but there was nothing they could do. The whole hand was black and leaking pus. They had to amputate it at the wrist to save my arm—and my life." Holt swiveled in his seat and faced the three Germans. "And that's the story of my short, sweet military career, and how I lost my hand." He blew a stream of smoke, looking at each of them in turn, and then shifted back around to the *Shiloh*'s wheel.

The three U-boatmen stood there in silence for nearly five minutes, listening to the hum of the trawler's engine and the churning of water beneath the hull. At last, Stuermer stepped forward, moved up beside Holt, and spread his hands on the console, looking out across the bow.

"I am sorry, Captain Holt," he said simply.

"Uh-huh," Holt replied. "Not as sorry as me."

Stuermer took a final drag from his cigarette and butted it in the overflowing ashtray that sat near the throttle levers. "Political circumstances have made us enemies," he said. "We cannot change that. But there is a difference between a soldier and a butcher. My men and I are soldiers. We do what needs to be done, but we fight by the rules of engagement. This *Gestapo* major you have described, this Fuhrmann, he is a psychopath, a criminal—"

"Was," Holt corrected. "As the Resistance guys were draggin' me out, I saw him lying by the front door in that fancy-dress dinner suit. There was a cigarette in a real nice black holder between his fingers, still burning. Hard for him to smoke it, though—he was missing his head." He snorted in satisfaction. "Fuhrmann must have been real popular with the Resistance boys. Looked like they used a whole clip on him."

"Then you have your revenge," Stuermer concluded, "at least in part. He was paid in full for what he did to you."

Holt looked at him. "No, he wasn't," he said, his voice hoarse. "It was too goddamn quick."

There was nothing to say to that. Stuermer held Holt's gaze for a moment, then looked back out the forward windshield. He tapped his fingers on the console briefly, then felt in his shirt pockets. He was out of cigarettes.

There was a nudge at his elbow, and he glanced down to see Holt holding out an open pack of Lucky Strikes. Surprised, he slid one out of the crumpled package. Holt flicked open his Zippo and held up the flame as Stuermer bent to take the light.

The American snapped the lighter shut. He didn't smile, didn't try to feign friendship, just spoke matter-of-factly: "I wanna thank you for gettin' Lucius out of there."

Behind the helm chair, leaning against the aft bulkhead, Bock and Wolfe exchanged glances. Stuermer nodded slowly. "We had no choice," he said. "One seaman cannot abandon another. Not when he has the ability to help."

"You said you'd cut his air hose if I made any trouble," Holt reminded him.

"Yes."

The American captain looked at the U-boat commander. "Would you have?"

Stuermer let a beat pass. "No."

"But I didn't know that."

The *Kapitänleutnant*'s thin smile appeared. "No," he said. "You didn't."

Holt said nothing, but the tortured lines in his face softened somewhat. Stuermer drew on his Lucky Strike. "All Germans are not like Major Fuhrmann, Captain," he said quietly.

"I saw," Holt replied. There was a pause, and he changed tack. "Them shafts and screws out there on the back deck. Lucius tells me they're from a U-boat."

There was no point in denying it. "Yes," Stuermer said.

"Uh-huh." Holt peered down at the compass and shifted the wheel a half point to starboard. "It seems to me that the only reason you boys would come out here like this and go to all the trouble of pullin' two screws off a wrecked U-boat would be that you want—no, *need*—to stick them back on another U-boat. Am I right?"

"Captain . . . ," Stuermer said.

"I know—you can't tell me," Holt went on. "But lemme ask you this: do you really think I'm just gonna sit around doin' nothing while you put a U-boat back out to sea? So you can sink more ships and kill more American sailors? Whadya think, I'm crazy or somethin'?"

Stuermer took a step backward. "No," he replied. His hand went into his pocket.

"Captain Holt," Bock said from across the bridge, "we're just trying to get home. We don't intend to do any hunting in the Gulf of Mexico or the Atlantic. If we make it back, and our commanders reassign us, then that's another story. But for now, we're noncombatant. We're no danger to any shipping."

"Not right now," Holt said. "But if you get back, and they refit you and send you up into the North Atlantic, you'll be sinkin' ships and killin' Americans, Brits, Canucks, and anyone else who serves on them convoys." He glanced over at Bock. "You ain't droppin' out of the war, buddy. You got no choice."

Stuermer stood off to one side, his hand still in his pocket, his face resigned. Wolfe and Lucius were light and dark mirror images of each other, big men standing erect now, watching and listening, their powerful arms folded across their chests. At the starboard end of the console, Jolene's eyes widened with apprehension. Bock cleared his throat.

"We did you a favor," he said. "We saved Lucius' life. We don't expect you to help us, but you *could* just let us go our own way, quietly. Can't you return the favor you owe?"

Holt blew a stream of smoke. "I just did," he said. "I let you know I can't."

Chapter
Twenty-five

Dekker watched over Winkler's shoulder as the senior radioman jotted down the Morse transmission that was coming through his headset. When he was done, he dropped the pencil on the notepad and pushed his glasses up on his forehead.

"That's it," he said. "What do you think?"

Dekker read the scrawl again: *"To K. Storm, K. Storm, K. Storm. Your message badly fragmented. Please repeat ASAP. Please repeat ASAP. Mr. Kaleu."*

"In English," Dekker muttered. "No encryption, of course . . ."

"We sent ours in English," Winkler said. "It's a reply in kind."

The burly chief furrowed his brows. "Another U-boat?"

"Possibly."

"But we can't know that, can we?"

Winkler sighed and scratched his chin. "There's the rub, Otto, as the Bard would say. I don't see how. If we reply, we might be able to establish contact with another boat that can help us, or we might attract the attention of American coastal defense units. This could be a false response from a tracking station trying to get a bearing on us. If we don't reply, we might be missing our best and perhaps only chance of getting out of here."

Dekker made a growling sound deep in his throat and

straightened up. He fished in his trouser pocket and
came up with a heavy coin. "My lucky Swiss franc," he
said. "Heads we transmit; tails we don't." He flipped the
coin into the air, caught it as it came down, and slapped
it onto the back of his hand.

"Heads," Winkler declared.

Dekker looked at the coin, then back at his fellow
officer, and nodded. "We send."

Winkler shrugged and readjusted his glasses on his
nose. "Send it is," he said, and reached for the Morse
key.

The chief leaned back against the doorjamb of the
radio room as Winkler transmitted their original message six times in rapid sequence, his fingers and the key
a single fast-moving blur. He finished the task in a couple of minutes and sat back from the radio desk, flexing
his hand.

"There," he said. "The damage is done." He smiled
ruefully. "We'll see if we get another response. If not,
I'll retransmit in half an hour. I think, however, that we
should limit this to two hours, total. Either we get a
verifiable identity from the sender of that message, or
we go radio silent. Our chances of turning ourselves into
a target increase every time we transmit."

"Agreed," Dekker replied.

Winkler took off his glasses and began to polish them
on his shirttail. "Just as a matter of interest, Otto, did
that coin actually come up heads?"

"You doubt me?" Dekker lifted an eyebrow. "I'm cut
to the quick, Jonas. Of course it came up heads."

"Why didn't you let me see it?" Winkler prodded.
"Maybe it was tails, but you really wanted to transmit,
regardless. You're not one to leave important decisions
to chance, my friend."

"I called it the way it fell: *heads*," Dekker insisted.
"It was pure luck which side of the coin turned up. And
I can prove it." He dug the franc out of his pocket and
tossed it to Winkler.

The radioman caught it and rotated it in his hand.
Then he laughed and held it up between two fingers.
"Pretty clever, Otto," he chuckled. The Swiss franc had

heads on both sides. "Remind me never to bet against you at the tables."

Their tension-relieving banter was interrupted by the sudden appearance of crewman Mohler, who slid down the main ladder into the control room from the conning tower. The *Schmeisser* machine pistol he'd been carrying while on watch was slung loosely across his back.

"Chief Dekker! *Puster* Winkler!" he called out, his voice hoarse with excitement. "Captain Stuermer is back! And he's brought a whole boat with him!"

Fetherstone-Pugh sat with both elbows propped up on the radio-intercept desk, his knuckles grinding into his temples. He was staring at the piece of paper on which he'd jotted down the immediate repeat broadcast of the strange communication to *Mr. Kaleu*—the transmission of which had apparently been prompted by his sending of his own carefully worded decoy message. The *fist*! He knew the fist! It was right there—right on the very fringes of his memory. . . .

At the chart-inscribed glass panel on the far side of the tracking room, a technician was marking down the first bearing in colored chalk. Radio techs were writing furiously, copying down additional bearings coming in from the secondary tracking stations—Biloxi, Pensacola, Galveston. Working out a triangulation.

He stared at the paper. *To Mr. Kaleu* . . .

Kaleu.

And then, suddenly, he had it.

His mind flashed back to a prewar exchange visit of naval cadets, soon after the 1936 Berlin Olympics, during which he and twenty classmates had toured the *Kriegsmarine* yards and docks in Kiel. He had heard the word *Kaleu* often then. It was the informal diminutive of *Kapitänleutnant*—"lieutenant commander"—used by German seamen when referring to the captain of their vessel, who in actual fact often held that lesser rank. "Jawohl, Herr Kaleu," "Nein, Herr Kaleu," "Danke, Herr Kaleu." . . .

The details that had remained so obstinately vague in Fetherstone-Pugh's memory now began to blossom into

sharp focus. There had been a U-boat operating off the
Channel Islands in 1940, a boat that had been spotted
on the surface numerous times by small British coastal-
patrol craft too lightly armed to engage her even if they
had had the turn of speed to run her down. This U-boat
had brazenly displayed her identifying letters in white
on her conning tower: U-111. And her radio operator
had possessed a unique fist—a fast, almost musical sending style that the Wrens and Fetherstone-Pugh had come
to know well.

When, by pure chance, a patrolling British Wellington
bomber had come upon the overconfident U-boat loiter-
ing on the surface and depth-charged her, reporting several direct hits, the Wrens had not expected to hear the
distinctive fist of the U-111's radio operator again. But
less than a month later, there it was—coming from another U-boat, unidentified this time. Without a doubt,
the U-111's *Puster* had survived his first boat's sinking.

Curious, Fetherstone-Pugh had sifted through a small
mountain of intelligence reports provided by the French
Resistance that contained, among other things, the crew
manifests of a number of individual U-boats operating
out of bases on the French coast. There had been a
manifest for the U-111, and it had identified the last
radio operator assigned to her as one *Funkmaat* Jonas
Winkler, a former flutist with the Berlin Philharmonic
Orchestra.

Fetherstone-Pugh raised his eyes and stared across the
room at the colored chalk glowing on the glass chart.
Little wonder, with all he'd been through in the past two
years, that the memory of a single North Atlantic U-
boatman's sending style had locked itself away in a dusty
corner of his mind. But here it had turned up again:
the unmistakable fist of Jonas Winkler, sending out an
unencrypted message in English on a high-frequency
military bandwidth.

He watched as the plotter behind the glass drew a
second bearing line in contrasting chalk from Biloxi
down across the mouth of the Mississippi River and out
into the Gulf of Mexico, intersecting the primary bearing

line from New Orleans and completing the triangulation. Fetherstone-Pugh blinked and looked again.

The unmistakable fist of U-boat radio officer Jonas Winkler was apparently transmitting obscure, repetitive messages from a location deep in the coastal swamps of southern Louisiana.

Holt's bloodshot eyes widened as he piloted the *Shiloh* out of Bayou Profond and into the large pond bordered by *les Isolates*' stilt shanties. The people of the tiny hidden community began to appear on catwalks and docks, eyeing yet another vessel from the outside world that had intruded upon their solitude. Lucius stood beside Holt at the wheel, one arm resting protectively behind him on the helm chair, ready to support his weight if the need arose. The skipper of the *Shiloh* had been having dizzy spells all the way up the twisting bayou from the open Gulf.

"Over there," Stuermer said, pointing. "Take her up alongside the starboard bow."

Lucius whistled quietly between his teeth as he took in the sleek, sharklike lines of the U-113's black hull. Even tied up between the tall cypress trees and draped from stem to stern with camouflage netting, she looked formidable. Holt's eyes lingered on the twin-barreled antiaircraft machine guns and the eighty-eight-millimeter deck cannon.

Stuermer had taken up a position behind the two Americans with his back against the aft bulkhead, one hand in his pocket on the butt of the Walther. He was being careful. After hearing Holt's remarks during the run inshore, he considered himself duly warned.

Wolfe and Bock exited the wheelhouse to man the *Shiloh*'s docking lines. The big torpedoman headed aft while Bock proceeded up to the bow, followed by Jolene. Holt watched them go, then turned around to see Stuermer looking at him.

"Hold your vessel steady, please, Captain," the German said quietly.

The U-boat was very close now. Holt smiled, turned

back to the wheel, and suddenly rammed the throttle lever full ahead with the *Shiloh*'s heavy bow pointing directly at the U-113's starboard forward quarter.

Stuermer was ready for that. In one motion, he drew the Walther and lunged forward, knocking Holt sideways into Lucius. As the American captain and his big mate stumbled into the bridge console, off balance, the U-boat commander yanked the throttle lever back and took the main engine out of gear. With the pistol leveled at Holt, he spun the wheel hard to port, looking coolly back and forth from the bridge windows to the two Americans as he ruddered the trawler up alongside the U-113 under her own momentum.

Bock and Wolfe, who'd been thrown off their feet by the *Shiloh*'s sudden acceleration, appeared simultaneously at the port bridge door, breathing hard.

"Everything under control, Captain?" Bock asked, noting the Walther in Stuermer's hand—and the two crouching men at which it was aimed.

"Absolutely," the *Kapitänleutnant* replied. There was a slight jolt as the *Shiloh* contacted the side of the U-113. Wolfe and Bock departed again to tend the lines, and Stuermer pressed the kill switch for the trawler's main engine. As the big diesel idled down and died, he lowered the Walther an inch or two. "Are you all right, Captain Holt?" he inquired, his voice very calm.

Holt straightened up and adjusted his head bandage. "Sure. Sure, I'm fine."

"Lucius?"

The black man nodded. "Uh-huh."

Stuermer smiled slightly. "It was—I'm trying to think of the correct expression—ah, yes, 'a good try.' "

Holt shrugged.

"Unfortunately," the *Kapitänleutnant* went on, "I can't permit you to interfere with the repairs that must now begin, and that will require my full attention. So you will be put under guard. Please refrain from attempting any more heroics. They might get you shot."

"Why didn't you shoot just now?" Holt asked. "Would've been easy."

Stuermer eyed him. "Because I didn't have to," he

said. He waved the Walther. "After you, gentlemen.
Step aboard *my* ship."

The *Kapitänleutnant* herded his two captives out the
starboard door of the wheelhouse and up onto the *Shiloh*'s rail. Slightly above them was the foredeck of the
U-113, now becoming increasingly crowded with crewmen who were emerging from the forward hatch and
mustering for work detail. Several of them stretched out
hands as Holt and Lucius stepped across the water gap,
followed by Stuermer. A guttural chorus of German-
speaking voices rose like a wave.

"Welcome back, Captain!"

"Good to see you, Captain!"

"Glad you're safe, sir! Do we go home now?"

Stuermer couldn't help but grin, the familiar company
buoying his spirits even more than he'd expected. "The
quicker we get these shafts installed," he announced in
German, "the quicker we go home."

There was a low cheer from the assembled men. As
it died away, Winkler and Dekker pushed their way
through the crowd.

"*Gott in Himmel*, Captain," Dekker exclaimed, shaking Stuermer's hand, "you did it."

"My sentiments as well, sir," added Winkler.

Stuermer nodded. "We were lucky, and we had good
help." He looked pointedly at Holt and Lucius. "Jonas,
these gentlemen are our unwilling guests. I want them
put ashore out of the way, under armed guard. Use two
men who can stay alert. Captain Holt and Mr. Dancer
are more than capable of getting into mischief if given
the opportunity." He smiled at Holt and switched to
English. "I am afraid Captain Holt doesn't think much
of me."

"Nothin' personal," Holt growled. He sounded as
though he half meant it.

Winkler examined the American briefly through his
thick glasses. "I'll see to it, sir," he said. "Mohler!"

The able seaman with the machine pistol appeared out
of the crowd immediately. "Here, *Puster* Winkler."

"Have Burkhardt draw a Schmeisser from the weapons locker and join us. You two have guard duty. We're

going ashore to find a spot in the shade where these gentlemen can cool their heels."

"Yes, sir."

As Mohler disappeared, Stuermer addressed Dekker: "Otto, we need that ballasting inversion we discussed—now. Are we still ready?"

"Yes, Captain," the chief replied. "I can have the men ashore and the skeleton crew below and in position whenever you give the command."

Stuermer smiled, reached out, and clapped Dekker on the shoulder. "Then let's do it."

"Yes, sir." The burly chief turned and began to shout commands, his harsh rasp of a voice echoing through the moss-hung cypress trees.

"That's the dumbest dang thing I ever seen or heard," Blodgett exclaimed, looking at the intersecting red, blue, green, and white chalk lines on the glass chart. "Face it, Feathers: you done got yourself a fix on a U-boat that's sittin' fifteen miles inshore in the state of Louisiana. Broadcastin' weird little joke messages in English, no less." He grinned, noisily chewing on a wad of Wrigley's finest. "You pull the alarm bell over this and you're gonna make one hellacious fool outta yourself, son."

"That area is riddled with uncharted waterways, Hiram," Fetherstone-Pugh retorted, not even trying to conceal his irritation.

"*Haww!*" the corpulent officer snorted. "*Waterways?* You ever seen a Louisiana bayou, Feathers? Most of 'em you can't even float a johnboat through without scrapin' the paint off the sides!"

"That doesn't mean a U-boat couldn't find a deep channel under cover of darkness and motor inland a few miles. That area is virtually uninhabited."

"But *fifteen miles?*"

Fetherstone-Pugh picked up a telephone receiver. "You should know as well as I do, Hiram—even if you don't—that the degree of error in this type of radio-bearing triangulation can be as high as twenty miles. With that in mind, I'm asking for two flights of patrol bombers to investigate both the inshore fix and the coastline to the south of it. The U-boat could actually be just offshore or hiding in one of the inlets."

Blodgett threw up his hands and rolled his eyes in mock horror. "What U-boat?" he exclaimed, looking around at his various cronies. "*What* U-boat?"

Patience shredding like wet tissue paper, Fetherstone-Pugh began to dial the emergency scramble number of the U.S. Navy and Coast Guard airfield in Houma, deep in the bayou country southwest of New Orleans.

Chapter
Twenty-six

"Now, Chief!" Stuermer shouted.

Up on the U-113's conning tower, Dekker threw his captain a quick salute and bent over the bridge speaking tube. His gruff voice was clearly audible on shore as he issued orders: "Pump fuel forward! Flood forward tanks!"

Spread out behind Stuermer on the banks of the little inlet, the bulk of the crew watched anxiously as the ballasting inversion commenced. The humming of pumps reverberated through the black hull plates as fuel and water were transferred forward, and gradually the sharp bow of the U-113 began to sink. The heavy mooring lines that had been rigged from her midships point to the massive cypress trees on either side of the inlet went taut, preventing her from sliding ahead into the pond.

As the bow submerged beneath the black-tea water, the stern rose correspondingly. Stuermer stalked swiftly along the bank, moving aft, watching the orientation of his vessel intently. The U-boat's slow pitch forward began to ease.

"Blow aft tanks!" Dekker shouted into the speaking tube.

Immediately, the hull rang with the blasting sound of compressed air being released, and two white geysers of foam erupted on either side of the U-113 just aft of her saddle tanks. The drum-tight mooring lines creaked and quivered as she canted forward even more, her stern rising partly clear of the water.

"All remaining ballast forward, Chief!" Stuermer called out, peering under the stern of the U-boat.

"Aye, sir!" Dekker bent to the speaking tube. "Transfer all remaining fuel forward! Flood all bow tanks completely!"

Her pumps and compressors thrumming, air bubbles still boiling up on either side of the aft deck, the U-113 rocked forward until her stem buried itself in the detritus at the bottom of the pond, some twelve meters below. The thick mooring lines amidships, taut as bridge cables, kept the central part of her hull from sinking beneath the surface despite her extreme angle.

"Come on, *come on*," Bock muttered urgently, standing beside Jolene in the grassy scrub. He dropped to one knee, eyeing the angle of the deck. She put a hand on his back and knelt with him.

The U-113 let out a series of metallic groans as her motion slowed. When her gradual forward pitch finally ceased, her stern had risen completely out of the water. Beneath it, revealed at last in daylight, her badly damaged bronze screws and steel shafts gleamed with green-and-orange oxidation. The through-hull glands had cleared the surface of the water by eighteen inches.

On the conning tower, Dekker's head and shoulders reappeared above the armor-plated bridge baffles. "Did we get enough incline, Captain?" he shouted.

Stuermer stood up and shook a fist triumphantly in the air. "We did, Otto! By about half a meter. Well done! Stabilize the boat at this angle as best you can and let's get to work on those shafts before something shifts."

"Aye, sir!" Dekker turned to face the mob of seamen crowding the edge of the inlet. "You heard the captain! Move your asses, boys! Machinists to the engine room— get those shafts uncoupled. Riggers, deploy the work rafts and tie them under the stern. I want that useless metal junk pulled off this boat within the hour!"

The crewmen went into action, dividing themselves into previously organized work details. Roughly a third

of them leaped back aboard the U-113 and hurried
below, while most of those remaining on shore began to
drag several ten-foot-square wooden rafts made of
lashed barrels and timbers toward the water. Several
other men started to free up the lines to the block-and-
tackle rigging that had been positioned twenty feet
above the stern, stretched between the two trees on opposite sides of the inlet.

Stuermer was walking toward Bock and Jolene when
he became aware of an odd vibration in the air. It took
several seconds for him to comprehend what it was. The
buzz of conversation generated by the working men died
away as the vibration rose rapidly to a high-pitched roar.

"*Alarrrmmm*!" Stuermer yelled, automatically using
the standard U-boat emergency command. "Aircraft approaching! Everyone under the nets *now*!"

Crewmen stripped to the waist dove in under the camouflage covering and lay still, craning their necks to look
upward through the dense foliage. The roar became
deafening, and then, like giant, dark blue birds of prey,
three U.S. Navy Catalina patrol bombers appeared less
than two hundred feet above the cypress treetops. Their
wings blotted out the sun as they passed directly overhead, casting huge, fleeting shadows across the camo
nets and the prostrate men beneath.

Stuermer rolled over in the coarse vegetation and
watched as the bombers disappeared behind the treetops
to the southeast, the combined roar of their engines fading to a low drone. A trickle of sweat ran down his
temple and stung the corner of his eye. He wiped it away
with the edge of his thumb.

"Do you think they saw us, Captain?" Wolfe's deep
voice was hoarse with tension. The big torpedoman had
ended up nearby during the mass scramble for cover.

Stuermer shook his head. "No. They'd be coming back
if they did." He gestured toward the pond. "With all
these huge trees forming such a dense canopy of leaves
over this entire area, I'm not sure that even the shanties
are visible from the air."

"Lucky for us," Wolfe muttered.

The *Kapitänleutnant* smiled thinly. "Indeed. Let's not

waste our luck." He got to his feet and took a deep breath. "Everyone carry on! But prepare to take cover if any more aircraft come our way!"

Wolfe stood up, brushing dead grass and burrs off his clothes. "Excuse me, sir," he said, touching his temple briefly with two fingers, "I have work to do."

"Carry on, Lothar," Stuermer replied. "But tell *Puster* Winkler that I want radar surveillance resumed. I don't want any planes surprising us again."

"Yes, Captain."

As Wolfe turned and trotted off toward the bow, the U-boat commander looked around for Bock. The exec was nowhere to be seen. Odd. Before the planes had overflown them, he'd seen Bock and Jolene standing together less than thirty feet away—beside the silver gray trunk of one of the giant cypresses that rose out of the swampy ground.

Men were moving back and forth, continuing the deployment of the work rafts and preparing the overhead rigging to lift out the first damaged propeller and shaft. Stuermer could see that at the far end of the clearing, sitting in the shade of an overhanging palmetto opposite the U-113's bow were Holt—smoking, as usual—and Lucius, guarded by crewmen Mohler and Burkhardt. But of Bock and the girl there was no sign.

Jolene must have gone off toward the settlement, Stuermer decided. Well, she was back where she belonged. And Bock . . . his young exec was probably below in the engine room, in the thick of the shaft-uncoupling operation. That would be right in character for him.

He stopped a crewman who was hurrying past with a coil of heavy rope draped across his shoulders and two large snatch blocks dangling from his hands. "Over there, Kurtz," he instructed. "Rig a pullback line from that tree directly opposite the stern."

"Yes, sir." As the sailor staggered off toward the head of the little inlet, Stuermer turned around just in time to see Papa Luc step out of the dense undergrowth. The tall Cajun strode forward, his gray white hair and beard a stark contrast with his rumpled black clothes. He was smiling, but something in his eyes made Stuermer feel for the butt of the Walther that was still in his jacket pocket.

The leader of *les Isolates* stopped in front of him. "So, you come back, eh?" he said. *"Très bien*—we keep our part of the bargain. Where the rest of my money at?"

Stuermer lifted an eyebrow. *"Your* money?" he replied. "I thought it was the community's money, my friend."

"That's what I mean." Papa Luc's eyes were like blue ice. "They do like I tell them, so when I say *my* money, I mean *our* money. Now, you about to fix your boat and get on your way. We kept our mouths shut about you bein' here, helped you find that trawler over yonder"—he pointed at the *Shiloh*, moored alongside the U-113—"so you could get your salvagin' done, and sold you food and supplies." His eyes narrowed. "Time for you to pay your debts."

"I told you," Stuermer said, shaking his head, "you get all the money and gold when we leave. Not before. But I will give you another small down payment. I think that two more bars—"

"Non!" Papa Luc interrupted angrily. "Once you get everything repaired, ain't nothin' to stop you from leavin', no! I want it *now!"*

The *Kapitänleutnant* folded his arms. "Sorry, my friend. You don't feed the dog until it's done its trick."

Papa Luc's face blackened. "You come with me," he said. "We gonna take a little walk."

"Where?"

"Not far," the Cajun replied. "Just through that brush over there."

Stuermer hesitated, then put his hand into his pocket and closed his fingers over the grip of the Walther. "All right," he said quietly.

Without saying anything more, Papa Luc turned and stalked off across the clearing. Stuermer let a good ten feet open up between them before following. The U-boat and the activity around it disappeared from view as they made their way into the thick undergrowth.

Stuermer followed Papa Luc along a narrow footpath

for nearly five minutes, bypassing sloughs of stagnant water and ducking under tangles of sphagnum moss. To the U-boat commander, accustomed but for brief periods of submersion to the space and the light of the open sea, the cypress swamp seemed to close in very quickly. The lush vegetation, dank moss, and towering tree trunks that rose like Doric columns out of the dark water to support the overhead leaf canopy effectively blocked out wind, sun, and sky. The only sound was the harsh, prehistoric croaking of a raven.

The *Kapitänleutnant* was about to tell Papa Luc that he would go no farther when the Cajun made a sudden sharp turn and disappeared behind a large cypress tree. Stuermer stopped in his tracks and pulled the Walther from his pocket. He waited for several seconds before speaking.

"*Que faites-vous,* Luc?" he called out. "What are you doing?"

There was no reply. Then, from behind a tangle of vines and moss some twenty feet farther down the trail, Bock stepped into view. The barrel of a hunting rifle was resting on his shoulder, the muzzle against his neck. At the other end of the rifle was Claude. Two more Cajuns, swarthy men with long black hair and unshaved faces, appeared next to him. Both carried rust-stained double-barreled shotguns.

"You see, *mon ami*?" Papa Luc's voice echoed through the stagnant air. "You play with me, maybe I play with you, eh?"

A fourth man, a trapper like the others, stepped from behind another cypress, pushing Jolene ahead of him. Her arms hung limply by her sides and her face was tilted upward, the fist tangled in her hair holding her head back. She grimaced and tried to kick backward at the man, but he merely sidestepped and gave her a vicious shake.

"Easy now, Serge," Papa Luc said. "Don't damage the gal. She just a little headstrong is all. She get her mind right once I give her the proper guidance." He slid halfway out from behind his tree. "Funny thing she wasn't on the U-boat like you told me, Claude," he con-

tinued, staring over at the trapper. Claude swallowed
hard. "But it don't make no never mind. She back
home now."

"What are you doing, Luc?" Stuermer called. "This
isn't necessary."

Papa Luc's eyes blazed. "I'm gonna tell *you* what's
necessary!" he shouted. "It's necessary for you to turn
over that money chest unless you want your man here
comin' back to you in little bitty *pieces*!"

"I told you," Stuermer said, "I can give you two bars.
There is no more on board. The rest is cached out in
the swamp."

"Where is it?"

"Out on the bottom of the bay. I have the coordinates
written down. We have to take the U-113 to the exact
spot and put a diver over the side to locate it and pick
it up. You would never find it yourself."

Papa Luc waved the four trappers back into the bush.
"Then you finish fixin' your boat, *mon ami*, go get it,
and bring it back here. Then you get your man back."

Stuermer hesitated. "Why are there patrol bombers
flying over *les Isolates*' camp?" he demanded. "If they
find us, you get nothing."

"They fly here; they fly there," Papa Luc said. "I
didn't bring them, no. But I might, if you don't pay your
debts." He backed into the brush after Bock, Jolene,
and the gun-wielding trappers. "One more day. And
then maybe your luck with planes changes, eh?"

And then, like the others, the tall Cajun was gone,
swallowed up by the silent, all-enveloping foliage.

The small group of *Isolates* and their two captives
trekked around the north end of the pond, taking a difficult, rarely used route that twisted through bogs, bram-
ble patches, and nearly impassable vine tangles. The U-
boat commander and his men, unfamiliar with the area,
would have little chance of following them through
such terrain.

The trail took them past the dilapidated, moss-covered
shanty that stood apart from the rest, built out over the
black water on rickety wooden legs where the north end

of the pond narrowed into an inland bayou. The four
trappers sloshed quickly past it with their eyes averted,
pushing Jolene and Bock roughly ahead of them. Papa
Luc stopped for a moment and looked darkly at the
shanty and the surrounding undergrowth but, seeing
nothing, moved on, grumbling.

As he followed the others, Estelle stepped out from
beneath the drooping limbs of a small swamp willow,
less than five feet from where he'd been standing. In
plain view, she watched Papa Luc's black-clad back
move off down the narrow trail, a broad grin creasing
her toadlike face. The Cajun leader had but to turn
around to find himself nearly face-to-face with her, but
he did not. She'd known he would not.

As Estelle watched the little group recede into the
brush, Jolene stumbled and fell to one knee. Instantly,
the young German officer—*Bock*, the old woman had
heard him called—stooped down and helped her to her
feet, a hand beneath her arm. Estelle caught the look
that passed between them as their eyes met. Then the
trappers pushed them apart, shouting angrily in French.
The young German's instinct was to hold his ground,
Estelle noticed. He did not like to be pushed.

Jolene's eyes lingered on him as they were prodded
on down the trail. The flush on her cheeks was apparent
even from this considerable distance, the old woman
thought. And Bock, regardless of the tight situation he
was in, was having trouble keeping his eyes off the slim
Creole girl. Estelle's grin grew even broader.

"Bon, ma chérie," she whispered aloud. "Someone for
you, at last."

There was a rustling sound in the ground cover
nearby, and the black cat she had thrown at Papa Luc
on the night he'd stormed into her shanty emerged from
a patch of brambles, its luminous green eyes staring up
at her. There was a small lizard dangling from its mouth.
Raising its tail and arching its back, the cat rubbed up
against the hem of the old woman's robe, meowed
loudly, and dropped its tiny victim at her feet.

Leaning heavily on her cane for support, Estelle bent
down and picked up the little reptile, pinching its tail

between a gnarled thumb and forefinger. Holding it up in front of her face, she examined it, squinting hard. The cat sat back on its haunches and followed every movement of the tiny corpse with unblinking eyes.

Estelle looked down. "You bring me a pretty present, *n'est-ce pas*?" The cat meowed once again. "Come on, now." The old woman turned and began to shuffle through the brush toward the lone shanty. The cat followed, picking its way delicately over the swampy ground as if its paws were satin slippers.

"Let's you and me think awhile about Jolene and Papa Luc, eh?"

Chapter
Twenty-seven

Stuermer knelt down on the bank opposite the U-113's uplifted stern and watched the repair in progress. A dozen seamen, stripped to the waist and balancing precariously on the makeshift work rafts, were muscling the first replacement propeller shaft into alignment with the port through-hull gland. The shaft and the screw were supported by several heavy lines that ran through the overhead block-and-tackle system stretching between the tall cypress trees on opposite sides of the inlet. It was far from a perfect rigging arrangement, and the seamen had hitched half a dozen tag lines to the shaft in an effort to pull it into place. The operation was accompanied by a stream of profanity and the requisite low-brow wisecracking about maneuvering the shaft into the hole.

Dekker, overseeing the installation from a vantage point on one of the rafts, was losing patience. "Together, *verdammt*, together! Do you want to be here all day, waiting for those Catalinas to show up again? You four in the back, lift straight up! Kurtz, Rathke, push left . . . *left!*"

There was a chorus of grunts and groans as the coupling end of the heavy shaft stabbed into the through-hull, stuck, and then slid forward into the engine room.

The chief snapped a finger through the air in a fast spiral. "Slack the holdback lines!" he barked. "*Slack!*"

A low cheer rose from the sweating men as the heavy steel column went all the way in and bottomed out with a metallic *boom*. Dekker pulled a dirty handkerchief from his back pocket and mopped his dripping forehead. "All right, boys," he said. "De-rig it."

Up on the bank, Stuermer shifted on his haunches as he lit a cigarette. "How long for the other shaft, Chief?" he asked.

Dekker puffed out his cheeks. "If it goes as well as this one, maybe an hour, Captain."

"Any difficulties making the couplings in the engine room?"

"No, sir. As you said, the U-113 and the U-115 came down the ways in Bremen almost on top of each other. All the fittings are the same."

The *Kapitänleutnant* rose to his feet and blew out a stream of smoke. "All right. Get the starboard shaft installed and then test run both screws. If we can, we'll leave under cover of darkness tonight."

"Home, sir?" Dekker inquired.

"Home, Otto."

The chief grinned and touched his grimy fingers to his forehead before turning back to the work party. "Let's go, let's go! Let's get that second shaft rigged before dark, eh?"

Stuermer walked forward along the bank to the gangplank, crossed over onto the U-boat's deck, and mounted the external ladder of the deeply tilted conning tower. Ascending to the bridge, he paused to search the surrounding sky through the camouflage netting, then butted his cigarette and climbed down through the hatch to the control room.

Winkler was sitting in the radio room, idly watching the circular radar screen, his thick glasses pushed up on his forehead. He straightened up slightly as Stuermer appeared in the narrow doorway.

"Any aircraft contacts, Jonas?" Stuermer asked.

"No, sir." There was an empty silence as the thin radioman stared at the bulkhead for a moment. "I suppose I shouldn't have sent out those English distress messages while you were away. I thought there might be a chance that we'd attract some help." He sounded very tired. "I think it's pretty clear that we were triangulated when I responded to that radio reply. It *must* have been a decoy. All of a sudden there were Catalinas right on top of us."

Stuermer shrugged, not quite smiling. "You and Chief Dekker both made the decision to transmit," he said. "You didn't know if I'd make it back. And anyway, the fix wasn't perfect; the planes seem to have missed us. They don't know exactly where we are, and we're not about to transmit again."

"If they think we're a U-boat," Winkler muttered, "and they didn't get a highly accurate fix on us, they'll probably spend most of their time searching over empty water out in the Gulf of Mexico. But they're looking for us now. They know *something* is in the area." He sighed. "It's my fault. I should have sat tight and waited for you."

Stuermer reached out and rested a hand briefly on Winkler's shoulder. "They won't catch us. We're going to slip out tonight, after dark. And then we'll be gone. Headed south, back to the Atlantic."

The radioman nodded. "Yes, sir," he said quietly.

"All right, then, Jonas." Stuermer stepped out into the passageway, ducking his head under the low jamb. "There'll be a meeting in my quarters in one hour. Get someone to fill in for you at the radar set."

"Yes, Captain."

Stuermer moved aft along the upward-sloping passageway and into the control room, which was deserted but for two ballast technicians standing ready by the compressed-air valves in the event that the U-boat began to shift. They nodded to him as he passed, and he touched the brim of his peaked white cap in return.

He climbed past the petty officers' quarters, the galley, and the aft head, slipping occasionally on the sloping metal grating underfoot, and entered the diesel-engine room. The compartment reeked of dirty oil and unburned fuel, the overhead piping and conduits dripping with condensation. The deck plates had been pulled up between the massive MAN diesels, and four grease-covered machinists were down in the bilges wielding pry bars and chain hoists, sweating like slaves as they struggled to complete the coupling of the newly installed port shaft.

Stuermer flashed his hard smile as he stepped past them. "Keep it up, lads. Good work." He worked his way farther aft into the next compartment, the electric-motor room. Here, too, the deck plates had been pulled up, and a half-dozen men were working on the shaft-clutching mechanisms of the twin *E-Maschinen*.

Lothar Wolfe was one of them. Stuermer leaned down and tapped him on the shoulder. The torpedoman finished tightening the nut he was working on before looking up, his face shining with sweat in the yellow light of the work lamps.

"Captain?"

Stuermer beckoned with a finger. "Did you get that diesel fuel transferred?"

The big man nodded. "Yes, sir. I put Endrass and two other men on it. He reported it done ten minutes ago."

"Good. How's the clutch looking?"

"It'll work, sir."

"Fine." Stuermer knelt on one knee. "I need you at a meeting in my quarters in forty-five minutes, Lothar." The hard, thin smile again. "See if you can't get the boys working on the second shaft by then, eh?"

"Aye, sir," Wolfe replied. "Forty-five minutes. I'll be there."

Stuermer got to his feet. "Very well. Carry on, Torpedoman."

Fetherstone-Pugh sipped his tea and looked over the rim of the cup at Blodgett, sitting at the radio desk opposite him and noisily cracking gum, a wide grin on his face. If there was a single annoying personal habit that the American officer had not yet demonstrated, the Englishman thought, he was at a loss to name it.

"Get any confirmations from them there patrols, Knowles?" Blodgett asked. "Any of them flyboys see anything that even *looks* like a U-boat?"

Knowles, at his listening station, looked regretfully at Fetherstone-Pugh before answering. "No, sir."

"Huh!" the heavyset officer went on. "No positive reports from—what? Twelve bombers?" He shook his head. "Reckon we're just burnin' up valuable aviation fuel here, chasin' echoes around the Loo-zee-anna coast."

Fetherstone-Pugh set his teacup down and picked up one of the direct lines to Houma's primary military airfield.

"You gonna call this foolishness off, Feathers?" Blodgett demanded. "Before you make us the laughin'stock of the entire Gulf Command?"

The Royal Navy officer looked down his long, aristocratic nose at him. "Actually, Hiram, I'm calling to recommend that they continue patrolling the target area in a crisscross pattern until tomorrow morning, from twenty miles inland to fifty miles offshore. They'll need time to prepare replacement flights as the first patrols run low on fuel." He pushed back his chair. "And as I'm tired of looking at *you*, I'm going to drive down there and check on the air patrols personally. Maybe I can narrow their search."

"Aw, for crissakes," Blodgett muttered.

Stuermer moved his legs aside to make more room as Wolfe crowded next to Dekker and Winkler into the tiny captain's quarters. The big torpedoman leaned up against the doorframe, mopping his dripping face with a gray towel. Metallic banging sounds echoed up the main passageway from the engine room, along with the muted conversation of working men.

"How long now?" Stuermer asked Dekker.

The chief engineer scratched the heavy stubble on his chin. "The external work is done, Captain. The shafts are in place, the screws secured, and the rudders and aft diving planes repaired. The rudders could be straighter, but they'll hold. Inside, all that's left is to repack the starboard through-hull gland so that it doesn't leak too badly when the shaft is turning, and to finish servicing the electric-motor clutches."

"We just got done with those," Wolfe interjected. "Ready to go. I don't know if the gland's been taken care of yet."

"That won't take long," Stuermer said. "As soon as it's done, Chief, I want the boat ballasted up onto an even keel again and made ready for sea." He smiled. "Time to try for home, gentlemen."

Winkler cleared his throat. "Wait. Have we all forgotten about our diesel-fuel situation? The tanks are nearly empty, remember?" He looked at Stuermer. "Captain, with the fuel we've got left, we won't even make the Straits of Florida."

"Relax, Jonas," Stuermer replied, glancing up at Wolfe. "I've solved that little difficulty."

"You found a few thousand liters of diesel fuel?" The radioman's expression was incredulous. "Where?"

"Wait a minute," Wolfe cut in suddenly. "Where's Lieutenant Bock? He should be here." His brow furrowed. "I haven't seen him for a couple of hours."

Stuermer looked up at him, then around the little room at each of them in turn.

"Lieutenant Bock," he said, "is something of a problem."

There was a brief silence. Dekker was the first to break it: "Problem, sir? Lieutenant Bock is a problem?"

The *Kapitänleutnant* nodded. "Papa Luc has him."

"What?" Dekker looked confused. "You mean he's captured him? Kidnapped him?"

"That's exactly what I mean."

Wolfe shifted agitatedly against the doorjamb. "Then let's go and get him back," he declared.

"How?" Stuermer asked.

"How, sir? I'll tell you how: we put together an armed shore party, find the right shack, and kick in the front door."

Stuermer shook his head. "We'd never find him. And I don't want any shooting started while the U-113 is still in this lagoon. If these people panic and decide to raise the alarm, we'll get caught in here or in the bayou on the way out to the Gulf of Mexico." He rubbed his eyes. "We're going to have to bargain with Papa Luc. He wants his money, his gold, in exchange for Lieutenant Bock. He's got him hidden somewhere—well out of our reach, you can count on it."

Wolfe chewed his lower lip. "If we only knew where he was being held," he said, "we might be able to surprise them."

There was a sudden rap on the passageway bulkhead, and the young oiler's assistant, Hofstetter, appeared at Wolfe's shoulder. "Captain," he said, "there's someone outside who wants to speak with you."

Stuermer's head came up. "Who is it? Papa Luc?"

Hofstetter shook his tousled head. "No, sir. It's the strangest-looking old woman I've ever seen."

Bock twisted around angrily as Claude shoved him through the front door of the clapboard church with the butt of his hunting rifle. The interior was dim and smelled of mold and rot, and up in the rafters several swallows took flight, disturbed by the noisy intrusion. Serge prodded Jolene across the threshold, followed by the two other trappers and Papa Luc.

The Cajun leader closed the two heavy arched doors with a bang and walked forward between the half-dozen pews to the small pulpit at the side of the nondescript altar. "Light me some lamps, *mes amis*," he ordered. Then he turned to face Jolene. "Come here, girl."

She shook her head and moved over to Bock's side, clutching his arm. The young exec looked surprised for a split second, then grasped her hand in his. Papa Luc's eyes seemed to smolder like black embers, and an ugly scowl twisted across his face.

"I said, come here, girl," he repeated. "Don't be defyin' me again." He gestured at Bock. "This outsider, this *Allemand*, he ain't gonna help you. One way or the other, he's leavin' this place, forever. Now, I'm tellin' you to come over here *right now*."

Jolene bit her lip and shook her head, pressing up against the young German officer. "*Non*," she said. "I ain't doin' what you tell me ever again."

Papa Luc strode forward abruptly. "By Jesus," he shouted, "you *are* a willful little creature—*c'est vrai!* Damn you, girl, come here to me now!"

Jolene cowered back, pulling Bock with her, but before the U-boat officer could brace himself to confront

Papa Luc, Claude had the stock of the rifle across his throat. The powerfully built trapper maneuvered him over to the nearest pew, stepped around its end, and yanked him back into the seat. Bock wheezed, scarcely able to breathe with the cold steel and hardwood of the gun nearly crushing his larynx.

Papa Luc had Jolene by the shoulders, shaking her. "I don't abide no disobedience from a child, and I don't abide none from my wife! The Good Book sayeth a woman shall obey her husband—"

He was cut off in mid-rant by the loud *crack* of Jolene's palm landing on his cheek. She fought with her eyes closed, kicking and flailing, but making no sound. Papa Luc shook her some more, shouting something incomprehensible, then grabbed her by the throat with one hand and began to rain blows upon her with the other. At first he struck with his open hand, but when this had little apparent effect he closed his fist and began to slug away in earnest. His eyes took on a mad, glazed appearance and spittle flew from his lips as he gasped out fragments of Scripture in time to the savage beating he was administering.

Bock had worked his fingers under the gun across his throat, and by pushing hard was able to ease the pressure on his airway. He kicked and bucked desperately in the pew, but to no avail. Claude had him pinned off balance, and the squat, stocky Cajun was too strong. The other three trappers stood by and watched in silence as Jolene's struggles grew progressively weaker, until finally Papa Luc's biblical mutterings ceased and the only sound was the dull thudding of his bony fist being driven, over and over, into her head and body.

For a full minute after she'd lost consciousness, he continued to hit her, holding her up by the throat like a rag doll. Then, his rage spent, he flung her away into the central aisle between the pews. She hit the wooden floor like a sack of wet flour and lay still, blood trickling from her nose and mouth.

Papa Luc stood in front of the pulpit, shaking as if with palsy, his breathing racked and shallow. His mad eyes fell on Bock, who'd stopped kicking and had craned

his neck around beneath Claude's gun to look over at
Jolene. Papa Luc covered the short distance between
them in two long strides. Delivering a vicious kick to
Bock's lower leg that twisted the young German sideways in the pew, he pointed at the unconscious girl.

"Get her cleaned up!" he shrieked. "I won't abide my
wife lookin' like some sloppy trash, no!" He kicked
Bock again. "Let him up, Claude! But if he moves
toward the door, shoot him, *tu comprends?*"

Bock lurched forward with a choking wheeze as
Claude released the gun's pressure on his Adam's apple.
It was a good thirty seconds before the room stopped
swimming and the red haze cleared from his eyes. When
he turned toward Jolene she was beginning to stir feebly,
looking like a small, broken child in her baggy hand-me-
down clothes.

Without looking at Papa Luc, he eased over to her,
carefully supported her head and neck, and rolled her
gently onto her side. The entire left side of her face was
puffy and turning purple, the skin split and bloody at
the eyebrow, cheekbone, and lip. Bock's own face darkened, and he turned to Serge, who was standing nearby
with his shotgun cradled loosely in his arms.

"Water," he said, tearing off a piece of his shirttail.
"Get me some water."

Chapter
Twenty-eight

The distant drone of Catalina engines faded away to nothing as another flight of patrolling bombers crisscrossed the swamps to the south of the U-113. On the steeply tilted conning tower, Stuermer and Dekker strained their eyes but could see only clear afternoon sky through the treetops and suspended camo netting.

The *Kapitänleutnant* shrugged. "All right, Chief. Level her."

Dekker turned to the speaking tube. "Transfer fuel amidships. Flood aft tanks one third. Blow forward tanks."

"Aye," came the disembodied reply. The vibration of machinery deep in the bowels of the U-boat intensified beneath their feet, and the blasting sound of compressed air echoed up through the open bridge hatch. Moments later, a huge discharge of bubbles roiled the surface directly over the vessel's sunken bow. There was a series of metallic creaks, and the U-113 began to move.

On the shore, Stuermer saw Holt and Lucius, still under guard, get to their feet and watch intently as the U-boat responded to the ballast shift. Like a slowly breaching whale she came up, the dark water ahead of the conning tower first bulging, then splitting and cascading off her foredeck in glassy sheets. The newly installed propellers, hurriedly wire-brushed clean of barnacles and oxidation and gleaming a dull bronze, sank out of sight beneath the descending stern. The U-113 surged back and forth a couple of times on her breast lines, then settled onto an even keel, perfectly balanced.

"Not bad, Otto," Stuermer commented. "Knowing that the damage has been repaired, she almost feels like a new boat." He looked up at the midafternoon sun. "We can't leave yet. You've got a few hours to run the engines and test the shaft rotation and rudder function. With all these Catalinas nosing around we can't slip her out into the pond to see how she handles, so you'll have to do the best you can while she's moored in here."

"I'll get it done, Captain," Dekker assured him.

"I know you will."

Winkler's face appeared in the bridge hatch, his glasses pushed up into his thin blond hair. "Metox shows radar impulses everywhere, Captain. The planes are just crisscrossing this general area, looking hard for something. We've definitely enabled them to get a partial fix on us." He shook his head. "This isn't routine. If they weren't pretty sure something was here, they wouldn't be going over the same ground time and time again. I've shut down our radar, just so there isn't any chance of them locating us with their own radar-detection devices."

"All right, Jonas." Stuermer moved to the external conning tower ladder and prepared to descend. "Carry on with systems checks, gentlemen, and we'll proceed as we discussed after sundown."

He climbed down the ladder and walked up the foredeck toward the bow. Mud and debris still clung to the stem where the U-113 had buried her nose in the bottom during the ballasting inversion. He shook his head slightly, still amazed that it had worked.

Holt and Lucius had sat back down on their shaded log and were watching him. Just off to one side Mohler and Burkhardt were, in turn, watching them, their *Schmeissers* cradled against their hips. Forced to do nothing but stay in one place for the entire day while activity buzzed around them, American captives and German guards alike looked hot and bored. Holt—not surprisingly, thought Stuermer—appeared particularly sullen. The blood on his head bandage had dried to a crusty brown and his face was pale, but he seemed steadier than he had aboard the *Shiloh* during the trip inshore.

The *Kapitänleutnant* stepped down onto the U-boat's port saddle tank and leaped to the bank. As he walked toward the prisoners he lit one of Bock's few remaining Turkish cigarettes and casually searched the nearby foliage. There was no trace of the old woman, Estelle, who'd come aboard briefly less than an hour earlier. Stuermer smiled. An interesting person, Estelle.

Lucius straightened as Stuermer drew near. "When you gonna let me take Mike to a doctor?" he rumbled. "I done what you asked."

"Soon," the U-boat commander replied. He looked at Holt for a moment. "But I don't think you have to worry, Lucius. Captain Holt seems to be holding his own."

The wiry American plucked his Lucky Strike from his lips and blew a stream of smoke. "This is gettin' old, Stuermer," he said. He gestured overhead. "You ain't gonna make it out of here, you know. Not with all them warbirds lookin' for you. It's a long way down that bayou and across the bay to the Gulf."

"Your opinion is noted, Captain," Stuermer replied.

"Look, pal, why don't you just give it up? Why get blown to smithereens for a lost cause? Germany's gonna lose the war sooner or later—that's a fact. Why get yourself killed for nothin'?"

The *Kapitänleutnant* smiled his thin smile. "That Germany will lose the war may be a fact to *you*, Captain Holt, but it is not a fact to me—or my men. We have been trained to win, and we will fight on until we do. If your home here in Louisiana was being bombed every day, and you had the means to fight back, would you refuse to do so? I think not."

Holt threw his hands into the air. "But that's different!" he exclaimed. "You guys—that tin-pot Hitler—*started* this whole fuckin' mess!"

"No," Stuermer said, "you Americans—and the British, and the French—started it . . . at Versailles in 1919."

He drew on his cigarette. "But that is history you don't want to hear—and at the moment, irrelevant. The fact is, Captain, my men and I are going to go home, or die trying. As I said, you'd do—no, you've *done*—the same."

Lucius laughed softly. "Every different man, he got a different point o' view," he said. He looked Stuermer up and down, a hint of sadness in his eyes. "Strange what a fella can tell hisself is true."

Stuermer cleared his throat. "At any rate, it is time for you to return to the *Shiloh* and prepare to separate her from my boat. I can't let you go on your way until we get clear, I'm afraid, so Seamen Mohler and Burkhardt will continue to accompany you while you move your trawler over to those cypress trees"—he indicated a shaded section of the bank some fifty yards from the U-113's bow—"and tie her up until I give you permission to leave." The *Kapitänleutnant* looked pointedly at Holt. "Do you understand?"

Holt did a tough-guy chew on his cigarette before answering. "Yeah. Yeah, sure."

"Good. I would like our association to end as pleasantly as it began," Stuermer said. "And I urge you not to attempt to interfere with my vessel's departure, Captain Holt. It would hardly be worth it."

"Uh huh," Holt replied.

Stuermer eyed him, then nodded at Mohler and Burkhardt, who both had a working command of English. "Escort Captain Holt and Mr. Dancer across the U-113 and back aboard the *Shiloh*," he instructed. "I want the trawler moved across the inlet and tied up as I described. If either of these gentlemen gives you any trouble, shoot them both."

Bock lifted Jolene's head carefully and brought the tin cup of water up to her mouth. She sipped carefully through her split and swollen lips, looking up at him all the while.

"There," he said. "Is that better?"

She smiled, then winced because it hurt. "Y-yeah." Her breathing was short and sharp, as if a rib was broken.

"Lie still, Jolene." Bock looked around for something to put beneath her head. The only thing within reach was an old burlap sack. He wadded it into a pillow. It was better than nothing.

"You know what?" Jolene asked weakly.

"No. What?"

"That's the first time you've ever called me by my name." She tried to smile again. "You say it kinda funny. 'Jolene.' "

"I'm sorry," Bock replied quietly. "I won't say it, then." He pressed a damp rag to the ugly bruises on the left side of her face. Her hand came up and grasped his.

"No," she whispered through her pain. "I like to hear you say it."

"Quiet!" Papa Luc shouted, pacing back and forth in front of the church altar. "Serge! Put a crack in that *Allemand*'s skull with your gun butt if he open up his mouth again!"

The swarthy Cajun trapper nodded and grinned down at Bock, showing a mouthful of crooked black teeth. The young German kept silent and continued to swab Jolene's battered face gently with the damp cloth.

Papa Luc paced over to the side of the church's small apse and squinted through the grimy window that looked out over the pond. "He got to make a move soon," he muttered. "Got to . . ."

The fiery orange disk of the sun was just dropping below the gnarled treetops to the west and an early-evening gloom had begun to shroud the pond. Papa Luc fixed his eyes on the dark patch of shoreline that marked the little inlet. As if in response to his mutterings, the patch appeared to move . . . and then the unmistakable silhouette of the U-boat, long and low, slid out into the center of the pond.

"Eh, bien," Papa Luc announced to no one in particular, "now we see. . . ."

The U-boat executed a smooth ninety-degree turn and came down the pond toward the cluster of shanties. Following close behind was the fishing trawler, running lights unlit and wheelhouse windows dark.

The church had a wooden dock built onto one side,

supported by crooked pilings and extending nearly thirty
feet out over the black water. Talking to himself under
his breath, Papa Luc hurried over to the side door and
opened it. He shot a look back at the trappers hovering
over Bock and Jolene.

"You watch him close, *comprenez-vous*? You bring
him out if I tell you. Claude, you watch Jolene. I don't
want no more trouble from that wicked child tonight."

On the conning tower of the U-113, Stuermer turned
and peered back through the gathering gloom at the *Shiloh*, following so close behind that her scruffy white bow
was almost touching the U-boat's stern. He couldn't see
into her darkened bridge, but inside, he knew, Holt was
standing at the wheel, Lucius beside him, with Mohler
and Burkhardt on guard close behind, weapons at the
ready.

He looked up anxiously. They were out from under
the shelter of the trees now, and although the first stars
were beginning to wink in the evening sky, it was not
completely dark. It had been some time since a flight
of bombers had passed nearby, but now the U-113 was
dangerously exposed . . . both to human sight and to the
probing, invisible eye of radar.

Stuermer bent to the control room speaking tube.
"Are we being hit by any radar impulses, Jonas?" he
asked. "Anything on Metox?"

There was a pause before the reply came. "No, Captain. I'd picked up some earlier, but they've moved off
to the south—probably over the water. We're clean at
the moment."

"Very well." Stuermer straightened up and adjusted
his peaked cap. The little buildings of the settlement
were close now, dark for the most part with the occasional glow of lantern light showing here and there.
There was no sign of human activity.

"The church," the *Kapitänleutnant* said quietly to Dekker, standing at his shoulder. "Estelle said they would
all be in the church." He squinted into the deepening
dusk. "Do you see it?"

The chief stared at the dark jumble of shanties on the

bank and shook his head. "Hard to tell. Maybe that one, the one with the longer dock."

"We'll try it." Stuermer bent to the speaking tube again. "Port rudder five degrees. Engines in neutral. Stand by to reverse engines."

The U-boat's bow drifted gradually to the left as the vessel coasted up under the overhanging cypress trees once more. Stuermer's eyes narrowed. There was a tall man standing on the end of the church dock, his white hair gleaming in the first pale light of the rising moon.

"Reverse engines one-third," Stuermer ordered. The steel plating underfoot shook slightly as the propellers bit in the opposite direction and cavitated. The U-113's forward motion slowed gradually to a halt, less than twenty feet from the dock. "Engines in neutral," the *Kapitänleutnant* said. He glanced back quickly. The *Shiloh* had also stopped and was lying adjacent to the starboard stern, her diesel idling.

"Time to bargain," Stuermer said, smiling grimly at Dekker. "I'm going up on the bow. Try to keep it close to the dock . . . but not too close."

At Houma Naval Airfield, Chief Petty Officer Alvin Kendall took his hands off the controls of his PBY-5 Catalina bomber, still chocked in place at the edge of the runway, and looked over his shoulder in annoyance at the unexpected passenger squeezing in behind him and his copilot. "Who the hell are you again?" he barked over the throbbing growl of his aircraft's twin twelve-hundred-horsepower Pratt & Whitney engines.

"Admiral's office, New Orleans," Fetherstone-Pugh called, struggling with the tangled straps of his seat harness. "Observation and assessment of patrolling tactics. You understand that I may ask you to diverge from your usual routine?"

Kendall continued with his preflight check. "Yeah, yeah," he grumbled. "I got the word from the CO."

Fetherstone-Pugh frowned and leaned forward, close to Kendall's ear. "What was that again, Chief Petty Officer?"

"Yes, sir," Kendall rephrased.

The Royal Navy lieutenant commander settled back into his uncomfortable fold-down seat. Another impudent Yank. He looked out at the night through the scarred Plexiglas of the cockpit windshield. The moon was full and rising, a great luminous ball hovering above the geometric lines of the airfield's blue and white runway lights.

Good, thought Fetherstone-Pugh. *A hunter's moon.*

Chapter
Twenty-nine

Stuermer walked up the foredeck of the U-113, past the battened-down eighty-eight-millimeter cannon, and halted just aft of her prow. Less than a dozen feet away, Papa Luc stood on the church dock, his long arms hanging loosely at his sides. The pale moonlight falling across his deep eye sockets and gaunt cheeks gave his face a mummified appearance. Casually, Stuermer lifted his left hand and waved.

"*Bonsoir*, Luc," he said. "I'd hoped I wouldn't have any trouble finding you."

"You got your wish," the tall Cajun replied.

"So it seems," Stuermer continued smoothly. "I believe we have one last piece of business to transact. An exchange."

Papa Luc scowled. "Maybe. If you got what I want. What *you* owe."

"Of course." The *Kapitänleutnant* walked back down the deck to the forward hatch. "Let me get it for you." He kicked the hatch cover three times with the heel of his seaboot. It swung open almost immediately, a cone of yellowish light from the interior flooding upward. The light quickly dimmed as something was thrust up into the circular opening from below. Stuermer bent down, seized a handle, and pulled the three-foot-long tool case up onto the deck—the same tool case that had contained the gold bars and the currency the *Kapitänleutnant* had shown to Papa Luc during their initial meeting.

Stuermer dragged the heavy case up to the bow and let the end he was supporting fall to the deck with a loud *boom*. He straightened up, panting slightly, and put a cigarette between his lips. "Your payment," he said, popping a wooden match into flame with his thumbnail. He paused to light the smoke. "Enough gold and cash to sink a pirogue."

Papa Luc stared at him. "You said you'd cached it. You said you had to go an' pick it up from the bottom of the bay."

"Did I?" Stuermer laughed and blew a stream of smoke into the night air. "Then I have a confession to make: it was here on board all the time." He held up his hand. "I thought I would spare you the temptation of knowing where it was while I was away from the boat. A harmless lie, designed to protect everyone. And now, it is all yours. You see? Everything has worked out, in the end."

"Bring it on over here," Papa Luc demanded.

"Of course, of course. But before I do, I would like to see Lieutenant Bock in the flesh, alive and unharmed." Stuermer drew on the cigarette. "That is only fair. You know what is in here"—he bumped the toe of his boot into the tool chest—"but I have no idea what you may have done to my executive officer. Since our working relationship has become somewhat . . . *strained* . . . you can hardly expect me to remit the balance of your payment without first seeing him."

For a moment, Papa Luc said nothing, merely stared across at Stuermer with eyes like two black coals. Then his hand twitched and he shouted over his shoulder: "Serge! *Ecoutez!* Bring out the *Allemand!*"

Good, Stuermer thought, *he's here*.

The side door of the church opened and Bock stepped out, followed by Serge and two of the other trappers. "Claude, he watchin' the girl, like you said!" one of them shouted to Papa Luc. Stuermer strained his eyes. It was hard to see in the darkness, but he was almost certain that the one called Serge had the muzzle of a shotgun or a rifle pressed directly against the back of Bock's neck. The other two were armed as well.

"I can't see him," Stuermer said to Papa Luc. "Tell them to bring him up here."

"Eh, Serge!" Papa Luc called. "You bring that *Allemand* to the foot of the dock, no closer." He glared at Stuermer. "That's all you gonna get, *mon ami*. You ain't dealin' with no fool. And let me tell you: the first sign of trouble—whatever else happens—Serge gonna blow that boy's head clean off at the shoulders." He pointed at the tool case. "Move your boat on over here and pass that chest up."

"All right," Stuermer replied. He turned slowly and raised a hand toward the conning tower, wondering how much more time he could buy. "Chief Dekker! Swing the bow up to the dock. Not too fast—we have a lot of weight behind us."

The throb of the electric motors intensified slightly through the soles of his seaboots as he turned to face Papa Luc again. His eyes roved over the dark shoreline, past Bock and the trappers, searching the shadows around the church, the underbrush, and the nearby trees.

The U-boat's bow had moved to within two feet of the rickety dock, and the deck vibration changed slightly as Dekker ordered a thrust reversal. The bow stopped swinging. The *Kapitänleutnant* and the leader of *les Isolates* stood in silence, eye to eye, virtually within arm's reach of each other.

Papa Luc's voice was hoarse, trembling: "Pass that chest over here. *Maintenant même*. Right now."

Stuermer hesitated, then stooped down to grasp the handle of the tool case. As he did so, he glanced toward the church once more—just in time to see the four small windows facing the dock suddenly illuminated from within by a strange flash of blue light.

From inside the church, there came a bloodcurdling scream.

Seconds later, the side door burst open and Claude reeled out into the night, shrieking and clawing at his head. His hair was on fire.

He fled past Bock and the trappers, who were too stunned to move, and out onto the dock, leaving a trail of smoke and sparks behind him. The shrieking was inhuman. As Papa Luc and Stuermer watched, transfixed, he ran off the edge of the dock and hit the black water with a sizzling splash.

Papa Luc's eyes were the size of saucers as he stared back at the church, his hands shaking. "*Estelle . . .*" he choked.

Behind Bock, Serge, staring at the bubbling spot in the water where Claude had just disappeared, let the muzzle of his shotgun slip from the base of the young German's neck down onto his right shoulder.

There was a sharp *crack*. Sparks flew off the shotgun's breech and the weapon spun into the air as if snatched away by an invisible spring. Serge doubled over with a cry of pain, clutching his stinging hands to his stomach.

Crack. The second trapper went down heavily as his right foot was knocked out from under him, a hole drilled neatly through it from top to bottom, dead center, just behind the toes.

Looking around wildly, the third trapper raised his shotgun and took aim at Bock, who had started to back away from the cringing Serge. It was a mistake.

Crack. The man's eyes bugged and his mouth fell open as the high-velocity slug punched through his sternum and out between his shoulder blades. The impact knocked him backward off his feet, his arms flying out sideways as he dropped the shotgun. He hit the damp ground with a thump, spread-eagled, and lay still.

Bock stood where he was, blinking, disoriented by the rapid sequence of events. He looked down at the two wounded trappers groaning in the dirt, and their very dead companion, then up at the church. The confused expression on his face cleared, and he started for the side door.

"*Lieutenant!*"

At the sound of Stuermer's voice, Bock halted in his tracks. He stared over at the U-113, her bow nearly touching the dock, and at his commanding officer. Then he glanced back toward the church.

Twenty feet up in the ancient willow tree to which Estelle had led him, and which had provided him with an unobstructed view of the church grounds, Lothar Wolfe snapped shut the bolt of his customized hunting rifle and slung the weapon across his back. With an agility that belied his size, the big torpedoman climbed down to the lowest limb and dropped to the ground.

"Lieutenant!" Stuermer shouted again. "Come on!"

At that moment, in the wheelhouse of the *Shiloh*, Holt whirled suddenly and delivered a pile-driving straight right to Burkhardt's chin, the U-boat seaman's attention having been diverted by the commotion on shore. Mohler was quick; as his comrade slumped to the floor, out cold, he stepped back and got his *Schmeisser* lined up on Holt's chest—almost.

Lucius' huge arms enveloped him from behind in a bear hug, tearing the machine pistol from his grasp. He struggled vainly as the powerful mate lifted him off his feet, half suffocating him and nearly cracking his ribs, and began to carry him out the port door of the wheelhouse. As his head swam, he heard the rising growl of the *Shiloh*'s main engine being throttled up.

The next thing he knew, the pressure around his chest was gone and he was falling. The fall was short. Mohler hit the water beside the stern of the U-113 flat on his back, which knocked what little breath he had left out of his lungs. He floundered to the surface, coughing, and seconds later Burkhardt's limp body splashed down nearly on top of him. The roar of the *Shiloh*'s diesel filled his ears as the trawler's stern swept past him, pulling away from the U-boat at high speed.

Up on the conning tower, Dekker spun around at the sound of the *Shiloh*'s revving engine. As the trawler curved away across the black water of the pond, heading for the entrance to the seaward bayou, the chief cursed fluently and turned back toward Stuermer. "Captain!" he yelled, pointing.

"I see!" the *Kapitänleutnant* shouted. "Go to diesel power; disengage electric motors! I want speed! Stand

by to back out of here with both engines full astern!"
He looked past the mute, immobile Papa Luc at Bock
and Wolfe, who by this time were pounding down the
narrow dock toward the U-boat at a dead run.

"Chief!" Stuermer shouted. "Both engines full astern,
now!"

On the dock, Papa Luc raised his arms as if to block
the passage of the two approaching crewmen. The *Kapitänleutnant* bent down swiftly, grabbed the handle of the
tool case, and swung it up onto the dock. The leader of
les Isolates looked over his shoulder as the metal trunk
thudded heavily onto the rough planking. As he did so,
Bock and Wolfe dashed past him unimpeded and leaped
across the water gap onto the U-113's foredeck.

Stuermer touched the brim of his peaked white cap
as the U-boat backed rapidly away from the dock, her
diesel ports billowing out acrid exhaust. "Adieu, Luc,"
he said simply.

The tall, withered-looking Cajun sank to his knees and
set a pair of trembling hands on top of the tool case as
Stuermer turned and ran along his vessel's foredeck
toward the conning tower.

Jolene stumbled and nearly fell as her toe caught
under an unseen root. Beside her, Estelle paused in her
steady forward shuffle and, gripping the girl's elbow between gnarled fingers, waited until Jolene had regained
her balance. The animal-bone charms dangling from Estelle's shawl clattered gently as she helped the injured
girl find her feet.

"Easy, child," she soothed. "Ain't no rush now. We
nearly there."

Jolene leaned on the old woman as another wave of
dizziness came and went. Her head was splitting, and
sharp pains lanced through her severely bruised torso
with each halting breath. Though it felt like an hour, it
had been only minutes since Estelle had surprised
Claude in the church, throwing a ball of blue fire in his
face when he'd pointed his rifle at her. As he'd fled out
the side door, screaming, his head wreathed in flames,
the wily old woman had ushered her out the front door

and into the nearby undergrowth. Behind them, the hollow crack of rifle shots had echoed through the night air.

A tear rolled down the side of Jolene's nose, and she looked at Estelle with brimming eyes, one of which was nearly swollen shut. "Did you see him, Estelle?" she asked, her voice breaking. "Did you see Erich? He didn't get shot, did he?"

The old woman reached up and gently stroked the ugly bruises on Jolene's face with her fingertips. "I didn't see, child," she said. "But that means . . . I didn't see him get shot, neither, eh?" She smiled faintly.

A quiet sob escaped the girl's lips. "He's gone, ain't he, Estelle?" Tears ran freely down her cheeks, glistening in the moonlight. "I'll never see him again."

Estelle took her hand and squeezed it. "Nothin' in this life is for certain, child," she whispered, and led her off into the undergrowth once more.

Chapter
Thirty

"Ha!" Holt gloated, steering with his stump between the top spindles of the *Shiloh*'s wheel, the throttle lever hard forward under his right hand. "Took those bastards by surprise. They won't even have that U-boat backed out and spun around before we make the mouth of the bayou. They can't run through all those tight turns as fast as we can."

Lucius was standing in the port doorway of the wheelhouse, looking aft. "Got some skinny water 'bout halfway to the bay, too," he said. "Maybe ten, twelve feet deep, no more. Betcha they scrape bottom there—slow 'em down some."

"Good, that'll make it easier for the navy to locate 'em." Holt plucked the mike off the ship-to-shore radio. He keyed it a couple of times, cleared his throat, and then frowned. "What the hell . . ." He keyed the mike again. "This thing turned on, Lucius?"

The big mate strode across the wheelhouse and examined the radio, flipping the on/off switch several times. "Yeah, Mike," he said. He patted the top of the housing. "But the tubes ain't warm. Somethin' wrong here . . ."

"Shit!" Holt swore. He banged the mike down on the console. "Check it out, will ya?"

Lucius released the unit's hold-down straps and spun it so that the back faced out. Unscrewing a couple of threaded cap nuts, he pulled the panel off, bent close, and peered inside. Then he blinked, looked up at Holt, and shook his head.

"I'll be damned," he said. "Look here." He turned the set around so that Holt could see inside. The working parts of the radio—tubes, wiring, delicate circuitry—had been neatly and thoroughly smashed. And there was something else, placed carefully just inside the housing. Lucius reached in with two fingers, extracted it, and held it up. It was one-half of a slender six-inch bar of gold.

Lucius rubbed his thumb over the rough-cut end. A few random flecks of gold dust came off on his skin. "Hacksaw," he muttered. A trace of a smile formed on his lips. "I'll be damned," he said again.

Holt stared at the gold bar, then back at the ruined radio. "Fuck," he said simply. There was a metallic *snick* and his Zippo flared as he lit a Lucky Strike, puffing furiously. He rammed his hand back down on the throttle, and the high-pitched roar of the *Shiloh*'s diesel jumped another decibel or two. Outside the port and starboard doors of the wheelhouse, the immense, dark cypress trees were looming very close now as the trawler foamed through the black water toward the bayou entrance.

"It don't matter about the radio," he said. "They ain't gonna catch us now. We'll beat them through the channel and across the bay, then cut behind the barrier islands where it's too shallow for 'em to follow. Get over nearer the shipping lanes. First boat or plane we spot, we'll fire off a handful of distress flares." He kicked his toe into the door of the storage cabinet beneath the bridge console. "Pull out a dozen or so of those red pistol flares. That big box on the bottom shelf, remember?"

Lucius squatted down on his haunches, opened the cabinet, and rummaged around momentarily. Then his head came up. "They ain't here, Mike."

"What?" Holt coughed out a billow of cigarette smoke. "Look again, dammit."

Lucius dug around. "Nope. Gone." He stood up and banged shut the cabinet door. "I recall 'em bein' there, but they sho' as hell gone now."

"That fuckin' Stuermer," Holt fumed through gritted teeth. "You can't trust them Krauts, you see? One sneaky goddamned sonofabitch."

The ghost of a smile reappeared on Lucius' ebony face. "Pretty smart," he observed. "But like you say, it don't matter." He moved over to the port door and gazed astern into the night. "They comin' now, all right . . . but they ain't gonna catch us."

Holt chewed on his Lucky Strike. "Not in *this* war, anyway," he growled.

"*Verdammt,*" Stuermer muttered softly, squinting into the hazy darkness, "they're going to get into the bayou ahead of us." He smacked his hand on the armored baffle of the conning tower. "I did *not* want that to happen."

Beside him, Bock watched as Mohler and another crewman helped the still-groggy Burkhardt down through the foredeck hatch. Twin lines of foam creamed off the U-113's sharp bow as she surged forward over the glassy black water of the pond, her twin MAN diesels turning at high rpm. As the U-boat bypassed the largest concentration of shanties in *les Isolates'* little settlement, roaring like a great metal dragon and trailing a long cloud of acrid exhaust, lights began to flicker on here and there.

"You'd have thought the shooting would have woken them up," Dekker said.

"Probably used to hearing people hunting at night," Bock suggested. "But not the sound of a U-boat making way across their pond at high speed."

"I'm sure," Dekker replied. "I'm going to the control room, Captain."

Stuermer nodded. "Keep an eye on the helm, Otto. We're going to be doing some fast maneuvering."

As Dekker descended out of sight, the *Kapitänleutnant* noticed Bock gazing back across the pond in the direction of the little church. "The girl, Jolene," the young exec said. "You didn't happen to see what happened to her, did you?"

Despite the tension of the pursuit, Stuermer's thin

smile appeared. "No," he replied. "She never came out of the church—not that I could see." He paused, peering ahead at the *Shiloh*'s broad white transom. The trawler was just beginning to disappear into the mouth of the narrow bayou. "But Estelle was going to take care of her, so I don't think you need to worry."

"Oh." Bock's voice sounded distant. "Good."

"And Erich . . ."

"Sir?"

"I need my executive officer with his mind on what he's doing."

Bock snapped to instantly. "Yes, Captain. Of course." He searched the darkness ahead, his eyes roving. "*Verdammt.* The trawler's gone. That bayou just swallowed her up." He glanced at Stuermer. "This isn't good, is it, sir? If Holt can get out into the bay and signal for help before we're in water deep enough to dive in, we aren't going to be able to hide from any attacking boats or planes. As a matter of fact"—Bock looked up anxiously at the starry night sky—"I can't imagine why he hasn't radioed a bomber patrol down on us by now."

Stuermer smiled. "I took care of that."

"He could even shoot off some distress flares. Attract patrols that way."

The *Kapitänleutnant* shook his head. "I took care of that, too. There is no conventional means of signaling for help aboard the *Shiloh*. Holt's on his own. And he's probably discovered it by now."

Bock shrugged helplessly. "Well, he's going to beat us out into the Gulf," he said. "There's a lot of traffic out there. All he has to do is hail any nearby vessel that has a working radio, and if he finds one before we can make it to deep water, we're going to get caught on the surface."

"He won't be able to reach the Gulf before we do," Stuermer said.

Bock looked at him. "I don't understand, Captain. The *Shiloh* can motor through that twisting bayou much more quickly than we can with our length and draft. We can't catch her now."

Stuermer's eyes glinted as he flipped up the cap on

the control room speaking tube and prepared to issue helm orders. "Yes, we can," he said, "and we will. Trust me."

After forty minutes in the air, Fetherstone-Pugh was nearly deafened by the omnipresent roar of the Catalina's Pratt & Whitney engines. Although the three-plane patrol group was flying at low altitude, what he was able to see of the swamps below amounted to an endless black void punctuated by the occasional gleam of moonlight reflecting off some unnamed body of water. To top it off, the Catalina's navigator/radar operator was getting no contacts on his scope that were not readily identifiable as coastal fishing vessels, and the pilot, Kendall, was exhibiting a sullen resentment of Fetherstone-Pugh's intrusion that rivaled Blodgett's. The Royal Navy officer found himself having to yell course variations at the top of his lungs to get any response.

He hunched over the grid map of southern Louisiana that was spread across his knees and examined it with a small red flashlight. Then he stared out through the Plexiglas at the darkness racing by. Somewhere out there, he knew, was Jonas Winkler. And where there was Jonas Winkler, there had to be a U-boat. There *had* to be.

He leaned forward, tapped the uncooperative Kendall on the shoulder, and shouted into his ear: "Turn to the southwest for fifteen minutes. I want to cover grid nineteen."

The pilot's cheeks puffed out as he let loose a weary sigh. Then he nodded to his copilot, twisted the controls, and banked the Catalina off through the night sky, chasing down the new bearing.

Holt spun the wheel as the *Shiloh* took the hairpin turn in the bayou at fourteen knots. Behind the wheelhouse, the upright outriggers jangled as they clipped an overhanging hank of sphagnum moss, tearing loose a big clump. Lucius stepped out to the port rail, looking up momentarily, then reentered the bridge.

"No problem," he said. "Jus' carryin' a little moss up there now."

"Nothin' to slow us down from here on out," Holt replied. "That shallow spot's comin' up. The bayou runs straight after that, all the way to the bay. We've got it—"

His voice faded abruptly as the main engine missed four times in a row and started to die. "*Goddammit!*" he cursed. He pumped the throttle lever back and forth as the big diesel began to idle, then sputter. The *Shiloh* settled low in the water as her speed fell off to nothing, and as Holt took the engine out of gear, desperately trying to reduce the load, she lost steerage way and drifted sideways, her starboard side crushing foliage and bracken along the bank with loud crackling sounds. Then, with a final cough, the diesel went completely dead.

"Lucius!" Holt yelled, but the mate was already out the door and heading for the engine-compartment access hatch on the back deck. Grabbing a small toolbox from a shelf on the aft bulkhead, Holt stumbled out after him.

Lucius had the hatch thrown back and was down beside the main engine before Holt set foot on the back deck. Sweat beaded on the big mate's bald head, shining in the moonlight, as he ran his skilled hands over the diesel, as sure of what he was touching in the pitch-darkness as a blind man reading Braille.

Holt dropped to his knees and set the toolbox down—*bang*—beside him. "What the hell is it?" he hissed. "Them fuckin' injectors again?"

Abruptly, Lucius stood up and climbed out of the compartment. "It can't be," he muttered. "It can't be. . . ."

He ran to the sounding vents flush-mounted to the deck on either side of the mast, unscrewed their water-tight bronze caps, and snatched a long, hash-marked wooden rod from its hangers beneath the port gunwale. Quickly, he inserted the measuring rod into first one vent, then the other, checking the levels in the *Shiloh*'s huge twin fuel tanks. When he turned to Holt, holding out the lower end of the rod, his expression was grim.

"We outta fuel, Mike," he said. The measuring rod was dry along its entire length. "Not a drop."

"*What?*" Holt's face went blank with shock. "We can't

be. We topped up for a long haul, remember? You're talkin' about thousands of gallons of diesel—"

He turned slowly and looked back up the bayou as the roaring sound of the U-113's thirsty MAN engines began to reverberate through the shadowy cypress trees, growing rapidly in intensity. Spooked night herons and ravens, croaking and cawing, fled their nocturnal perches as the unfamiliar racket filled the air.

"—fuel," the wiry captain finished, his voice a hoarse whisper.

Chapter
Thirty-one

"Helm, hard to port!" Stuermer barked into the speaking tube. "Port engine, reverse, three-quarter speed. Starboard engine, ahead one-half." He and Bock ducked as the scraggly branches of a willow scraped first over the forward antiaircraft gun and then the armored plate of the bridge's wind baffle. The U-113, too long by far to be driving down the narrow bayou as quickly as she was, swung awkwardly through the tight bend, her counterrotating screws churning hard and crabbing her stern to starboard. With full port rudder, she came close to spinning on the axis of her conning tower—but not quite. Her steel bow crackled through the undergrowth on the bayou's western bank, tearing loose vines and briars and snapping off small saplings.

"Bloody hell," Bock breathed, eyeing the narrow margin by which the bow would miss an upcoming fully grown cypress, "too tight in here, Captain."

The U-boat listed slightly to starboard as the central part of her keel rode up over a shallow spot near the eastern bank, then leveled again as she eased through the turn into deeper water. Stuermer let go a sigh of relief and pushed his white cap up on his forehead.

"We still have to slide over that one extremely shallow spot," he said, "but after that, it's a fairly straight run down to the bay."

"As I recall, that's just ahead, isn't it, sir?"

"Yes." Stuermer bent to the speaking tube. "Helm amidships. Both engines ahead one-third."

The U-113 steadied herself in the center of the narrow waterway as she continued to glide forward, the brush and the trees on either side of her seemingly close enough to touch. As Bock peered at the black water ahead, a thick log lying on a bare patch of light-colored soil on the western bank came into view, illuminated by a shaft of moonlight. The bow of the U-boat drew abreast of the bare patch, and without warning the log—all fourteen feet of it—came to life, launching itself through the air for fully half its length and hitting the water with a tremendous slap. The alligator thrashed its scaly tail once across the surface in a wide arc, and disappeared.

"Helm, port two degrees," Stuermer ordered. The bow began to track slowly through a gradual turn to the left, keeping in line with the center of the channel. The *Kapitänleutnant* kept a sharp eye on the orientation of his boat until the bayou straightened again. "Helm amidships."

"Captain," Bock said, squinting into the darkness ahead, "you were right. There she is."

Stuermer stared down the bayou. "That's certainly the *Shiloh*," he replied. "She's right on top of that shallow spot we have to slide over." He bent to the tube. "Port and starboard engines, full astern!" As the pitch of the MAN diesels changed yet again, slowing the U-113's forward progress, Stuermer frowned and shaded his eyes against the gleam of the moon overhead. "Something's not right," he said, straining to see through the darkness.

Jonas Winkler's head appeared in the bridge hatch. "Permission to come up, Captain."

"Granted, Jonas." Stuermer continued to stare at the dim outline of the *Shiloh*.

"Our radar is still off, sir," the slender radioman reported. "I got a distant contact on Metox just now. There are still patrols in the air, probing with their own radar. None are close at the moment, but they're around. I strongly suggest that we make it to water deep enough to submerge in before dawn—or risk the conse-

quences." He pushed his Coke bottle glasses up into his
limp, thinning blond hair and moved up beside Bock,
who continued to gaze out into the night. "What are we
looking at?"

The exec pointed ahead. "The *Shiloh*, see? We've
caught up to her, for some reason. Now we have to slide
past her if we're going to reach the Gulf before morning." He drummed his fingers on the wind baffle. "It
looks like Holt's got her anchored directly in the middle
of the bayou, right on top of that shallow spot."

"He probably hopes he can block us in," Winkler surmised. "But with our weight, we should be able to just
push him aside, eh?"

"I'm sure of it," Bock replied. "What I don't understand is why he stopped and let us catch him." He
looked over at Stuermer. "Surely he can't be thinking
he can turn this into some kind of fight?"

"No, he's not," the *Kapitänleutnant* said. "He's out of
fuel." He glanced over at his surprised exec. "I know
because I ordered the contents of both his diesel tanks
pumped over to the U-113 while the *Shiloh* was moored
alongside during the shaft and screw repair." He smiled.
"You missed that meeting, Erich—being in the company
of Papa Luc at the time."

"Ahh," Winkler said. "*That's* where the diesel we're
running on came from. Enough to get us home,
Captain?"

"All the way," Stuermer replied, turning back toward
the *Shiloh*, "if we can get past Captain Holt and his
trawler." He lifted a pair of Zeiss binoculars to his eyes
and began to focus them.

Bock shrugged. "He can't stop us, sir. Without power,
he can't even try to ram us. All we have to do is nudge
him off to the side and we're through. There's isn't anything he can do."

Stuermer slowly lowered the binoculars. "Yes, there
is, Lieutenant. There is one thing. And he's done it."

Bock looked at him. "Sir?"

The *Kapitänleutnant* passed him the Zeiss glasses.
"Have a look."

The U-113's forward drift ceased entirely as Bock

raised the binoculars and centered the *Shiloh* in the viewing field. At first he thought he was seeing things, and adjusted the focus in and out several times. But his eyes had not deceived him.

The trawler's mast and its net outriggers still reached skyward between the overhanging cypress trees. Her upward-angling bow pulpit and boxy wheelhouse were still visible in the pale moonlight. But that was all.

The rest of the *Shiloh*—massive hull, decks, winches, and engines—lay beneath the surface of the water. Holt and Lucius, no doubt by opening all her sea cocks, had sunk the trawler across the narrowest and shallowest part of the bayou, completely blocking it off. They were both standing on the wheelhouse roof, staring at the approaching U-boat, black water brimming through the windows and the doors of the bridge two feet below them.

"*Mein Gott*," Bock muttered. "That crazy bastard Holt has sunk his own boat. Right across the channel." He focused the binoculars on the American captain's features, which were clearly visible now in the moonlight.

The coal of a Lucky Strike glowed briefly. Behind it, the expression on Holt's haggard face was a mixture of anger, desperation, and triumph.

Papa Luc had been kneeling on the church dock in front of the open tool case for nearly thirty minutes, staring blankly at the contents like a man in a trance. Ashore, Serge and the other surviving trapper—the one with the punctured foot—had long since hobbled off into the brush. The unfortunate Cajun who'd aimed his shotgun at Bock, earning himself an instantaneous bullet through the sternum from Wolfe, lay spread-eagled on his back where he'd fallen, his sightless eyes staring up at the star-encrusted night sky. Of Claude there was no sign; he'd never resurfaced after plunging off the dock into the inky water, his head ablaze.

Slowly, rigidly, Papa Luc reached inside the case and withdrew the single item it contained. Then, eyes glazed and mouth hanging open, he rose to his feet and lurched stiffly back along the dock toward shore, zombielike, his arms dangling loosely by his sides. He stumbled off the wooden planks onto the swampy ground, gaining speed, and headed for the narrow trail that led off into the brush toward the north end of the pond. As he did so, an incoherent stream of biblical quotations and vague obscenities began to spill from his lips.

By the time he was fifty feet into the dripping undergrowth, his mutterings had become shouts and he was crashing along in a near frenzy, heedless of the thorny vines and brambles tearing at his hair and clothes.

In his clenched right hand, he held the only thing the tool case had contained: a fetish consisting of a rawhide thong on which had been strung the tiny skulls of birds, reptiles, and small mammals.

It was less than a quarter mile to Estelle's shanty.

Chapter
Thirty-two

Once again, Stuermer stood on the bow of the U-113, Winkler a few feet behind him carrying a heaving line and lead. Up on the conning tower, Bock was leaning over the control room speaking tube, quietly issuing maneuvering orders as the U-boat inched forward. Beside him, Lothar Wolfe, summoned hurriedly to the bridge, slid a shell into the breech of his hunting rifle, keeping the weapon just out of sight below the top edge of the armored wind baffle.

"Watch Holt," Bock muttered. "I'm pretty sure we confiscated all his guns when we were aboard the *Shiloh* offshore, but there's no way to be certain. He's paranoid enough to have pistols stuffed into the icebox."

"Why is the captain even bothering to talk to him?" Wolfe growled irritably. "We're wasting precious time. It looks as though there's enough water between the trawler's bow and the bank for us to squeeze past."

Bock shook his head. "It may be too shallow, Lothar. The tide is low right now, and the deepest part of the channel is in the center. We might go hard aground trying to bull our way through there. The captain wants to nose up close and take a sounding with the heaving line."

"That crazy Holt," Wolfe said. "There's something wrong with his brain. We may have taken all his guns, but I wouldn't put it past him to try throwing knives or even rocks if someone gets within range—like the captain, for instance."

"That's what you're up here for," Bock replied shortly. "Keep an eye on him."

As the U-boat's bow drifted to within twenty feet of the sunken *Shiloh*, Stuermer pushed his white cap up on his forehead and regarded Holt wearily. "What have you done, Captain?" he called. "I have no time for this." He half turned and spoke quietly over his shoulder to Winkler: "Take a few soundings off the bow, Jonas. We need a full four meters."

"Aye, sir." The radioman moved forward, swung the lead, and heaved it into the black water with a loud *plop*.

Holt was grinning maniacally, his Lucky Strike clenched between his front teeth. "I told you, Stuermer— I ain't lettin' you take this U-boat back to sea so you can kill more Allied sailors." He glanced at his watch. "Gonna be light in a few hours. You listen real hard and you can hear the engines of them patrol planes now and again. They're still around, and there ain't much tree cover here. They're gonna spot you real quick come sunup. Ain't that so, Lucius?"

The black mate nodded slowly. "Like a whale in a bluegill pond."

"How deep, Jonas?" Stuermer asked quietly.

The radioman heaved the lead again—*plop*. "Barely two meters, sir. We'll never get by here."

"Look, pal," Holt declared, "why don't you just give me the keys to that thing and call it a day? It's over."

Stuermer looked at him. "It's never over."

Holt's voice rose several pitches. "You're blocked in, Stuermer! You'll never get around me!"

Stuermer began to turn away, back toward the conning tower. "Then I'll go through you," he said quietly. He put a hand on Winkler's shoulder. "Come on, Jonas."

His eyes wild, Holt reached behind the wooden shield of the starboard running light. "*You goddamn Kraut!*" he yelled, spittle flying from his lips. "*I gave you a chance!*" In one fast motion, he yanked up the *Schmeis-*

ser machine pistol that Burkhardt had dropped in the wheelhouse.

Winkler, still facing forward, saw the weapon come up level with Stuermer's shoulder blades as the *Kapitänleutnant* walked past him toward the conning tower. The senior radioman threw himself against Stuermer's back as the night air was shattered by the blast of the machine gun. His momentum drove the U-boat commander onto his face on the foredeck plates.

"Full astern!" Bock shouted, as Wolfe's hunting rifle cracked beside him. "Both engines!"

The big torpedoman's unerring shot deflected off a nearly invisible mast support cable just in front of Holt, a split second before it would have punched through his right temple. It whiz-snapped past his ear—and then Lucius crashed into him from the side with all his weight, driving him off the roof of the wheelhouse. The two Americans hit the black bayou water with a loud splash as Wolfe's second and third rounds splintered the starboard running light and the wooden base of the radio antenna in quick succession.

Wolfe ratcheted another shell into the firing chamber of his rifle and sighted through the scope a fourth time, but Holt and Lucius managed—just—to flounder behind the wheelhouse before he zeroed in on them. He put the shot into the dark water at the corner of the half-sunken structure anyway, the slug kicking up a skiff of white spray.

The U-113 was backing away rapidly now, beginning to skew sideways as she approached the previous turn in the bayou. Already, they were several hundred yards from the sunken *Shiloh*. Bock glanced aft quickly and, seeing the increasing misalignment, shouted orders into the speaking tube: "Both engines, forward, one-quarter speed!" The U-boat shuddered as she slowed to a halt, white foam churning out from beneath her stern.

Sprawled on the foredeck, dazed, Stuermer shook his head and attempted to get up. As he did so, Winkler's weight slipped off his back. The radioman slumped to the deck beside the *Kapitänleutnant* like a sack of potatoes, lying on his side.

Stuermer rolled over and got a hand under Winkler's head, supporting it. There was blood on the slender man's pale lips, but no indication of a wound on the front of his shirt. Gripping his shoulder, Stuermer pulled him gently forward and checked his back.

The thin gray cotton was soaked with blood, welling freely from four ragged punctures that were stitched across the radioman's back from armpit to armpit. By reflex, the U-boat commander pressed his hand to two of the holes, trying to stem the flow. With every beat of his heart, Jonas Winkler's lifeblood, hot and wet, pumped out through Stuermer's desperately groping fingers.

"Jonas," Stuermer whispered, his voice stricken. He shook the dying man gently, still trying to hold in the life that was leaking away beneath his hand, and turned his face upward.

Winkler's glasses were broken, hanging askew across the bridge of his nose, and several limp strands of blond hair had fallen over his high forehead. The blood coming from his mouth had slicked his chin and run down his neck. But his eyes were still clear, bright with awareness, and he was smiling.

"A life for a life, Yitzhak," he said softly. Then his head sagged off to one side in Stuermer's hand, and the light in his eyes faded away.

The U-boat commander barely heard the clang of the foredeck hatch opening a few feet away. It was not until he felt the firm hands of seamen pulling him to his feet that the shocked numbness left him and he was able to refocus. Unsteadily, he backed away several steps, his eyes on Winkler's lifeless body.

"Are you all right, Captain?" It was Mohler, looking at him anxiously.

"Yes," Stuermer replied, regaining his composure. "Take *Puster* Winkler below and secure his body in one of the berths."

"Aye, sir."

As the knot of seamen bent in unison to pick up the body of their dead officer, Stuermer turned and headed for the conning tower. Bock watched him come, relieved that his commander was walking under his own power, apparently unhurt. There was no need to wonder about Jonas. Bock had seen plenty of dead men in his short life. Later, perhaps, there would be time enough for grieving.

Stuermer came up the external ladder two rungs at a time and stepped into the bridge. On Bock's opposite side, Wolfe was peering through the scope of his rifle, his arms braced on top of the wind baffle. "I don't see them," he muttered. "They're staying behind the wheelhouse." He looked over at Stuermer. "Mr. Winkler, sir. Is he—?"

"Dead," Stuermer said.

"I'm sorry, Captain. I was too slow. And I missed three times."

Bock stepped in: "No, you weren't, Lothar. Holt was too fast, and then Lucius had them both in the water in the blink of an eye."

"Still . . ." the big torpedoman said quietly. He looked back through the scope. "I know they're back behind the wheelhouse."

Stuermer put his hands on top of the wind baffle and gazed across the black water at the *Shiloh*, his mouth set in a hard line. "Don't bother with the rifle, Lothar," he said. "We're through wasting time on Captain Holt." He glanced at Bock. "How long until dawn?"

The exec consulted his wristwatch. "About two hours, sir."

Stuermer nodded slowly. "Mm. Barely enough time to make deep water."

"Captain," Bock said. "We've still got to get around that sunken trawler. The water's too shallow to push past on either side, and she's too big for us to just ram her. We'd get hung up in the wreckage, maybe even damage our bow."

"You're right on all counts, Erich," the U-boat commander replied. "And we don't have time to waste trying to break her apart with our deck cannon."

"Only one option, then, sir."

Stuermer nodded again. "Correct. Load an eel into tube one."

*   *   *

"What the hell's that fuckin' Kraut doing?" Holt
wheezed, exasperated. He was beginning to shake with
cold, huddled in the water behind the *Shiloh*'s sunken
wheelhouse. His head wound had started to bleed again.

Lucius thought for a moment, then began to haul himself up on the roof. "Lemme go look. You keep low,
now."

"*Wait!*" Holt hissed, taken off guard. "Don't go up
there. . . ."

But Lucius was on top of the wheelhouse, water dripping from his clothes, before Holt could seize a leg and
haul him back. The mate had seen that it was Wolfe in
the conning tower handling the rifle, just as it had been
Wolfe in the tree near the church. The German seemed
selective about his targets, and somehow Lucius had a
gut feeling that he wouldn't end up getting shot just
for climbing into view—unarmed—and having a quick
look around.

The big man steadied himself on the slippery roof with
a hand on the radio antenna and stared up the bayou at
the barely discernible outline of the U-boat. It had
backed off to the last tight turn in the narrow waterway,
a distance of at least four hundred yards, Lucius estimated. *Maybe*, he thought, *they're gonna take a real long
run at us. Try to ram on through . . .*

A pale wash of moonlight passed over the conning
tower as the U-boat rotated slowly, its bow lining up
directly on the *Shiloh*. For a couple of seconds, Lucius
was sure he could see several of the men on the bridge
waving their arms in the air . . . waving him and Holt
off to one side. . . .

And then, as if hit by a bolt of lightning, he realized
what was going to happen.

"Mike! *Mike!*" he shouted, scrambling to the back
edge of the wheelhouse roof. "We gotta get away from
the boat! Swim to the bank! *They fixin' to fire a
torpedo!*"

Wolfe continued to wave off Lucius as Stuermer
leaned down to the speaking tube. "I want the eel set

to run at a depth of two meters," he ordered. "No deeper." He looked up. "Ready, Exec?"

Bock's eyes were glued to the UZO targeting binoculars, mounted on their metal post in the center of the bridge and connected to the U-boat's firing computer. "I have the *Shiloh* dead center, sir."

"They're swimming to the bank," Wolfe said, lowering his arms. "I can just barely see them in the moonlight."

Stuermer took one of Bock's dark-papered cigarettes out of his jacket pocket and put it between his lips. "Let me know when they climb out."

"The concussion would kill them if they were in the water that close," Bock muttered softly, hunched behind the UZO, concentrating.

"Correct," Stuermer said, lighting the Turkish smoke.

"Not that I give a damn about Holt, at this point." The exec's voice was bitter.

"They're on the bank, Captain," Wolfe reported.

The U-boat commander looked down the bayou, exhaling a cloud of smoke.

"*Los*," he ordered.

Chapter
Thirty-three

The U-113 bucked slightly as the twenty-two-foot-long, thirty-five-hundred-pound G7e torpedo hissed out of the port bow tube, ejected by a blast of compressed air. It left no bubble trail as it hurtled off down the bayou at nearly forty knots, its main propeller driven by powerful electric batteries. At the tip of the warhead, a miniature second prop spun at high rpm, activated by the torpedo's forward motion through the water.

At a range of three hundred yards, a threaded screw attached to the tiny front propeller spun all the way in, arming the five hundred kilos of high-explosive torpex contained within the warhead. At four hundred and six yards, at a depth of eight feet, the nose of the warhead hit the side of the *Shiloh*, firing off the torpedo's internal Pi-G7H impact pistol.

The torpex warhead detonated with a shattering explosion, disintegrating the entire center section of the sunken trawler's hull. Seasoned cypress planks and stout ribs that had weathered thirty years of storms in the Gulf of Mexico were turned instantly into wet sawdust and splinters, the debris erupting skyward in a two-hundred-foot plume of white water. A split second behind the initial detonation, the *Shiloh*'s two huge empty diesel tanks, heavy with fumes and only partly flooded, went up in a massive secondary explosion. An orange-white fireball that spanned the bayou burst upward, charring the great cypress trees on both banks and boiling into the night sky like a miniature sun.

Holt and Lucius, like the foliage around them, were flattened by the blast, the intense heat of the fireball scorching their clothes and hair and sucking the breath out of their lungs. Twenty feet back from the edge of the bayou, they lay dazed and deafened in a tangled ruin of smoking leaves and blackened branches. Overhead, the cloud of flame swirled and seethed in on itself as it tumbled upward.

Before the last fragments of debris had rained back down to earth, the U-113 was surging forward, putting on speed as she lined up her sharp bow with the center of the channel. On either bank, the immolated trees and brush flickered along the dark stretch of water, a gauntlet of fire.

Seven hundred and fifty feet above the treetops, in the cockpit of CPO Alvin Kendall's lead Catalina bomber, Fetherstone-Pugh craned his neck and stared in disbelief at the mushroom cloud of flame that had just erupted from the pitch-black swamp, not more than two miles ahead and slightly to port.

"Jeesus H. Christ!" Kendall exclaimed. "What the hell is that?"

Fetherstone-Pugh clapped the pilot hard on the shoulder. "Over there! Take us over there!"

Nodding to his copilot, Kendall banked the big plane hard and put the nose on the swirling remnants of the fiery column. The two trailing Catalinas followed suit, closing formation behind the lead bomber's port and starboard wingtips. Within seconds, Fetherstone-Pugh could make out two parallel lines of burning vegetation and, in between, moonlight glinting off the black water of a bayou.

"You're fitted with a Leigh Light!" he shouted at Kendall. "Turn it on!"

The pilot hit a switch and instantly the twenty-four-inch, fifty-million-candlepower carbon arc searchlight mounted beneath the nose of the aircraft sent a concentrated beam of white light flaring downward. The circle of illumination danced rapidly over the moss-hung cypress tops . . . over the dark surface of the bayou—curiously disturbed and churning with ringlets of milky foam. . . .

And over the sharp, gray black hull and turretlike conning tower of a U-boat, fleeing down the narrow waterway at full throttle toward the Gulf of Mexico.

"Lucius," Holt gasped, rolling over in the charred underbrush and spitting out cinders. The air was thick with ash; it was impossible not to ingest it with every breath. "Are you all right?" He reached out and shook the big mate by the shoulder.

"*Damn*," Lucius groaned. "If hell be anything like that, I don't wanna go."

Holt hacked violently and spat again, on all fours, his head drooping. Lucius looked at him and started to chuckle, a deep, rasping sound.

"What's funny?" Holt grunted.

"You," the mate said. "People gonna mistake us fo' brothers."

"Howzat?"

Lucius propped himself up on his elbows. "You black as me right now, an' damn near as bald, too." He managed a grin. "You got soot all over your face, an' that wall o' fire done burned off most of your hair."

"Huh." Holt was about to retort when the thrumming sound of diesel engines in high gear, approaching rapidly, caught his attention. He turned toward the bayou, some fifteen feet away, and sat up. Lucius heaved himself to one knee, his charred shirt smoking.

In the flickering light of the burning undergrowth, the conning tower of the U-boat was just passing by, directly over what little remained of the *Shiloh*. Stuermer, Bock, and Wolfe were clearly visible on the bridge. As Holt and Lucius watched, the lean U-boat commander spotted them on the bank, let his eyes linger for a moment, and touched the brim of his white cap in a military salute. Beside him, Wolfe raised a hand briefly, looking at Lucius. The black mate lifted his in return, acknowledging the man who had pulled him from the sunken off-shore wreck less than two days earlier.

And then the U-boat was past them, sliding rapidly down the bayou like some great lost shark in search of the sea. The darkness, underbrush, and cypress trunks closed in behind it until, at last, it disappeared from view, the throb of its engines fading into the night.

Holt turned to Lucius and opened his mouth to speak—but at that moment the swamp was suddenly inundated with dazzling white light, and the ground shook with the roar of six Pratt & Whitney engines as Kendall's formation of Catalina bombers, doing nearly two hundred knots at treetop level, overflew the site of the *Shiloh*'s destruction.

"Not that damned Leigh Light again!" Bock exclaimed, ducking out of reflex as the three Catalinas passed over the fast-moving U-boat like a trio of giant black condors. The deafening racket of their engines sent vibrations through the steel plate of the conning tower. "Just like those Wellingtons over the North Sea!"

"Lothar—" Stuermer began, but the big torpedoman was already out on the *Wintergarten* behind one of the twin-barreled antiaircraft machine guns, racking ammunition into the weapon's breech. Seconds later, Bock leaped down beside him to man the other gun.

"Get Mohler up here!" Stuermer shouted into the speaking tube. "Helm! Full port rudder! Both engines, maintain full speed ahead!" He ducked behind the wind baffle as the conning tower crashed through a low-hanging cypress branch, twigs snapping, sheaves of sphagnum moss tearing free on the periscope housing and gun barrels. The U-113 careened around another bend in the bayou, listing hard to starboard and scraping the western bank.

The Catalinas were coming around, all three of them now with Leigh Lights on. The powerful, concentrated beams stabbed downward, searching this way and that as the copilots manipulated them on their gimballed mounts. Then, as if guided by a homing signal, the three columns of light swung together simultaneously, locking onto the U-113's conning tower. The trio of bombers swarmed into a loose attack formation, one staggered behind another at varying altitudes in an attempt to confuse their quarry's antiaircraft gunners.

Wolfe swung his heavy weapon sternward and lined it up on the apex of the nearest light beam, less than a mile distant and closing fast. Bock did the same, squinting through his gun's ring sight, his shoulders trembling with tension. The U-113 glanced off the muddy bank yet again as Stuermer piloted her at nearly unmanageable speed through another turn in the ever-widening bayou.

"The lights!" Stuermer shouted to Wolfe and Bock. "Knock the planes down if you can, but try to put out those *verdammt* lights!"

By way of direct reply, Wolfe opened fire, the two-centimeter machine gun chugging out one gracefully arcing orange red tracer bullet for every four rounds fired. Bock joined in a second later, and the night sky became streaked with thin, lethal ribbons of light. Watching the dark waterway ahead, Stuermer covered his ears against the deafening racket of the guns and yelled steering orders into the speaking tube.

The U-113 slewed into another turn as the lead Catalina roared overhead, its wide black wings blotting out the stars. As it overflew them, Wolfe and Bock tracked the plane, swinging their machine guns rapidly through a high-angled arc as they continued to fire. Stuermer braced himself against the armored baffle as the U-boat listed to starboard once more with her rudders hard over; he knew that somewhere in the night sky overhead, a stick of bombs had been released.

The turn saved the U-113. Kendall, piloting the lead plane, could not see the bayou just ahead of the U-boat and had not anticipated her hard turn to port. In a perfectly straight line, his four surface bombs walked off into the saw grass away from their intended target, detonating in quick succession.

Port and starboard behind Kendall's bomber, slightly higher, the other two Catalinas suddenly found themselves out of alignment, the U-boat unexpectedly curving off to the east, following the bayou. Banking hard, they tried to salvage the bombing run, but their speed was too great and they both overshot the fleeing German, their track too far to the west by several hundred yards.

As the trailing Catalina leveled out, Wolfe's final burst raked across the underside of its nose, sending armor-piercing slugs punching up through the thin metal of the fuselage. The pilot and the copilot recoiled violently in their seats as most of the instrument panel disintegrated under their hands, fragments of glass and steel flying. Beneath them, the twenty-four-inch lens of their aircraft's Leigh Light exploded into a million tiny shards, its powerful column of light winking out.

Wolfe stepped back from the shoulder rests of his smoking machine gun as the attacking Catalinas wheeled around in a wide turn, the third plane faltering, sideslipping, its searchlight gone. He grinned over at Stuermer. "One *verdammt* light for you, Captain!" he called.

"We're going to need a lot more shooting just like that, Lothar!" Stuermer responded. His face was grim as he watched the two remaining beams of light track off to the west, then to the north, circling around. "Get ready!"

Mohler's head appeared in the hatchway. "Seaman Mohler reporting, sir."

"Man Lieutenant Bock's gun!" the *Kapitänleutnant* ordered. "Erich! Take over the conn! The helm needs steering orders for this turn coming up!"

"Yes, sir!" Leaving the machine gun, Bock hurried into position behind the control room speaking tube. The dark, pillarlike cypresses that lined the turn ahead were rushing toward the U-113's bow with frightening speed. "Helm, hard port rudder!" the exec yelled, his eyes wide, desperately trying to gauge the angle of the upcoming bend in the bayou. "Starboard engine, maintain full ahead! Port engine, neutral!"

There was a series of loud clacking sounds as Wolfe and Mohler locked down the breeches of their machine guns and racked fresh ammunition into them, both men staring intently at the two probing beams of light that were lining up on them less than a mile distant. Bock leaned on the wind baffle as the U-boat listed to starboard, driving hard into the turn. He glanced over at Stuermer as the *Kapitänleutnant* swung his legs down into the open bridge hatchway.

"I need something from below!" Stuermer shouted. "Maintain as much speed as possible through these next three turns, and for God's sake keep your head down! I'll be right back!"

"Aye, sir!" Bock replied sharply, but the U-boat commander had already dropped through the tight circular opening.

Chapter
Thirty-four

Gasping for breath, his long white hair flying and his eyes wild, Papa Luc burst from the brush near Estelle's stilt shanty. The tiny dwelling was completely dark, the water lapping quietly against its rotting support pilings. The leader of *les Isolates* staggered against a tree, sweat pouring down his face, and hurled the animal-skull fetish he'd found in Stuermer's tool case onto the front porch. It bounced off the aging planks, slid, and dropped into the black water. *Ploof.*

"*Where are you, old witch?*" Papa Luc screamed. "*I know you're here, par Dieu!*"

Not waiting for an answer, he started for the narrow wooden catwalk that spanned the swampy, fetid water between the bank and the shanty's low dock. His feet skidded out from under him in the muck and he went down with a loud splat, arms flailing. Enraged, cursing incoherently, he dragged himself out of the stinking mud and stumbled onto the catwalk.

"*I'm coming for you, Estelle! And you, too, little Jolene! There ain't no place you can hide from me, no!*"

On the corner of the dock was a chopping block; an old sawed-off cypress stump that Estelle used to behead chickens. Embedded in its crosshatched surface was a rusty five-pound ax. Papa Luc stepped off the catwalk, seized its well-worn handle, and wrenched it free.

"I have something here for you! Salvation! Salvation for your evil souls!"

He walked unsteadily to the front door and twisted the latch. It was locked. Raising the ax, he swung two-handedly and landed a blow to the thick cypress panel that made it jump on its hinges. The booming crash echoed across the still waters of the pond.

"That's the angel of death knockin' for you both, you hear?" Papa Luc lifted the ax a second time. *"Listen! Here he comes again!"*

The rusty blade crashed into the door once more, splitting one of the central planks and making the entire shanty tremble on its stilts. With a screech, Estelle's black cat darted out from beneath the porch, leaped onto the catwalk, and fled into the bushes lining the muddy shore.

"Ah-haaa! The witch's familiar! Run away, demon! Run before the choppin' starts!"

Papa Luc began to batter the heavy door repeatedly, windmilling the ax in a state of near frenzy. His eyes had gone glassy and his convulsing mouth chanted out a bizarre mantra.

"Chop, chop, chop, chop . . ."

With a ragged splintering sound, the door broke in two and swung partly open, sagging off its rusty hinges. The tall Cajun stood back for a moment, wheezing in air. Then he brought the ax up above his shoulder with both hands, ready to strike, and forced his way through the shattered planks into the shanty's interior.

As before, it was pitch-black inside. But Papa Luc strode across the central room without hesitation, muttering to himself, and drove his shoulder against the closed door to Estelle's back room. When it wouldn't give, he took a step back, swung the ax, and began to laugh: a thin, deranged cackle that came from high in his throat.

Crash!

The laughter grew louder.

Crash!

Louder still.

Crash!

"Hey, Luc!"

Papa Luc froze in midswing at the sound of the voice, the insane cackle dying on his lips. Eyes wide and staring, his mouth hanging open, he turned slowly toward the splintered front door, listening.

"You ain't too smart, are you, Luc? Why you beatin' on that door when it ain't even locked?" Estelle's voice seemed to be coming from outside the shanty. But it wasn't only the old woman Papa Luc wanted. He dropped a hand to the heavy wrought-iron latch and twisted. It clicked free instantly, the door creaking open several inches. Hefting the ax, he peered inside. The last rays of the low moon illuminated the tiny room through a narrow window. Jolene was not there.

"Luuuuc!" Estelle's distant voice was sardonic, mocking.

Papa Luc turned and stumbled back across the main room, forcing his way through the broken remnants of the front door and out onto the porch. There he paused, momentarily distracted by what sounded like the rumbling of a Gulf thunderstorm off to the south . . . a strange storm, with thunderclaps that were sharp and explosive and seemed to occur in groups of four.

"You get lost, Luc?"

Refocusing, the leader of *les Isolates* followed the voice around to the side of the shanty. The narrow, sagging plank that Estelle used for a bridge still extended from the side porch to the shore. Twenty or thirty feet beyond it, in a little clearing at the end of an arched natural tunnel of brambles, stood Estelle herself, small and stooped in the moonlight.

The mad gleam in Papa Luc's eyes intensified. Without thinking, he lunged out onto the narrow plank, making for shore with great lurching strides. The makeshift bridge bowed and twisted under his weight, and three-quarters of the way across he lost his balance, pitching off with a strangled yell. He landed on his side in three-inch-deep water, sinking more than two feet into the reeking black muck and humus below.

"*Aaggghhh!*" he shrieked, feeling the sucking pull of the saturated mud. Still holding on to the ax, he groped desperately for a cluster of protruding roots on relatively solid ground, just within arm's reach, while Estelle's unmistakable chuckle echoed in his ears: "Heh heh heh!"

Had he fallen a few inches farther from shore, the quicksand—quick *mud*—would have claimed him. But the cypress roots were strong, and he had the strength of his fear and fury. Slowly, grudgingly, the viscous mud released his torso, his legs, and finally his feet with a series of wet sucking sounds. Gasping, covered in slime, he staggered to his feet, still gripping the ax.

"Oh, you got outta there, eh, Luc? Must be on account of you're so foul even the swamp don't want you."

Papa Luc stumbled toward the mocking voice, making his way into the tunnel of brambles. Estelle hadn't moved. She still stood in the little clearing at the far end, her wizened form bathed in moonlight. Grinning insanely, Papa Luc brandished the ax and moved forward.

He drew to within ten feet of the old woman before he noticed another small opening in the brambles, off to the left. In the center of it, Jolene sat on a cypress stump, her swollen, battered face impassive, half covered by shadow.

"You," Papa Luc hissed. "Ungrateful child. I'll show you what it means to defy me, *par Dieu!"*

Jolene sat there without expression, watching him.

The tall Cajun came forward through the brambles, the moonlight glinting off the checked blade of his ax. Slowly, he brought it up.

"Evil girl," he whispered, grinning, his eyes like saucers.

Jolene didn't move.

Papa Luc took a long step toward her and lifted the ax high above his head, bracing himself to strike. His shoe landed on something that crackled underfoot like a dry branch and he hesitated, glancing down.

He was standing in a garden of small, round bladders, each one impaled on what appeared to be a hollow reed. His feet had made deep imprints in the soft, sticky earth, and a thick black fluid was oozing rapidly into these.

The pungent smell of sulfur, crude oil, and methane rose around his head.

He stared back at Jolene. The Creole girl's brutalized face was immobile, her gaze flat and hard. Then the brambles off to his right rustled and parted, and Estelle was there, her small black eyes glinting up at him like pellets of obsidian.

Papa Luc gaped at her. The skin around his eyes and mouth drew back in an inhuman leer and he raised the ax over his head.

"Au revoir, Luc," Estelle hissed, and her right arm snapped out straight.

There was a scratching sound, and a long tongue of blue flame licked down toward the deranged man's feet. Instantly, the methane fumes rising from the petroleum-soaked earth ignited, which in turn set fire to the entire small oil seep. With an ear-splitting screech, a yellow-and-blue inferno erupted from the ground, completely engulfing Papa Luc.

He thrashed wildly for a few seconds, a distorted black figure at the center of a pillar of fire. There was no sound but a blast-furnace-like roar. Then his frantic silhouette collapsed into a dark, shapeless lump at the base of the conflagration and began to disintegrate rapidly under the intense heat.

Estelle moved up beside Jolene, who had leaped backward off the cypress stump as the earth around Papa Luc burst into flame. The Creole girl took the old woman's hand, and the two of them stood together in the flickering shadows, faces impassive, silently watching as his remains were steadily consumed.

Five minutes later, the surface gases and raw petroleum of the seep had burned away, and there was nothing left but the blackened head of the ax, its handle gone, lying in the center of a smoking circle of charred earth.

Jolene began to tremble violently. Estelle patted her hand, tucked it into the crook of her own arm, and began to lead her back toward the little stilt shanty. As she did, the air suddenly shook with the rolling sounds of far-off thunder. A strange thunder, sharp and explosive.

Estelle frowned as the distant echoes died away. No Gulf thunderstorm had ever sounded like that. She glanced over at Jolene. The Creole girl was staring past the black treetops to the south and into the night sky, her eyes glistening.

"Erich," she whispered.

Chapter
Thirty-five

Admiral Richard Zacharias let the telephone on the night table ring seven times before he rolled over in bed and picked it up. Blearily, he eyed the fluorescent hands on the alarm clock. Four oh two in the goddamned morning. This had better be good.

"Zacharias," he growled. "What the deuce is so important that it couldn't wait another ninety minutes until I got up?"

"Admiral, sir, sorry to wake you early, but I'd knew you'd want to know what we've got—"

"Who the hell is this?" Zacharias interrupted, immediately annoyed by the slippery drawl at the other end of the line. "Identify yourself, man."

"Blodgett, sir," the voice went on. "In charge of the tracking room."

The admiral rubbed his eyes, the fog of sleep clearing rapidly. "Blodgett? Yes, yes—of course. Well, what is it?"

There was a breathless pause as Blodgett gathered himself. "Sir. We've located a U-boat near the head of a large inlet in the coastal swamps south of New Orleans. A flight of Catalinas out of Houma has it under attack as we speak. I've requested that a dozen more sub-killin' planes be scrambled, as well as patrol vessels redirected toward the route the Kraut's most likely to take tryin' to get out to the Gulf. It's a runnin' firefight down there right now, sir. He's already shot down one Catalina and damaged another."

Zacharias was sitting upright on the edge of the bed, completely awake. "You've got a U-boat? Here? *Inshore?* How'd you find him?"

Blodgett cleared his throat. "Well, sir—I just thought that we oughta keep checkin' on a strange signal we'd isolated earlier. We'd taken a look earlier in the day, but I had a hunch we needed to keep the patrols flyin' until morning, at least—have 'em tighten up their search grid. Better safe than sorry, you know, sir?"

"Absolutely," Zacharias replied. "And it paid off, Blodgett. Good work. By the way, where's Fetherstone-Pugh? He mentioned something about this to me, as I recall."

"He's . . . not here, sir. He, ah, left early. Said somethin' about gettin' a drink."

Zacharias frowned. "I didn't know he drank."

"Well, Admiral, sir—I just thought that one of us had better stay here and keep an eye on the war, if you get my meanin', sir."

"I do." Zacharias cleared his throat. "Stay on it, Blodgett, and keep me updated. I'll be in my office by five thirty. I'll want a complete update from you at five thirty-one, understood?"

"Yes, sir. But I think we've got us one dead Kraut. If the flyboys don't let him slip out into deep water before dawn, he's ours."

"Good. We could use a solid kill." The admiral got to his feet and scratched himself through his navy blue silk pajamas. "Outstanding, Blodgett. Stay on it. If this thing comes out looking pretty in the report, there may be a commendation in it for you."

Zacharias could almost hear Blodgett grinning through the phone line. "Yes, sir, Admiral," he said crisply, and hung up.

Mohler was dead at his antiaircraft gun, crumpled forward with his arms entangled in the recoil pads, the exposed back of his neck streaked with blood. Beside him on the *Wintergarten*, Wolfe swung his own weapon sternward yet again as the two relentless Catalinas, now with only one functioning searchlight between them, banked through the night sky to the east, circuiting around for another attack run. It was easier now to pick out their silhouettes, Bock noticed, as he prepared to bark more steering orders into the speaking tube. Dawn was coming.

"Helm! Five degrees starboard rudder! Both engines maintain full speed ahead!" He eyed the circling planes grimly. "Where's my other gunner? I need him up here *now!*"

"Burkhardt reporting, sir!" The seaman clambered out of the bridge hatch. "I'm sorry I'm late, Lieutenant. That last stick of bombs sprang the external door on one of the forward torpedo tubes. We were flooding badly for a few minutes. We had to yank the eel back out and seal the internal tube hatch."

"Very well, Burkhardt," Bock replied. "Take over Mohler's gun."

"Aye, sir." The crewman hurried out onto the *Wintergarten* and pulled Mohler free of the machine gun's recoil pads. His mouth tightened as his dead comrade's head lolled back in his arms. Moving quickly, he laid the body down just inside the armored baffle that shielded the aft end of the bridge.

"Here they come!" Wolfe rasped as Burkhardt stepped back behind his gun, nestling his shoulders against the recoil pads.

Alvin Kendall's lead Catalina came in low and fast, the Cyclops eye of its Leigh Light glaring on the U-113's conning tower. The second bomber was close behind, offset to port. Out of the corner of his eye, Kendall could see the burning wreckage of the Catalina that the U-boat gunners had shot down; it was lying in the saw grass to the northwest. The sight filled him with a cold fury.

Neither plane had any depth charges or surface bombs left. Due to the unpredictable high-speed turns the U-boat was making as it fled down the bayou, not a single dropped explosive had found its mark. Several had been close, but none had inflicted more than minor damage.

Now, until backup planes arrived, the attack would consist of multiple passes with side-mounted blister guns raking the U-boat from stem to stern, probing for her Achilles' heel.

"Center your fire on the conning tower!" Kendall radioed his gunners. "Take out the Krauts manning those antiaircraft weapons!"

A low vibration shook the frame of the Catalina as the blister guns began their harsh chattering. In response, clusters of red tracer shells began to float up from the U-boat's gun platform, slowly at first, then gaining speed and flashing past the windshield, filling the sky with streaks of hot light.

As the big plane rushed forward, Fetherstone-Pugh, leaning over Kendall's shoulder, could see a double line of explosive geysers march diagonally across the bayou and intersect the U-boat at the conning tower. In the glare of the Leigh Light, the bridge and the gun support superstructure seemed to dissolve into a cloud of paint dust, sparks, and flying metal fragments. Then the Catalina was past the target, banking up and around in the silvering predawn sky.

Down on the U-113's *Wintergarten*, as the second bomber droned by, Burkhardt emptied the remains of his magazine at it, scoring some hits on the tail, then stepped back from his gun, breathing hard.

"Lothar!" he gasped. "Did you see that? I punched some holes in that bastard's ass, I think!" He looked around at the shell-torn gun platform and bridge. At the conn, Bock was just regaining his feet, shouting terse orders into the speaking tube. The armored baffle surrounding him was riddled with bullet strikes, and the Metox antenna was nothing but a twisted mess of splintered wood and wire.

Wolfe's twin-barreled antiaircraft gun was canted upward at a steep angle, its rotating mount cracked. The plate-steel shield that afforded the gunner some protection had been ripped back and one of the weapon's recoil pads was dangling from a broken strut. Nothing remained of the hand railing on that side of the *Wintergarten*.

And Lothar Wolfe was gone.

Burkhardt blinked, uncomprehending, then looked down onto the aft deck. Nothing. He stared back at the black water rushing by the U-boat, port and starboard. Nothing.

"Lieutenant!" he yelled, pointing helplessly at Wolfe's unmanned gun.

Bock glanced around. His face fell as he realized what Burkhardt was telling him. The big torpedoman, the crack-shot hunter from the Black Forest, was lost. It wasn't possible. Lothar Wolfe was one of those indestructible men who could not be killed. He was too tough, too fast, too smart . . . too *alive.*

The young exec turned away, fixing his eyes on the bayou ahead. There was nothing to be done. Nothing to be done but fight on.

Then, as the drone of the approaching Catalinas began to fill his ears, a single huge cypress tree on a tiny point of land appeared just off the starboard bow. A tree with a large spike driven into its trunk, slightly higher than a man's head. And beyond it, under the pink-and-silver dawn sky, the bay's flat expanse stretched off to the south and into the open waters of the Gulf of Mexico.

Bock whirled as Stuermer climbed rapidly out of the hatch, followed by Dekker and the nervous, adolescent oiler's assistant, Hofstetter. "Captain," the exec shouted, "we've made it!" He pointed forward excitedly. "The bay!"

"Don't count on it," Dekker said grimly, looking aft. He clapped Hofstetter on the shoulder, propelling him toward Wolfe's damaged gun. "Get on that weapon, boy. If it still works, we're going to need it."

As the U-113 charged out of the mouth of Bayou Profond and into the bay at full throttle, Stuermer, Bock, Dekker, Burkhardt, and Hofstetter stared astern, past the two onrushing Catalinas. Far behind them, at a distance of perhaps seven miles, an entire squadron of identical bombers was strung out above the horizon—over a dozen black specks growing larger by the second as they homed in on the U-113.

"M-mein Gott," Hofstetter exclaimed, his boyish voice

high, breaking. But he hauled his damaged machine gun around on its broken mount and racked a belt of ammunition into the breech.

Stuermer's eyes flickered everywhere at once, then settled on Dekker. "Chief!" he barked, "take the conn! Exec, you come with me!" He stepped out onto the external conning tower ladder and slid down to the deck below. Without hesitation, Bock followed.

As his feet hit the steel plates with a thump, Stuermer grabbed him by the lapels of his battle jacket and shoved him up against the side of the conning tower, eyeing the two Catalinas that were rapidly overtaking the U-boat by the stern.

Bock blinked at him in surprise. "I'm all right, sir! They aren't firing yet! What do you want me to do?"

Stuermer wrenched open the exec's jacket, pulled an oilpaper envelope from his own pocket, and stuffed it in against Bock's chest. Then he yanked the lapels closed once more, still gripping them tightly.

Bock stared into his captain's hard eyes in utter confusion. And then, just for a moment, Kurt Stuermer's gaze softened. The deep seams in his face, carved there by years of unrelenting strain, lessened slightly. And as he leaned back and looked Bock up and down, his familiar thin, wry smile appeared. Tainted, perhaps, with a hint of sadness.

Then he leaned in close. "Erich," he said. "Find the girl. Find Jolene."

Bock blinked again. "Wha-what, sir?" But his response was lost in the hammering of the U-113's antiaircraft guns as they opened up on the two bombers closing in over the stern.

Shell strikes from the blister guns of the first plane clanged against the far side of the conning tower and stitched a string of jagged holes across the deck as Stuermer crowded Bock up against the steel plates. The Catalina roared overhead, the twin guns on the U-boat's *Wintergarten* keeping up their withering fire.

And as they did, *Kapitänleutnant* Kurt Stuermer yanked his young exec away from the conning tower, spun him around, and threw him backward off the side of the U-113. Bock's astonished yell was cut short as he hit the dark, muddy water of the bay headfirst.

By the time he managed to flounder to the surface, coughing and spitting, the U-boat had already slid by, her twin screws thrumming. Their turbulence spun Bock in the water, forcing him to pull hard to stay on the surface. He kicked away from the hissing wake, staring in disbelief as the U-113 drove on down the bay, her stern shrinking with each passing second.

"Captain!" he yelled, spotting Stuermer's lean form on the external ladder to the bridge. But his voice was lost to his own ears as the second Catalina passed overhead, engines roaring and blister guns spitting out a deadly staccato.

Chapter
Thirty-six

Bock took a dozen desperate strokes after the U-113 before the futility of what he was doing sank in. Treading water, he watched helplessly as the vessel carrying his comrades-in-arms—men with whom he shared a bond of loyalty as strong as that between blood brothers—raced off to the south across the glimmering surface of the bay, ruffled now by the gentle stirring of dawn breezes. The harsh *taktaktaktaktaktaktak* of heavy machine gun fire echoed across the water, and Bock could make out small puffs of cordite smoke erupting from the *Wintergarten* as tracer bullets streaked upward.

A wavelet slapped him in the face, reminding him of his own situation. He swiveled his head, looking around. The upper edge of the sun was just beginning to rise over the low line of mangroves to the east, its first rays throwing a cool pink light across the bay. Behind him, to the north, the shore was closest, the mouth of Bayou Profond less than a quarter mile distant. The tall cypress tree on its western point provided a convenient landmark.

As Bock turned away from the fleeing U-boat and began to breaststroke toward shore, the first reinforcement wave of Catalina bombers thundered overhead. The young exec stopped swimming, hoping a lone, motionless man wouldn't be noticed in the shadowy water, and rolled onto his side, looking upward.

The first wave went by, followed closely by the second.

Bock counted thirteen of the big, lumbering twin-engine planes, their wing racks heavy with depth charges and surface bombs. Though there was no way to be sure, something told him that he hadn't been spotted, that every eye was on the escaping U-boat ahead—still under attack by the first two Catalinas.

As the two wavering lines of bombers droned on southward in pursuit of their quarry, Bock turned away from the U-113 for the last time and began to pull through the murky water toward the tall cypress at the mouth of Bayou Profond.

"Helm!" Dekker bellowed into the speaking tube, grabbing the edge of the wind baffle as the U-boat caromed off the edge of an invisible mudbank. *"Keep the verdammt boat on course! If we run hard aground now, we're lost!"* His rugged face pale, streaked with cordite soot, he looked over at Stuermer as the *Kapitänleutnant* stepped off the top of the external ladder and back into the bridge. "Where's Bock?" he asked, breathing hard.

"Dead," Stuermer replied. He held Dekker's gaze for a moment. "He took a burst through the chest on that last pass. It nearly cut him in two. He went over the side."

The chief stared at him in shock, his mouth going slack. "Not Bock . . . ," he muttered. Then he gathered himself, set his jaw, and surveyed the featureless water ahead. "Jonas, Lothar, now Erich . . . ," he said bitterly. "There aren't going to be many of us left."

"There are *forty-seven* of us left, Chief Engineer," Stuermer retorted. "And we're going home."

Dekker looked back at him, and as the thunderous roar of more than two dozen Pratt & Whitney engines filled his ears, he smiled slowly and nodded. "Aye, Captain."

Kendall's bomber banked in toward the U-boat's stern once more, just ahead of the first wave of reinforcement aircraft. Behind him, Fetherstone-Pugh crowded forward, trying to watch the approach through the Plexiglas windscreen, his weight on the pilot's shoulder.

"Will you get the fuck *off* me?" Kendall snapped,
shrugging his unwanted passenger away. "Can't you see
I'm tryin' to work?" As Fetherstone-Pugh shifted to the
side, the pilot pushed the controls forward and sent the Catalina into a shallow dive. "One more pass," he snarled.
"One more good lick at this sonofabitch before the boys
behind us blow him outta the water . . ."

"I can't believe you didn't stop him back in the
bayou," Fetherstone-Pugh said loudly, his arch tones
thick with frustration. "He had no room to maneuver in
there. Now he'll be in the open Gulf in five minutes,
deep enough to dive." His long nose wrinkled in disgust.
"Bloody hell, don't you Yanks ever conduct practice
bombing runs?"

"Goddammit!" Kendall yelled, twisting around in his
seat. "If you don't shut up back there, I swear to Christ
I'm gonna—"

The rest of his words were drowned out as the blister
guns opened up, their chugging rattle combining with
the roar of the engines. Fetherstone-Pugh caught a
glimpse of the U-boat's conning tower sweeping by the
lower edge of the windscreen, its gray black paint pock-
marked by numerous bullet strikes.

All at once, the Catalina shook as though its tail had
just been fed into a giant set of grinding gears. There
was an ear-splitting *powpowpowpowpow*, and the cockpit floor exploded in a welter of sparks, dust, and jagged
chips of aluminum. Simultaneously, the side window
next to the copilot blew out, sending fragments of Plexiglas whirling through the interior. The harsh smell of
burned wiring filled the air, in spite of the slipstream
howling past the shattered panel.

The big plane fell off to the east, going down rapidly
by her port wing. It was a full minute before Kendall,
fighting desperately with the controls, could bring her
level again, less than fifty feet above the bay. The pilot
blinked cold sweat out of his eyes. Enough was enough.
Babying the Catalina around, he came onto a direct
heading for Houma Airfield.

In the seat beside him, his copilot had a gloved hand

to his head. "Riley!" Kendall barked, not daring to let go of the controls. "You okay?"

The copilot looked at him and grinned, nodding. He moved his hand slightly to reveal the huge, bloody flap of forehead skin that he was holding in place. Then he squinted calmly out the forward windscreen, settled his free hand on his own controls, and proceeded to help Kendall keep the aircraft level.

Kendall's throat mike and headset were still working. Quickly, he checked the rest of his crew. Both gunners and the navigator were still alive and unhurt. With a sigh of relief, he settled back and allowed himself to concentrate on getting the damaged bomber home.

"Hey, Al," Riley called, looking back in his seat. "This guy don't look so good."

"What?" Kendall glanced over his shoulder. His mind on his crew, he'd forgotten about his extra passenger. Well, he might be a British-sounding pain in the ass, but on *this* flight he was Kendall's responsibility.

"Hey, pal," the pilot shouted, not quite able to see the man directly behind him. "You okay? Talk to me. You hit?"

There was no answer. Lieutenant Commander Trevor Fetherstone-Pugh sat belted into place in his small seat with his head cocked back, his mouth open and his eyes wide and staring. There was blood bubbling from a small patch of torn cloth at the front of his jacket collar.

The single two-centimeter bullet that had killed him instantly had punched through the thin skin of the Catalina's boatlike underside, perforated the cockpit floor, passed through his small fold-down seat, hit him in the rectum, traveled upward through his body, and exploded from his throat just below the Adam's apple.

The U-113 was just passing the low barrier islands and sandbars that guarded the wide mouth of the bay when the Catalinas caught up to her. Contrary to the late Lieutenant Commander Fetherstone-Pugh's hasty assessment, the American pilots were, in fact, cool, deadly competent, and very well versed in air-to-sea combat tactics.

The bombers attacked in groups of three: two aircraft flanking the U-boat port and starboard, raking the conning tower with their blister guns and forcing the German antiaircraft gunners to divide their fire, while a third plane, slightly behind the other two, came in directly for a depth charge run.

"Forget the strafing planes!" Stuermer shouted at Hofstetter, stepping over Burkhardt's smoking, bullet-riddled body and seizing the grips of the heavy machine gun he'd been manning. "Concentrate on the one that's lining up on us!" He swung the two-centimeter around and began firing.

Wide-eyed, his face the color of the foam curling off the U-113's sharp bow, the young oiler's assistant hauled his own weapon around and doubled the barrage his captain was putting up. As the two flanking Catalinas thundered by, their blister guns rattling, the *Wintergarten* and the bridge became a blinding hell of bullet strikes, paint dust, steel shrapnel, and tumbling brass shell casings—underscored by a furious din of hot metallic clangs and the *whizzzsnap* of flying slugs.

Somehow, miraculously, Stuermer and Hofstetter remained on their feet, returning fire. Dekker, at the conn, took a small splinter of steel in the hand. He hardly felt it. The strafing ceased as the first two Catalinas bypassed the U-113, but the conning tower continued to shake with the recoil of the two antiaircraft guns on the *Wintergarten*. Dekker watched helplessly as the third bomber came in low, directly in line with the U-boat's keel, the air in front of it crisscrossed with flickering red tracer trails. There was no room to maneuver in the narrow channel. No way for the enemy pilot to miss.

And then Stuermer's and Hofstetter's fire drifted down and converged on the Catalina's forward windscreen. For a second or two, the tracers appeared to float directly into the cockpit—and a small puff of smoke and shattered Plexiglas blew back over the top of the fuselage and the wing. The Catalina wobbled imperceptibly.

It roared over the stern, over the conning tower, over the bow, and on ahead without releasing a single bomb or depth charge. Stunned, Dekker stared as the apparently undamaged plane continued on a straight course for another quarter mile or so, then slipped sideways, going down by its starboard wingtip. Slowly, gracefully, it banked over and dove straight into the water in a churning explosion of white spray.

Elated, the chief bent to the speaking tube. "Control room! What depth now?"

"It just dropped off, sir!" came the reply. "Nineteen meters and getting deeper!"

God in heaven, Dekker thought, his mind racing, *we're going to make it*. He looked astern at the swarming, circling bombers. *Or at least we'll get a chance to die under the sea, instead of being shot to pieces on the surface like a chunk of flotsam.*

Hofstetter was panting as though he'd just run five miles, his chubby, youthful face flushed with fear and excitement. He looked over at Stuermer—already sighting in on the next trio of planes and leaning hard on his gun, his shoulders braced against the recoil pads.

"I did it, Captain!" he said hoarsely, not quite believing his own words. "Did you see me? I got him, sir!"

Stuermer looked over at him, his face drawn and grim. Then he nodded, and for a second the thin smile appeared. "Yes, you did, Seaman Hofstetter," he replied. "Very good work. No one could have done better."

Hofstetter's own smile of gratitude went from ear to ear. "Thank you, sir," he whispered, certain that at that particular moment he would have followed Kurt Stuermer through the gates of hell itself.

"*Captain!*" Dekker yelled. "*Twenty-six meters of water, sir!*"

"*Dive, Chief!*" the *Kapitänleutnant* shouted back. The rising drone of the attacking planes, boring in to strafe from the flanks, was drowned out by the rattle of Stuermer's machine gun. Hofstetter sighted in on the starboard Catalina as a line of bullet-geysers began to race across the surface of the water toward the conning tower.

In a flurry of paint dust and shrapnel, hits and misses, the burst cut across the *Wintergarten* like a scythe. When

Stuermer's vision cleared, the two strafing planes had flown past and the U-113 was slanting forward in a crash dive, her foredeck already submerged and water boiling up against the front of her conning tower.

Hofstetter was lying on his back against the remaining hand railing, his arms and legs at unnatural angles. He was staring straight up, his adolescent face registering blank shock. His pelvis was no longer attached to his torso; the two were now separated by a bloody, gore-filled gap of more than six inches.

A shadow of pain fled across Stuermer's hard features, but he wasted no time with the dead boy. "Get below, Otto!" he shouted, lunging toward the bridge. The third Catalina was locked into its bombing run, the howl of its Pratt & Whitney engines reverberating off the armor-plated wind baffles.

Dekker dropped through the hatch just as Stuermer reached the periscope housing. Water began to pour into the bridge through the scuppers as the U-113 drove for the bottom, the huge batlike shape of the attacking bomber hovering just aft of her up-kicked stern. *Too late*, Stuermer thought, as he slid down into the bridge hatchway in a foot of swirling seawater. *For us.*

The Catalina came in barely seventy-five feet off the water, releasing her stick of four depth charges. The first can hit the stern of the U-boat, bounced up, and exploded harmlessly in the air. Without the density of water to create its killing shock wave, it was little more than a giant firecracker.

The second, third, and fourth charges splashed down along the length of the U-113, bracketing her perfectly, port and starboard, at intervals of thirty-eight feet. The 250-pound Mark VII canisters sank at sixteen feet per second, their pressure-sensitive hydrostatic fuses distorting rapidly with the increasing depth. Damaging if detonated within fifty feet of a U-boat's pressure hull, they were lethal if closer than twenty-five.

There was a dull *clunk* as the fourth charge, tumbling downward, hit the top of the conning tower. The third and second charges, farther astern, narrowly missed the bulging saddle tanks to port and starboard as the U-113 charged ahead through the muddy depths, leveling herself out at fifty-two feet—a mere ten feet from the uneven, shallowing bottom.

"Verdammt," Dekker breathed, eyeing the gauges in the control room. "We're going to get it, boys. Hold on. . . ."

Stuermer came slithering down the ladder from the conning tower compartment, soaking wet and breathing hard. His foot skidded out and he fell to one knee, gripping the ladder uprights, bracing himself. . . .

But no explosions came. Instead, there was a violent, jarring impact and the U-boat tilted upward, her propellers thumping into the muddy bottom and sending an ugly vibration through the hull.

"Stabilize!" Stuermer shouted, his eyes darting to the depth gauge. "We're skidding on bottom! Level her out four meters shallower, Chief! *But keep us below the surface!*"

"We hit a mudbank, sir!" the helmsman cried. "Water depth went from twenty-six meters to eighteen without warning!"

"Bloody Louisiana coast," Dekker fumed. "The bottom changes in this cursed place every time the tide goes in and out. Too much sediment and muck!" He cranked furiously on a series of bulkhead-mounted bronze wheels, adjusting the boat's trim.

"Helm," Stuermer ordered. "Veer hard to starboard. Come onto course one-seven-five degrees." He glanced over his shoulder, his face very pale. "Otto. Maintain depth at seventeen meters until we get into deeper water, then stay within six meters of the bottom. We'll try to zigzag and lose them."

"The water's too shallow," one of the younger planesmen whimpered. "They'll see our swirl!"

"Shut up, Bergen!" Dekker barked. "See to your station, boy! The captain knows what he's doing!" He glanced over at Stuermer, a thick eyebrow raised as if to ask, *don't you?*

"What happened to the depth charges?" the helmsman wondered aloud. "We heard one hit the conning tower." He glanced quickly over his shoulder at

Stuermer. "They had to have dropped at least four, didn't they, Captain? I only heard one go off, very faintly. It didn't even shake us."

"That one may have detonated prematurely in the air, I think," Stuermer replied, abandoning the etiquette of total control room silence, orders excepted. "The other three, I'm not sure. They can't all have been duds. . . ."

Many dozens of yards astern, tumbling along the mudbank in the U-113's turbulent wake, the deadly canisters remained unexploded, their pressure fuses stressed but still intact. In the desperate scramble to load the additional Catalinas with depth charges and get them off the tarmac at Houma Airfield, no one had considered that they would be in pursuit of a U-boat fleeing through *inshore* waters.

With the exception of the canisters carried by Kendall's flight on their special inland patrol, the depth charges in the airfield armory were intended for use in deep *offshore* waters, where a diving U-boat would typically attain a depth of nearly one hundred feet before an attacking plane could get close enough to drop a stick over its swirl. And the hydrostatic fuses, adjusted by the armorers in accordance with current U.S. Navy tactical policy, were preset to go off at the anticipated escape depth—one hundred feet.

As the turbulence from the escaping U-113's screws died away, the depth charges that had been dropped with such lethal accuracy by the onrushing Catalina stopped tumbling and came to rest on the underwater mudbank . . . at a nondetonating depth of sixty-nine and one-half feet.

The atmosphere in the U-boat's control room was becoming thick and humid—redolent of perspiration and fear. No one spoke. The thrumming of the electric motors, the occasional creaking complaint from the hull plates, the *drip, drip, drip* of water from the conning tower compartment hatch, and the forced breathing of frightened men seemed to echo at unnatural volume through the entire boat.

"Helm," Stuermer said quietly, his voice very controlled, "go to one-nine-five degrees. Full speed ahead on the electric motors. We've zigged. Now we'll zag."

"Aye, sir," the helmsman replied, adjusting his course.

"Depth of water?" Stuermer inquired.

"We've got twenty-nine meters now," Dekker reported. "Using bow and stern planes to keep her close to the bottom." He spun one of the bronze ballast control wheels. "Adjusting trim."

"Why aren't there any more explosions?" the terrified planesman opined. "They can't have given up! There were a dozen bombers on us!"

Dekker didn't even bother disciplining the boy. "Don't worry," he growled. "I'm sure they're still there."

Stuermer was leaning heavily on the control room ladder, water dripping from his soaked battle jacket onto the deck plates. "For some reason, they're not saturating the water around us with depth charges," he said. "I don't know why. They had us cold. But we're not looking a gift horse in the mouth. Helm, go to one-six-five degrees. Maintain full speed ahead."

For another fifteen minutes, the U-113 continued to zigzag out into the open Gulf of Mexico, working her way into progressively deeper water. And for the first ten of those fifteen minutes, a madly circling swarm of Catalina bombers dropped depth charge after depth charge along her projected course, many of the lethal canisters sinking past her a scant six feet to one side before coming to rest on the bottom, always at less than their detonating depth of one hundred feet.

Infuriated, frustrated, the pilots realized very quickly why their weapons were not exploding, but there was little they could do about it. With the U-boat submerged, there was nothing to shoot at with their blister guns. In the turbid, mud brown coastal Louisiana water, they were unable to track their quarry visually even though it could not be running more than twenty feet or so below the surface. And with no way to reset their depth charges' pressure-sensitive detonators while in flight, their primary U-boat-killing weapons were useless. The airwaves turned blue as pilot after pilot alternately cursed his luck, his armorers, and the U.S. Navy in general, and radioed bitterly for surface ships to continue the hunt offshore.

"Bottom now thirty-five meters," one of the ballast techs reported. "Boat depth: twenty-seven meters."

"Mein Gott," Dekker muttered. "We've made it. We're alive." He looked over at Stuermer, still standing rigidly beside the ladder, in disbelief. "You did it, Kurt. We're *alive*."

Stuermer's thin, hard smile appeared, and he nodded. "Yes. We are," he said—and sank down the ladder to his knees.

Dekker uttered an exclamation of alarm and moved to his side, supporting him. His eyes on the gauges, he hadn't noticed that the puddle of seawater in which Stuermer had been standing was tinged with red, as were his soaking-wet battle jacket and pants. The U-boat commander winced as Dekker twisted him slightly, getting an arm under his back.

"Easy, Otto," he said quietly. His battle jacket fell open, revealing a bullet-torn mass of bloody flesh that had been his stomach.

"Get the cook in here with his medical kit!" Dekker screamed. He tried to find a place to put his hand, to stem the flow of blood and tissue that was oozing out of Stuermer's gut, but could find nothing to grasp—there were no edges to pull together, no holes to cover. Nothing but sticky, shredded meat.

"Kurt . . . ," Dekker said, his voice breaking. He pulled his captain closer, gripping his shoulders. He was vaguely aware of the sound of shouting in the forward passageway, of the patter of running feet. Someone dropped a medical kit to the deck beside him, fumbling with the latches.

Stuermer's blood spread out beneath him in a fast-widening puddle, mingling with the seawater on the control room floor. The U-113 heaved slightly, listing to port. A half-dozen red rivulets ran sideways across the deck plates, pooling against the trim panels.

The U-boat commander looked up at his chief engineer and smiled one last time. Not the thin, weary smile of the war-hardened soldier, but a full, boyish smile of friendship that drove the lines of care and pain from his face. Slowly, he grasped Dekker's sleeve and tugged on it.

"Your boat, Otto," he whispered. "Take her home."

Then his hand fell away, his head sagged back, and his gray green eyes closed.

Dekker stared at him, blinking. Then, gently, he let him slip to the deck.

"Aye, Captain," he said. He looked up and around at the faces in the control room, mostly young, all frightened, yet resolute. They were gazing back at him. At the man to whom command had just fallen.

"Home," Otto Dekker repeated. "*Home*."

At that moment, the U-113, following the contour of the bottom out into the open Gulf, descended past the thirty-one-meter level—just over one hundred feet deep.

The hydrostatic fuse of the Mark VII depth charge that had hit the conning tower and become lodged on the bridge between the starboard wind baffle and the periscope housing fired off, detonating the canister's 250 pounds of high explosive.

An instantaneous pressure wave equivalent to fifty thousand atmospheres moved outward from the center of the explosion at the speed of sound.

The conning tower of the U-113 split down the middle as if hacked open by a giant ax. The pressure hull bulged outward, cracking open longitudinally from bow to stern on both sides. With a great, dying gasp, the life-sustaining atmosphere within the U-boat belched out through the gaping central wound, joining the expanding gases of the initial explosion as they blew toward the surface.

Seconds later, the U-113 nosed down and plowed bow first into the soft, muddy bottom of the Gulf of Mexico. Her momentum drove her along another two hundred feet, scraping out a deep trench in the seafloor, until at last she came to a halt.

One final shudder, a slow, agonizing roll to starboard, and she laid her shattered conning tower down in the sticky, grasping mud.

And the cold, and the dark, and the silence closed in around her.

Sitting with his back against the immense lone cypress tree on the point of land at the mouth of Bayou Profond, Erich Bock continued to search the horizon to the south. He had not taken his eyes off the head of the bay and the Gulf of Mexico beyond since reaching dry ground, waterlogged and exhausted. After buzzing over the site of the U-113's crash dive with futile energy for more than half an hour, dropping depth charges that, inexplicably, did not explode, the Catalinas had banked off to the north, heading inland. Still Bock watched. Hoping for . . . something.

And then his sharp eyes caught a faraway movement, in deep water, just in front of the horizon line. The unmistakable, boiling white eruption of a depth charge going off. He'd seen many of them in the North Sea, the English Channel, the Gulf Stream—had been their intended victim too many times to count. Too many times to even want to count.

Something stabbed him in the breastbone, seized him by the throat. A freezing claw sank into his vitals, twisting. . . .

And he *knew*.

He sat there under the cypress tree for a long time, staring out at the empty horizon as the sun traveled across the sky and the shadows lengthened.

Expecting nothing.

Hoping for nothing.

And then something made him turn and look back up the shimmering black bayou, and as he did so, a small, low pirogue slid into view around the nearest bend . . .

. . . paddled with quick, sure strokes by a slim figure in baggy hand-me-down clothes and a battered, wide-brimmed fedora. . . .

Epilogue

The early-morning sun was burning the mist off the bayou water below the back deck of Oswald's Beer, Bait, and Gas when Al Mandy leaned across the cable spool, uncapped the second scotch bottle, and split the last golden inch of single-malt it contained between his glass and mine. Then he sat back, recrossed his stiff legs, and raised the tumbler briefly in my direction.

"The end," he said.

I looked at him, shaking my head slowly. "Incredible. Just incredible." I rolled my own whisky tumbler on the top of the cable spool, watching the multifaceted glass and the amber liquor within catch the sunlight. "But hardly the end."

Al chuckled and sipped his scotch. "I leave somethin' out, *mon ami*?"

"A lot of things." I hardly knew where to begin. "I dove on that wreck yesterday, and it was in fifty feet of water. But back in 1943 it must have been over a hundred feet deep to detonate the depth charge that was caught in its bridge, the way you claim. How—"

"Hurricanes," Al said. "I been watchin' her move from here to there for forty-five years. Storms, flood currents—they been bowlin' her across the bottom, buryin' her sometimes, uncoverin' her a couple years later, ever since the war. Since I knew where she went down, I've always been able to keep track of her."

"The navy never found her? At the time, they would have given their eyeteeth for the chance to salvage an operational U-boat, wouldn't they?"

"You're forgettin'," Al pointed out, "they never realized they'd sunk her. They thought she got away clean. The Catalinas went home and reported that none of their depth charges had fired, and the U-boat had disappeared."

I nodded. "Right, right." I shook my head again. "There were *no* survivors from the U-113? No one got out?"

The old man took a long swallow of scotch. "Not a one," he said softly.

"Well, what happened to *les Isolates*? That whole community out in the deep swamp? Technically, what they did was treason. Trading with and giving refuge to the enemy. The military wasn't interested in what a U-boat was doing up in a bayou waterway? They didn't investigate?"

Al waved my speculations away. "Ah, no. The authorities never knew about the resupplyin' of the U-boat. When the navy flyers first caught up to it, it was nearly at the head of the bay. They never realized how far up the bayou it had been.

"Fetherstone-Pugh had been killed, and Blodgett was never organized enough to figure out what had gone on. It didn't stop him from gettin' the credit the Brit deserved, though. He was awarded the Distinguished Service Medal for his part in locatin' the U-113. Politically expedient for Admiral Zacharias to have one of his own men decorated. Blodgett received several promotions, then died in 1948 from eatin' bad oysters in the French Quarter." Al grinned. "Oh, yes. I've looked into *everything* over the years.

"And you have to understand: to people like *les Isolates*, livin' far removed from regular society and government authority, what they were doin' was just what they'd done since the time of Jean Lafitte—bartering, trading, smuggling. It didn't matter who it was with, just that it was good business. It was a way of life in the deep bayous." He laughed. "It still is, for some people."

"Are they still there?"

"No." Al shook his head. "After Papa Luc was done in, it dawned on the more reasonable folks among 'em that there was a bigger world out there. After the war, the younger ones drifted off to the cities, to another kind of life. The old ones just died. America got prosperous, *mon ami*. There was radio, television, better communications. There was money for social improvements. The government went into a lot of isolated, backward places like the hills of Tennessee and the deep swamps of Louisiana and educated the people. Showed them a new way of life. By 1955, *les Isolates* were just a memory."

I sipped my scotch, feeling it burn against the back of my throat. "What about some of the others? For instance, what happened to Mike Holt? Lucius?"

"Holt went back to Venice and wrangled another trawler out of the bankers. He got some money from the government after the war on account of his missin' hand and was able to keep a pretty fair fishin' operation going for a few years. But he never beat the bottle: he died of cirrhosis of the liver in 1960. Lucius worked with him right until the end, tryin' to take care of him like he was his kid brother or something." Al laughed, shaking his head. "I never could figure out why he was so loyal. Something in the past just welded them together. No matter how bad Holt got with the booze, Lucius was always there to pick him up out of the gutter. After Holt died, the boat they shared went to him. He worked it for a few more years."

"I think I'd have liked Lucius," I said. "From the way you've described him, he was a class act. What happened to him?"

"He lived to be ninety-one years old," Al replied. "Died just a few years back in a veterans' home in Mississippi. He was a World War *One* vet, remember." He laughed again. "And I'll tell you something else about him in a moment—been savin' it for a surprise."

I smiled. "Okay. But look, how about Estelle? Jolene?"

"They say Estelle went on just as she always had,

livin' by herself in that lonely shanty for about another six or seven years after the war ended. Then one morning, the story goes, she came out onto her dock, got into a pirogue with her black cat, and paddled off into the swamp. No one ever saw her again."

"And Jolene?"

"She—well, look, let me tell you that other thing about Lucius first. He—"

There was a sudden thumping of boots on the wooden catwalk that led to the little establishment's parking lot. A moment later, the captain of the oil field workboat that had brought my crew and me back to the docks the previous night appeared around the corner, looking fresh from a good night's sleep—unlike myself, I had little doubt.

I waved a hand at him. "'Mornin', Cap."

"Hey," he said to me, smiling. He regarded Al Mandy with fond exasperation. "Pop—what the hell d'you think you're doin', stayin' out drinkin' all night long like you were twenty years old? You're gonna kill yourself, and then Ma's gonna kill *me*."

Al drained the last of his whisky, looking stubborn. "She'll keep," he declared. "I'm not quite done yet."

"Maybe she'll keep and maybe she won't," remarked a smooth female voice from the corner of the restaurant.

I swiveled in my chair as an elegant Creole woman with a full head of silver gray hair, cut short, stepped off the catwalk onto the back porch. She was truly striking, with a graceful, erect carriage, high cheekbones, and dark, almond-shaped eyes. Despite her age, barely a line creased her milk-chocolate complexion. Her navy blue dress-and-jacket ensemble fitted her slender frame so well that it appeared almost formal. But her walk as she came forward was athletic and relaxed—the walk of a person comfortable in her clothes and skin.

I was impressed. It would have been difficult to imagine a woman more effortlessly regal. From head to toe, she looked ageless.

I got shakily to my feet. "Ma'am." I said with a nod,

and sat back down. Too much scotch and no sleep isn't good for the legs.

She smiled at me and then put a hand on Al's shoulder. "Don't you think you could use a little breakfast and a nap?" she asked gently.

"As soon as I'm done," the old man replied. He patted her hand. "Sit down, *chère.*"

As the woman took a seat, smoothing her dress across her knees, Al continued: "About Lucius—just after the *Shiloh* was torpedoed, he and Holt were makin' their way along the shore of the bayou, tryin' to get out to the coast. They came on an abandoned pirogue in the brush, along with a couple of rotten paddles. It leaked, but it floated, and it was better than bushwhackin' through the undergrowth, so they slipped it into the water and began paddlin' down the bayou.

"About three miles from the mouth of Bayou Profond, Lucius spotted Lothar Wolfe lying across a log near the bank. He was shot up, unconscious—but alive."

I straightened in my chair. "He was blown off the gun deck of the U-113 during one of the Catalina attacks in the bayou. One minute he was there; the next he was gone—I think that was what you said."

"That's right. But he wasn't killed. At first Holt wanted to leave him, but Lucius talked him around. They hauled him into the pirogue, more dead than alive, and paddled with him all the way down the bayou, across the bay, along the outer coastline, and up the Mississippi shipping channel to Venice. They got him to a doctor—under a fake name—and made up some story about a boiler explosion in a factory."

I nodded. "They were paying him back for saving Lucius' life when he got trapped in the wreckage of Schecter's U-boat."

"Exactly. He made a full recovery, worked quietly as a farmhand for a few years until the war ended, and then went back to Germany in 1948. He built a successful business manufacturing custom-made hunting rifles— some of them are now worth hundreds of thousands of dollars to collectors—got married, had seven sons, and died happily in bed in his big home in Heidelberg in 1982. I talked with him often over the years, after I finally tracked him down."

"Holt never told anyone what he knew?" I asked. "Neither did Lucius?"

"Never," Al said. He frowned pensively. "Something about Stuermer, Bock, Wolfe—the Germans he went head-to-head with over here—seemed to cancel out, to some degree, the self-destructive hatred he carried for the Nazis who'd maimed him in that Gestapo prison in France. The U-boatmen were the enemy, and yet he liked them. I think the contradiction must have tormented him until the end of his days."

"Seems as though he was predisposed toward it," I observed. "Not too tightly wrapped to start with. Although I have to confess, if I'd gone through what he did, I might have been even more of a basket case."

"No tellin'," Al agreed.

I drained the last of my scotch and set the tumbler down. The sun was becoming hot on my aching head, and I could tell that the old man was losing steam as well. It had been a long night. With a deep sigh, I stretched my arms and looked at Al Mandy directly.

"Well, Al," I said. "That leaves you."

The lines of age at the corners of Al's dark eyes crinkled in amusement. But he said nothing.

"*Al Mandy,*" I went on. "Very close to *Allemand*—the French word for 'German.'"

The old man, the elegant woman sitting beside him, and the middle-aged workboat captain standing nearby all smiled.

"Kurt," Al said, holding out his hand. "You have that letter I asked for?" He tipped his head at the boat captain. "My son, Kurt Mandy."

"I see." *Kurt Mandy.* Things were rapidly becoming clearer. "You knew where the U-113 was," I said to the younger man. "You knew we were going to dive on it. Probably identify it positively as a U-boat."

The workboat captain nodded. "My dad and I been trackin' that wreck since I was a child. Nobody ever bothered with it. Disturbed it." He grinned at me, a hint of challenge in his gaze. "Until now."

I shrugged and grinned back, holding his eye. "It was my job. It was leaking oil."

The boat captain retracted his attitude a bit and smiled. "Well, we all got to do our jobs, I guess." He reached inside his shirt and passed a brown manila envelope to his father, then leaned back on the wooden railing that surrounded the patio deck.

"Thanks, Kurt," Al said. He opened the end of the envelope, looking at me.

"Before you go any further," I said, "I have to ask you: why did Kurt Stuermer throw Erich Bock over the side of the U-113 as she started across the bay? Surely you don't expect me to believe that an experienced naval commander would push one of his best men—an experienced senior lieutenant—off his vessel, when he would very likely need that man's skills to get that vessel safely back across an entire ocean—just for the love of a girl he'd met only days earlier? Combat captains aren't that sentimental."

The corners of the elegant woman's mouth tightened slightly in annoyance. "What a cynical person you are, Mr. Mannock. At your age, you should still have some romance lingering in your heart."

"I'm afraid I'm the product of a rather cynical and unromantic age, ma'am," I said. "But that was a bit harsh, I admit. I apologize." I smiled and looked back at Al. "I just don't see Stuermer pushing Bock off the U-boat unless . . . he felt that they had no chance, that they were all going to die and he wanted to save him, or—"

"Your speculations are all wrong, *mon ami*," Al interrupted. "Kurt Stuermer *never* gave in, *never* gave up hope. And he expected those around him to do the same—to follow his example, and do their duty." He pulled a sheet of writing paper, yellow with age, from the manila envelope. "Here," he said, sliding it toward me across the top of the cable spool, "read this."

I picked up the brittle page and examined it. There was no letterhead; the body was handwritten in black ink, the small script elegant and readable in the Old World fashion, in contrast to the illegible pseudomedical scrawl affected by so many North Americans. Sitting back in my chair, I began to read:

September 14, 1943

Dear Erich,

I have chosen to set pen to paper in English, as I fear you are fated to speak it for the rest of your days.

If you are reading this, it is because I have apparently abandoned you—marooned you—somewhere on the coast of the United States. You may have had to watch as the U-113 put out to sea without you, and for the pain and confusion this must have caused, I deeply apologize. In my professional and personal opinion, you are one of the finest young officers the Ubootwaffe has ever produced; in every way, your performance of your duty has been exemplary. When I report you killed in action upon our return to Lorient, I will do so with the recommendation that you be awarded the Iron Cross for extraordinary bravery and service to the fatherland.

Why? you must be asking. Nothing makes any sense. Why has my captain treated me in such a way? What have I done to deserve this?

You have done nothing to deserve what I must tell you now. During the long hours that we have spent limping northward through the Gulf of Mexico toward the coast of Louisiana, I have racked my brains for words that would make this easier for you to hear. Now we are less than a day from the Mississippi River, and I have found none. No elegant, magical phrases that will pass on knowledge without pain. So I must simply tell you.

During our last rendezvous with Captain Kessler aboard the U-395, east of the Windward Passage, he asked me to come to his cabin. He had information concerning you, Erich, that disturbed him greatly, and that he felt he must pass on to me. In doing so, he put himself at considerable risk, for it was information of the sort that can cause a man who repeats it—given the current state of affairs in Germany—to disappear. But I do not need to remind you how much Hans Kessler liked you. I say "liked" because, sadly, I fear that Captain Kessler and the crew of the U-395—like so many of our friends and comrades-in-arms—now lie at the bottom of the Atlantic. I may be wrong. But something tells me that I am not.

This is what Hans Kessler told me: last month, the Gestapo arrested your father and uncles for attempting to smuggle fifty-seven Jewish men, women, and children out of Germany by concealing them aboard your family's three fishing vessels. Their intention was to transport them across the Baltic from Kiel to neutral Sweden, where they would be landed on the coast southwest of Stockholm.

The Gestapo caught your father and uncles at the docks red-handed, with the Jews hidden in the fish holds of the three trawlers. Apparently, this would have been their third such trip; they had already smuggled an estimated one hundred other people to safety in Sweden. But someone informed. A neighbor, I am told—a person with whom your father had done business for years. I do not know his name. This is what the glorious Third Reich has become, Erich: a place where friends betray friends—a place where, having devoured the rest of Europe, we now turn on each other.

The Gestapo decided to make an example of your entire family. Your father and uncles were put up against the wall of the Fisherman's Memorial in Kiel and shot. Your mother and sister were arrested in your family home and "shot while resisting detainment" in the military car that was transporting them to prison. Your family home was pillaged, then burned to the ground.

A similar fate, Kessler warned me, awaits you upon your return from this patrol. Himmler and Goebbels themselves have a hand in this. They have convinced

Hitler of the deterrent power of wiping out an entire German family sympathetic to the Jews, even if one of its members is a decorated U-boat officer. The frantic protests of every senior officer in the Kriegsmarine— including Dönitz himself—have fallen on deaf ears. You must be sacrificed, the führer has decided, as an object lesson in what happens to German families who entertain notions of assisting Jews to escape.

You cannot go home, Erich. Not ever. There is nothing to go home to.

And now you know why I have left you on the shores of America. I could never forgive myself if I let you return to your death. And I know that you would not leave the U-113 of your own volition. Quite the contrary. If I was in your place, I would fight tooth and nail to get home, just to reassure myself that it could not be true—that it was all some horrible mistake.

But it is true. And your only hope is to stay in America. You speak the language. You have relations in the north. You are young, smart, and tough. You can take another name, keep your head low. This war will not last forever, and in spite of what my military training would have me believe, my human heart tells me that you—and not I—will have a home on the winning side when it is all over.

It has been a privilege to serve with you aboard the U-113. Perhaps, many years from now, we may meet each other again. Perhaps it will be in Paris, at a café along the Seine. Or perhaps it will be in New York, after a Broadway show, at a small, fine restaurant in the heart of the city. And perhaps we will laugh, and drink too much Schnapps, and tell each other stories we already know by heart, of fallen friends and hard-won battles in a war long ago.

Perhaps.

Remember me as I will remember you, Erich, and always consider me

Your captain, and your friend,

Kurt Stuermer

I gazed at the signature for a long time after I finished reading, examining the bold, controlled pen strokes, trying to absorb from them the essence of the man who'd signed the letter nearly fifty years before. His words echoed in my ears as if they had been spoken aloud. Slowly, carefully, I folded the aging paper along its existing creases and handed it back to Al Mandy.

"You see," he said, touching a finger to his empty whisky glass, then looking out at the sparkling surface of the Gulf of Mexico, "Captain Stuermer and I have our drink, together, every month. And for the first time in fifty years, I've brought a guest—you."

I smiled, swallowing the odd lump that was thickening in my throat.

Al kept looking out at the Gulf. "I never went north, never contacted my relatives in New Jersey. There was no point. I had to become another man. The Bocks of Kiel, Germany, all died in the war." He looked over at the beautiful, silver-haired Creole woman sitting next to him, and took her hand. "Jolene gave me my new name: *Allemand* she always called me—it became *Al Mandy,* as you guessed."

I smiled at the woman. "Jolene," I said. She nodded, smiling back.

Something else was happening. Al's thick Cajun accent was disappearing. His English was becoming clipped, his voice harsher, the delivery more from the back of the throat.

"I lived with *les Isolates* for a couple of years, until the war ended, and then moved with Jolene into the small bayou towns—Larose, Dulac. I took the fishing knowledge I'd acquired from my father and bought a shrimper, then a trawler, then another and another. I bought a small cannery. Kurt, our son, was born in 1950.

"Always, I kept a watch on the U-113. I tended it like a grave, because that was what it was—what it still is . . . the grave of my captain, my comrades-in-arms—my friends. A war grave."

He looked at me suddenly, his eyes bright and hard, devoid of the fog of age and fatigue. "And I do not want the Coast Guard to contract some oil field barge to scrap it out, piece by piece, as a so-called hazard to shipping or the environment. Not while I'm still breathing. I want it left there. I want them left there. At rest in their iron coffin. At *peace*." The eyes took on a hint of desperation. "Can you understand that?"

I looked at him, and Jolene, and their son. I didn't have to think about it very long. "Well, the Coast Guard isn't going to bother hiring a scrapping barge to pick up one rusty oil barrel, which is what my report will say was causing the slick when I hand it in on Tuesday."

Jolene reached across the table and put her hand on top of mine. "You aren't going to tell them that there's a U-boat out there?"

"U-boat?" I said. "What U-boat?"

Al's smile went from ear to ear. Jolene sat back, her eyes moist with relief. Beside his mother, Kurt Mandy nodded approvingly, but with concern on his face.

"Thank you," he said. "Thank you, for my father's sake. But what about your buddies—the guys who were out on the divin' job with you? Didn't you tell one of 'em—what's his name?—Gaston?—didn't you tell him there was something big down there? What about him?"

"Two weeks and twenty-five six-packs from now, Gaston Messier won't remember a thing about this job," I replied. "Don't worry."

Jolene wiped the corner of her eye with her little finger. "Thank you," she said softly.

Al Mandy got to his feet, a little unsteadily, and drew himself erect. He squared his shoulders, military style—and suddenly it was as if half a century had fallen away from him. The man who stood in front of me was in his early twenties, straight as a lance, his eyes sharp, his face hard and alert.

"You know who I am," he said, extending his hand, "but I would like to introduce myself formally, if I may."

I nodded and got to my feet. Clasping the hand, I shook with him, gazing at his weather-beaten face as a multitude of emotions passed across it: loss, regret, old pain . . . and iron pride. His grip was the same.

Like iron.

"*Oberleutnant* Erich Bock, of the *Kriegsmarine* attack

boat U-113," he said, the thick Cajun accent at last giving way completely to the guttural inflections of a native tongue long unspoken. His dark eyes shone, frosted over with memory. "I am pleased to meet you."

John Mannock is a former commercial oil field diver and boat captain whose work has taken him to the far corners of the world. In the early 1980s, he served in the military in an infantry reconnaissance unit, and was deployed on peacekeeping operations in Lebanon and Central America. He has also been a construction welder, journalist, teacher, and professional jazz musician. He and his wife of twenty years live in the Florida Keys when they are not on the road doing research. To learn more about John Mannock's writing, please visit his Web site at www.johnmannock.com.